NAKED AMBITION

A Thriller

Rick Pullen

VIRGINIA BEACH
CAPE CHARLES

Naked Ambition

by Richard G. Pullen

ISBN 978-1-63393-741-3

Published by

◣ köehlerbooks™

210 60th Street
Virginia Beach, VA 23451
800-435-4811
www.koehlerbooks.com

For Dad

The best man I've ever known.

To Tom
Best Wishes
Rick Pullen
1/1/16

Acknowledgments

Thanks, Red.

Thanks to my editors, Barbara Esstman, Diane Krause, and Lorin Oberweger, whose advice and direction were crucial in developing this novel.

Thanks to Ron Sauder of Secant Publishing and JJ McNabb for steering me in the right direction. And thanks so much to the Royal Writers Secret Society for your invaluable advice and an excuse to down another beer. This book is much better for it.

I also owe a debt to Matthew Stennes, who explained how the Justice Department's Public Integrity Section struggles to achieve the impossible in an underfunded, undermanned, cramped office high above Fourteenth Street. Now that's a Hobbs Act violation if ever I saw one.

Coletta Kemper—here's to great conversation and Corona Lights over lunch on a hot August afternoon at Penn Quarter Sports Tavern discussing how to resolve the court scene. You were there at the beginning. And thanks to the Tavern staff for indulging our many requests for fish tacos and for placing my best side on your webpage.

And thanks to my daughter Jill Howard, who read innumerable rewrites, always with a sense of enthusiasm, and texted corrections long after midnight. Thanks also to my daughter "Congressman" Kelsey Laye for your suggestions and meticulous read-through.

And then there's Dave Bayard, who fulfilled his lifelong ambition of becoming a sleazy politician without ever running for elective office. (It happens.) His liberal donation to First Children's Hospital in Washington, DC, secured him naming rights and a villainous place in thriller lore. (I hope.) Thanks for your generosity.

Finally, thanks to Cherie for putting up with this for so long and for reading so many unfinished drafts. There's no past tense about you, Red.

1

When his secret was secure and his brain afire, Beck was alive. Fueled by a rush of adrenaline, his mind would not rest. But it was not always that way. Like now. Oh man, especially like now.

Grateful to finally be home in the solace of his cluttered condominium after a turbulent morning flight back to Washington, Beck was cranking through a chilling novel and a second Corona Light. He'd suffered through five interminable days in a fleabag in Flyover, America. And for what? The stale beer? The stench of cigarettes? No, it was the lumpy bed and the low-pitched rumble of the sputtering air conditioner. Or maybe the all-night, ragtag symphony of truckers braking at the intersection just outside his hotel. Yeah. That was it. Had to be. The price of admission to his world.

His cell phone rang. Not now, he thought.

He'd just reached the climax, where the hero discovered his beautiful accomplice was an enemy spy. Finally, Beck would learn. . .

The damn thing rang again.

He glared at it, vibrating on his coffee table, willing it to shut up and stop dancing.

The caller ID was blocked. Shit. He looked back at the page, determined to finish the chapter, but his eyes refused to focus. His DNA was nothing if not determined. God, he hated that about himself.

"Yeah?" he grumbled into the phone.

"Beck Rikki?"

"Yeah."

"The reporter for the *Post-Examiner*?"

"Maybe. Who's calling?"

"Daniel Fahy, head of the public integrity section at Justice. Your office said I could reach you at this number. I'd like to speak with you privately."

"About?"

"I'd rather not say over the phone. Can we meet?"

Not another crackpot, thought Beck. He'd just finished a frustrating week hounding false leads. He didn't need this right now. "Got a thing about phones?"

"It would be more appropriate to discuss what I have to say face to face."

"How do I know that?"

"You'll just have to trust me."

"Why should I? I haven't a clue who you are."

"I just told you."

Beck groaned softly. He needed to talk to the city desk about giving out his number. "Look, I've had a bad week. Lost my appetite for wild goose chase. Throw me a bone."

"Are you always this difficult?"

"Occupational hazard. You always this secretive?"

"Occupational hazard."

Beck leaned back on his couch and stared at the ceiling, waiting. Not another smart-ass government bureaucrat whining about his abusive boss. Why do these loons always call a reporter instead of HR?

Fahy fell silent, but Beck heard other voices and muffled laughter in the background. "You still there?"

"I'm thinking," Fahy said.

Beck heard more laughter. "That's okay. While you're at your party, I'm sitting here quietly engrossed in one of the best novels I've read all year. I've got nothing better to do with my time than to listen to *your* silence on *my* end of *your* phone call."

"Okay. Okay. I think I've run across a bribery scheme involving a very important public official—a *very important* public official. Interested?"

Beck sat up straight. "I could be. How important is important?"

"Near the top of the Washington food chain."

"Meaning?"

"He looks in the mirror every morning and imagines he sees the president."

"That's half of Washington."

"He's already taken the measurements of the Oval Office and ordered new carpet."

Beck felt his brain spark. It was like striking a match. Then just as quickly, the familiar refrain of his defenses jumped in to douse the flames.

"Why tell me?" he asked. "I thought you Justice guys liked to do this sort of investigation in the shadows. You hate the press."

"I've got my reasons. I'll make you a deal. I'll not only give you what I think is a story, but I'll explain my motivation for calling you when we meet. Fair enough?"

"Not fair, but it's enough." Beck had to play ball. He'd just about gone crazy over the past several months. It had been too long since he had published a significant investigative piece. His editors had been hounding him. One even suggested he be assigned to a regular beat again. A beat? For the most decorated investigative reporter at the paper? How humiliating.

Fahy suggested breakfast the next day and gave Beck directions to a restaurant south of Old Town Alexandria on US Route 1, a good ten miles outside of Washington.

"How will I recognize you?"

"Don't worry," Fahy said. "You will." And hung up.

2

Beck eyed his cell phone. What the hell? Who was this guy Fahy? He'd heard a rasp, maybe a hint of an Irish or Scottish accent? Languages weren't his thing. Even his exasperated journalism prof once told him English was his second language.

No mind. He grabbed his laptop and googled Daniel Fahy. Sure enough, he was the director of the Justice Department unit that prosecuted dirty politicians. He graduated fourth in his class at Georgetown Law and, according to an old Nicky Allen *Politico* story, had a reputation as a Boy Scout—a government do-gooder. An oxymoron, at best, in this town, Beck thought.

A couple of clicks later, he pulled up some old *Post-Examiner* stories from the newspaper's morgue. Same thing. A feature a few years back mentioned Fahy's reputation for prosecuting wayward politicians. His investigations didn't make him popular in Washington, but they did make him politically untouchable.

"Red?" Beck did not look up at his writing assistant sitting in the far corner of his living room but continued scanning his computer screen. "This guy might be legit."

He checked the article's byline. Shit. Kerry Rabidan. Her newsroom moniker was Rabid Dog—she was that good. But lacking enough seniority to own her job, the paper downsized her a year ago. Union rules. She now worked for the rival *News-Times*, Washington's other daily newspaper. Damn, he thought, can't call the competition for background.

"Red, why is the head of the Justice Department public integrity section really calling me at home?"

Beck stood and walked back into his living room. He sank into the soft brown couch and felt the expensive speckled leather cushions sigh beneath him.

He shoved a week's worth of old newspapers into a pile atop his crowded coffee table and created a soft landing for his feet. He noted his Italian shoes were badly scuffed. Must have been from dogging dead ends around Flyover, he thought. It was all he had to show for a week's worth of hard labor.

Beck leaned into his neglected Corona Light and took a swig. Good. It was still cold. He wiped his mouth and mustache with his sleeve.

Red faced the fireplace near Beck's whodunit wall—a floor to ceiling collection of autographed Lawrence Block mysteries, as well as first-edition Dashiell Hammett and Raymond Chandler detective novels. Beck especially liked his Michael Connelly novels, but he recognized himself more as a character in one of Carl Hiaasen's offbeat beach capers. Five hardback copies of his own nonfiction work were scattered in no particular order on the bottom shelf along with several Jimmy Buffett books. Thank god the maid was coming tomorrow. She'd make order of his chaos.

Beck stared at Red as she sat in silence. He thought about the possibilities of the phone call. If Fahy really did have the goods, Beck knew he and Red might quickly be back on top. He wanted nothing more. A big story meant he would not face the agony of backsliding into the mundane trappings of covering a beat like most of his newsroom colleagues. And most important, there would be no threat of anyone finding out about Red. Their secret would remain secure. A big story meant they could continue to work together in private, here, in his man-cave sanctuary. He had worked too hard with too little talent to get this far. He needed a big score, and he needed Red's help to make it happen.

God, he was glad they'd met. Even if they hadn't collaborated in months, without her clandestine assistance, he would have never become one of Washington's most successful investigative reporters. Beck had never shared a byline with her, but he credited Red with organizing his thoughts, helping him with two Pulitzer Prize nominations, and shaping his two books into *New York Times* best sellers. She was always the first one he acknowledged in his books.

Twelve years ago, his career had been in the toilet. No Justice Department officials were calling then, requesting secret meetings. He had been a snarl of dangling participles and disjointed gerunds demanding industrial-strength editing from the city desk.

But then, thanks to a half-price Labor Day sale on all-leather furniture, Red had entered his life.

Their accidental partnership had begun about a week after he had brought her home. He'd paced the floor, wearing a path in his oriental rug and reading a draft out loud, struggling to craft a story for the weekend national news section. He had then turned his attention to Red for a moment, and something had suddenly clicked. The words had flowed easily. He hadn't realized it at the time, but he had found his muse—and a half-priced one at that.

Considering his level of writing talent, maybe that was appropriate. His writing wasn't poetry, but it was close enough.

Suddenly, he had been welcomed on the front page. It had been embarrassing—no, outright humiliating—but Red had saved his career.

He gazed across the room at her—his empty leather reading chair nestled comfortably in the corner. Beck felt that queasy sensation in his stomach, the one he got when he wasn't certain of his facts. "Red, you think Fahy could be setting us up?"

3

Daniel Fahy hung up and slipped his cell phone back into his suit coat pocket. He worried if he'd overstepped by calling a reporter. Then he glanced up, toward a commotion across the hotel lobby. The doors to F Street swung open, ushering in a whiff of steamy summer downpour, followed by a strong gust of Senator David Bayard. Bayard strode across the plush lobby of the W Hotel, two young aides drafting in his wake.

Fahy felt desperate. He knew he was losing his battle to rein in Bayard before the senator won his party's presidential nomination. If he didn't do something quickly, Bayard would likely escape justice forever. Fahy took a big breath and felt helpless watching his target from afar.

The lobby was unusually crowded. Dozens of bangle-laden tourists huddled boisterously near the first-floor alcohol supply to escape the violent afternoon thunderstorm that had cleared the rooftop terrace lounge. Halfway across the lobby, Bayard stopped suddenly to greet a designer couple dressed in black and white and clinging to martini glasses filled with unmet expectations. The trio created a traffic jam in the boutique hotel's packed corridor. Bayard gave the woman a peck on the cheek and pumped the man's hand, shaking his martini far more than the bartender had ever intended.

Perched across the room, cradled in a cushioned velvet chair near the Fifteenth Street lobby entrance, Fahy felt silly at his feeble attempt at amateur sleuthing while he watched his prey with a bit of awe. The alpha male was establishing his exceptionalism.

The senator stepped back from the couple, nodding in a well-practiced farewell gesture, and slipped away into the glittering, damp-haired crowd, heading in the direction of the lobby bar. Unlike the throng, he showed no signs he had just stepped from Washington's summer steam bath. His groomed graying hair—turned premature blond at some high-priced salon—along with his crisp tailored suit hugging his slim, athletic frame belied both his age and the weather.

Bayard shook three more bejeweled hands as he eased through the throng of slinky summer dresses and brass-button sports jackets, each time grabbing a forearm and practically jamming its reluctant hand into his palm.

Fahy recognized the insatiable urge for political sustenance. So far, he had remained immune to the Washington epidemic—the incurable need for recognition that seemed to accompany political power. He preferred to wield whatever power he possessed quietly and remain anonymous.

He studied his quarry. Bayard appeared obsessed with grabbing the ultimate brass ring— preaching God, family, and lower taxes—all the while using his elective office to grow his personal wealth. Bayard's government financial disclosure reports suggested it. Fahy needed to somehow prove it. And he needed to prove it quickly before Bayard took down the entire Republican Party.

Bayard slapped another back and finally slithered next to a whale of a man sitting at the end of the bar. Built like a former college football player—*former* being the operative word—the Whale wore a crumpled, navy, chalk-stripe suit and hovered over his latest round. How many tumblers had it been? Fahy had lost count.

The senator talked briefly with the man, and then motioned with his thumb over his shoulder toward the well-heeled couples behind him. Both men laughed, but Fahy could make out none of it above the genial roar of the raucous crowd, whose volume had risen with their alcohol consumption.

The Whale stood, as big a man as Fahy had imagined. His belly cascaded over his belt as he reached into his trouser pocket and withdrew a shimmering money clip. He extracted two bills and slapped them on the bar.

Bayard turned briefly to his two young aides, told them something, and then swiveled, briefly resting his hand on the big man's shoulder. The two men then walked together across the black-and-white marble lobby to the nearby elevator and slipped through its ornate doors, leaving the two young assistants at the bar.

Fahy eyed the electronic display on the lobby wall above the elevator. The elevator did not stop until it reached the rooftop lounge. He rose from his chair, folded the newspaper he had used as a prop, and strode toward the elevator, dodging several small gatherings. It was not unlike his morning commute, darting in and out of traffic on the Beltway, always in a rush to get to the Justice Department.

He needed to hurry. For what, exactly, he wasn't sure. But he felt he was running out of options.

In moments, he sat unnoticed and uncomfortable under the still-dripping canopy shielding the rooftop terrace, posted in a chair far across the expanse of damp, empty tables and chairs from the Whale and the Republican senator from New Jersey. He smiled to himself. Thanks to the storm, the empty rooftop lounge offered not only an unfettered view of the presidential candidate, but a stillness that enabled him to make out bits of their conversation—even from across the steamy patio.

Thank god for Mother Nature, he thought. She's a Republican.

Bayard nursed a glass of clear liquid on the rocks. The Whale appeared to have arranged for another tumbler of brown liquor. Fahy suspected single malt Scotch, the preferred drink of the power elite. Washington was so cliché—a city of red-tie conformity and uniform egocentric comportment. The drinks rested on the high-top table between them, mere props as both men leaned in, engulfed in conversation.

Fahy partially hid behind his wilting copy of the day's *Post-Examiner* as the waiter brought him iced tea. Spy craft, he had to admit, was not his forte. He strained to hear and bit his lip, hoping for something—a clue of some sort. He wiped his brow. His suit was starting to stick to him. Was he just nervous or was it the loitering humidity?

He looked up again over his newspaper. Would they recognize him? But the two men—busy chatting and laughing—paid him no attention.

The Whale made a grand gesture, extending his arm out over the balcony's iron railing toward the White House, whose roof and top floor loomed a block away. Fahy felt he could reach out and touch the executive mansion from his chair. He imagined Bayard did too. But this had to be as close as the senator got.

Bayard looked toward the White House and smiled.

It might as well have a "For Sale" sign planted on the South Lawn, Fahy thought.

Bayard had slithered through his fingers again and again, and now the Republican convention was just days away. If Bayard got the nomination, he would be placing a substantial down payment on the First Family residence. If elected and subsequently exposed, Fahy was sure Bayard would destroy the Republican Party. Fahy could kick himself. Had he done a better job, the New Jersey senator would never have gotten this close.

Bayard must have intentionally chosen his seat next to the rooftop railing. Literally, nothing stood between him and the White House.

"Shoot. You're kidding. You're killing me, man," the Whale cackled. The words echoed throughout the empty lounge.

Fahy smiled and immediately looked at his watch, marking the time. Maybe this time, he thought. Just maybe.

Bayard leaned on the railing and spied the White House as if affirming his future ownership.

Perfect, thought Fahy. He had no idea the White House was spying right back.

4

The bulky green backpacks appeared to be stacked randomly about five feet high on a bed of silver needles against a Sitka tree that towered over a stand of firs. The packs were visible from the open field.

Stupid kids, thought Gardener. They were supposed to camouflage the damn things.

In the darkness of night, they probably hadn't realized how exposed the bags were to the open field. That, or they were just too eager to get the hell out of there before sunrise. He thought about it. Probably the latter.

Through his powerful riflescope, he eyed the bags and for the third time this morning swept his viewfinder across the field. Always checking. He could never be too careful.

Then he caught a blur of movement. He stopped and slowly backtracked with his scope. There. There it was—a Mountie walking slowly along the tree line through the tall grass and wildflowers, staring into the forest, no more than twenty yards from the stack. Gardener studied him closely. It appeared he had not yet spotted the backpacks. Maybe there was still a chance.

And then he noticed it. Damn. The lawman had a dog. That was it. He was done. The canine would surely pick up a scent. He immediately thought about his own position. If the wind changed, the animal would quickly find him as well. Damn it. The entire mission was now at risk. He was looking at millions sitting under that tree, and he needed it badly. The boss did not take failure lightly.

Had the Mounties already discovered their decoy deliveries, as intended? Those were supposed to divert the constables miles away over into the next district, far from this, the real haul. The law should be forty miles from here in the next valley. Yet here he was. How the hell did he get here? Was he tipped off or did he just stumble into it? Did it really matter at this point?

Gardener was crouched in the tall grass, watching the money. He had been as still as the spruces and pines for the past half hour, something he had learned years ago when he was a guerrilla in South America. Now he was the next link in the money's circuitous journey back home.

He looked for the Mountie's partner. He thought they always traveled in pairs. From his crouch position, Gardener slowly studied the field through his scope with his good eye. He was in his realm sitting alone in a field of tall grass, buttercups, fireweed, and elephant head. His real name wasn't even Gardener, but everyone called him that because of his love of beautiful flowers and the joy he found in running his hands through thick, rich soil. Even in the trade, everyone knew how he could bring new life to abused plants. So it was convenient to go by Gardener. It was better not to use his given name.

He felt the warmth of the early morning sun at his back. He turned, forgetting how low the sun was in the sky. It blinded his view as he scanned for additional lawmen. He looked away and held his breath. He closed his eyes and listened for anything beyond the sunlight. Only the nervous pulsing of blood through his veins interrupted. He picked up nothing but the irritating chirping of crickets. He hated crickets.

Then from his flank he heard the distinct calls of geese, grouse, and maybe a magpie or two. He turned back around. The only man-made sounds were right in front of him, about fifty yards away. In the morning stillness, he could easily pick up the steady crunch of dead needles and the snapping of twigs as the Mountie trudged after his dog along the edge of the trees, pushing dead branches and brush aside as he deliberately edged forward.

Gardener scanned the valley back and forth with his scope. Still nothing. Then there was more movement. The dog had found the money. It was barking and wagging its tail with urgency.

The Mountie turned toward him and quickly surveyed the field. Gardener paused for just a millisecond, then quickly ducked, losing his balance and slamming his left elbow on the ground. Had he been seen?

Then he heard a sound he did not recognize and slowly raised his head. The Mounty was tearing through the bags. Gardener recognized zippers grinding open, the ripping of paper, and the thud of the heavy packs being tossed to the barren forest floor. And the dog. He could hear the dog still whimpering with excitement.

The Mountie must be new, thought Gardener. Probably his first major haul. No fears of a booby trap or nothing. Son of a bitch, he wouldn't know a booby trap if it smacked him right upside the head. Gardener smiled at the thought and stifled a laugh. Must figure he's safe by now.

Gardener did one more quick sweep of the valley. Still nothing. Then he returned to watch patiently through his scope as the constable stopped, turned, and stepped away from the bags of cash and looked toward the field again.

He kept his head just below the top of the wildflowers and didn't move. Through the scope, the Mountie appeared to be only a few feet away. His face was reddened, partially covered in acne. He was a baby-faced kid, thought Gardener. Not even stubble on his chin. Hell, he had a nephew his age.

They were face to face. It was like the Mountie was staring right at him. Almost as if he could see him crouched in the grass. Creepy, he thought. What was the minimum age for joining the Mounties anyway?

Then there was a sudden look of recognition on the Mountie's face. Gardener had been made. The Mountie quickly grabbed for his belt. It was a radio. He started lifting it to his ear. Gardener squeezed the trigger, and a second later, the Mountie's head exploded into a red spray of blood and tissue fanning out over the quiet field of fireweed, glorious harebells, and tall grasses.

The pop of the rifle had broken the morning calm. Then silence echoed again. Gardener heard the rustle of God's beautiful bounty waving ever so slightly in the light breeze across the valley floor. There was not even a whimper from the dog.

Yep, thought Gardener, wouldn't know a booby trap if it smacked him right upside the head.

WHEELS UP FOR THE PRIVATE Gulfstream G450 jet at precisely 4:30 p.m. The pilot had filed his flight plan for yet another trip for an affluent businessman and his family headed to Mexico on vacation. In a week, the plane would return to Canada with two trunks of fashion samples for the mother's small family boutique.

Last month, two Canadian businessmen longed for a week of fishing on Ascension Bay on the Yucatán Peninsula. A week later, they returned with coolers full of bonefish, tarpon, and snook. Next month, it would be a rock musician finishing up a five-concert tour in Canada and heading home to Mexico City.

There were no plans to return to Canada after that. Planning too far in advance was risky.

The small private airstrip, a hundred miles from Vancouver, British Columbia, was strategically located for its runs to Mexico and Central America. The Gulfstream did not have to refuel in the United States, which allowed it to veer out over the Pacific Ocean and avoid US airspace. That was deliberate, because the "Cash Cow," as its owners dubbed it, was crammed with seventeen suitcases stuffed with American one hundred dollar bills.

The most dangerous part of the trip was over—escaping the United States into Canada. Cash was bulky and difficult to hide from authorities, but most of the border stood unprotected and easily passable, unlike Mexico, which was monitored constantly. The Gulfstream owners—a shell corporation out of Venezuela—preferred human mules with backpacks to make the crossing.

Now with their hoard secure onboard, the pilot pushed forward on the stick, and the plane leveled out. On the horizon, he saw the green Pacific Ocean melding into the blue sky. It was difficult to tell where they met. He watched the approaching coastline and the whitecaps and fishing boats offshore. The vessels bobbed like tiny toys in a bathtub.

In a little over seven hours, the bank manager at a friendly Mexican bank would open his back door in the middle of the night for his special client and welcome him in. Welcome indeed. The bank charged exorbitant fees to deposit foreign cash in exchange for asking no questions about its origin.

Once in the banking system, the money flowed as easily as water, beginning a long circuitous journey through several South American financial institutions. It changed form—from bulky paper bills requiring human mules or aircraft to transport them, to computer digits carried on the backs of electrons passing at the speed of light. The funds moved with a few computer keystrokes from latitude to latitude, thousands of miles in seconds, making it impossible for authorities to trace. Only a few knew its true destination.

On several occasions, the pilot overheard the owners call the Cash Cow's flight "the circle of life" because the money, they said, would someday circle right back to where it had come from. They were never more specific, and he wasn't about to ask any questions. Like everyone else in the organization, he was well paid to keep his mouth shut and his eyes averted. He knew what would happen if he didn't.

5

A few hours after returning from the W Hotel, Fahy uploaded the audio file he'd requested from Homeland Security. He double-checked to ensure it was set at the precise time noted on his watch. He immediately recognized the voices of Senator David Bayard and the Whale, Bayard's Chief of Staff Doug Jones, as they percolated up, electronically separated from the din of background noise that always surrounded the White House.

The audio came from speakers wired to Fahy's office computer, the sound as unmistakable and precise as if the two men sat next to him. He knew he shouldn't be in awe of the quality of the White House surveillance operation, or how easy it was to pull up electronic files from Homeland Security, and yet he couldn't help himself.

Since 9/11, everything had changed. Washington was a city under electronic siege. Audio and video monitors loomed everywhere. Bomb-sniffing equipment hid at all major entrances to the city. A truck carrying a large explosive couldn't get within three thousand feet of the White House or the Capitol without being detected. Hell, Fahy knew he couldn't walk into a doughnut shop on Fourteenth Street for a cup of his favorite Texas-style coffee without being recorded by at least three different cameras.

Washington had copied London, the archetype of surveillance, and then raised the bar. If not entirely original, then it was at least a sign of America's consistent need to flex its superiority. The thought made Fahy grin.

He adjusted the volume on his computer.

"Shoot. You're kidding. You're killing me, man." The boisterous recorded voice of Jones made Fahy jump as it burst from his computer speakers.

"That was subtle," said Fahy, hitting the "Pause" button. He looked across his desk at FBI Special Agent Patrick McCauley, who tilted his head in a knowing fashion. Fahy forced a nervous smile. "This better be good. I've been waiting for a long time for a break in this case." He busied himself adjusting the speaker volume.

McCauley had called in the morning, notifying Fahy of Bayard's meeting at the W Hotel and saying he also had new information on the investigation he wanted to share after his shift. His timing was impeccable. Fahy had just received the recording from Homeland Security.

Fahy clicked the "Play" button again.

"No, you're killing *me*, man. Washington was built on sweetheart deals," Bayard said.

Fahy felt like an impatient child about to open the biggest present under the tree on Christmas morning. Maybe this recording would finally reveal a clue he needed to piece the Bayard puzzle together. He knew he might have something when he heard the fat man's expletives on the terrace of the W Hotel. Ballistic-laden words like *shoot* and *kill* guaranteed every word of the conversation would be recorded. And depending on the severity of the perceived threat, the computers had either alerted officials immediately or relayed a message to a low-level agent for later review.

"Jesus, I hate Washington summers," Jones said. "*Shoot*, Dave. These summers are *murder*."

"Dougie, how long has the staff been handlin' this?"

"They've been digging through your finances for nearly a year. We've got to be prepared to release them publicly soon. When you win the nomination next week, we can't avoid releasing more information. We'll be pressing the Dems to do the same."

"So what's your issue?"

"You've made a lot of money—all legal, mind you—but based on your knowledge of what happens on Capitol Hill. If we go public with your finances, the Democrats will blast you with insider trading charges. The race is too close for that kind of distraction."

Fahy leaned in to one of the speakers to listen closer.

"My investments are all legal," Bayard said.

"Insider trading based on your knowledge of pending legislation *was* legal," Jones replied.

"Just because that White House bastard Bill Croom pressured us to change the ethics rules, doesn't mean I broke the law."

"But it looks bad. And if they get ahold of this Grand Cayman thing, you're toast."

Fahy clicked on the "Pause" button again. "The Grand Cayman thing?" Fahy turned to McCauley. "Is that what you wanted to talk about?"

McCauley looked up from the speakers. "Maybe."

Fahy looked at him briefly, silently questioning his response, and then clicked the "Play" button again on his computer screen.

"How do I keep the public—and nosy reporters—from digging deeper into my investments?" asked Bayard.

"Senator, let's face it, most reporters add two and two and get chocolate. You think those dim bulbs could ever figure out any of this? But the opposition's another matter. They're the smart guys in the room."

"So you think we can cover up my crony capitalism?" Bayard laughed. "Crony capitalism. Who came up with that phrase anyway?"

"It's this Lamurr lease in the Caribbean—in Grand Cayman—that I've got trouble with. We can't let it see the light of day. I've come up with a pretty simple plan, and well, if I do say so myself, it's rather ingenious."

"I'm listening."

Fahy watched the audio signal bounce up and down on his computer screen. He was enjoying every minute of this conversation.

"We have your lawyers put the offshore stuff in a blind trust, and it disappears altogether from your public financial disclosure report."

Jones's voice practically crackled from the computer. "The Senate rules don't require public disclosure of any details from a blind trust."

"They don't?"

"Not a word."

"I hadn't thought of that. You're a friggin' genius."

"I'll get the lawyers to make the trust retroactive to last year and move the island assets in there now."

"Is that legal?"

"Do we care at this point? If any nosy reporters ever catch wind of it, we'll be long past the due date on this election and can finesse it a dozen different ways. We're talking reporters after all. They don't know chocolate from vanilla, and we'll feed 'em strawberry." Jones was laughing.

"What?" The technology made the conversation so vivid; Fahy could almost hear the puzzled look on Bayard's face.

"It's just so perfect," Jones continued, his voice rising half an octave. "I love the irony."

"Irony?"

"Sure. The public thinks you're clear of all conflicts of interest by putting your assets in a blind trust because someone else controls your investments—" Jones was wheezing and laughing at the same time. "When—when—in fact we're just *hiding* your conflicts of interest from the public in a blind trust."

They both broke into laughter.

"Dougie, you're *killing* me."

Fahy clicked the file closed and swiveled in his desk chair to face the tall man seated across from him.

"This is the break I've been looking for," Fahy said. "I've been trying to nail this bastard for years."

6

"There's more," McCauley said. "I called around. I talked to a friend of a friend who knows a real estate agent. Bayard leases his property on Grand Cayman to a commercial enterprise." McCauley eased back in his chair. He looked relaxed with his legs crossed. "Then my friend of a friend dug up copies of Bayard's incorporation papers. That's where it gets interesting."

"Friend of a friend?" Fahy cracked a slight smile at what the FBI special agent had just said.

"Friend of a friend."

"So I struggle to get approval to prosecute cases and you can move forward finding friends in the Caymans?"

"Strictly unofficial, I assure you. We have ways." McCauley nodded. "Granted, we will need our own sandals on the ground to verify anything."

"And you volunteered, of course."

McCauley grinned for the first time. "I think we have an opening."

"Remind me the next time I need a parking ticket fixed," said Fahy.

"Parking tickets? Maybe not. But this Bayard case . . ."

Fahy sat back and studied McCauley, a well-maintained man like himself. Today, however, Fahy, felt weary, a bit rumpled in his shirt-sleeves and rep tie while eyeing the younger McCauley in his tailored suit and still sporting the athletic build of a college basketball player.

Fahy had been pursuing Bayard for what seemed like forever, and now, upon hearing McCauley had new information, he wondered if he had done the right thing by calling the reporter. Was he short-circuiting McCauley's efforts? He trusted McCauley, if not the rest of the FBI. Was he in too much of a hurry to press his case before the fall election? Maybe he just wouldn't show up tomorrow for breakfast.

But if he relied on the plodding, methodical efforts of the FBI, an indictment would come long after the presidential election. Once in power, presidents had inexhaustible resources to fight or delay a Justice probe. Fahy realized he couldn't afford that. Bayard could destroy his party for decades to come.

Fahy knew making an end run around the FBI was always dangerous. It could backfire. It could destroy his career. And it could wreck his case against Bayard. The more he thought about it, the more he didn't like his odds.

But he had fought terrible odds his entire career, and most of the time he came out on top—except with Bayard. He resented politicians who took advantage of the public purse, making themselves rich off public service. It was one reason he thought he was so good at his job. He had seen the same behavior in numerous federal and local officials, and he knew where to look for skeletons. Eventually, they all slipped up. Fahy had been biding his time, patiently waiting for Bayard. Now, finally, he saw an opening.

McCauley pulled a notebook from his blue suit jacket and flipped the pages on his knee. "Cayman is one of those offshore tax havens," he said. "Our senator from New Jersey funnels the lease payments on his waterfront property from a company called Sunrise Meridian through his own corporation, Jersey Shore Ltd."

"Cute."

"Yeah. I thought you'd like that one. And he appears to be reporting only a fraction of his earnings as income."

"Oh?"

"I picked up a copy of his old tax returns from the IRS. Bayard and his wife are the sole owners of Jersey Shore. Now take a look at this contract—the lines I circled in red."

McCauley reached his long arm across Fahy's massive mahogany desk and handed him a half-dozen folded sheets of paper, his tanned wrist extending far beyond the limits of the white fabric of his cuff-linked sleeve. "Look at the lease price."

Fahy fumbled for his reading glasses and thumbed through the pages until he came across the highlighted number. "Twenty-five thousand dollars? A month?"

"Precisely."

"That's three hundred thousand dollars a year." Fahy shook his head in disbelief. This was bigger than he thought. Bayard was more corrupt than even he had imagined. Fahy felt acid percolate in his stomach. He needed to find his pills. What a son of a bitch, he thought.

Yet he felt giddy, knowing he finally was making progress on the case. He wondered again if he should talk to the reporter. He looked up at McCauley.

"So far the income doesn't show up on his tax returns," McCauley said. "But those are two years old. He got an extension this year and has yet to file, so we won't know anything until October—if it shows up at all."

"The law states pretty clearly that he must report all overseas income. If he doesn't report it, he's guilty of a crime," Fahy said.

"Can he hide it in the corporation?" McCauley asked.

"He could. It's offshore. How would we know? Anyone can disguise income. Where does the money come from? That's the real question. And who are these Sunrise Meridian people who are leasing his property? No matter how he disguises it from the IRS, if the money comes from a government contractor his Senate committee oversees, it could very well be a Hobbs Act violation."

"And Homeland Security's recording just now tied it directly to Lamurr Technologies," McCauley said.

Fahy stood up slowly and walked to the window. His small office was discreetly housed on the top floor of an aging, nondescript office building several blocks from the Justice Department's stately stone temple, ascending majestically above Pennsylvania and Constitution Avenues. He looked down on the bumper-to-bumper traffic waiting impatiently, trapped on the steaming asphalt on Fourteenth Street. Rush hour was in full swing, cars backed up in both directions on the sweltering asphalt. The perception that the city shut down in August was a political myth. Congress may be out of session, and the president may be relaxing at Martha's Vineyard, but Fahy was still here in Washington, and the corroded gears of government kept ceaselessly grinding on.

"I'm not ready to talk to Bayard or his staff yet." Fahy spoke directly to the window, as if McCauley wasn't there. "I don't want to spook them. This is too politically charged. The Republican convention is days away. We need to dig deeper, and we need to be very discreet. This Jersey Shore company must be the key. If we can tie that to Lamurr, it would be a crime—a clear case of bribery."

"And with Bayard's fingerprints all over the Pentagon contract, it wouldn't be hard to show intent. The contract language is written so tightly that only Lamurr and its competitor, Serodynne Corporation, are even bidding on it. And who knows what type of pressure Bayard is putting on the Pentagon brass to award the contract to a friend?"

"If Lamurr is a friend," cautioned Fahy. "We need to do our homework and confirm our suspicions are correct. There could be some explanation to explain away a bribe. If he's guilty, I want a solid case. I want to nail the bastard. I don't want him to wheedle out this time."

"On the surface, both Lamurr and Serodynne seem clean," McCauley said. "I'm meeting with a Serodynne official tomorrow to see if they are part of this. So far, I've found nothing."

"Is that wise? You meeting with Serodynne? You could be tipping off the competition. There's a hell of a lot of money at stake here. Billions."

Fahy worried. What if the financial ties spread to Serodynne? Would McCauley's poking around blow their case?

"We need to ascertain just how widespread or isolated this scheme is. Bayard could be on the take from both companies," McCauley said.

"It's better questioning the competition than showing our hand to Bayard or to the Lamurr people right now."

McCauley joined Fahy at the window and towered over him. Fahy wondered if the agent's size intimidated people or if it was a disadvantage in his line of work since he always stood out in a crowd.

They looked down at the street and not at each other.

McCauley spoke again. "The bureau doesn't want to waste its time if Justice won't prosecute. It's a politically hypersensitive case. My bosses get that."

"All of our cases are, aren't they?" Fahy looked up at his colleague.

"Yeah, but this one is about as big as they get. The only thing bigger would be going after a sitting president."

Yes, thought Fahy. And if this is done the FBI way, that could be a real possibility.

A year from now that could turn into a constitutional nightmare. It could be the Watergate scandal all over again. But most likely it would just result in a lot of Justice Department officials getting fired, including himself.

"You were an actor in college, weren't you? You've done undercover work. Can't you use some of that ability to persuade your bosses this is worth pursuing?"

"Not without some department reassurance from you," McCauley said. "They'll never go for it."

"Then we have a problem. I went to Oliver yesterday, and he refuses to move the case forward without more evidence."

"Oliver?"

"Yeah."

Fahy had taken over the public integrity section seven years ago when Jackson Oliver moved to the White House to become assistant special counsel to newly elected President William Croom. Oliver returned to Justice six years later to head Justice's Criminal Division, overseeing Fahy's unit as well as others.

"But isn't this your decision?" McCauley stepped back. Fahy could see concern in McCauley's narrowing expression.

"It is, and it isn't. Technically, yes. Politically, no. It almost takes an act of God just to get a wiretap on an elected official these days. You thought going after Bayard would be easy? If Bayard weren't running for president, I would still have a tough time getting the green light to escalate this to the next level. Imagine what it's like now, with him inches away from the White House. Oliver gives a guy in Bayard's position a wide berth."

Fahy moved slowly back to his desk. His sciatica was giving him fits from too many sit-ups. After his youngest went off to college a year ago, his wife had left him for a girlfriend she had been playing tennis with for four years. That's when he began spending his early mornings at the gym.

"If Bayard wins the presidency, do you realize what he could do to this department? He names some toady as attorney general, and the guy sweeps in here and fires everybody who isn't a Bayard loyalist. Any investigation we start now could easily be shut down immediately after the inauguration. It happens all the time during a transition. We must be very careful and politically sensitive."

Fahy knew that wasn't the whole truth. But he couldn't tell McCauley everything. Truth was, he didn't completely trust the FBI. It was just as political as the rest of the Justice Department. And there was no way Oliver would allow the investigation to go forward; he said he did not want to put the department at risk.

More like Oliver didn't want to put his own political career at risk, thought Fahy.

But he couldn't tell McCauley that. He needed him now to continue pursuing the investigation.

McCauley flipped to another page on his pad, walking back toward his chair as he read his notes. "The attorney who incorporated both Sunrise Meridian and Bayard's Jersey Shore is a Roger Kindred."

"So?"

"You don't think it's a bit strange that the landlord and the tenant he's leasing his property to for twenty-five thousand a month are incorporated by the same attorney?"

"Well, yes and no. It's a small island. And remember, lawyers will work for either side of a transaction, and sometimes both. We're whores to the corporate wallet. But yes, it certainly ties them closer together and makes you wonder."

"Well, it gets even better than that. It gets personal."

"Oh?" Fahy leaned forward, positioning his elbows on his desk, looking directly into McCauley's eyes.

"Your boss. Jackson Oliver. Kindred is his half brother."

"Holy shit."

7

A perfect spot for anyone to meet unseen, thought Beck, as he pulled into a crumbling parking lot next to an old strip shopping center on US Route 1. The highway was once the main east coast route from Maine to Key West, but it had grown seedy after I-95 opened in the early 1960s. He parked next to a drywall contractor's battered white crew cab, "Fairfax Dry Wall" painted in faded red lettering on the door. Beck stepped out of his classic Volvo C70 convertible onto loose pavement eaten away by leaking engine oil. He stood in the middle of the low-profile immigrant community inhaling a whiff of diesel fuel. Beck looked around the parking lot at a desolate moonscape of potholes and faded, nearly invisible line markings of old parking spaces. He locked his doors.

The restaurant wore its age on its sleeve. At least the peeling paint had been scraped from the cinder-block walls, leaving a patina of speckled blue and white. The lit red Plexiglas restaurant sign had seen better days. It read "Rant." Beck grinned and wondered if that was appropriate. He figured he would soon find out.

The wooden front door could use a coat of paint, thought Beck.

It opened with a whining hinge and closed with a clanging bell. Scratchy, upbeat Latin music blared from a small black plastic AM radio high on the wall behind the lunch counter, fighting for shelf space with brown packages of spare white paper napkins. A bare silver wire served as a makeshift antenna and stretched tightly from the radio to a thumbtack on the top shelf.

Five Latinos, garbed in plaster-splattered T-shirts and jeans and wearing heavy work boots, sat on stools at the long lunch counter. They drank tiny cups of espresso and talked in bursts of Spanish, then laughed. Beck didn't understand a word.

He spotted Fahy immediately in the back of the dining room. They were the only white guys in the place—probably the only ones speaking English. He navigated a hodgepodge of mismatched chairs and made his way to a Formica-covered table with scratched chrome trim and legs. It reminded Beck of his family's kitchen table when he was a boy.

Fahy sat with his back to the wall. His wrinkled, blue, plaid shirt was at odds with his white hair, which stood unbending like a field of wheat stalks after it had been harvested.

They shook hands. Fahy did not stand. Fahy had the sad eyes of an overworked government bureaucrat and the soft features and lines of age, yet the taunt body of an athlete.

"How'd you find this place?" Beck asked.

Fahy motioned for him to sit. "Five years ago, I met Councilman Barry Marion here when we were investigating corruption on the DC city council."

"Isn't that a full-time job?"

"Just about," Fahy replied.

"So you have the same idea today. We're keeping a low profile."

"Something like that."

Fahy slid a large tan envelope across the table and scanned the restaurant over Beck's shoulder. Beck opened it.

"It's a Form 302 FBI report," Fahy said.

Several lines were blacked out. Beck looked up, pointing at the missing words.

"Everything you need to get started is there," Fahy said. "The redacted material is classified national security information. It's a confidential FBI report on Senator David Bayard of New Jersey. He's involved in some offshore financial scheme that doesn't appear kosher. We're not sure where it leads."

"The senator who's running for president?"

"The same."

Beck looked at Fahy for a long, awkward moment saying nothing. Then a stocky, large-breasted, black-haired waitress in a too-tight blouse waddled up to the table and rescued him. Beck covered the papers with the envelope. Fahy looked up at her as she leaned over, her black bra edging out of her white blouse and doing its best to keep her cavernous cleavage from spilling out onto the table. She pulled a pencil from the beehive atop her head and aimed it at a small pad of paper. Beck noticed Fahy's eyes were also leveled at her chest.

She wheezed from the exertion of crossing the room. Beck recognized her perfume. Cigarette. Menthol.

"The sausage and eggs are the best," Fahy said. "Nothing fancy." He ordered.

Surprised to see some Anglo food choices on the menu, Beck ordered corned beef hash.

The waitress left a pot of coffee and a plate of toast behind. The toast went untouched. The coffee was strong. They drank it black.

"Nice pencil," Fahy said, shifting his glance to the waitress who had retreated across the room. Beck smiled, acknowledging the crude attempt to bond over the opposite sex.

Fahy told Beck of his suspicions about Senator Bayard taking bribes from Lamurr Technologies, which was bidding on a large Pentagon contract. He told him that his boss, Jackson Oliver, had effectively killed the investigation.

"But doesn't the Pentagon contracting office have the last word on who wins a contract?" Beck asked.

"On paper, of course. But that's not really how it works. The Pentagon brass know where their money comes from, so they do the bidding of Congress, even when it's to their own detriment. Why do you think

Eisenhower warned of the growing influence of the military-industrial complex? And that was more than fifty years ago."

The brass wouldn't risk alienating Bayard, Fahy explained. It was all outlined in the investigative documents in the envelope. He kept glancing around the restaurant. The place was quickly emptying of construction workers.

Fahy's gift came with two conditions: Beck could never reveal him as his source nor reveal that Beck actually owned or saw the memorandum now in the envelope.

Beck couldn't believe his luck. If any of this were true, he had the beginnings of one helluva story. He didn't see how Fahy's terms would impede him from writing anything, so he readily agreed. Still, Beck felt uneasy. "Why are you doing this?"

"My hands are tied. I'm hoping you can find the truth."

That seemed to corroborate what Beck had read about Fahy. He was a man who did not appear to fear taking extraordinary risks to resolve corruption cases. Beck sensed he was Fahy's last resort. No doubt Fahy had exhausted all other avenues if he was turning to a reporter. Still, Beck wasn't used to such high-powered people leaking him information. This was no low-level, disgruntled bureaucrat he was talking to.

"You don't have many friends in this town, do you?" Beck asked.

"A few. It comes with the territory. My office is not popular with either end of Pennsylvania Avenue or anywhere in between."

"Lonely job."

"It takes a certain kind of person. I guess I qualify."

Beck recognized the breed. They shared official Washington's mutual hostility and respect. In a sense, they played similar roles. But he wasn't on the public payroll. He didn't have a boss burying his best work. Beck felt a tinge of sympathy for the man sitting across from him.

"What makes you tick? I've read about you. They call you the Boy Scout."

"Somebody's got to do the right thing in this town—too few actually do anymore."

"I get that. I became a reporter for the same reason. Now it seems a bit naive."

"Maybe we both are."

Beck shifted his attention to the contents of the large envelope. He involuntarily tapped his foot under the table. He shifted in his seat. It was no longer the strong black coffee that was giving him a buzz, but that old familiar euphoric feeling that the hunt was on. This was better than sex. If he found anything—even the smallest hint of a big story— he knew he would never let it go until he had shredded every outstanding lead, every avenue.

Fahy handed Beck a small folded piece of paper. "If you need to reach me, use this number. Leave a message. Make it sound innocuous, a routine call from a reporter that my department knows I would never return. Make it sound like you've never met me. If the voice mail is ever seized, I don't want it to sound like we have any connection. Leave me a number where I can reach you. I will call you back and make arrangements to meet again, but I won't discuss this over the phone. Agreed?"

"Agreed."

"Then we're done here." Fahy gulped down his coffee. He shifted in his seat.

Beck then broached the one question he'd been yearning to ask since he had sat down. "Why leak this to me? Why not another reporter?" By handing over that envelope, Fahy must have broken a slew of federal laws and probably violated every legal ethics tenet he'd learned since matriculating law school.

"Reputation," Fahy said. "I asked around. You're the most ruthless reporter at the *Post-Examiner.*"

"Ruthless?"

"All right, relentless."

Flattery bought Fahy two eggs over easy, sausage, uneaten toast, and strong black coffee.

8

Geneva Kemper had finished a quick meeting and was scanning the morning paper when her administrative assistant interrupted to announce a visitor.

A very tall man with a hint of a goatee, probably in his late thirties, strode into her corner office. He had broad shoulders and a small waist. No doubt a fitness buff, she thought.

"Patrick McCauley." He offered a firm hand as she stood and stepped from behind her desk to welcome him.

Geneva had a strong grip, yet she noticed her visitor did not try to crush her fingers as some men did. A gentleman, she thought. And a nice-looking one.

Though she could have chosen the small conference table in the corner of her office for a visit from the FBI, Geneva preferred her territorial position of power, behind her desk. This was her court.

She watched McCauley quickly scan her grip and grin wall to the left of her desk. There were dozens of obligatory vanity photos of her shaking hands with various senators and congressmen—and even a few presidents—all prominently displayed. He seemed to be looking for someone, but then quickly turned his head and looked straight into her eyes.

"We're doing a routine inquiry, and I wanted to ask you a few questions," McCauley said as he made himself comfortable in her visitor's chair. "I appreciate you agreeing to meet with me on such short notice." He sounded bored.

"I'm sorry I didn't return your call yesterday. I was on a flight from Minneapolis."

"Your corporate headquarters, right?"

"I see you've done your homework."

"We try." He smiled.

"I'm always happy to help the FBI." That was dumb, she thought, but what else could she say?

"Just so you know, this is a confidential inquiry, so we ask you not to discuss it with anyone. If you feel uncomfortable at any time, however, we can stop, and you can consult with your legal counsel or have one present."

"I've got nothing to hide." Geneva leaned back in her chair, her hands folded in her lap. What was this all about?

"Mind if I take a few notes?" He whipped out a small notebook and pen from his suit jacket, not waiting for an answer.

She eyed him but said nothing. He was probably a gym rat—one with a slightly crooked nose, probably earned in a boxing match or a pickup basketball game after work, she thought. His vigor stirred something inside her. It had been a while. She had to remind herself to pay attention to the issue at hand.

"For the record, your name is Geneva Gordon Kemper, correct?"

"Correct."

"Gordon's an unusual name for a woman."

"It was my mother's maiden name. I'm part Scot. German on my father's side—the Kemper part. I kept my name when I got married."

"I see. And you're married to . . ."

"Senator Michael Harvey . . . really, Agent McCauley, you know all of this from your files, I'm sure. I'm a registered lobbyist. My complete background is on file in the Capitol. Let's skip the investigatory foreplay." What was this guy up to? Was he hoping she would slip up? Was he trying to catch her in a lie? What was the deal here?

He looked up from his notebook and into her eyes. "Do you know Senator David Bayard?"

"Of course. He's chairman of the Senate Armed Services Committee."

"Ever give him any political contributions?"

"All the time. Serodynne has numerous Pentagon contracts. I give both personal and Serodynne political action committee contributions to Senator Bayard's campaigns and also to every member of the committee. It's all in the public record."

McCauley adjusted his athletic frame in her chair. "Have you ever been to an out-of-town retreat with Senator Bayard or his staff?"

"Not that I can remember. I'll be happy to check our records if you'd like." What was he fishing for?

"Have you ever socialized with the senator?"

She explained her husband dealt with Senator Bayard as part of his job, but they did not routinely socialize privately as a couple with the senator and his wife.

"Have you ever heard of his retreats with lobbyists in the Caribbean?"

"No, but I wish I had. I'd love to find some excuse to do business down there, especially in the colder months. Although now that it's August, I feel Canada calling."

McCauley exaggerated a polite grin, a sure sign her clumsy attempt at humor fell flat, Geneva thought. She needed to not overreach.

Keep your answers simple, she told herself.

McCauley looked down at his notes and continued in his dry monotone. "Have you ever been to the Caribbean?"

"Sure, my husband and I have been all over—the Bahamas, Aruba, Puerto Rico, Grand Cayman, Saint John, Saint Bart's, Saint Martin, Anguilla. I think that covers the past twenty years."

"When was the last time you were in Grand Cayman?"

"Hmmm. Five years ago maybe? Yes. I think it was about that long ago. Why?"

"The senator apparently has invested in some commercial property down there. I was wondering if you or your company had ever done business with any of his Caribbean investments or businesses."

"I never knew he had anything going in the Caribbean. I'll have to ask him about it." Geneva instinctively leaned forward, clasping her hands together on her desk. She noticed McCauley eyeing the large diamond on her left hand. She instinctively covered it with her right. She wondered where this was going.

McCauley then grilled her on her out-of-town business trips, none of which were tied to Senator Bayard and all of which she assumed he was already familiar with from examining her lobbyist filings at the Capitol. She hedged on dates and specifics, not wanting to be caught in any discrepancies. She couldn't believe the FBI would come after her for some minor travel infraction. Would it?

"I go to New York on a fairly regular basis," Geneva said. "I meet with investment bankers quarterly. In fact, I've got an appointment with them tomorrow. They want to keep up with our government contracting so they can tell their clients we are still a good investment. Just routine stuff."

McCauley leaned forward in his chair, his big, dark eyes almost penetrating her. "Serodynne Corporation is competing with the Lamurr Technologies for a big contract on some new drone technology for the air force. Yes?"

"Well, that's certainly no secret. It's a one-hundred-billion-dollar, seven-year deal. Certainly would be our largest contract ever. Serodynne and Lamurr are the only two companies in the US with the capacity to manufacture them." Was this what this interview was about? Geneva was careful not to bite her lip or show any sign of nervousness.

She shifted into lobbyist infomercial. "In fact, I believe we have a much greater capacity than Lamurr to meet the Pentagon's target dates. I've made sure to mention that to the generals, the Pentagon contracting office, and several members of Congress. Our contracting team is all over it."

"So you think your chances are good?"

"Of course." Geneva's mind started to race. What was he after?

"So Serodynne doesn't do any business with Senator Bayard?"

"No. Our only financial connection with him is political campaign contributions. We're as generous as the law allows."

That was the second time he'd asked that question. She brushed her bangs out of her eyes and rested her elbows on her desk.

"Are you aware of any financial relationship between the senator and Lamurr Technologies?" he asked.

"If I were, I'd pick up the phone and call you. Not only would it be unethical and illegal, but it would be against Serodynne's best economic interests to compete in some rigged bidding contest. What do you know that I don't know?" Geneva twisted her diamond ring.

"Like I said, this is just a routine review. Since the senator is running for president, the crazies come out of the woodwork, forcing us to scrutinize all of the potential candidates' finances a little closer. You wouldn't believe all of the crackpots out there with conspiracy theories. I've been in the agency for thirteen years and, every four years, it's the same thing all over again."

Crazies. Yes, she'd met a few in Washington during her career. But was McCauley being honest or was he trying to conceal what he was really up to?

McCauley rose from his chair. "I don't want to take up any more of your time, but I may be back in touch with you with some follow-up questions, if you don't mind."

His gaze penetrated her. Another place, another time, she told herself, but not under these circumstances.

"Not at all," she blurted out a little too loudly.

"But if you would keep our conversation between us, the bureau would appreciate it. We are still looking into this matter."

"I understand, but I may need to tell our corporate counsel. We are a publicly traded company."

They shook hands again, and his handshake was once more cordial and not overbearing. Geneva closed her office door behind him and leaned against it, breathing deeply. She stared at the wall and then sat back in her chair.

What just happened? She was well paid to play political chess in this town and be three moves ahead of the competition. She hadn't seen this one coming. What was the senator up to? What was going on in the Caribbean? Was her contract bid in jeopardy because Lamurr was paying off the senator? It had to be the contract, she thought. If Lamurr had an inside track with the senator, years of her work would be wasted. Her job would be in jeopardy. She shuddered and sat at her desk, her face in her hands.

Washington was a dirty town where people didn't always play by the rules, but this . . . this was beyond anything she had ever dealt with. She brushed the hair out of her face and picked up her desk phone. She dialed Minneapolis headquarters. She recounted her conversation with McCauley to Serodynne's legal counsel, Sue Nijelski.

"Don't say a thing about this tomorrow when you meet with the investment bankers," Nijelski said. "Nothing has been confirmed. You don't know for sure anything is going on. The last thing we need is for our stock to crash based on false rumors. You need to find the truth."

After some pleasantries about Nijelski's husband's latest wine find, they hung up.

Geneva sat at her desk in thought. Find the truth. How in the world would she do that?

Geneva's administrative assistant buzzed her. "Your brunch is in twenty minutes."

McCauley's bombshell had totally disoriented her. She had forgotten about meeting with Ellen Elizabeth. She needed time to focus, but now was not the time. Geneva grabbed her handbag and jacket and raced out the door.

9

Throughout brunch with her college roommate Ellen Elizabeth Howard—one of many Washington hostesses who greased the wheels of politics by throwing parties and fund-raisers for the powerful at her Georgetown home—Geneva couldn't get the conversation with the FBI agent
out of her head.

"What's bothering you?" Ellen Elizabeth finally asked, her husky
Georgia drawl lingering a half step behind her.

"Apparent, huh?"

"Duh."

"Its just work. I'm trying to figure out my next move. I had a disturb-
ing meeting just before I came here." She didn't want to talk about the
FBI, not even with her best friend. "Ellen Elizabeth, how long have we
known each other?"

"Geneva—" Ellen Elizabeth paused and tilted her head. She had a
curious look on her face. "What do you mean? Since college of course.
And then when we both worked on the Hill for those two obscure
congressmen."

"What ever happened to them?"

"I think they both were disappointed—or maybe overwhelmed—
and went home after a few years."

"That's unusual. They didn't cash in."

"Jen, why are you changing the subject? Why are we having this conversation? What happened to you today?"

"I don't think I can look at another blue pinstripe suit." Geneva looked away from her friend and stared blankly across the dining room.

There was a long pause as she fumbled for her water glass and took a sip.

"Need to talk? Jen, you know I'm always available if you need to talk."

"I appreciate that. I'm just stumped about what to do right now." Geneva secretly examined the large gold bracelet her husband Harv— she always called him Harv—had given her on her thirty-fifth birthday. It glistened in the sun's light, which filtered through the large palms by the window, shielding the restaurant's patrons from the street. Her bling reminded her of an earlier, happier time.

Today, the two friends met at the new bistro in Washington's Penn Quarter, only a few blocks from Geneva's condo. After scrutinizing the lavish brunch menu, they each ordered a different version of Eggs Benedict and a glass of champagne. Glancing around the bistro, Geneva noted it was similar in design to the latest stark, modern interiors favored by designers in their never-ending quest to set the latest trend. Eating out in Washington was similar to its pandering politics. It was all about the fashionable experience, she thought, and had little to do with the actual ingredients.

"Are you okay with your job?" asked Ellen Elizabeth. "You know, you've talked for years about hanging up your lobbyist spurs. Is it time? Do you still think about that?"

"Too often, but things aren't great between Harv and me right now, and now I have to deal with these problems at the office. I'm tiring of the Washington conceit. But if Harv and I don't work out, I can't afford to quit right now." There. She'd said it. She'd bottled up feelings about her marriage struggles for too long.

"I didn't know it was that bad." Ellen Elizabeth spoke slowly. Her eyes narrowed, and she reached across the table and placed her hand over Geneva's.

"He's a lovely man," Geneva said, "but I need to be desired again."

"I'm sorry, Jen. I hope you can work it out. Maybe a new job would help your relationship. Maybe get out of this rat race. Why not give it up? Try something else?"

"What would I do?"

"Retire to that beach you always dream about."

"At forty-two?"

"People do it all the time. No more Armani suits. Just a teeny-weeny bikini—or for you, something less—much less."

Geneva grinned at the thought. A vision filled her mind of lying naked under a clear blue sky on some private beach feeling the warm sun radiate on her bare skin with the sound of gentle waves lapping the shore. What a cliché, she thought.

But it was her cliché. It was her ambition, and that's all that mattered. She desperately needed to clear her mind and get off the Washington treadmill while she was still young enough to enjoy life. She'd seen enough of the never-ending churn of the struggle for power.

And yet now she faced the possibility of losing the biggest deal of her life and being forced out of her job, and she realized she couldn't afford to leave. And she was all too aware she'd become too comfortable with a life she despised. She enjoyed the perks of power and money like everyone else, yet she yearned to go back to something simpler.

"You know me too well," Geneva said, looking back to her friend.

"But I could never get you to come out of the closet." Ellen Elizabeth grinned.

"You're the one who put me there, remember?"

They both laughed, and Geneva thought back to their sophomore year, when Ellen Elizabeth labeled her a closet nudist. If she wasn't sneaking up to the roof of the dorm for the perfect tan, Geneva was prancing around their room in the buff. She was frequently found at her desk, stark naked, or laid out naked on her dorm bunk with her thick brown hair pulled back in a ponytail, reading her economics text. And since men were restricted on her floor to visiting hours, Geneva was never worried about them getting a cheap thrill.

She had grown up a child of the diplomatic service and frequented nude and topless beaches with her family around the world. She and her brother swam nude together in the Mediterranean with their mother and thought nothing of it.

"You weren't a real nudist—" Ellen Elizabeth said.

"Just a closet one," they both chimed in, finishing a line they had laughed at over for years. Ellen Elizabeth dabbed her napkin to her lips. "So you're coming on Thursday?"

"Yes, but Harv has to make a quick run to Wyoming. His scheduler screwed up his calendar and booked him for a campaign fund-raiser for one of his colleagues on the same day as your party. He's still trying to take over the Senate Republican Campaign Committee, so he can't miss this trip. I'm afraid he'll have to bail on you. I'm sorry."

"It's my fault for trying to put a party together at the end of August. I've never tried this before, when Congress is out of session. But I thought with the party conventions this year, there would be plenty of members in town to put a little soiree together. I figured I'd have no competition."

"Most members, I think, prefer Washington over their backwater districts," Geneva said. "The power heats their blood. Harv's no different. He'd much rather enjoy the trappings of Washington than spend a month back home. Normally, we go to the Cape or Canada or the Outer Banks this time of year. But no, this year I'm stuck here. Harv is spending his days on the telephone raising money for fellow senators or attending fund-raisers in preparation for the convention."

"You're really unhappy."

"Right now Wyoming for a day sounds better than being trapped in this swamp."

They both laughed, but Geneva could tell from Ellen Elizabeth's strained expression that she understood there was nothing funny about it. Friends, she thought, sometimes communicate true feelings in such strange, indirect ways.

Ellen Elizabeth interrupted Geneva's train of thought and continued her own. "I started out with three congressmen and two senators.

I'm down to one of each. But I've got some pretty good administration officials." She sighed.

"It will still be a great party." Now it was Geneva's turn to offer comfort. Strange how Ellen Elizabeth was anxious about the next few days while she was fretful about the rest of her life. This time she reached out and squeezed her college roommate's hand, thankful for one true friend in this town. "I can't wait to see the fireworks between Congressman Joy and that reporter, Beck Rikki," Geneva said.

"Oh? They have issues?" Ellen Elizabeth put down her champagne glass and brushed strands of blonde hair out of her face. She looked up at Geneva.

"You hadn't heard?" Geneva said. "A while back, Rikki wrote a story about one of Joy's pet projects he'd stuffed in the appropriations bill. It was buried in the *Post-Examiner*, but the local paper in Nebraska picked it up and splashed it on its front page. The publicity in his district forced Joy to withdraw his amendment. He was mad as hell. This was a favor to some big contributor."

"Oops. I need to change my seating chart. I had them sitting together."

Geneva paused. She had an idea. She leaned forward, placing her elbows on the table and holding her water glass in both hands. "Ellen Elizabeth, would you seat me next to Rikki? I've never met him. I've read some of his articles and heard a little about him. I'd like to take his measure."

"You're doing me a huge favor, Jen."

Geneva took a sip of her water and wondered if it was the other way around. Maybe Mr. Rikki could prove useful. Maybe a newspaper reporter was what she needed to help her with her Pentagon problem. Maybe, she thought, she could find her way out of this mess.

10

The next morning Geneva arrived at the lower Manhattan office of her investment banker nearly fifteen minutes early to give herself enough time to deal with lobby security and wait for the creaking elevators as they gasped to reach the twenty-seventh floor. She hated to be late for appointments. She needed a few moments beforehand to mentally prep herself.

A receptionist escorted Geneva into one of the investment bank's smaller conference rooms. The only light came from a window overlooking the Hudson River. Steel-rimmed photographs of partners and favored clients ringing the opening bell at the New York Stock Exchange covered the dark gray walls. Other photos showed the partners with celebrities and politicians. Geneva shivered. The room made her cold.

"Geneva, good to see you," boomed George Bernstein, offering his hand as he entered the room. He and Geneva had been meeting for nearly a decade, beginning back when he was in his fifties and actually ran the place. A tall, younger man stepped into the room. Bernstein turned toward him. "You remember Keith Crocker, our young associate."

"Of course," Geneva replied. "We had a very pleasant lunch the last time I was here." She shook his hand.

"We've decided to make him chief analyst on your account."

Geneva studied Crocker more closely: in his midtwenties, sandy blond hair, slender, and a bit gangly. Not bad looking, she thought, especially if she were fifteen years younger.

"How's the writing coming?" Geneva asked him. At their last lunch meeting, they talked for a nearly an hour about literature. Crocker was a poet and wannabe novelist.

He blushed. "I've still got a long way to go."

"We call him our resident poet laureate," Bernstein said, his grin flapping across his fleshy face. She could not help but notice the turned-up corners of his cardboard smile. He was a slippery bore, and as far as she could tell, not even much of a stockbroker. She understood she was being downgraded by the firm and handed off to the farm team.

As they sat, bankers Robert Gettlin and Peter Lamarca joined the meeting—all familiar faces. All but Crocker were dressed in expensive Italian or Savile Row suits.

Geneva distributed a summary of government contracts she was bidding on. It included two small cybersecurity proposals and Serodynne's multibillion-dollar contract submission for the unmanned aerial vehicles. They walked through the numbers.

She could do this over the telephone, but her career as a lobbyist had taught her the importance of face time. She wanted to personally explain how government contracts worked and assure them Serodynne was in a healthy financial position. She needed to snow these investment bankers, which wouldn't be easy. One wrong word could cost her company tens of millions of dollars in the stock market. It was imperative Serodynne's stock price not fall right now, yet one sniff of a problem could send company shares tumbling.

On the Acela train the night before, Geneva had formulated the beginnings of a plan to ensure Serodynne won the Pentagon contract. Her first step would be convincing these bankers Serodynne was about to win its biggest contract ever.

"So," Crocker said, "your stock is trading at nearly thirty-two percent over its balance sheet valuation in anticipation of Serodynne winning the drone contract later this year. What if it doesn't happen?"

"It's not a drone contract," she explained, slipping into her lobbyist spiel. "It's a proposal to build unmanned aerial vehicles. Drones have preset flight patterns. Unmanned aerial vehicles are actively piloted by an air force pilot, but from the ground. In fact, it usually requires two pilots. The first one is at the runway from where the aircraft takes off and lands. That pilot then hands over control of the aircraft to a pilot in North Dakota, who handles the craft while it's in flight."

"Okay, but what if you fail to get the contract?"

"We don't anticipate that." She shifted into lobbyist warp drive. "We obviously have what we believe to be the inside track on this. Our delivery record and capacity are better than Lamurr's. Our R & D folks work hand in glove with the Pentagon, and our knowledge base means we can move quickly. Lamurr couldn't possibly gear up to deliver on the fast-track schedule the Pentagon is demanding. The air force generals and the contracting office know this, but they have to consider more than one bidder, and Lamurr would be stupid not to bid. We are quite confident in our chances to win the contract."

Geneva saw this same technique successfully employed on the Sunday morning political talk shows. When asked a question, she would ignore it and go straight into her canned speech. It worked for powerful politicians. Why not for her?

She studied Crocker. The strategy seemed to be working.

She shifted the focus of the conversation from Serodynne's finances to Lamurr, making her competitor out to be nothing more than convenient window dressing for Serodynne's future world domination of the drone market—or as Geneva reminded them, unmanned aerial vehicles.

"And what about private commercial contracts?" Crocker asked.

"As you know, that's not my area. But I'm told we have several pending with four Fortune 500 companies and two European firms. We are even talking with the Chinese on some more basic technology and have been in constant contact with clients in Brazil. We also just started talks with the Saudis. These contracts could be worth hundreds of millions, maybe even billions, to our company."

Crocker continued. "Your last quarterly earnings statement was down from expectations. If you don't win this Pentagon contract, your next quarter will look even worse. What are you doing to prepare should you lose the Pentagon contract to Lamurr?" His glance locked onto hers.

Geneva pivoted toward the other partners and then thought better of it and stared directly into Crocker's eyes. He knew something about the investigation. In an instant, he had turned the tables on her. Was she wrong about him?

"How do you . . ." She trailed off, her mind racing. He couldn't know. The FBI wouldn't go near an investment bank for fear of spooking the market. What was he after?

"How do I—" Crocker paused. "What?"

"How could you . . ." Words escaped her. Slow down. Be deliberate and pull it together, she told herself. "How do you create such expectations? We are profitable. We are growing. We have no doubt we will win the contract. The Street is fickle with its forecasts."

She again looked over at the partners. Bernstein glanced at his watch and motioned to Crocker. "Well, as you can see, Keith here has been doing his homework. He's a tough questioner."

"Perfectly legitimate questions," Geneva said. "Anyone for lunch today? Any takers? My treat."

The senior partners demurred; two had early afternoon tee times, and the other had lunch plans. But Crocker accepted. She slipped her sheets of numbers into her slim leather briefcase and said her perfunctory good-byes to the partners. They seemed most eager to get to their golf games and early afternoon cocktails.

She had managed to put Crocker in his place in front of the partners. Apparently his promotion to chief analyst had given him the balls to show off his knowledge. She liked that. But she had come too close to inadvertently blurting out her secret. She needed to be more careful. Crocker might be a minor leaguer, but he also might be a deceptively good player. She would need to watch herself—and him—over lunch.

11

The elevator was crowded and again seemed to take forever. Finally, Geneva and Keith emerged and walked across the street to a steak house where they had dined the last time she was here. Dark, with white silken-edged waiters and black cotton tablecloths, it operated like Wall Street: an arrogance of efficiency, subtle discretion, a touch of boisterous banter, and always, always expensive. It reminded her of many of Washington's exclusive haunts, places she had come to despise. But at least here the tables were deliberately placed far apart, affording each diner a sense of privacy for doing deals. Geneva liked that and thought it would grant her the opportunity to size up Crocker. They were certainly friendly, but how much could she trust him? She had a notion of a plan she had formulated on the train yesterday, and she needed an investment banker's help to pull it off. Could Crocker meet her needs?

This was their third lunch together, and they had talked by phone often about investment matters. Through these phone conversations, Geneva felt they had formed a friendly enough bond. She certainly understood the importance of relationships and worked them daily on Capitol Hill and along the long, scuffed corridors of the federal bureaucracy. Building them with investment bankers was really no different.

It took only a few questions about Crocker's writing to send him on a circuitous detour about his quest to get published and the crazy demands of book publishers and literary agents. She could tell her encouragement endeared her to him.

She had wined and dined the entire investment team up until six months ago. Since then, they had ducked out, leaving lunch up to Crocker. Bernstein and his cronies talked nonstop finance and the latest news of that day's market. Even though she had a degree in economics and could keep up with the dialogue, she grew weary of money matters after the first five minutes. She appreciated that Crocker had a life beyond lower Manhattan.

"Keith, you don't strike me as your typical type A investment banker. You're not like the others on Wall Street."

"You noticed?"

He laughed. She smiled.

"Between you and me," he said, "this job is my means to an end. Once I make a killing, I'm out of here. I'll move to South Carolina or Florida, or maybe I'll have enough money to buy a shack on a Caribbean island somewhere and start my writing career."

"Not going to do the starving artist thing? Pay your dues as a waiter so you can stay up late at night and write?"

"That sounds more like an actor. And why should I? It's a new world out there. I've got my plan, and I've got ready access to money. Real money. That's why I'm here. The partners know I'm not willing to put in the hours to make partner in ten years. They keep me because they need someone with my brains who can analyze the information from five different angles and not just sell crap investments to unsuspecting clients."

"You sound like you've got this all figured out."

"I wish. The firm's money is in sales, not my area of expertise," he continued. "But they need good analytics to keep their clients from fleeing to the competition. Most of the firm is nothing but salesmen who analyzed common stocks twenty-five years ago. All of the firms are looking for bright kids like me who can dissect the new creative derivative investments, which are nothing more than stocks on steroids. But in the end, it's still all about selling and what gives the firm the highest commissions, and I don't fit that mold. They know that. They'll use me for a few years, and I hope, I'll use them."

"Sounds a little cynical, but it also sounds as if the only way your job's in jeopardy is if you quit."

Keith smiled. "You might say that."

She ordered cabernet. He ordered a Bud. Not a sophisticated drink, she thought, not even an import or a microbrew. She glanced at his pin-stripe suit. Strictly off the rack. But he was young. He would change as his bank account did if he stuck around. They all did.

"Just how much do you want out?" she asked.

"I'm twenty-six. If I could work just one big deal, I could retire with two or three million by the time I'm thirty—that's all I want."

"You have a nest egg?"

"Not much. I just got started last year. I've got about thirty-five thousand in a money market, and another twenty in stocks that I can leverage into about one hundred twenty on a sure trade using stock options. I'm still analyzing companies, looking for that one sweet deal where I can make a killing."

"Sounds risky."

"If I want to quit in three or four years, I have to take big risks. If I fail, I start over. I'm young enough. I'm smart enough to minimize the risks. That's why I haven't made my move yet—I'm still looking. And please, don't say anything back at the office."

"I thought you discussed it with Bernstein."

"Not that part. He only knows I don't want to go for partner and I won't be around forever. I don't want anyone piggybacking on my great investment—when I find it. Remember, I need to make a killing to get out of here."

She assured him their conversation would go no farther than their table and then ordered a second round to go with their entrees. He'd ordered a rib eye. Geneva chose the steak salad. They talked about investment banking, and she kept subtly shifting the conversation back to what he really wanted out of life.

She hesitated and took another bite of salad. They had a good relationship, but was that enough? For god's sake, they had known each other for only eight months. Yet, he had confided in her about his plan and even his personal finances. When he became wealthy, no doubt he would be more circumspect. Yet, they were friendly confidants, she assured herself.

She flirted with him, complimenting him on his independence and his desire for a different life. She liked his inquisitive mind. He smiled, and his eyes drifted down to her chest.

Wow, she thought. Is he interested? I wonder if he's got the balls to hit on me. She felt a faint shiver dance through her body. No, she told herself. He's too young.

She probed deeper into his personal life. How would his dad react to Keith checking out of Wall Street? Hadn't he just split with his girlfriend of three months? He said he lived simply to save money to invest, and he was up every morning at five o'clock and wrote for two hours before he showered and shaved.

This kid was focused and driven and wanted to get out—just what she needed. She recognized they were looking for the same thing. This just might work, she thought.

Just as she prepared to go on the full charm offensive, he brought it back to business.

"To be honest, Geneva, I'm not sure your company is in as good a shape as you think, or at least its condition isn't as good as you let on. I need to spend more time with the numbers, but I might be forced to recommend to our clients that they sell the stock."

She saw her opening. "What would it take for you to recommend a buy or hold instead?"

"The stock is already selling at a high price in anticipation of the Pentagon contract."

"The unmanned aircraft contract." She smiled.

"Yes, the *unmanned aircraft* contract. I'm not sure, though, how I could come up with a buy recommendation on Serodynne stock. The price is just too high. You expecting some of those commercial contracts to come through and raise the value of the company?"

"What if I could deliver that deal you're looking for that would allow you to write for the rest of your life—no financial worries ever again?"

He fell silent. He gazed into her eyes. She watched his expression run the gamut from wide-eyed astonishment to wrinkled brow realization. He quickly looked around the restaurant before turning back to Geneva.

"You're serious?" He fingered his half-full beer glass.

"I could be." She watched him closely.

His eyes widened. He grinned and looked down at his beer.

"It would involve risk," she said, "as well as your pledge of complete confidentiality. And there is no guarantee, but the odds are pretty good. The upside could be huge. And like you said earlier, you're young. If it fails, you look for the next deal." She looked intently at his eyes. He was looking down, eyes leveled at her chest, yet she could tell he was elsewhere, thinking, contemplating what she had just said.

He looked back up at her. "I'm willing to listen."

"Then we need to talk more."

And they did. For the next hour, she laid out her plan, almost in a whisper at their table as the waiters scurried about, occasionally stopping by to ask if they needed anything. Each time she waved them off. She asked Keith dozens of questions about the workings of his office, explaining she needed to understand how it operated if her plan stood a chance. At first he didn't understand, but then she could see excitement in his eyes as she laid out the details. He began to fidget in his chair so much that at one point she reached out and laid her hand on his forearm and told him to calm down.

He was a strange concoction of creative enthusiasm and financial zeal. As long as she could keep his creative passions in check and focus his financial acumen where she needed it, she thought, this might have a slim chance of working.

12

Geneva's meeting with Keith lasted more than two hours, yet a cooperative cab driver delivered her in time to Penn Station where she made the three o'clock train back to Washington. After a brief swim in the pool, she now lounged naked on the terrace of her Pennsylvania Avenue penthouse. The sun's rays warmed her soul, while a soft breeze bathed her in freedom.

She loved the feeling, and her rooftop location gave her complete privacy, even from presidential helicopters, whose flight path over the Potomac, nearly a mile away, ferried the president regularly between the White House and Andrews Air Force Base. She wondered if the spy satellites over the city ever focused in on her. Maybe some air force satellite jockey staring at a big screen in a bunker in Colorado was getting his jollies in real time, she thought. It took all kinds.

She glanced down on the Navy Memorial thirteen floors below, a circular plaza dedicated to sailors around the world. Across Pennsylvania Avenue, she gazed at the shadows cast by the giant granite columns of the National Archives building. It always gave her goose bumps knowing the nation's history and official secrets were kept there, along with one of her own.

On their first date, Harv had taken her on a private tour of the building after closing time. It was a curious gesture, she thought, until he surprised her with a lavish private four-course dinner on the roof terrace. After it became dark and the waitstaff left, they made love under the stars. But it was during dinner that she first eyed the penthouse across the avenue, which a year later they would occupy as their new home. But that was in a happier time.

She yearned to look beyond the National Archives and gazed at a faraway place that existed only in her imagination. It was not real, just like much of the nation's capital. Washington's Mall and national monuments might be built over an old rancid swamp, but official Washington cleverly paved over it long ago to glorify itself in time-honored granite and marble. Granite for strength and marble for polish. Who were they kidding? Washington had neither, she thought, but it cornered the market on self-delusion—the renewable biofuel that kept the city humming.

She took another sip of her martini and closed her eyes, content to have the sun's heat engulf her body—a momentary real-time escape from political Disneyland. She lay back in the lounge chair as she felt her own sweat mix with the pool's chlorine. It was drying her skin. She sat up quickly and slathered on sunscreen. The sweet smell of coconuts toyed with her senses. She swept her bangs to the side and pinned her damp hair back off her neck and shoulders.

Geneva looked at the beads of sweat dripping down the narrow valley between her breasts. The valley of the shadow of death, she reminded herself. She winced at the thought. She knew she could still turn a man's head, yet her body did nothing to lure her husband's advances. She grabbed a towel and erased her perspiration, rubbing her skin until it started to hurt.

Geneva propped her sunglasses on her forehead and reached for the daily *Post-Examiner*. It felt grainy, almost dusty, and began turning yellow less than sixteen hours after rolling off the presses.

The news was retro: the same old stories about upcoming legislative battles on Capitol Hill; the same tired stories about the presidential campaign. The names changed every four years. The debates never did. And no, this year's presidential election was no more important than any previous one, but the flood of political campaign commercials was aimed at convincing voters otherwise. She was so tired of it all, and she had to get out. Now she saw her chance.

She closed her eyes again. A horn blared in the post–rush hour traffic. She felt a trickle of sweat run down her belly to between her thighs. Tranquility was scarce in the city, but she cherished her spot atop it all. Then another post–rush hour sound: the distinct clack of the front door bell rung twice.

She raised her eyes and lowered her sunglasses. She swung her legs over the side of her lounge chair, sliding her feet into her sandals. She strode across the hot stone patio and wondered if any neighbor might catch a glimpse of her bare bottom from this vantage point far above the city's hypocrisy and partisan thuggery. Inside her brightly colored living room, the air-conditioning gave her a sudden chill. Mother Nature's radiant heat was no match for a blast of man-made cold air.

She grabbed her black yukata—the one splashed with vibrant pink flowers—off the back of the white cloth couch and slipped it on. The light weave clung to her damp skin. She wrapped the cloth belt around her waist and then thought better of it and untied it, letting her robe hang open.

She heard the wall clock chime once for seven thirty as she entered Harv's bedroom. His tie was already off and three buttons of his shirt undone. A small fund-raiser had been penciled in on his evening agenda. A senator's life really wasn't his own Tuesday through Thursday, she thought, even when Congress was out of session.

Geneva had forgotten he was coming home early tonight. Harv loved the Senate, and most nights, he wasn't home until after nine. She was saddened he'd crashed her solitude, but she was glad he was home. They needed to talk.

"Scotch?" she asked.

"It's been a hard day, Jen. I had wine at the reception. I don't want to switch." He leaned down and kissed her on the forehead.

She looked into his pale green eyes, then reached up and ran her fingers through his long, thick, white hair. "Harv, you need a haircut."

"First thing tomorrow, dear."

"You might want to ask him to cut it a little shorter this time."

"Much sun today?"

"It's very hot, just the way I like it."

A cabernet waited for him on the balcony when he joined her in his black linen robe, closing the living room French doors behind him. Wine meant a Cohiba cigar—his latest supply, a gift from President William Croom.

"He's one of the few Republicans I can work with," the president had whispered in Geneva's ear at a White House dinner five years ago. Croom showed his appreciation with occasional private conversations on the White House Truman balcony. Just the two of them, smoking Cubans, even though boxes of the cigars were still banned in the United States. Geneva knew the Cuban issue was just another constituency to be managed at election time. The two politicians weren't going to let a trivial law deny them a momentary pleasure.

She clipped the end of his cigar and placed it next to his wineglass on the small glass-top patio table between them. She loved the aroma of a good cigar—not the cheap ones that often served as shorthand for backroom deals. She preferred to smoke Padron 1964 Anniversary Churchills. As for a good cigar, size did matter, she thought. She flicked the lighter and held it up toward Harv, her supple, evenly tanned skin covering his mottled wrist as she steadied his hand. She then lit her own and grabbed her martini.

"Harv, I had a strange meeting yesterday with an FBI agent."

"FBI?"

"He was asking about Dave Bayard. He implied something is going on with my bid on the Pentagon contract. It could be in jeopardy."

"I thought you had a huge advantage over those Lamurr people."

"We should. Lamurr's track record in the sky is not very good."

"And Bayard's committee, no doubt, will have its fingers all over the contract."

"No doubt."

"Can't say I'm surprised. Bayard is all about Bayard. And if the FBI is interested, it's more than politics. They must suspect something. He's running for president, for Christ's sakes. You just don't know what kind of deal that bastard would come up with to secure the nomination."

"The agent said this happens every four years during a presidential campaign. Something about all of the crazies coming out of the woodwork."

"Hogwash. He's downplaying it, trying to make you think it's routine. The FBI doesn't walk into your office unless its suspicions are pretty damned strong. There is something there, and I'd be worried if I were you." Harv drew deeply on his Cohiba, not looking at her, and exhaled.

She shuddered. He just confirmed her fears—all of them. "I'm pretty sure Lamurr is paying him off," Geneva said. "At least the FBI agent implied that. We can't compete with that. We maxed out our contributions to his presidential campaign."

"Are you willing to go any further? Take Lamurr on its own turf?"

"Come on, Harv. We're based in Minneapolis. The guys out there don't have a clue how to play Washington. They still believe in their junior high civics texts. My hands are tied. I've hit the limit of what I can do."

"Legally."

"Obviously." She felt unease coarse through her veins. Harv was fortifying every suspicion she'd had in the last thirty-six hours.

"That's why I've always supported my old pal Ford Patton for president over that slimy bastard Bayard. He's not on the take the way Bayard is. I think Ford will do well at the convention, but he needs to keep an eye on Bayard. He may need Bayard on the ticket to keep New Jersey in the fold. Bayard could fuck him over if he isn't on the ticket."

"Strange bedfellows."

"Exactly, and they never stop fucking over anyone who's not in bed with them."

"Washington's version of safe sex."

They laughed. It was good to hear Harv laugh. What had happened to their fun together?

"It makes no sense for Bayard to take a payoff in exchange for a contract, no matter how big it is," Harv said. "There's plenty to be made on the Hill. My god, the lobbyists are practically shoving stock tips down my shorts on a daily basis, and they give us cheap access to those super-profitable IPOs. You're either a damned fool or damned honest if you can't get rich in this town after Election Day. And we sure know Bayard doesn't qualify as one or the other."

"And he still gets their campaign contributions on top of all of that legal graft."

"Exactly, my dear. It's a great system."

"Still? What about Bill Croom's push to get Congress to change its insider trading rules for members a few years back?"

"Window dressing, dear, nothing more. Neither the Senate nor the House Ethics Committees will be any more aggressive in the future at ferreting out ethics violations or corruption. What you don't realize, dear, is a year after the insider trading rules were enacted, we gutted them before they took effect without even a floor vote. The public had no clue. One thing you've never accepted about Congress, Jen, is how exceptionally adept we are at tap-dancing around the public's latest per-ceived outrage. We simply convince voters the problem has been taken care of."

She cocked her head slightly and looked at him. He was right. What politicians did and what the public perceived were miles apart—just as Congress intended.

Geneva stirred her olive and took a sip of her martini. She liked it dirty. As she turned to set it down on the small table, her robe gaped open and slipped off her thigh, revealing her long, tanned legs all the way up to her hip. She looked toward Harv. He paid no attention. Instead, he looked into the darkening sky and blew out yet another stream of smoke from his cigar.

She felt a chill. Her understanding of their relationship was all too apparent. She pulled the gown back over her legs. Harv continued his monologue.

"The ethics committees don't investigate the ethics of members of Congress. They defend them."

"Nothing ever changes here, does it?"

"Insider trading and unethical behavior are very difficult to prove. We can always argue we traded on the day's headlines. The difference, of course, is we know what tomorrow's headlines will be. The voters aren't concerned with a little graft. They're angry we accomplish so damned little."

"I've never heard you talk this way," Geneva said. "You're not getting fed up with this town too, are you? I can't imagine you would call it quits." She wondered if there could be a future for them after all.

"Don't kid yourself, dear. No, I love having a staff at my fingertips to do anything I ask, even picking up my dry-cleaning. I like power. I'm all too human. I married you, when you were my beautiful young staffer—and I appreciate that you take care of yourself and you are still beautiful. Would you have ever married an old guy like me twenty years ago if I weren't a US senator?"

"Harv, we would never have met if you weren't a US senator."

"Nice dodge, dear. But you get my point. Lobbyists, staff, the news media—they all want my attention. Who would I be if I left my job? Who would care about my opinion?"

Geneva said nothing, but instead took a draw on her cigar and blew out a stream of smoke. No, she thought. There is no future here. Not for them. Not for her.

"I know, they say get out before you're shoved out, but at sixty-six, I feel I still have a good game. There's no one on the horizon able to take me down—although there are plenty in the Senate who would love to. And if one of these Republicans wins the presidency this fall, we not only own the Senate and the House, but the presidency. It's a whole new ball game. Bill Croom is nice enough, but he's still a Dem.

Imagine what I can do with my committee with a Republican in the White House."

"It's all about power," Geneva said. "Harv, nothing seems to change here. Just new labels on the same old battles—over and over and over again. One congressional session blurs into another." Just like her life, she thought, an endless run on a treadmill going nowhere. She thought of her earlier conversation with Keith and the plan they were hatching. Harv only hardened her resolve to see it through.

"Dear, Washington is all about never-ending turmoil."

"My job security."

"And mine. If we move too quickly, your profession won't have a need to give us all of that lovely campaign cash."

She smiled at him and relit his cigar. It had gone out during his monologue. Even though the fire in their relationship had dimmed, she still enjoyed the tiny gestures, like pouring his wine and lighting his cigar. He always seemed so appreciative of those small intimacies. But she didn't kid herself. She realized she was grasping for something that was no longer there.

They sat in silence, above the city lights, enjoying the stars. Geneva turned away and looked over the other buildings down Pennsylvania Avenue toward the Capitol, its lit white dome shining like a beacon.

Harv began again, but her thoughts were drawn to the light. Why had she married this man, Senator Michael Harvey? What had she seen in him back then? She had been only twenty-three, and he had been forty-six. For the first sixteen years, she had been convinced it was a wonderful union. But over the last four, Harv had grown disinterested, especially in any physical relationship, as she had entered what she considered her sexual prime.

She turned her head back to him. Only the orange glow of Harv's cigar was visible, and it moved rhythmically up and down as Harv talked, waving his hand in the air. She shifted her stare back to the light.

Because of their age difference, she was not interested in children and, truthfully, never had the urge after her brother's sudden death when she was a teenager. Did she want to avoid the pain again of loving someone so much? She'd never really considered that, but now that she looked at Harv puffing away, she realized maybe she'd married him because he was safe—and distant. And it didn't hurt, she reminded herself, that he provided her with instant access to money and prestige. And because of their age difference, no one ever inquired about them having children. And now they slept in separate rooms.

Was it just two years ago, while gathering his suits for the cleaners, she had discovered the condoms in his pocket? There was only one reason a man who had a vasectomy more than a decade earlier would use condoms. She still felt the ache of betrayal as she watched him in full soliloquy. But the pain had softened. Time had gradually healed it, just as it had for the loss of her brother. Maybe, she thought, she had gotten too close to Harv as well.

She took a drag on her cigar and blew out a violent line of gray smoke.

"So what do you say, Jen . . . dear? Dear, you there?" Harv was addressing her.

"Oh sorry," Geneva said. "It's late. My mind was wandering."

"About?"

She paused, and they looked in each other's directions in the dark. He turned more toward her, and she heard the stretched fabric make a cracking sound as it strained against the lounge chair's frame. The light from the Capitol Dome flickered a reflection in Harv's eyes for the briefest of moments before his face was hidden in the shadows. She knew he was looking at her, and then she heard a soft, invisible sigh. He was still waiting for an answer.

"You know. That FBI business."

"It's really got you worried," he said.

"It's my life."

"Don't you worry. It'll be fine." He reached out and caressed her knee through her robe and then pulled away as if realizing he had overstepped an invisible boundary. They had never spoken of his infidelity, but he must have figured she knew. His behavior was telling. This was the first time he had touched her in a long time. Too long, she thought.

It was all so humiliating. She wanted more. She wanted to feel alive again and escape this hollow emptiness she experienced with Harv. It was time, she told herself, to confront him about his cheating. Her meeting with Keith had convinced her she must start looking out for her own needs. She blamed herself for allowing men to have far too much influence in her life—whether it was her brother's death, Senator Bayard's bribes, or Harv's infidelities. She had to stop reacting to their behavior and take charge of her own.

And she'd start with Harv. It was time she told him she was going to find herself a lover.

13

As he made his way to his desk, Beck spied Nancy Moore across the massive newsroom in conversation with one of her editors at the copydesk. She was supposed to meet earlier this morning with Managing Editor Robert Ely Baker and her equals about his story. He was curious what they had decided.

He had barely sat down and managed a sip of his Starbucks before she was hovering over his lair, a desktop hodgepodge of empty Styrofoam cups, stacked newspapers, and file folders. Somewhere hiding in that mess was a computer screen and keyboard.

"What's with the necktie?" she asked.

"I've got one of those Georgetown parties tonight."

"Got a jacket to go with it?"

"Somewhere around here."

Nancy leaned over his desk and looked at the floor. "Ooooh. Shoes that match. I'm impressed."

Beck strained to hide a grin.

"Whose party?"

"An old friend from college. She's got some congressmen she wants to impress."

"So what are you? The bartender or the bait?"

"I'm the life of the party."

"Yeah. Right. Don't let it ruin your beauty sleep tonight. You look like you need it. You look like shit, and we have a lot of work to do."

"Really, boss, you worry way too much about my beauty regimen."

"My pleasure. Always here to help. Anything new on Bayard?"

Beck stared at the stack of papers on his desk and shuffled through them. "I've learned he's made a lot of money being a US senator."

"Yeah, so what's new there?"

"Well, you asked." Beck leaned back in his chair, propping the heels of his shoes on the only available corner of his desk. His toe unknowingly skimmed a coffee-stained empty Styrofoam cup, sending it floating in midair and then crashing to the floor—without a sound. Nancy acted like she didn't notice.

"Baker wants news. Not the obvious. They all do that. Look, we have a short calendar here. The Republican National Convention starts the day after tomorrow. We all agreed in the editors' meeting this morning that we've got to move quickly if we are going to get a story ready long before the election."

"Long before? What's the rush?"

"God, it's so obvious you've never covered the political beat. Look, Sherlock, we can't run a story like this too close to the election. We lose all credibility. It will look like a partisan hatchet job. You don't think this newspaper will endorse the Republicans, do you?"

"But the newsroom is separate from the editorial department."

"Tell that to the public. Tell that to Fox News."

"Shit." Beck dropped his legs from his desk and sat erect.

"That pretty much sums it up. Your ass is on the line with this one unless you get the goods on Bayard in time—that is, if he's on the party ticket. And the odds are he will be. So you've got two, maybe three weeks—tops."

"Two weeks?"

"You got it, Watson. Get your butt in gear and uncover my story. And pick up your trash off the floor. You need one of those road signs that barks 'Beware of Rockslides' on your desk." Nancy walked away, stopped, and turned around. "And don't forget when you're out there in the real world, you're representing a great institution."

"Which one?" Beck asked. "The newspaper or you?"

Nancy smiled. "Which one's more important?"

"That's a loaded question."

"It's only your career on the line."

Beck detected a smile in her voice. Her deadpan expression gave her away for sure. Their eyes locked. The ridicule in her voice gave him a warm feeling. She was one tough newspaperwoman, and he loved her for it. She had an instinct for the big story and even acquiesced to his messy desk filing system. What more could he ask of her? Well, he guessed, she didn't have to mother him so or pretend she wasn't manipulating him to get her way. They were partners in their crazy world, and she never failed to clear a path for him in the minefield of petty newsroom politics. His stories got the same front-page play as the reporters who covered the White House and congressional beats. He knew he was her favorite among the staff. Sometimes he thought she knew him better than he knew himself. It was uncanny how she seemed to always know what he was thinking just before he did.

Nancy turned away and broke into a purposeful stride. "And straighten your tie before you leave," she said over her shoulder.

14

The pilot had just landed the Gulfstream on a new private runway and guessed it was maybe a hundred miles east of the Andes, give or take ten miles. He sighed, thinking it had been a rough ride and wishing he were still having fun back in Mexico City. He never looked forward to the turbulence caused by skimming over the mountains, and on top of that, he'd dodged two thunderstorms, not thirty miles apart, just before landing. Relieved to finally be on the ground, he sat in a comfortable leather chair, admiring what all of those suitcases of cash could buy, and stared out the window at a strange sight.

Though in the middle of nowhere in the Amazon rain forest, with lush green jungle not a hundred feet from the runway, he sat in a tastefully decorated, air-conditioned office. It was all part of a small, modern complex connected to the airplane hangar. There was a small kitchen and even a cot in the other room where he could catch some sleep before his next flight.

It was his first time at this airstrip, but he knew to taxi into the shiny new hangar before shutting down his engines. No satellite or drone in the sky could see the crew on the ground when they unloaded and reloaded the aircraft with a roof over their heads.

He looked around the room at the expensive furnishings. His cargo certainly could afford a lot of nice things. He hadn't raised his rates in more than a year, but maybe it was time to talk to them again about more money. They certainly could afford it. He was the one taking all of the risk, whether dodging bad weather or suspicious aircraft—to say nothing of the imminent possibility of arrest.

Movement through the glass caught his eye. Light clothing was the norm in this region of Colombia, but the man standing outside in the white linen suit and white straw fedora was an oddity. Under the gray sky, he looked like a character from one of those exotic black-and-white movies from the 1940s he used to watch late at night.

The pilot couldn't understand how the dark-skinned man kept his suit so spotless out in the jungle. The gentleman could have just come from the dry cleaners, but there was no such creature comfort anywhere nearby. All of the other men, packing and unloading the small, battered, Japanese-made pickup trucks, were uniformly attired in stained, sweat-drenched T-shirts and ragged pants.

The man in white gave instructions to a worker dragging long, green palm fronds and carrying a machete. He obviously had been clearing overgrowth nearby. It must be a constant battle to keep the jungle from encroaching on the runway and grounds, thought the pilot.

The conversation grew heated. The white-suited man, obviously the supervisor, waved his arms and pointed at the ragtag laborers, but the pilot could hear none of it over the sound of the air conditioner spewing out a steady stream of dry cool air.

The supervisor waved one of the laborers over to join them. A burly man, with big muscles outlined under his white-turned-gray soaked T-shirt, walked over. The supervisor, now with hands on hips, yelled and gestured. Then he poked his finger in the big man's sweaty chest. The laborer bowed his head in submission as the yelling continued. Then he looked up, vigorously shaking his head, and appeared to be pleading with the supervisor.

The supervisor stomped his right foot several times on the newly laid asphalt runway and again pointed at the man, this time with two fingers, as if lecturing him. He then backed away several feet, pulled a gun from his suit waistband, and waved it at the pleading man. They continued to argue, both with arms gesturing wildly in the air.

The pilot reached into his lightweight, nylon bomber jacket for a cigarette and lit it, once again cursing the nasty habit he had picked up after taking this job. The woman who had approached him at a pilot hangout near Alberta two years ago said she was looking for someone who could fly larger corporate jets from Canada to as far south as Argentina. Triple his pay, the pilot was promised. Shit, he'd never been to South America, but for that kind of money, he was happy to fly anywhere.

Outside the window, the supervisor waved the gun again and pointed it downward. He shook it, emphasizing the ground. The laborer slowly got down on his knees holding his fingers locked together, pleading. The supervisor walked behind him and kept walking away, but the man on his knees did not turn around to plead more. He just closed his eyes and sobbed. He rocked back and forth with his hands on his thighs and appeared to be praying.

The white suit signaled the worker who had been clearing brush. The worker walked up behind the kneeling man with his machete and took one lightning-fast, powerful swing.

The pilot quickly shifted his glance from the window. But that changed nothing. He had to look. Blood flew into the air as the razor-sharp machete made a straight, clean cut. Then the head of the kneeling man tumbled to the tarmac. The man's body collapsed to the side, almost in slow motion, in the direction of the swing. It slumped on the pavement, spurting blood everywhere, staining the new runway. The machete blade gleamed bright red, and blood splattered all over its accomplice's filthy T-shirt. He bent down and wiped the blade on the dead man's trouser leg.

The man in the white suit, now some thirty feet away, had never looked back. He walked up to the five-man crew, who had all paused outside the hangar, watching. They were stunned. They edged back as the supervisor approached. He clapped quickly, signaling the bewildered men to get back to work unloading their trucks. They jumped immediately, disappearing into the hangar.

It was as if nothing had happened.

The pilot had never seen a man murdered in cold blood before, and so brutally. He looked for an ashtray. There was none. Then he saw the sign on the wall. "No Smoking."

He quickly mashed his cigarette on the side of a metal trash can and looked through the window again at the supervisor, careful not to glance toward the lifeless body on the ground. What had the poor bastard done to deserve this? Probably stolen a few extra dollars for his family.

Well, at least he now understood how the supervisor kept his white suit spotless. And no, now was not the time to ask for more money.

15

Geneva took a taxi straight from work to Ellen Elizabeth's. She never considered driving herself since parking in Georgetown was practically nonexistent. She kept extra clothes in her office closet for the numerous evening political fund-raisers, charitable events, and cocktail parties that were part of the grease that kept Washington running. Over the years, she had learned to make her eveningwear easy. She wore a black suit to the office and simply changed from a gray blouse to a black one—one revealing a little cleavage. A little bling and sexier pumps, and she was ready to go. The men got off easy. They went straight from the office dressed in dark suits, white shirts, and power ties.

Tonight she was hoping her outfit would accomplish its intended purpose and help her attract a certain man. She felt a bit nervous, almost like being on a first date. How did she even remember that feeling from so long ago? Yet this was a first date of sorts. It was a recruiting mission, although she had no clue what she was doing.

By the time she arrived, ten people mingled in their red, white, and charcoal gray as a butler led her into Ellen Elizabeth's old Georgian mansion. Geneva stepped gingerly, her high heels clacking on the marble checkerboard entryway. Guests gathered in the main living room across the large entry hall from a temporary bar set up in the dining room.

She saw the graying eminence of Congressman Kelsey Joy, holding court in the corner under a large tapestry clinging to the wall, and recognized a couple of congressional staffers chatting in the middle of the room. Joy, a middling member of one of the agriculture subcommittees, was of no concern to her, so she stepped onto the oriental rug that defined the living room and reintroduced herself to the staffers. She made small talk for five minutes and then excused herself, saying she needed to find the bar. Geneva had learned to talk with the unimportant people before finding her way to the bar—her excuse to cut the conversation short and move on. She thought of it as her updated rendition of looking over someone's shoulder for the most important person in the room—a Washington tradition.

She spotted Beck Rikki across the entry hall in the dining room. He looked taller and more slender than he appeared on television. She had heard the television camera added ten pounds. Apparently, it was true. At least this wouldn't be painful. From a distance, he was a bit of a hunk.

Rikki was in an animated conversation with a CNN senior producer, a petite, attractive woman Geneva recognized, but whose name momentarily slipped her mind—a gaff not acceptable in her line of work. Then they split. The producer made a beeline for a political consultant who had just entered the room. Beck headed toward the bar. An interesting juxtaposition of styles, thought Geneva. Who really was the more aggressive journalist?

Geneva wondered if she could drop hints to Rikki about Senator Bayard being on the take. Would Rikki bite? She'd not really dealt with reporters before. Was it like lobbying a congressman? Could she show her hand? She knew one thing. Reporters, especially investigative ones like Rikki, always seemed to suspect everyone's motives. Politicians didn't care as long as you handed them a check.

Nice hair, she thought. A little shaggy on his collar perhaps. But what was with that droopy brown mustache? Tall, maybe a little over six feet, he appeared to have a nice butt beneath his charcoal-gray suit jacket. And the way he walked. She tried not to stare as he strode across the room toward the bar, his gait like a panther—smooth, effortless, in charge. From this distance, he reeked of confidence—a brash journalist for sure. She hadn't paid much attention the few times she had spied him on some cable news show, usually to talk about a story or book he had just written. But now she was intrigued.

She stepped through the foyer and took a few steps toward the bar. "Hi, I'm Geneva Kemper," she said, extending her hand.

Rikki turned to her, switching his mixed drink to his left hand. "Oops, sorry," he said, reaching out to greet her. "Beck Rikki."

His hand was cold and clammy. Geneva recoiled momentarily, then realizing he was juggling a cocktail, recovered: "You're with the *Post-Examiner*?"

"Guilty as charged."

"I've read your byline. You do good work."

"Thanks. I recognize you from somewhere, but I'm sorry, I don't recall your name."

"I'm Geneva Kemper, with Serodynne Corporation. I'm a lobbyist."

"Ah yes. Aren't you married to—"

"Senator Mike Harvey."

"I've read about you in our Style section," Rikki said. "But I promise, I've never written a word of it."

"Your paper has been very kind to me. I have no complaints, except maybe for the photographs. Your photographers never get my best side."

"From where I stand, I'd say the photographers don't have to worry about that."

"You're flirting, Mr. Rikki."

"Guilty as charged again."

They made direct eye contact, followed by a short moment of silence. His eyes were pale blue. Was he staring at her? She looked away and began to grin. Wow, this was going to be fun. He's attractive and charming. She felt her jitters relax.

"You need a drink. What can I get you?" he asked.

"Vodka tonic. Thank you."

He turned to the bartender, who was rearranging glasses and bottles of beer on the backbar. While Beck was getting her drink, Geneva scanned the room. Congressman Joy appeared to have taken up permanent residency in the living room, expounding on the day's events to anyone willing to listen. She looked beyond Joy to see who else was there. The party had grown to about thirty people. She hoped that wouldn't interfere with her attempt to monopolize Rikki's attention.

"Here you go." She turned back as Rikki handed her a vodka tonic.

"So, Mr. Rikki, you must have an interesting job."

"Beck, please. Only police officers call me Mr. Rikki."

"Do you meet a lot of them in your job?"

"Only when I drive too fast."

"Speed limits not your thing?"

"No limits are my thing. In a way, we reporters are just like politicians. We like to make our own rules."

"At a heavy cost to your wallet, no doubt."

"No doubt. Between the speeding tickets and the hikes in my insurance premiums—yep. Kinda expensive after a while."

"No chance of reform, I take it."

"I'm afraid not. I have to constantly race to keep up with what's going on behind the scenes in this town. That's where you've got an advantage on me. You're a participant. I'm merely an observer."

He certainly seemed confident enough, she thought, and rather charming. "Don't be modest, Mr. Rikki."

"Beck," he corrected her.

"Beck, your reputation is quite well known. Weren't you on the *New York Times* best-seller list?"

"I've done okay."

A waiter banging a small chime rang cocktails to a close.

"It was nice meeting you," Beck said.

"You too." She would let him discover on his own that they were tablemates. She turned away. That was unexpected. She had no experience with reporters. They all seemed so callous and boastful on television, yet Beck was a strange combination of modesty and confidence. She wondered just who was charming whom.

Ellen Elizabeth led the crowd to her conservatory filled with exotic ferns and a small koi pond. It was still light outside, making the formal gardens visible through the large glass walls. Oval tables covered with white tablecloths and flower centerpieces, probably from Ellen Elizabeth's garden, decorated the expansive room. Each table had seating for eight. Geneva smiled at the arrangement; her friend entertained with such ease.

She saw Congressman Joy and Senator Jesse Zadlo from Texas, who had just arrived, led to two tables at the far end of the room. Well, she knew where she *wasn't* sitting. Eager to get things rolling, she found the seating chart on an easel near the doorway and slipped into her chair long before Beck reached the table.

"Well, we meet again. What a pleasure," he said when he saw her.

She extended her hand in a playful manner feigning formality, and he gently grasped it as if meeting for the first time—this time holding on far longer than necessary. This time his hand was gentle and warm. She liked his touch and felt sad to let go.

Their other tablemates consisted of three congressional staffers and two lobbyists—the equivalent of the kids' table at Thanksgiving dinner. The seat on the other side of Beck was supposedly a no-show, not uncommon with Washington dinner parties. Geneva however, knew the real story. At her request, Ellen Elizabeth had guaranteed the chair next to Beck would remain empty—the place card a ghost guest—giving Geneva exclusive face time with the reporter.

"Do you know Ellen Elizabeth?" she asked.

"We actually met briefly one summer at the University of Tennessee. She took some summer classes and interned at the school newspaper, the *Daily Beacon*. I was trying my hand at photography at the time, so we worked on some of the same stories."

"I remember. Her family is from East Tennessee—Greenville, I believe."

"Or as they say in Tennessee, '*Green*-vul.' I'm a graduate of the UT College of Communications. I think they call it the College of Media or Information or something like that now. It's all about digital these days."

"You speak Tennessean?"

"Not anymore. I'm a southern half-breed. Mom from Richmond. Dad from Chicago. A couple of aging hippies. I grew up in Richmond. Still have a sister there. As for work, I'm fortunate I've still got a job. I've navigated the paper's downsizing. We used to have a big investigative team. Now we are all solo artists. I'm lucky. I no longer have a beat position. I just write what I want."

"Why is that?" Geneva quickly sipped her water and took the measure of her table for any obligations. The other guests were all engaged in conversations. Good, she thought. She needed time with Beck. She needed to gain his trust.

"It's funny," he continued. "People come out of the woodwork with stories once they realize you're willing to investigate and won't burn them."

"Meaning?" The waiter poured Geneva a glass of red wine.

"Well, first off, most reporters are just lazy. I'm certainly susceptible. But I learned early on to follow up on every string of information. That takes work. Once you get the reputation as a reporter who will actually dig, all of the nutcases in the city start calling with tips about the conspiracy of the week."

"And you follow up on every one?"

"Every one. It takes time. Sometimes I won't make that phone call for a month, especially when I'm on another big story. Most times, the tip was malarkey, and a simple phone call ends it. But sometimes that phone call launches a new adventure."

Beck looked out over the room and stroked his mustache. She wondered what he was thinking and if it was the right time to bring up the Bayard issue. And just how would she do that? *Oh, by the way, Beck, I have a story for you about a dirty presidential candidate.* No. That certainly wouldn't do. She needed to bide her time and figure out a good approach.

Beck began again. "My work is Alice in Wonderland. I just keep opening doors until one leads someplace. One of my biggest stories—in fact, it was about the Pentagon getting ripped off—came from one of my favorite crazy sources. Do you remember the Nordact Arms muni-tions scandal a few years back?"

"That was you?"

"Yep. But I didn't follow up on the tip for about three weeks. I kicked myself that I hadn't jumped on it sooner, but I literally had to go through a dozen other totally worthless tips before I got to it."

"That was a huge story. Weren't you up for a Pulitzer for that?"

"Yep. That was one of my first really big stories. I'd done a lot of investigations prior, but they didn't move public policy the way that one did."

"That makes you one of the most dangerous people in this town." The thought excited her and gave her confidence that Beck was the right man for the job.

"Thanks for the compliment, but my editor will assure you I put my pants on one leg at a time and tend to spill coffee all over my desk—just like everyone else." Beck took a sip of his wine and munched down on a breadstick. "Okay, your turn, Geneva. Tell me about you."

"You're so much more interesting. Call me Jen, please."

"Okay, Jen, stop stealing my methods of avoidance."

"Guilty as charged." There was something about this man. She couldn't put her finger on it, but she was thoroughly captivated by their conversation.

"I'm a military brat," she said. "Grew up all over the world. My dad transferred to the state department as some sort of military liaison later in his career. Frankly, I think he was a spook, but he would never say. We were all over Europe and South America. I never made it to Asia."

Beck visually perked up when she mentioned her father was a spy. Interesting, she thought, how a reporter's mind must work. He must always be looking for a story. Another point in his favor.

"I came back to the States for college," she continued. "I went to school here at GW, got the political bug, worked on the Hill, and met my husband. I couldn't work for him after we married, so I got a job lobby-ing. Three companies later, I'm one of the lobbyists for Serodynne. It's interesting work." No, not really, she thought. Her job was a grind and she dealt with jerks on a daily basis.

"You must be good at your job."

"I'd like to think so, but you know, Washington is a shark tank and things change quickly."

"Frankly, I don't know how you keep up with it all. Do you ever get tired of this scene and just want to say chuck it and sit in a beach bar for the rest of your life?"

"Oh, you have no idea."

Beck laughed. "Maybe we have something in common."

"Really? Tell me more." She dabbed her lips with her napkin, placed it in her lap, and crunched down on her breadstick, never taking her eyes off him.

"Oh, it's just that it all seems the same over time."

"You ever see the movie *Groundhog Day* where the main character lives the same day over and over again?" she asked.

"Exactly. That's Washington. Don't get me wrong. I love the chase—putting all of the puzzle pieces together to create a big story. But all of the puzzles form the same self-serving picture, the same typical corruption."

He paused and took another swig of the red wine. "In college, I wanted to be Perry Mason, the hottest defense lawyer around. Then I realized that defense lawyers represented the scum of the earth, and most of their clients were guilty. Kinda blew the image for me. In my sophomore year, I took a journalism course and was hooked. I discovered investigative reporting, and soon realized I could be judge, jury, and prosecutor. So who needed to be a lawyer?"

"I like your logic." Maybe reporters aren't so bad after all—at least this one, she thought.

As waiters laid the main course plates in front of them, their conversation ceased, but their eyes lingered on each other. Geneva looked down and blushed, realizing she had forgotten to eat her salad. She quickly grabbed her glass of wine, took a sip, and looked away. Beck picked up the conversation again, and they talked nonstop for the next half hour, managing to eat a few bites in between sentences.

Before the dessert course, Ellen Elizabeth stood and thanked everyone for coming, then pointed out the elected members of Congress in attendance, who stood as the group applauded. They each made a few remarks about the upcoming political conventions and congressional elections and quickly sat down. The party broke right at 9:00 p.m., a Washington rule of the game. Geneva realized she and Beck had virtually ignored everyone else at their table the entire evening. She hoped that worked in her favor.

"Share a cab?" Beck asked.

"Love to," Geneva said. "I'm heading to Pennsylvania Avenue." Senator Bayard, she reasoned, could wait a little while. She needed to find the proper opening, but what she really wanted was to get to know Beck.

"I'm going to Old Town, so you're not much out of the way."

16

The air had cooled considerably since the sun had gone down. Now in the low seventies, the humidity seemed to have disappeared, giving Washington a temporary reprieve from late summer's steamy countenance. Enjoying the cool night air, they walked two blocks to Wisconsin Avenue to hail a taxi.

Geneva navigated the uneven brick sidewalks in her four-inch heels with the skill of a woman who knew the gentrified neighborhood well. She noted Beck kept a slow, deliberate pace—not really a necessity, she reasoned, but she appreciated the gesture. He said something about women torturing themselves instead of wearing sensible shoes, and she wondered about the choice herself.

Geneva was glad she hadn't reserved her car service for the evening. She would have missed spending a little more time with Beck. The second taxi passing by did a U-turn and pulled up to the curve. The Indian driver smiled and greeted them in broken English. Geneva knew exactly why he was so eager to dodge traffic to pick them up. A well-dressed white couple in Georgetown made for a safe bet at night, and they were almost always good tippers.

Beck asked for her address. They sat in silence, looking out the window as they turned onto M Street in the direction toward downtown. She didn't want this moment to end. She felt something—his shaggy hair, his droopy mustache. He was different.

"You know what I really need?" she said.

"What?"

"I need a drink. You have time for a nightcap?"

"Sure. Where would you like to go?"

"I'd love a cigar and a brandy."

"You're kidding. You like cigars?"

"Why? Have I broken some sacred rule?"

"No. I think it's great. I love them. Let's have cigars. But where? The cigar bar downtown will make you smell like a chimney for a week."

"I know. I was there once. Too little room, too little time, too many cigars."

"If I'm not being too forward, I have a great balcony where I enjoy a smoke. And the brandy's a bargain."

"You're on. That sounds like fun." She felt a thrill. Again it was like a first date, but the jitters were different. She was happy to be in his company instead of dreading it. And he smoked cigars. Who'da thought?

Beck directed the cabbie down Fourteenth Street across the Potomac and down the G.W. Parkway to Old Town Alexandria.

Geneva glanced at him. Had she been too forward?

He turned her way. "So how did you become a cigar smoker? It's not exactly a woman's sport."

"Well. I work in a man's world. Long ago, I told myself if I wanted to be successful in Washington, then I needed to be in the room. So I play golf, drink scotch, and play poker. I even know how to ride a Harley."

"Really?"

"And I watch sports."

"And who are your favorite teams?"

"Oh, come on. I have to be a Nationals and Redskins fan, no matter how good or bad they are."

"Not the home state teams?"

"That's Harv's problem. Not mine." That was awkward. She had just brought reality crashing down on her little fantasy. What was she doing? This could never work. Could it? Why did she bring her husband into the conversation? Stupid, stupid, stupid.

She could tell Beck was attracted to her, or at least he enjoyed harmless flirting. Had she just thoughtlessly smothered a potential fire or was she just kidding herself? She stared at her wedding band. Damn it. She had to be more careful. She might have messed up her chance with him, but she couldn't afford to slip up nudging him toward Senator Bayard. She had too much at stake.

They fell silent. That did not bode well for the rest of the evening.

GENEVA WAS RELIEVED WHEN THE cab arrived at Beck's condo. Their attention was diverted, and Harv's essence no longer lingered in the air.

Beck lived in a six-story brick building near the Braddock Road metro station edging along Alexandria's historic area.

"I love Old Town," Beck said. "It's a mixture of one-hundred-and-fifty-year-old mansions and town houses mixed in with condominiums like mine. I almost bought a condo on the Potomac, until a jet flew over, landing at Reagan National Airport while the Realtor was showing it to me. The view was beautiful, but the noise—worse than the newsroom. I was renting this at the time, so when it went on the market, I settled for privacy and convenience instead."

They rode the elevator to the third floor, and Beck led Geneva through his front door. The living room had a comfortable overstuffed leather couch. Good quality, Geneva thought. He must make a pretty good living.

A pile of books was stacked neatly on an end table. A large wingback leather chair stood in the corner, next to another small table stacked with books. So this is what a big deal journalist's home looks like, she thought. It seemed to fit with what little she knew of him.

"Now here's the best part." He walked across the living room to a set of French doors, then swung them open with gusto, proudly revealing a large balcony. "I got the corner unit and have twice the balcony. And since it's still summer, I've got total privacy. The pin oak makes it impossible to see my neighbors."

The slender branches of a large tree came within arm's reach of his balcony. Geneva leaned on the railing and could barely make out the yards of several homes that backed up to the building.

"I sit out here at night and enjoy a cigar. Sometimes the neighbors have a barbecue outside, and I can enjoy the aroma."

She noticed Beck smiling at the thought. He ducked inside, leaving her alone to take in the balmy evening. She closed her eyes momentarily, luxuriating in the temperate air against her skin. The luscious feeling made her body tingle.

Beck quickly returned with two brandies. He handed her one and then exited again, this time returning with a cigar humidor.

"What's your choice?"

"You have any Padrons? Sixty-fours?"

"And twenty-sixes," he chimed in. "Naturals, not maduros."

"You have good taste."

"Apparently, we both do."

He handed her a 1964 Anniversary Padron. He chose the 1926.

"Before I get started, do you mind if I get comfortable?" Geneva asked. It had been a long day. She'd given up on anything more than a cigar with him tonight. Might as well make herself comfortable.

"Well, I suppose not." Beck raised an eyebrow. "Bathroom's at the end of the hall on the left."

A FEW MINUTES LATER, Geneva padded barefoot back to the balcony and sat on his couch, curling her legs under as her skirt rode up her thighs. Beck noticed they were now bare. God was she a babe, he thought.

His eyes quickly traveled up to her satin blouse, whose neckline teased him with a hint of cleavage. It clung loosely over her curves, but remained faithful to every peak and valley of her figure. There was no doubt she was no longer wearing a bra. Beck looked away quickly, aware he was staring, but his glance apparently did not go unnoticed.

"My business uniform chafes after a long day," Geneva said. "I need to wind down and ditch the political armor."

Beck looked into her eyes, careful not to let his gaze drop lower. "So you're a jeans and sweats kind of gal."

"Not exactly. I'm more of a minimalist." She turned away to light her cigar, offering no further explanation.

Beck was already puffing away. He looked at the blue smoke he exhaled against the night's blackness. He desperately needed a distraction. She was turning him on. He continued his gaze into the darkness.

"What a peaceful spot," she said. "Hidden in the middle of the city, you've found a little slice of paradise."

"It helps. I do a lot of my work here." He turned to her. "It's quiet, no newsroom bustle. I get jazzed with the energy of the newsroom, but writing takes a lot of time and research, and I have moments when I just need quiet. Half of my job is reading old files and documents. It's really not glamorous. It's laborious. To be honest, I'm nothing more than a nerd hanging out in dusty old libraries."

"If you're a nerd, I'm Cleopatra."

"The makeup may be a little off, but you're certainly attractive enough."

"Are you flirting with me?"

"Ms. Kemper, I believe I am."

Leaning back against the end of the sofa, he watched her closely. At the other end, she leaned forward toward him with her arm over the back of the sofa, her blouse gaping open and her brandy in her other hand.

Should he make a move? She's married. Better not, he thought. Was she sending a signal? He couldn't tell, but he sure was receiving one. Maybe he should confront the elephant in the room.

"So tell me about your husband. It must be interesting to be married to a US senator."

"Not really. It's actually kind of boring. But I'd rather talk about something else. Your life must be so much more interesting. I'd really like to know what a writer does exactly. Until tonight, I didn't know any writers."

Interesting, he thought. She didn't want to talk about the husband. A good sign?

"Well, I'm happy to be your first." Ugh. Did he really say that? "It's simple." Beck shifted on the patio sofa. "I pace the floor wearing out the carpet and talking to myself until I come up with just the right words. But most of journalism—at least for me—is in the reporting. Writing comes late in the game."

He looked down at his drink as he raised it to his lips attempting to scan her body unnoticed. His eyes traveled up her curves, trying not to linger too long on her bare, tanned legs or the contour of her nipples straining under her clingy blouse. Was she doing this intentionally to him or was she a woman more interested in her own comfort than worried about what signals she might be emitting? What was he reading here?

They sat on Beck's pale yellow patio sofa and talked politics, religion, and Washington ways. But never once did they touch on the third pillar of nonpolite company conversation—sex. Was it that obvious?

He poured them a second brandy. She accepted hers gladly. An hour later, they were still talking, and the cigars were a memory.

Beck caught himself staring into her face several times. Her dark lashes cradled her wide-set eyes, which seemed to dance excitedly as she talked. The curve of her mouth was so inviting that at one point he lost track of their conversation. He was thinking what it would be like to kiss her. And then he caught himself. Stop it. She's married. The last married woman he'd had an affair with did not end well. He didn't need that again.

FINALLY, SHE STOOD. "This has been really nice." It was late, Geneva thought. They couldn't talk all night.

"Can I get you anything?" Beck asked.

"A cab. I think I should be going. This evening turned out to be nothing like I expected. Thank you for a wonderful time."

"I wasn't prepared for this either. I've never met a woman like you."

"I hope that's good."

"Oh, it's good."

They looked intently at each other and reached out for a good night embrace. It was quick, and they separated, but she refused to let go of his arm.

"Beck."

She looked into his eyes, and he wrinkled his brow, questioning. "Beck, this evening was too good."

He smiled widely.

She reached behind his neck and pulled him toward her. Their lips met, tentatively. Then, in a frenzy of motion, they were fused together. She grabbed his face with both hands and kissed him harder. Beck responded, wrapping his arms around her back. His hands wandered, and he cupped her bottom and pulled her hips to him. She wrapped her leg around his, slamming his leg between her thighs. A wave of warmth rose from her groin at the feel of his hard body pressed against her softness.

Her heart pounded. She couldn't breathe. She grabbed his forearms and pushed away.

"Sorry," said Beck. "I shouldn't have, but—"

"No, silly. You literally took my breath away. Do you have a bed?"

A broad smile crossed his face. She stared into his eyes and unbuttoned his shirt. She ran her hands over his chest, feeling the hairs between her fingers. She kissed him again and began to unleash his belt.

He fumbled with the buttons on her blouse, but to no avail.

"Here, let me." She finished unbuttoning and opened her blouse. He gasped at the sight of her breasts. He cupped her soft flesh in his palm. She felt her nipples harden as he caressed her, and she shivered with excitement.

She reached into his boxers. He shuddered. They groped and pawed at each other feverishly. His hand reached under her skirt. She felt him pause momentarily as he discovered only her soft bare skin. She grinned at the thought. She'd forgotten how much fun it was to surprise a man.

She looked up at him. "Don't you think we should go inside?"

He led her to his bedroom. They left the light on as they stripped and then stood for a moment. She eyed his naked body, trying not to look too long, but it had been decades since she had seen a naked man other than her husband. She pushed him to the bed, grabbed him, and climbed on top impaling her body on his. She leaned down and raked her hardened nipples across his chest. Then she leaned back and took him for a long, late-night ride.

GENEVA WAS JUST WAKING UP when she noticed Beck at the foot of the bed, standing, fastening his belt. He was already dressed and showered. Her hair was tussled and in her eyes, which were half-open. Her lips were dry.

She moaned, mourning the morning and the sun's rays filtering through the bedroom window shutters. "Hey. I know guys are supposed to quietly sneak away before dawn and before we wake up, but that really isn't necessary. This is your place, you know."

Beck looked at her and grinned. "I have an early meeting with my editor. I know this isn't the right way to do this. I guess we need to talk. This is a bit awkward."

"Ah . . . sure. Sorry. I'm not really awake yet."

"Coffee's on the kitchen counter." He sat on the side of the bed. "I really enjoyed last night. I don't know what your situation is, but I would love to see you again."

"Me too."

"I'll call you later."

"That's what they all say."

"No, I mean it." He leaned over and kissed her. She reached for him. The sheet fell away revealing her breasts and belly. She pressed against him. He gently brushed her flesh with the back of his hand. "I'm sorry. I really have to go."

Beck caressed her breast one last time and kissed her hard.

She let go of his neck and fell back into bed. And he was gone.

She lay there, remembering last night and realized how sore she was. It had been a long time. She smiled at the thought. She drew the sheet over her body. His scent lingered. What a surprising and delightful man. He turned what could have been an incredibly boring evening into one of her best nights ever. What was it about this guy?

The first part of her mission was accomplished. She had gained his confidence—well, she'd gained a lot more than that and would likely feel the effects of her late-night workout the rest of the day. Last night was totally unexpected. This lovely man had deflected her attention. That wasn't a bad thing, but it wasn't a good thing either. How could she breach the subject of Senator Bayard without Beck thinking she slept with him in exchange for a favor? This was Washington, after all.

17

A senator's wife. What was he thinking? The only meeting Beck had that morning was with a large espresso. The third cup of Starbucks finally green-lighted his synapses. He was thinking caffeinated again.

"You look like shit," said Nancy as he trudged into the office.

"I feel like it."

"Must have been a good party."

Beck didn't answer. They met in one of the conference rooms and spread out four pounds of documents that Beck had collected from various nonprofit watchdogs and government agencies over the last two days. It was the beginning of his investigation, and like many of them, he wasn't quite sure what he was searching for yet. But if his source was correct, the documents would give him a hint. Later that morning Beck cabbed to Capitol Hill to find some missing pages that must have stuck together when he copied the originals.

On his way back to the office, his cell phone rang. The screen said it was Geneva. He had forgotten they had exchanged numbers. Why'd he do that? He ignored it, and the phone signaled she'd left a message. He stared blankly through the taxi window, feeling guilty. He said he'd call her. But a senator's wife. Was he crazy? He thought about last night. Those big, beautiful, wide-set brown eyes. Those dimples when she curled her mouth. Her long brown hair smelled like roses, and her bangs tickled his face when she leaned over to kiss him. And that body. Wow, she rubbed it up against him like a purring cat.

Where had she been all of his life? Oh yeah. That's right. She was somebody's wife—a senator's.

WHEN HE RETURNED to the office, he and Nancy sat in the glass-walled conference room next to the newsroom and scrutinized the documents a second time.

"I don't see anything here," Beck said.

"Agreed. The reality is, we've got a hundred different rabbit holes to explore. We need to narrow our possibilities, or we'll never finish a story in time for the election. The fastest way to get to the truth is to send you packing to Grand Cayman. Maybe you can come back with something that points us in the right direction."

"But we haven't even scratched the surface here yet. We need to explore the Pentagon angle. And what about Lamurr? I'd be going to Cayman blind without more background."

"Have you looked at a calendar lately? We've got a presidential election in short order. We need to move now."

"But—"

"But what? Jeez. I've never seen a reporter so reluctant to take an all-expenses-paid vacation to a beautiful island like Grand Cayman."

"It's not that. I just feel like there are so many loose ends."

"Duh. Look, while you're gone, I'll ask Leslie Werstein to snoop around the Pentagon and grab as much of the contract proposal information as she can find. And I'll get the business staff to dig up everything they've got on Lamurr. I'll do that just for you. Just to massage that restless imagination of yours. I'll ladle it on a silver platter. It will be sitting on that disaster of a desk of yours when you return. You can then bury yourself up to your ears in contract minutiae. Satisfied?"

Beck nodded.

"And who was that guy at Justice?" Nancy asked.

"Jackson Oliver."

"Yeah, we'll run some background on him too. Any other avenues you can suggest we attack while you're on vacation?"

"I think you've got it covered." She was right. If they were going to get this story in time, they needed to work in tandem with other reporters on her team.

"Glad we could accommodate you. At least someone is gonna work around here while you're enjoying the sun. You just figure out how to prove Bayard is a crook. I want the front page. Above the fold. I want to dominate the web page and the newspaper app."

"And if he's not?"

"Don't come back here trying to justify all of those margaritas on your expense account. God, I hate sending reporters on free vacations while I'm stuck here in the newsroom. Just make it easy for me to justify your expense account to Baker. And don't enjoy it too much. That's an order." Nancy smiled.

"It's off-season. Who wants to go there in August?"

"Yeah, right. The beach in August. Rough assignment. Try not to get swept away by a hurricane or come back with a sunburn."

"This could take a while."

"Yeah, right."

Beck felt better. He couldn't wait to dig through island land records and find Bayard's property, and he'd be doing it sooner than expected. Nancy, as usual, covered all the bases. She wanted that story before Election Day. Now it was going to be his head if he failed to deliver.

He spent the rest of his day in the newspaper morgue, combing through old Bayard news clippings, immersing himself in the senator's political history. Beck wanted to know his prey. He cornered John Jeffrey, one of the political reporters on the national desk, and grilled him.

"Bayard was a relative latecomer to the race last year," Jeffrey said. "He surprised a lot of people with his ability to so quickly raise enough campaign cash to be competitive. It was unusual. Money is the mother's milk of political legitimacy, and he seemed to have no problem raising it. People were obviously looking for alternatives to the candidates already announced. He's now second in the convention delegate hunt in what was originally a five-candidate race."

Jeffery explained that Senator Diana Lee from Florida was in third place. She was everybody's favorite for the vice presidential nomination. The Republican establishment was talking about a need to balance the ticket with a woman. What they weren't saying aloud was they needed Florida to win.

"That puts extra pressure on Bayard to win the nomination. Otherwise, he might not get picked to be number two on the ticket," Jeffrey said.

"Even I get that," Beck said, "and I don't cover politics."

His cell rang. Beck excused himself and walked to his desk. He answered on the fourth ring.

"It's Geneva. Can we talk this evening?"

"Ah, sure." Oh god, he thought. What do I do?

"Your place? Seven okay?"

"Okay. Sure."

"I'll see you then." She hung up.

It sounded like a business call, he thought. There was no "I had a wonderful evening" or "Hi, how are you?" chatter. Maybe she decided it was just a one-night stand. He felt his stomach ease.

Beck thought about his wayward love life and lack of commitment. Since his early college years, he had the reputation as the two-month wonder—if he dated a woman for more than two months, his friends would start to wonder.

That's all this was. It would be over shortly. It was just a one-night fling and some of the best sex he ever had. Maybe that was it. Great sex. Beck sighed and grinned at the thought.

But there was something more. He didn't remember this feeling. Infatuation maybe? No. That, he remembered. He was an expert at infatuation.

Who was he kidding? He liked her. He liked her a lot. Maybe more than he should—more than he could comfortably handle right now.

What was it about this Geneva Kemper? He did not need this entanglement, and yet he somehow did. He wanted her. Was it the thrill of the forbidden? Hell, he'd had affairs with married women before. What made this one so special?

18

When Beck returned to his condo, the bed was made. The coffee mugs were cleaned and resting on his stainless steel drying rack in the kitchen. He walked out to the balcony. Though the ashes were still in his large cigar ashtray, the glasses were gone. He checked the dishwasher and found she'd placed them inside. Obviously, she didn't know where he put his ashes.

It felt intrusive. He stopped himself. Are you kidding? You had sex with her last night exposing everything you've got, and you're concerned about her playing house while you're gone? Get real.

One of his notepads was out of place on the kitchen counter. "Thank you for last night. —J," it read.

He stared at the note. His insecurities welled up.

"Red, what have I done?" he said aloud, turning toward his reading chair.

Red served many purposes, usually helping him organize his thoughts. But this evening, he knew he asked the impossible: helping him understand a woman. Beck understood only one female, and he was looking right at her. Red was good at figuring out motives, inserting paragraphs into long stories, and finding just the right word. But how could she help him with Geneva?

He paced the floor. "When she gets here, I'll just tell her we can't do this. I'm not getting involved with a senator's wife. Okay, so she's great in bed, and she likes sports, and she loves cigars, and she's smart, and she's got a great body, and she's good in bed, and she's, well, she's great in bed.

God, can she kiss. Red, that's not enough. I like this woman, but she's married. She's coming over to break it off anyway. That'll be fine. Maybe just another roll in the sack before I say good-bye. No, that will just complicate things further. I need a cup of coffee. Gotta think straight."

TEN MINUTES LATER, Geneva pressed the intercom downstairs. He buzzed her up. It was awkward.

She just stood there, looking beautiful in the hallway, her hair smoothly curving around her face. She had obviously come from the office, dressed in a stylish, fitted blouse and dark pencil skirt. Beck didn't know anything about women's fashion, but he knew she sure looked good.

Her wide mouth curled up into a grin when he motioned her through the door. After she crossed the threshold, she turned to him and embraced him. This time, the kiss was less aggressive, less desperate.

"I think we need to talk," Beck said. He was not used to being pursued.

"I'm the one who needs to talk," Geneva said. "I owe you an explanation. You must be wondering what a married woman, especially one in my position, is doing in your bed."

"The thought had crossed my mind."

"This is serious." She glared at him with a raised, well-manicured eyebrow. "I know this happened suddenly, but I don't regret it. I'm sure you're worried about us being found out, but you needn't be. My husband and I have an understanding. We're free to pursue a sex life outside of our relationship."

She said sex and not love. That was substantial. The muscles in the back of his neck relaxed.

"My husband is no longer interested in sex with me. He's found someone else. We've been married for twenty years, and we've spent the last four in separate beds. He doesn't want a divorce. Politically, publicly, that would hurt him. And quite frankly, we are still both very fond of each other. We love each other. But he has his life on the Hill, and I have mine. We appear together at public events and still make the gossip pages in your newspaper and the *News-Times*. We keep up a good front."

"That sounds like half of Washington."

"We wondered when we got married if the twenty-four years separating us would become an issue. But I have to hand it to Harv, until the past four years, he was very young at heart and kept me very satisfied. We had a great marriage, but then the relationship faded."

"But last night—" She paused and slowly shook her head, never taking her eyes off his. "I hadn't had sex in more than three years." Her eyes were pleading with him. "Beck, I'm only forty-two, and solo sex just doesn't cut it. I'm not dead yet, and you're a very, very attractive, intelligent—and as I found out last night—an extremely sexy man. I don't want to give you up. Maybe we have a chance at a relationship. Maybe not. Right now, I'm willing to settle for one of those friends-with-benefits sexual relationships. All I ask is that you give us a chance."

Beck looked into her eyes. For the first time, he realized they were amber, not brown. Her irises sparkled with hints of yellow starbursts, almost transparent. She slowly blinked her long, black lashes twice, attempting to stop a tear, awaiting his reply. He felt himself giving in. "Before you arrived, I asked myself, 'What the fuck am I doing?' And I still don't have an answer. I was convinced that ending this before it began was the best option for both of us. I don't know. I just don't know."

"Then let's give it a try." She walked over to the living room couch and dropped her jacket on the arm. Her back to him, she paused and looked at a painting of palm trees by the water's edge he had hung above his couch. It was mounted behind a rustic white window frame giving the impression of looking through a window at the beach.

She stood, fiddling with her blouse, and then turned and dropped it to the floor. He gasped at her nakedness. She knew she had his number. He was defeated before this battle began, and right now he was more than willing to give in.

"You're manipulating me."

"I would certainly hope so."

GENEVA DIVIDED MEN into many categories over the years. Some liked asses, others legs. Some went strictly for the eyes.

Beck was a breast man. Most men were. She had Beck pegged immediately and delivered what he wanted. If she wanted him, it was important to know what bait to dangle.

Throughout years on the party circuit, she had grown used to men's furtive glances at her low-cut cocktail dresses. A few of her gowns even made the gossip columns. She enjoyed the attention. It gave her power over her male counterparts, power she learned to use as a lobbyist.

Geneva slept with none of the men she lobbied. However, she had had many offers and had been tempted in her last few years of celibacy. She knew instinctively if she ever crossed that line with any of them, her influence would vanish. Instead, she flirted and watched their reaction, which only enhanced her influence.

Beck seemed different. And yet, in other ways, he was just like all of the other men. He had an air of confidence that nearly all men in Washington possessed, but he also had a quirky boyish charm. He showed a glint of vulnerability, of decency, that she didn't come across very often in the nation's capital.

The more they talked last night, the more she wanted to talk. He had a way of drawing her out. He listened. Was that just a reporter's trick or was he truly engaged and nonjudgmental? She wanted to believe the latter.

Their second round of lovemaking was less desperate. They took their time exploring each other's body, finding the other's pleasure zones and exposing their own. They took turns giving massages before consummating their passion.

Geneva enjoyed his hands wandering over her skin. She also enjoyed feeling every one of the muscles in his back ripple as she touched him. She enjoyed letting go and allowing him to take control. She especially enjoyed his desire for her, something she had missed for a long time.

Beck was not the bulky athletic type, but he was strong and fit. He had no six-pack across his abdomen like those magazine models, but his stomach was flat and firm. And he seemed to lack vanity.

To her, he seemed more in tune with himself than other men. She wouldn't quite call him overly sensitive, but she did think he was kind. Maybe even thoughtful. Men, she realized, just didn't get women. They had no idea how women manipulated them to their will.

She watched her power at work as she touched his thigh. She liked that she could make him so helpless. Beck brushed his fingers across her nipples. A tingle surged through her body. He rolled on top of her. She spread her thighs and welcomed him with open arms.

They made love for more than a half hour. Beck made sure she was satisfied before rolling over and falling asleep with the evening sun spilling through the blinds. Geneva could not sleep and rose to go to the bathroom. She looked at him naked, partially wound up in the sheets. God, he was good-looking, she thought, even with that silly mustache that tickled her thighs. She felt her emotions taking over. Senator Bayard could wait a while.

BECK AWOKE TO AN EMPTY BED. He stumbled into his living room in search of Geneva. He spied her through his French doors lounging naked on his patio sofa, a bottle of his wine on the side table. That reminded him he was still naked. He felt silly walking around his apartment in the nude, so he went back to his bedroom, slipped on his boxers, and joined her.

The laughter of distant children filtered through the trees that hid Beck's balcony from the neighbors. The only outsiders to see them were small birds that hopped from branch to branch chirping furiously at his presence. Beck stood, watching. He could almost reach out and touch them. One jumped to his bird feeder, which hung by a wire from the ceiling in an effort to fend off his pesky squirrel neighbors.

"This is almost like your own tropical rain forest," Geneva said. "Come join me." She patted the cushion on the yellow sofa.

"Am I properly dressed?"

"Don't ridicule me, Mr. Boxer Shorts." She shook her head in mock disgust. "When I have the opportunity, I always ditch the outfit. I'm more comfortable this way. Does that bother you?" She sat on a large, white bathroom towel spread across the cushions. He sat down beside her.

"I have a beautiful naked woman next to me and I'm uncomfortable? Does it bother me? Maybe a little. I'm just not used to women lying around so casually naked. I hope you don't mind if I stare."

"Stare all you want. Didn't you know that nude is the new black?" She looked at him with a smirk and then turned serious. "I think I told you I'm a military brat. My dad, I really do think, was some sort of spook. But whatever his job, we moved around the world from embassy to embassy. When I was young, my mother would take my brother and me to the beach. As you know, much of the rest of the world isn't as hung up on nudity as we Americans. So I was maybe four or five and my brother a year older, and we would play on the beach nude and think nothing of it. My mother would always go topless, and nearly all of the women on the beach were topless or completely naked. It was normal.

"The locations changed as we got older, but the beaches never really did. It was the most wonderful time of my life. My brother and I were playing in the sun and swimming in the sea till we were exhausted. We then slept on our towels on the sand before we would play in the sea again. Not a care in the world.

"My dad's last assignment was in the Middle East. They are not quite so forgiving about nudity, so our beach fun came to a halt."

Beck laughed. "I'll say. So what happened next?"

Geneva frowned. "My life took a bad turn. Dad had another year to go on his tour before returning to the States, so my brother decided to delay college for a year and stay over with us. The local butcher had some special cuts for my mom. My brother went into town to pick them up. A political protest spilled out of the main square. Protestors threw rocks at the police, and they returned fire with rubber bullets and tear gas. My brother got caught in the middle of the crowd and was killed when a rubber bullet struck him in the temple."

"Oh my god. That's awful." Beck placed his hand over hers.

Geneva looked at his balcony floor. "My family was devastated. I was scheduled to attend George Washington University that fall, and my folks had another year of their tour, but the State Department quickly shipped us all back to Washington. They wanted to minimize any political fallout. We buried my brother here in Virginia, and I've been in Washington ever since."

"I'm sorry."

Geneva pulled her hand away. "My mother was never the same. We never went to the beach again. She drank. She took antidepressants for years. My dad tried to carry on as best he could, but he couldn't hold it all together either and died shortly after they retired to Florida. I lived on campus here and discovered Washington nightlife and politics. It was the only thing at that time that gave me a thrill and took my mind off my brother and family."

Their eyes locked on each other. "That's terrible about your brother. It must have been extremely painful."

"It was. He was fun and so full of life, and I felt so bad. I had trouble fitting in at college. I spent six months in therapy trying to figure out why I was different from all of the other college girls—why I didn't like to wear clothes. Finally, my therapist pointed to my time on the beach with my mom and brother. Subconsciously, she said, I was trying to relive my happy youth. Honestly, I just enjoy the freedom and comfort of being clothes free—that's what the real nudists call it—in the privacy of my own home."

"Do friends and family know of your habit?"

"A few. Harv, of course. He sees me all the time. And a handful of girlfriends. But it's not like we sit around naked together. This is America. I wear a bathrobe or lose-fitting blouse and skirt when they are around. They know I have an overall tan and how I get it. I'm not embarrassed."

"I must admit, I've never met a woman like you. You smoke cigars. You prance around the room in the buff. I'll bite. Let's see where this relationship goes."

Two chirping birds interrupted them, one on the roof of Beck's small hanging birdhouse, the other on its perch. Beck and Geneva looked up at the noise. They seemed to be having a conversation.

She turned back to him. "Now what about you, Mr. Rikki? I've laid myself bare."

"Literally."

Tiny crow's-feet were lightly etched at the edges of Geneva's wide eyes as she grinned. Her dimples accentuated the corners of her mouth. "No, really. What is your story?"

"Nothing really. Grew up in Richmond, Virginia. Went to college in Tennessee where I met our friend Ellen Elizabeth. Began work at a couple of suburban newspapers outside of DC before I landed a job at the *Post-Examiner*."

"How do I get a man to talk more about himself? In this town, I usually can't get them to stop blathering on and on about how great and powerful they are. You, on the other hand, have a two-sentence history."

"I'm a journalist. We're all about brevity."

"Come on."

"No girlfriend, if that's what you mean."

"I wasn't probing."

"Oh, there's Red."

"Red?"

"My chair." Beck pointed over his shoulder. "She's about as close to a girlfriend as I have at the moment."

"A chair? What makes Red so special?"

"That's between Red and me."

"Why the reluctance to talk about a chair?"

Beck hesitated and looked into her eyes. Should he tell her? It was just so damned embarrassing and made him feel so vulnerable. Finally, he got up from the balcony sofa and stepped into his living room. He returned with a book, opened it to the acknowledgments page, and handed it to Geneva. "This is my latest."

She read aloud. "I must first thank Red. Without her help, not a word in this book would have appeared on the page." She put the book down. "I don't get it."

"Promise you won't laugh."

"Promise." With her index finger, Geneva swiped her finger across her tongue and made a small cross on the bare skin above her breasts.

"I've never told anyone this. I'm not quite sure why I'm telling you . . . it's a long story . . . but I talk to her."

"Your chair?" Geneva did not change her expression but gazed directly into Beck's eyes.

He turned away. Now he'd gone and done it. He could feel her ridicule coming. "It's complicated." He hesitated. "When I was a kid, I was dyslexic. I was a very slow reader. I didn't read an entire children's book until the fifth grade. So reading and writing were always difficult for me. My parents—God bless 'em—began shoving the newspaper in front of me. I started with the comics and progressed to the sports page. I later graduated to the advice columns, where I learned about sex and dysfunctional families. And even later, I started reading the front page and became a news junkie. By the time I got to college, I gobbled up books. But my writing was rudimentary, probably because I came to reading so late."

Geneva's eyes glistened. Beck saw empathy in her expression instead of the ridicule he had expected. There was an awkward silence.

"So there I was, a news junkie who wanted more than anything to become a newspaper reporter, but I couldn't write worth a damn. So I became the next best thing, the best goddamn investigative reporter ever. You didn't have to be a great stylist if you created stories that blew the doors off City Hall. Editors always compensated for my lack of skills in exchange for the big score—until I came to the *Post-Examiner.*"

He turned to her. "I had some good stories early in my career, but they still put me on probation and told me to find a writing coach or I'd likely lose my job or end up on some suburban beat forever."

"Did you?"

"Lose my job? Course not. I'm still there."

"You know what I mean."

"Do you know how embarrassing that would have been? Me, a reporter at one of the best newspapers in the nation, working with a writing coach? I'd have been the laughing stock of the profession. So I tried to self-medicate. One thing led to another, and I began talking out my stories, which helped me organize and polish them. It's how I write my big stories today. I pace the floor and, well," Beck stammered, "and I—I talk it out with Red. So you understand my need to keep this between us." He felt like he was pleading with her. "I don't wish to be mocked. Not in this town."

"You're serious? So you're telling me your chair proofs your stories?"

They stared at each other. Beck bit his lower lip and then spoke. "Not proof. Just helps to write and rewrite my drafts."

Geneva leaned over and wrapped her arms around him, burying her face in his bare chest. Beck felt tears against his skin. He hugged her hard for a long time.

Finally, he pushed her back and looked at her again. "So you're okay with this?"

She gave him a broad grin. "Every artist needs his muse. I admit I'm a little jealous. I don't like sharing you with another woman. But I'll let it go just this once. But why the name Red? She's a brown leather chair."

"Oh that." Beck shook his head. "It's a joke. Red is my reading chair. Red, or r-e-a-d, is the past tense of the word read. Red is female because I enjoy sitting in her lap. For that reason alone, I almost named her Luxury."

"That is so cornball."

"Writer's joke."

She leaned in and kissed him. He kissed back even harder. He did not want their embrace to end. He liked the feel of her in his arms and her skin touching his. His hand slipped down to cup her bottom, and his body hardened against her. Finally, she pushed back.

"I can't. I'm really sore," she said.

Beck hesitated. "Share that bottle of wine?" He nodded at the bottle she had left open and her half-empty glass.

She smiled, picked up her glass, and offered it to him.

"I've got several in the kitchen," he said.

THE EVENING SUN HAD FADED to night. Beck flipped on the balcony light as he returned from the kitchen and filled his glass. Geneva felt a slight chill as the air began to cool. She had not intended to tell her life story tonight or to learn his. Now she was torn. She liked this man, liked him a lot. But she knew she needed to circle back and discuss her suspicions about Senator Bayard. But when? She needed the right moment.

"You and Red working on any big stories together?"

"Just started a new investigation. Don't know where it's going. But I'm on a tight deadline."

"Anything you can talk about?"

"Just a member of Congress. Don't know anything yet."

"How do you investigate someone?"

"I just dig into documents. Interview people. Call sources. It's not rocket science. But you have to be good at seeing how disparate things may be tied together."

"Well, I hope it doesn't interfere with us getting to know each other."

"It may. I'm leaving on a business trip tomorrow."

"Bummer. Where to?"

"I've got to go to Grand Cayman in the Caribbean, of all places. Usually I go to exotic locales like Indianapolis or Billings, Montana. So this will be a nice break."

"Going to get any real work done?"

"Yeah. I'm looking into some real estate deal."

Congressman? Cayman? Real estate deal? Could it be? She thought about it. Could he already be working on her story? If so, what an incredible streak of luck. She wouldn't have to choose between a relationship with this wonderful man and her first order of business—leaking him Bayard's story. The last thing she wanted was for Beck to question her motives. Okay, so she originally approached him about a story. She looked at him sitting there in his boxers. She never counted on this happening.

"That sounds like a tough assignment." She hesitated, determined not to raise his suspicions. "All of that sand and sun. Don't you think you should take along an assistant? I could keep you warm."

"It's plenty warm down there already."

"I could cool you off."

"I don't think that's possible."

"I could carry your briefcase."

"I leave tomorrow."

"I could be ready."

"You're serious?"

"I could be."

"What about your husband? Your job?"

"As I said before, we have an understanding. Besides, he's at the Republican convention. And as far as my job goes, I'm in a holding pattern. Every Republican's already out of town or leaving today. I can easily take some time off."

"You really are serious."

"Just because you've seen my naked butt doesn't mean I'm not a serious person."

19

Eight couples, all dressed in tropical print pastels, stood in line ahead of Geneva and Beck at the Coral Sunset Hotel, awaiting check-in. Some fidgeted while others hovered over the front desk, forever hopeful that would somehow speed up the process. Geneva eyed a small, deeply tanned woman behind the counter who apologized to anyone within earshot about the delay. She was alone, she said, because her colleague had taken ill an hour earlier.

The woman hammered at her computer terminal and glared at the ancient matrix printer, waiting impatiently for it to spit out room information one line at a time. She pounded staples to paper as if she were squashing tropical bugs.

Island fever caught on island time, thought Geneva. A beautiful sunny day—who wouldn't want to go home early with a slight case of sun and salt breeze?

Geneva's eyes wandered around the grand lobby with its bright hues and indoor palm trees. Large exotic fish swam lazily in a pond, which featured a splashing fountain at one end. Encircling the lobby were a coffee shop, restaurant, clothing store, and gift shop. A flawed attempt to keep tourist dollars from leaving the building, she thought. The attraction was outside on Cayman's snowy-white Seven Mile Beach.

It had been a while since she had experienced island time, and Geneva still felt remnants of the sharp edges of Washington under her skin. The first blast of humidity as she and Beck stepped off the plane at the tiny Grand Cayman airport hit her like a viral infection, invading her lungs and triggering the first symptoms of island fever.

Her stride slowed, suddenly less deliberate. Her shoulders slumped slightly. Perspiration made her blouse cling to her body. She pulled the hair off her neck and tied it in a ponytail. As they left the airport to pick up the rental car, Beck had paused and asked if she was feeling okay.

"Never better." She belonged here in a beautiful island setting far from Washington's frenetic political battles that accomplished nothing more than determining who gained the temporary upper hand.

The second leg of their flight from Charlotte had been smooth. Geneva had upgraded them to first class using her frequent flyer miles, and Beck seemed to appreciate being able to stretch out on the longer portion of the trip. They enjoyed complimentary Bloody Marys, watched a movie on Beck's laptop, and then read and slept.

"Reservation for Rikki," Beck said when they finally reached the lone clerk behind the registration desk.

"Do you have a penthouse available?" Geneva asked.

"Yes, miss, we do," the clerk said.

"How much more?"

"Only one hundred dollars at this time of year."

Hurricane season, Geneva thought. Might as well take advantage of it. "We'll take it," she said, not seeking Beck's approval.

He grinned and shrugged.

She handed the clerk her American Express card and turned to Beck. "My treat."

"Thank you, Mr. and Mrs. Kemper," said the clerk, handing them room keys after the printer dawdled in near-record island time.

Geneva and Beck glanced at each other. Beck raised an eyebrow but said nothing. Geneva rolled her eyes.

BECK TIPPED THE BELLMAN and shooed him out the door of their room before he could point out all the amenities. Geneva immediately stepped through the side French doors onto the expansive rooftop terrace that must have been forty feet long. A masonry wall along the far side and rear of the terrace blocked crosswinds and provided plenty of privacy. Very good, she thought. Atop a glass table stood a tall vase of brilliantly colored tropical flowers that indulged her senses with a confectionary aroma, like blending the sweetness of chocolate with salt—the combination magnifying the scent of the ocean breeze.

The afternoon sun was intense, with only a few wisps of clouds in the sky. In the distance, the sky and the pale green water merged into a seamless horizon. Even from six stories up, she could see the sandy bottom of the Caribbean where swimmers splashed near couples walking languidly, hand in hand, along the beach. The gentle waves of the sea softly pulsed like a metronome, slowing life's rhythm.

GENEVA QUIETLY SLIPPED BACK inside while Beck stepped to the railing and leaned over to take in the scene. The slight breeze filled his nostrils with its tender sting. He closed his eyes and felt the sun's hot rays braise his face.

A moment later, he heard the French doors open and turned to see Geneva with her hair pulled up under a wide-brimmed straw hat and wearing sunglasses—and nothing else. She carried a towel, the novel she had begun after leaving Charlotte, and a tube of sunscreen. "I always need to find my private oasis," she said. "It's like your balcony at home. Private, comfortable—"

"But home doesn't have this view," Beck said, sweeping his arm out to the water below. Then he turned back to her, lowered his voice, and sighed. "Or this view."

Dark sunglasses hid her eyes, but Geneva's smile said it all.

"Could you put lotion on my back?" She laid her towel on the large daybed, which was shielded from the sun by an oversize umbrella.

He didn't say a word but walked over and sat beside her. She lay on her stomach. He started with the back of her neck and arms, then her back. He took a long time rubbing it in on her backside.

"Don't you think you've got that covered, dear?"

"I don't want you to sunburn here. This is precious real estate."

He moved down inside her upper thighs. Her body quivered from his touch. Her skin was soft, smooth, and unblemished. Her tan was light, but there. And no tan lines. He continued down her calves. They were firm. He finished with her feet and manicured toes. He took his time.

"That feels nice," Geneva said.

"It sure does," said Beck.

She turned over. "I think I can handle the rest. Come join me." She rubbed lotion on her skin and then lay back and closed her eyes. He stripped and stretched out next to her under the umbrella. He placed his hand on her thigh and did not move. So this was what her nudist thing is all about, he thought. I could get used to this.

BECK WAS STUDYING an island map and reading his notes when Geneva awoke. At about five o'clock, they showered and ventured out to the beach. Though the sun dropped into the sky, the temperature was going nowhere.

This was the first time Beck had seen Geneva in a swimsuit. He admired the top of her black bikini, held up with thin spaghetti straps and sporting white piping that drew attention to her ample cleavage. She wore a thin, white, cotton cover-up that didn't cover up much at all. He wore his yellow trunks and a blue Hawaiian shirt his sister had given him for Christmas.

They swam for a while. The clear water magnified the sandy bottom, making it appear shallower than it was. Beck could see his feet through the pale water. Geneva swam up to him, put her arms around his neck, and kissed him. He tasted the salt on her lips. Even with wet hair, she was still beautiful. She remained a mystery to him, but he figured it would just take time to fully understand her. He found her unusually honest and totally open. It was like her attitude toward nudity. She had nothing to hide.

"Now," she said, "can you feel why I don't like to swim with clothes on?"

He hadn't ever thought about it. But yes, his suit felt clammy. A few minutes later, when they stepped out of the water, he noticed right away. His suit clung to him. He was starting to understand.

STILL IN THEIR DAMP SUITS, they stopped at a nearby beach bar for dinner and gazed at the simmering orange sun sink into the green ocean.

"So what is your agenda for tomorrow?" Geneva asked.

"I'm looking into Senator David Bayard. Know him?"

Geneva had stabbed her fork into a chunk of grouper and paused midlift. It was true. Beck was working on her story.

"Know him?" Beck repeated.

"Uh, I've met him. Can't say I know him."

"There are some real estate transactions—trying to find out if he has ties to a company called Lamurr Technologies."

She paused, her grouper still hung in limbo between her mouth and her plate. Finally, she took a bite. She felt her body tense. Would he be pissed the moment he learned of her connection? He was going to find out sooner or later. That mind of his would put it all together. So how should she handle this?

"Excuse me. I need to visit the ladies' room." As soon as she entered the restroom, she found a stall and locked the door behind her. She sat, thinking, filled with dread. This man meant more to her than she had bargained for. Getting her life together and escaping Washington was her top priority. Now this relationship and her own plans were headed for a major collision.

Obviously, she's not the only one in Washington with suspicions about Bayard. But who would have given Beck the story? What did he know? He certainly didn't know about her connection. Or did he? Could he be playing her all of this time? Maybe he was just pretending to be this wonderful, kind man only because he wanted more than just sex. She immediately realized the irony. Imagine, a man wanting more than sex. But if true, she might end up on the front page with Senator Bayard. She wouldn't put it past a newspaper reporter. They're mostly scum, just like politicians.

But that didn't feel like Beck. She'd witnessed the kindness in his eyes. Yet they were eyes filled with the same ugly ambition of so many others in Washington. She would need to keep her guard up around him. No, she wouldn't mention anything to him right now. Maybe she was wrong to be so suspicious. She hoped so. But until she knew the truth, she would keep silent.

Finally she returned to the table and sat in silence. She poked at her grouper. It was cold.

"Hello?" Beck stretched the word out like a piece of saltwater taffy.

"Sorry."

"Something bothering you?"

"I'm a bit distracted." What to say? *Concentrate,* she told herself. "I think I might have gotten sand in my suit where it doesn't belong." Lame. Did he buy it?

"I guess skinny-dipping is healthier for you."

She smiled but said nothing.

"So where was I? Oh yeah. Tomorrow I want to check out a piece of property the senator owns on the water and then follow up with a check on land records at the government building."

"Sounds like a blast."

"Hmm. I detect a hint of sarcasm in your voice. Wait and see. You have no idea how lucky you are to see a real investigative reporter in action—to see the naked underbelly of an exciting profession. It's really sexy stuff."

"Can't wait," she said, her mouth now full of fish.

"I bet you can't."

"I could lie on the patio while you run around the island. I'm reading a good novel."

"And miss all the fun? Not a chance. You promised to assist, remember? I want my money's worth."

I think I just got mine, Geneva thought. "Well, there are other ways I could assist you."

"Just hang onto that thought, lady." Their eyes met. His wicked grin said it all.

In celebration of their surroundings, Beck ordered two drinks with little umbrellas.

"Oh, come on," Geneva said, fingering hers. "I thought these went out with the Dark Ages." Here he goes again with his cornball ways, she thought. I'm a sucker for this guy.

"Humor me."

After downing their island concoctions, they weaved back to their hotel, arm in arm. It had been a long day of travel and sun. Tomorrow would be all work. They were naked and in bed before ten o'clock. Beck fell silent, spooning with Geneva, his arm wrapped around her body, his hand on her belly.

Geneva lay awake. Who was this man? He was nothing like she had originally imagined. And now he was conducting her investigation. She liked him. Too much so, she thought. And sooner or later, he would learn the truth about her corporate ties to the Bayard story. She didn't want to think about that—about the possibility that her own ambition directly conflicted with his. She had to figure out how to make this all work.

His hand moved to cup her breast. She placed her hand over his and held it tightly to her chest. She didn't want to let him go.

20

The next morning, Beck appointed Geneva navigator. She took full command of the map they had grabbed at the rental car company. At the wheel of their white compact Ford, he negotiated the left-hand side of the road. They weaved through the narrow streets of George Town, leaving behind Seven Mile Beach and their hotel. Beck found driving on the left fairly intuitive with the rental car's steering wheel on the right, but he still struggled with his first roundabout. But Geneva's directions and vivid oral and hand signals ("This lane! There! No there! Left!") ensured they would survive their first morning on the island.

They cruised a two-lane road heading east along the southern coast, edging the perimeter of the island. It curved inland at Bodden Town. From there, they made their way along Frank Sound on the southern side, slowly passing rocky cliffs along the shoreline and then sandy beaches. Waves broke over the coral reefs a few hundred yards offshore. The road turned west, and the lanes straightened out along the north- ern coast, heading toward Rum Point. Beck slowed the car.

"It should be up here on the right somewhere," he said.

Bayard's was a huge three-story pale-yellow stucco house that dwarfed the neighbors. Beck turned into the driveway of a smaller home next door.

"What are you doing?" she asked.

"Watch me." He stepped out of the car.

Geneva followed, but she stayed back and leaned on the hood of the compact car. It was hot, but her flowing, yellow-flowered sundress protected her legs and body from the heat of the metal. She placed her hands on her thighs to keep her dress from flying up in the slight breeze.

Beck turned to her and tilted his head, looking down at her strategically placed hands.

"I'm a closet nudist, not a flasher," she said.

He pointed his index finger to the side of his head.

She shook her head dismissively.

"I can't help staring. You're just so beautiful."

Her smirk turned into a genuine smile.

Wearing a blue baseball cap advertising Kalik Bahamian beer and yellow sunglasses that matched the shade of Geneva's sundress, he stepped up to the front screen door and knocked. A short white-haired man with sun-damaged skin shuffled to the entrance.

"We seem to be lost and were hoping you could help us," Beck said. "We're looking for an address." He gave the man the number.

"Why, that's right next door," the man said, pointing to the large house.

"Do you know if it's for rent?"

"No. The owner told me it's been leased."

"Shoot. My wife and I wanted to rent it. Would you know the owner's name? Maybe we could lease at a later date."

"Nice guy named Bayard. Not easy to reach though. It's the damnedest thing. Ain't nobody ever around."

"It's empty?"

"Oh, they come down maybe every few months or so for a weekend, but why would anybody rent it and then not be there more often than that? Some people just got more money than they have a right to, I suppose. The only people I see over there on a regular basis are the gardener and the property manager. Both come by once a week or so."

"Do you think it would be okay to look it over? My wife and I were really hoping to rent it. A friend told us about it."

"Don't bother me none. Ain't gonna bother them none neither, I suppose. Nobody's there."

"We're only going to be a couple of minutes. Mind if I leave my car in your drive?"

"No bother. Go right ahead."

Beck thanked the man, and he and Geneva walked to the sea. A five-foot concrete retaining wall rose from the beach, giving the false impression of protection from Mother Nature's wrath. They climbed seven stone steps to a palatial tiled terrace overlooking the ocean, easily forty feet deep and as wide as the house. The sun reflected off the large windows overlooking the terrace, acting like mirrors, making it impossible to see inside.

Geneva took off her straw hat and sunglasses and leaned against the glass to peer inside. She glimpsed expensive patio furniture stacked in the middle of the room and chair cushions piled on a couch. "I feel like a Peeping Tom," she said.

The room was large and the interior furniture typical light-colored beach fare. Only the pictures on the walls gave the room personality. She spotted some photos of what appeared to be the senator along with family and friends, but they were too far away to make out any details.

They stepped around to the side of the house by the road and found a three-car garage adjacent to a large entry porch. Both faced a manicured lawn and U-shaped paved drive.

"Nice place," Beck said.

"Beachy. Not ostentatious," Geneva replied. "It's big, but it's still comfortable. The senator has good taste."

The old man stood outside, watching from his front porch, when Beck and Geneva finally walked back across his yard to retrieve their car.

"I'd sure like to rent it," Beck said. "Do you know how we reach the property manager?"

"Like I told ya, I think it's rented for the year," the old man said.

"Well, maybe next year."

The man disappeared in his house and stepped back onto his front porch a moment later, handing Beck a scrap of paper.

"His name's Casper Agee. Nice fella. Old as me. A bit scatterbrained. He sorta looks like that genius guy, Einstein. Hair out to here." He held his hands far from his head. "He's got an office over in George Town, not too far from the airport."

"Thank you, mister . . . ?"

"Bridges," the man said.

"I recognize the accent but can't place it," Beck said.

"Texas. San Antonio. You?"

"I'm Beck Rikki from Washington, DC."

"Where all them damned politicians is from?"

"Guilty as charged."

Beck shook the man's hand, and they left.

Back in the car, Geneva rolled her eyes at him. "You're quite the actor. I'm now your wife, and we want to rent a very expensive house. You're rather clever."

Beck grinned. He had his moments. "Stretching the truth to get at the truth isn't all bad, although my editors would frown. They want everything on the up and up, but out in the real world, sometimes you need to use your wits to dig out the truth. A little sleight of hand does no harm. Besides, the hotel clerk already has us married. I thought I should acknowledge our Cayman nuptials."

"And stopping at the neighbor's?"

"I didn't know if anyone would be watching and call the cops on a couple of trespassers. So I decided to give us a legitimate excuse for looking around. Instead of a suspicious neighbor, we have a cooperative one."

She turned to him and caught his glance. "You know, you're not as dumb as you look."

"Deception comes with the job. I work in Washington, remember."

"So who do you deceive next?"

"Follow my lead, lady. Just follow my lead."

21

Beck called Casper Agee, trying to hear him over the blast of the small car's overworked air conditioner. The air conditioner was cold. The rental agent's response, lukewarm. He couldn't meet until eleven thirty the following morning.

"That gives us the rest of the day to search land records," Beck told Geneva.

"Sounds thrilling." She smirked.

"Sarcasm? Really? About doing God's work?"

"But land records?"

"Hey, it's this land." Beck nodded at the palms and lush green underbrush on the passing sand dunes as he kept two hands on the wheel. "In my business, we call it a paper trail. Just watch. It's better than a movie. Promise."

"I hope you brought the popcorn."

They wound back across the island's narrow sunburned roads to George Town and hunted down the Land Registry Office. Beck was familiar with US land records but unsure what he faced in this British colony. He found a stout, aging clerk who explained how the records were organized. They were similar enough. He shouldn't have problems doing his research.

"Will tax stamps on the deeds give me the value of the property?" Beck asked the clerk.

"Not only the property value. Our records also contain tax stamps for leases," she explained. The clerk handed Beck a map of the island

and corresponding tax rates and then led him and Geneva to a large room with rows of floor to ceiling shelves of dusty deed books and rows of almost-new computers on a long oak table in the middle of the room. She left them on their own.

It was similar to a court clerk's office back home, Beck thought. The newer deeds were now on a computer; the older ones in the oversize printed volumes. The computer would do. At most, he figured, he needed to look at land records going back a decade.

"What did that woman just say?" Geneva asked.

"It's simple," Beck replied. "We can determine real estate values as well as the values of property rental leases from land deeds on file right here."

"So?"

"Just hang with me. This is where the fun begins."

"You were right a while back." Geneva shook her head and snickered at him.

"About what?"

"You really are a nerd."

Beck sighed loudly, making sure she caught his feigned annoyance. He immediately went to work. He sat at one of the computer terminals and clicked the keyboard. "Look here." He pointed to the screen as Geneva peered over his shoulder. "Jersey Shore Ltd. purchased the house four years ago from a company called Sunrise Meridian."

He noticed the page menu allowed him to search other government records, so he pulled up the buyer's incorporation papers. "Right here. See. Bayard and his wife are sole owners of Jersey Shore." Beck typed in more, and another document popped up on the screen. "Aha. Check this out. The seller, Sunrise Meridian, is a subsidiary of a company called XAX Ltd. in Venezuela. And isn't this nice. They even provide a full list of all of Sunrise Meridian's corporate officers. They're all from Venezuela too. See, I told you this would be fun."

Geneva sat in the chair beside him in front of an adjacent computer. "Okay, so Bayard sets up a family business to buy his house."

"Patience. Being an investigative reporter takes time and perseverance. One fact at a time. Each piece of evidence leads to the next question."

"Which is?"

Beck wondered how she could be so clueless. Was she just not paying attention or was she deliberately provoking him? "The question is who is this Venezuelan company and why did they use a subsidiary to sell Bayard the house? Are they connected to that Pentagon contract bid? If so, I think I just may have my story."

He checked his cell and called Nancy at the office.

"Is Woodard still in South America? Could he check some business records for me?" Bobby Woodard was a long-time foreign correspondent for the *Post-Examiner*.

"Shit," Nancy said. "I was talking to the international desk this morning. Jim McKnight told me Woodard just finished covering an oil ministries meeting in Caracas and left yesterday."

"You got contact info? I'll see if he can get ahold of one of his stringers to dig out some details." Beck hoped Bobby had a decent stringer correspondent in Caracas.

Beck gave her all of the XAX information he had and did his best to pronounce the Sunrise Meridian officers' names, which were in Spanish. He finally gave up and spelled them individually. Oh, how he regretted not being more diligent in Professor Harding's Spanish 101. Damn, had he only known how important being bilingual would be in the twenty-first century.

Nancy told him to call her back tomorrow and hung up. Beck explained the conversation to Geneva.

"So you think this Sunrise Meridian company is tied to my contract—our contract—if this XAX company has a Bayard connection," Geneva said.

"Precisely."

"Well, then, we just have to wait for word from your office. We're done for the day."

"Hardly." Beck shook his head in mocking frustration. "We need to see what else is hidden in these documents."

Since his assistant seemed bored, it was time to put her to work. Beck showed Geneva how to thumb through ten years of land deed indexes. She worked the computer and quickly found Sunrise Meridian owned a dozen other properties on the island. He then explained how to trace the deeds back to a previous owner and follow that trail back for decades.

She dug in and picked up on the process quickly. After a few miscues learning the system, she got so interested in one property she traced its ownership back to the old deed books. She pulled three of them from their berths on the wall and followed the paper trail until it ran out more than one hundred years ago. She carried each large book in front of her at her waist like a clothes basket filled with clean towels. They were so heavy, she stood on tiptoes to ease them onto the slanted countertop where she could open and read them.

Beck watched her from behind as her sundress rode up the back of her tanned legs when she lifted the books. God, she was a beautiful distraction, he thought. He was glad to see her finally engage in his passion. Now if he could just curb his own so they wouldn't end up in bed all afternoon.

"I hate to admit it, but this is kinda fun, like a treasure hunt," she said a few moments later as she sat back in her chair in front of the computer. "A new discovery on every page. I can see how you might get hooked on doing this type of thing. It's like tracing a family tree, only it's a piece of land. Too bad a woman can't use this method to research the dirt on her man's history. This only proves helpful finding the dirt under his feet."

"Ooooh. That sounds dangerous," Beck said. "Not sure many guys would like their past deeds recorded."

"Imagine all of the heartache we could avoid." She was typing as she talked.

"If it helps at all, you're not just looking through deeds, but deeds of trust."

"Even better," she said. "Of course then the question becomes academic. What woman ever trusted a man's deeds?" She did not acknowledge her failed wisecrack, but kept her eyes concentrated on her screen and feverishly pounded her keyboard.

Beck turned to his own terminal and quickly found Sunrise Meridian had recently sold off four of its properties: a condo, the house on the ocean, some acreage, and a shopping center—all to Bayard's Jersey Shore company. He printed copies of all of the transactions.

"Look at these," he said, handing the pages to Geneva. "According to these deeds of trust, Bayard purchased eight million dollars worth of property in four years. Where in the world did he get that kind of money?"

"His combined mortgage payments for all of those properties would cost him more than his monthly salary," Geneva said.

Now she was starting to tune in, Beck thought. "And his financial disclosure documents back in DC show his net worth at no more than two million dollars. Something doesn't fit."

Geneva was still looking over the paper copies. "And look at this. Look who the lender is."

"Let me see that." Beck grabbed the pages out of her hands. "I can't believe it." The answer was right in front of him, but he had been so blinded by Bayard's name on all of the deeds of trust, he hadn't read through the documents to find the most important name. "Son of a bitch. Not only did Sunrise Meridian sell Bayard the properties, it financed them as well. Good catch."

"But what does that mean?" Geneva looked at him as if she were lost again.

"Maybe nothing and maybe everything. Find out if Bayard leases out all of these properties."

Geneva keyed in the information and quickly found Sunrise Meridian was leasing back all of them.

"Bingo. Print it out," said Beck. "I have a hunch if we do the math, we will get to the bottom of this scam very quickly."

"What do you think you will find?" Geneva asked as they waited for all of the documents to print.

"What if Sunrise Meridian leases the properties back for the same amount of money—or more—as Bayard's monthly mortgage payments to Sunrise?" Beck asked.

"Oh, I get it."

"Exactly. They're actually giving Bayard the real estate for free—for nothing—but he's covered his ass by making it look like he's buying it. It's just a fancy, more complicated form of bribery instead of stuffing dollar bills in his pocket. But it's still a bribe."

"A very big bribe."

"In exchange for some very big numbers in the Pentagon contract." Beck did the math on his cell phone. "Look at this." He showed Geneva the figures. "The rents paid to Bayard are higher than his mortgage payments to Sunrise Meridian." Beck could feel the adrenaline running through his veins. "I can't believe it. He's really doing it."

Geneva looked at him. He could tell she was puzzled. "Beck? What's wrong?" she asked.

"I'm not sure what I expected, but I just really didn't think he would actually do it. It's just so big. So audacious. This guy's got the biggest balls of any politician I've ever seen in my entire career. It's so presumptuous. I've never seen a payoff this gigantic. The money we are talking about is crazy. It's in the millions. And he thought he could actually get away with it."

"Well, he has up until now," Geneva said.

"Yes, but as you discovered, it's all documented. Maybe you were wrong. Maybe you can dig into a man's past."

Beck was still trying to wrap his arms around what they had found. Right here in this sunshine-drenched island playground just outside the United States, an American politician has created an international operation to enrich himself while running for president. What exactly does that mean?

"We still don't know who is behind all of this money," Geneva said. "Who is this XAX?"

"We need to wait to hear from Nancy. Maybe Bobby's stringer will pick up some clues down in Venezuela."

Geneva wrinkled her brow and gazed at Beck.

"What?" he asked.

"I don't know if this is important." Geneva hesitated, uncertainty on her face. "I noticed all of the documents were filed by the same law firm, Roger Kindred and Associates. Does that mean anything?"

"What did you find?"

"Roger Kindred incorporated both the seller, Sunrise Meridian Ltd., and the buyer, Jersey Shore Ltd. His law firm also filed all of the deeds. It's like he's the only lawyer on this island."

"That can't be a coincidence," Beck said. "That must be the local connection." Beck felt like kicking himself. He hadn't been paying close enough attention. Geneva was turning out to be a very able assistant as well as a beautiful distraction.

Without saying a word, he stood and walked over to the clerk and grabbed a dog-eared paper telephone book sitting atop her desk. She glanced up at him showing little interest. He found Kindred's office number and punched it in his cell phone. While the phone was ringing, he handed the clerk his copies, and she tallied what he owed on a scratch pad. He held the phone to his ear as it continued to ring and managed to pay the clerk before someone finally answered.

Kindred's secretary said he would be free at three o'clock the following day to discuss Mr. Rikki's interest in buying real estate. He hung up and turned to find Geneva practically in his face.

"More playacting? Who are we this time?" she asked.

"Just a tourist interested in buying some real estate," he said. "Be good to me, or I won't let you attend my next performance."

"But don't I have a supporting role? After all, I am your leading lady."

More than you know, thought Beck. "Good point. I guess your understudy isn't available."

"Humph." Geneva displayed a facetious pout that slowly grew into a broad grin. "Are we done yet? I'd like to take you back to the hotel and do awful things to you. I'll be your understudy—until I decide to get on top."

If only, thought Beck. "Not yet. Let's go to the beach."

"Skinny-dipping?"

"Don't tempt me."

They headed out the door for their rental car. In the middle of the parking lot, Beck realized he was empty-handed. "Did you pick up the copies by any chance?"

"I thought you did."

"Hell. Be right back." He tossed her the car keys so she could get out of the heat. Beck then bounded up the stairs and pushed through the government building's heavy door. He startled the clerk who was still seated at her desk and now on the phone. She quickly hung up in midsentence.

"Sorry. I left my copies." He looked to her in affirmation and gestured at the stack on the edge of her otherwise clear desk.

She looked at him with a forced smile, her eyes creased under her wire-rimmed glasses. He grabbed his copies, slapped the rolled-up pages on his wrist, and nodded a thank-you to her. Then he pivoted and walked out.

Funny, he thought, he was almost certain he heard her say the name Bayard over the phone.

22

Beck pressed hard on the gas pedal. He took the curves and straightaways in the small rental car like a grand prix driver, heading back in the direction of Bayard's waterfront mansion. He was comfortable now driving on the left and decided to use it to his advantage, zigzagging along the south side of the island again.

Geneva grasped the handle above her door and pressed her right hand against the dashboard to steady herself. "Beck, really."

"Sorry. I can't wait for the next clue," he said. "Mystery buff in me, I guess." He slowed down.

Beck had copied the plat of the acreage Bayard purchased and brought it with them. Future building lots and roads were outlined, and he remembered a winding road that bisected the property. He found it on his island map, and in just twenty minutes, he was braking the rental car, searching for a wide enough space to pull over.

They stepped out of the Ford into the sizzling sunshine and humid air. A breeze gave a hint of relief. Beck slipped on his baseball cap and looked around. Geneva tugged on her wide-brimmed straw hat and tucked her hair up underneath.

He looked down at the plat. "Well, this is it," he said. His arm swung out in the direction of the vacant land covered occasionally with tall brush and scrub pines climbing rugged sand dunes.

"This is what?"

Beck said nothing but continued to gaze across the acreage. "This is my Pulitzer Prize." An air of triumph filled his voice.

"Your what?"

"This is the real bribe," Beck said. "The house was nothing. This is worth millions today and tens of millions tomorrow. Bayard has set himself up for the good life. This is forty-seven acres of prime land just begging to be developed. Close to a hundred building lots here."

He nodded to one of the large sand dunes. "Look over there. On the other side should be the Caribbean. According to this plat, there is more than two thousand feet of water frontage on this parcel. That's almost half a mile long. You know what that's worth?"

"I haven't a clue."

"More money than you or I will see in a lifetime."

"But how can he afford this?"

Beck leaned against the warm hood of the car looking down again at the plat and then at Geneva. "He can't. Don't you see? He holds this land for as long as he needs while its value skyrockets, and all the while the Venezuelan company is paying the bills."

"How do you know that?"

"The rents on the other properties pay him enough to bankroll the real prize—this land. The other real estate is a smoke screen. Its only purpose is to provide him with enough cash flow to pay for this. He pays nothing out of pocket, and yet he now owns all of this." Beck again swept his arm across the horizon as he spoke and then rested one hand on his hip.

"Come with me," he said. They followed a path leading up the dune, and Geneva quickly fell behind, her sandals being sucked into the deep soft sand with each step. Short, wind-blown trees and scattered green shrubs held the dune together as the breeze swirled a low mist of sand at her feet.

Beck quickly scaled it, his powerful runner's legs thrusting his sneakers ankle deep with each step. Geneva took off her sandals and struggled barefoot, falling to her knees twice in the cascading sand.

"Beck," she called. He turned to see her on all fours. Her hands buried in the sand. Her hair askew and her knees and sundress disappearing in the white softness. From his angle above her, he looked down the top of her skimpy sundress and saw her large breasts swaying. He felt a momentary thrill.

"Beck. Please," she said. He realized he hadn't moved and quickly descended the hill to help her. "Sometimes you can be the biggest jerk."

"Sorry. My head was elsewhere." He helped her to her feet. God I am a jerk, he told himself. He held her hand and almost lifted her up the sand dune. Finally at the top, they could see the Caribbean several hundred yards away. It was a developer's dream.

He wrapped his arm around her waist, held her tightly, and felt her body ease.

"So he owns all of this," she said.

Beck looked at the paper in his other hand. "Yep. All of it."

They walked hand in hand through the sand dunes and the brush. Beyond a small dune next to the road, they found a freshly painted sign that had blown down, hidden by overgrown bushes. "Crystal Shores Estates," it read. "Future green estates developed by Sunrise Meridian."

"Look at this," Beck said. "They didn't even try to disguise the connection. I guess he thought no one down here would ever notice."

Beck pulled a small digital camera from his pocket and took several pictures. He then stepped back and took shots of the acreage. Finally, he turned with the sun at his back and took a shot of Geneva, standing with her hand securing her floppy straw hat and her face hidden by her windswept hair and large sunglasses. She playfully primped and posed, and he took several more shots.

"Nice," he said. Over her right shoulder, he saw a flicker of light in the distance. What was that? Beck was curious and zoomed in with his camera lens. About two hundred yards down the road standing behind a parked white car was a figure dressed in white wearing a white straw hat. There was another sudden glint of sparkling sun. A reflection? Binoculars, thought Beck. Someone was watching them.

He said nothing to Geneva, who was still enjoying preening for the camera.

23

Back at the hotel, Geneva ducked her head under the shower spray, rinsing away a layer of sand, dust, and perspiration. The afternoon's heat had nearly sapped her energy, but the feeling of the cool water pummeling her pores reinvigorated her. She lathered lavender soap all over her body. Suddenly, she felt Beck's hands on her hips, his body behind her. Her heart raced in anticipation. She had not heard him enter the large walk-in shower. She liked the feeling of his wet, slippery self against her and handed him the bar of soap over her shoulder. He immediately began to rub her back, then her breasts, and then much more.

LATER THAT EVENING, refreshed and exhilarated from their lengthy lovemaking, she and Beck stepped into a café built on a pier over the Caribbean Sea. She requested a table next to the water, and the young hostess obliged. From their perch, they watched the pale green ocean slapping against the pilings below. The violent clash of salt water against concrete formed rings of foam that glided gently up to the white sandy beach. Lights under the pier attracted tarpon, which provided much of the evening's entertainment. The floor show was fed by diners who dropped bread crumbs in the water, prompting the big fish to frenetically hurl themselves into a lightning-quick battle for the morsels. Above, on the pier, a band played island sounds syncopated by steel drums under a small canvas canopy.

Geneva suggested cocktails before dinner, then they ordered a bottle of white wine to go with the Caribbean lobster. The meat was more succulent than the northern lobster she had grown accustomed to with

Harv on their many trips to Martha's Vineyard and Bar Harbor. Somehow everything tasted better with Beck. And she needed to be sure to eat enough tonight so the alcohol did not affect her. This evening she was determined to get her man drunk, or at least drunk enough to give him a hangover in the morning. She needed him to sleep late while she carried out part of her and Keith's plan.

Beck downed a couple of beers and then switched to the wine. She kept his glass full while barely touching her own. Halfway through dinner, he excused himself to hit the men's room, just as the waiter arrived with another bottle of wine and poured two glasses. She ordered another beer for Beck and then extended her hand over the railing and gently poured her hardly touched glass into the sea. It was a shame, she thought. It was rather good. Maybe the tarpon would enjoy it. The thought of a drunken fish wallowing in the clear, warm water below brought a smile to her face.

As soon as Beck returned, she grabbed his hand. "Let's dance."

He gave her a puzzled look but did not resist. They moved in rhythm on the tiny dance floor. Geneva ground her hips to a salsa tune, and her light flowered skirt whirled in the air around her. She wondered if she was revealing too much of her long, tanned legs, but then she decided she did not care. She was having too much fun.

Beck played along, dancing and clapping to the beat beside her, but moving more in place as if to admire her show.

She liked him watching her, but then he grabbed her hand and spun her around. They moved in unison as if they had been dancing together for years. Beck led her through a few provocative moves that verged on spectacle. It surprised her he could move with such grace and ease. She was learning something new about this intriguing man and realized she really didn't know him at all.

Other couples stepped aside to watch Beck lead Geneva through several improvised moves. She loved dancing, especially to a throbbing Latin beat, and she enjoyed the attention of Beck and the other diners. It had been too long since she felt this way.

Finally spent, they returned to their table.

"I love this music," Geneva said.

"I love the beat. It makes me want to move."

"You moved pretty well out there."

"I've never met a woman who could dance like that."

"I've never met a man who knew how to lead. You make it so easy, and you make me look good."

Beck was sweating and downed his wine to cool off. He grabbed the beer Geneva had ordered and gulped it down as well. He again excused himself to visit the men's room.

Geneva began to worry. Beck was holding his liquor rather well. She ordered two shots of a bourbon liqueur, Jeremiah Weed, as a nightcap, and waited for him to return.

Beck stared at her wineglass. It was empty. His was still full. He gulped it down. "Lady, you're drinking quite a lot tonight," he said. "Better pace yourself."

"I'm okay."

"And what have we here?" He eyed the two shot glasses filled to the brim with brown liquid.

"Guaranteed to help us sleep," Geneva said, raising her glass to him. Their shot glasses clinked, and he swallowed the liquor in a single gulp. Geneva sipped.

"And what if I don't want to sleep tonight?"

She smiled at him.

"That burns," Beck said.

Geneva put her hand to her mouth, struggling to swallow. She finally nodded in agreement. "Yes. But it makes you feel soooo good."

"You gonna finish that?"

"I can't."

Beck picked up her shot glass and drained it. "Wow. Good stuff," he said loudly. "What's that called again?"

"Jeremiah Weed."

"Good stuff," he repeated.

A short time later, they left the café and walked arm in arm back to the hotel. She noticed the streets were rather quiet tonight. No one was around except for a tall man in a white suit across the street. She wondered where everyone was. She would rather be back dancing at the pier, but she realized Beck was in no shape to continue.

Beck stumbled entering the hotel lobby. Geneva steadied him, holding his arm. She barely got him into the elevator and down the hall to their room. She sat him on the bed and helped him undress before he collapsed in the sheets. He was snoring loudly before she stripped and entered their bathroom to remove her makeup and wash her face.

24

Beck awoke to an empty bed. After stumbling into the bathroom, he splashed water on his face and squinted into the mirror. He didn't like what he saw. His eyes were red, and his cheeks were puffy. He could hear Nancy's voice in the back of his head saying he looked like shit.

He felt like it too. He walked slowly into the living room, steadying himself with his hand on the back of the couch. Geneva wasn't there. He shuffled out to the patio. Not there either.

A cool breeze struck him head-on. He looked down, realizing he was standing naked on the patio—Geneva's influence. He could feel himself smile at the thought of her. But where was she? In his fog, he managed to find the kitchen and search the cabinets for an aspirin when he heard the front door open.

"Anyone alive?" came a familiar voice.

"I'm in here."

GENEVA ENTERED CARRYING AN overflowing grocery bag. "I bought you breakfast. Fresh fruit, bagels, eggs, skim milk, and veggies. I thought I'd make you an omelet."

She placed the bag on the counter, and Beck pulled her into his arms and attempted to kiss her. He felt wobbly.

"Whoa, boy." Geneva pushed back to elude his morning breath. She surveyed the damage. "Babe, why don't you jump in the shower while I make you breakfast?"

Looking at the floor, he ran his hand slowly through his already tussled hair and gently moved his head back and forth. Geneva gave him a hard shove toward the bedroom.

When she heard the shower running, she slipped into the bedroom and found her suitcase. She pulled an envelope of papers from her purse, gathered on her morning quest, and slipped them into a zippered compartment of her luggage.

She had entered the first bank when its doors opened, and then stood among the first customers at two others. She opened accounts at three different banks and was still back at their penthouse before ten o'clock. She would need these accounts later and could not risk Beck finding out.

It bothered her to keep secrets from him. Maybe if she knew him better, she might not keep her plan with Keith a secret. She might even seek Beck's help. She was growing more enamored every day. Beck's adventurous side made her feel giddy, and she loved the feeling. But he was still a driven reporter always probing into other people's business. She had to keep that in mind. She didn't know just how far he might go for a story. Would her secret be safe with him? Was anything off-limits to a reporter?

25

Unlike his belly, which appeared to be held up with suspenders, Casper Agee's wild fringe of white hair defied gravity. He welcomed Beck and Geneva into his clutter, clearing magazines and stuffed paper files from two office chairs to make a place for them.

"So you want to rent that senator of yours place," he said.

"Well, we'd sure like to consider it and maybe others," Beck responded.

"The Bayard place is leased through the end of the year, or maybe it's two years? I need to check on that. But from what I remember, I think the renters want to extend the lease." Agee removed the eyeglasses perched on top of his head, pulled a handkerchief from his back pocket, and began cleaning the lenses.

"It's such a great place. Do you think the tenant would give up the lease?"

"I could talk with them."

"Mind if we do?"

"A lawyer in town drafted the lease. His name is . . . oh, jeez, his name is—ah, yes—it's Roger Kindle. No, that's not right." He tapped his index finger on the edge of his desk. "It's Kindred, Roger Kindred. Nice fella. I work with him from time to time. Not many lawyers in George Town that aren't on the insurance and banking gravy train. Roger does a lot of that too, but also enjoys real estate. He dabbles and invests."

"Don't all lawyers?" Beck asked.

"Roger also hires me and folks like me to manage his clients' properties and find renters. He found this tenant, if you can call them that." Agee held his glasses in his lap, continuing to clean them. "That house on the water is used as some sort of executive retreat for some South American company. The executives come up from Brazil every once in a while. No, that's not right. It's Venezuela, I think. But they are hardly ever there. I check on the place regularly for Roger. Once a week. Sometimes every other week. But, that's not unusual in these parts." Agee paused and scratched his head, leaving his hair even more unwieldy. "There are lots of expensive properties with part-time residents—lots of folk with money around here who have nothing better to do than to buy a place and let it sit empty. It makes more work for us. But it keeps us employed, you know?"

Geneva had been sitting patiently, playing her role as Mrs. Silent Agreeable Wife, when Agee turned to her. "So, Mrs. Rikki, you like the island?"

"Very much," she said. "We still want to look at some other islands, but this one appears to be our first choice."

Beck looked at her. She didn't even need a script. She was a better actress than she let on. "When I was at the land records office looking for different properties, I saw Senator Bayard also owns a condo somewhere," he said. "Any chance it's available? If it's half as nice as the house, maybe it would fit our needs."

"Actually, I think Sunrise Meridian is renting that one too. Lemme check." Agee swiveled in his chair and faced a two-drawer file cabinet next to his desk, paused, and then turned back. "Now where did I put my glasses?"

He continued to rub the lenses with his handkerchief.

"Uh, in your hands." Beck motioned toward Agee's lap.

"Oh, right. Thanks." He perched them on his nose, turned again, pulled a file from the second drawer, and flipped through several pages. "Yep. They're paying a premium to have it available. I remember this now. I was involved in the signing 'cause Mr. Kindred was off island."

"Does Bayard own anything that Sunrise Meridian isn't leasing?"

"No doubt he's got a really close business relationship with them."

"What about the acreage on the east end of the island?"

"Don't know much about that. Your senator Bayard fella is working with Mr. Kindred on that one. I saw a plat once, but Mr. Kindred handles all of those sales. Doesn't let anyone else on the island sell them 'cause he says he wants to attract buyers from off island. If you ask me, I think he just wants all of the legal fees and commissions for himself. Probably charges more that way too. Funny how he holds that one close to the vest. It's the only property he doesn't let others in the local real estate community sell. That's a bit odd now that I think about it."

Agee took off his glasses and polished the lenses again. He then looked up at Beck and Geneva. "Maybe you'd be interested in one of those lots."

"The price would have to be right." Beck looked over at Geneva. She struggled not to break out in laughter. He couldn't decide if Agee was a senile old fool or a cunning operator. Whatever he was, Beck was determined to play along. "I saw Bayard even owns a shopping center. Don't tell me Sunrise Meridian leases that too."

"Not quite. If I remember correctly, from time to time the company rented out some of the empty storefronts. Haven't paid them much attention, but I don't think they ever used them for any retail. I think they set up an office in one once and used some for temporary storage. Those units don't go vacant for long. There isn't enough commercial space around. That's where you'll find Kindred's office, in the shopping center.

"Look," Agee continued, "you seem awfully interested in this Kindred fella. He's not the only one on the island selling and leasing real estate. I've got plenty of other properties."

"We had our heart set on Senator Bayard's house on the ocean," Geneva said.

"When we drove by, my wife fell in love with it," Beck added. "If we decide Grand Cayman will be our winter home, I guess we will have to persuade the senator to lease it to us. Maybe Mr. Kindred could persuade him."

"Good luck with that one," Agee said. "I think if I were you I'd try to buy one of those lots he owns on the ocean. Might be easier."

"YOU THINK HE BOUGHT IT?" Geneva asked as they hopped into their car. "You almost had me convinced."

"Good, 'cause this Kindred guy won't be so easy. He's a lawyer, and if he's involved in this, he'll have his antenna on full alert."

"Lawyers. They're all a bunch of liars and cheats."

"Isn't your husband one?"

"Yes. But he hasn't practiced in years. He's a twofer—a lawyer and a politician—two of the least beloved occupations in America."

"Followed closely behind in popularity by lobbyists and reporters." Beck laughed at his own joke.

"You're right. We all deserve one another." Geneva sounded serious.

Bringing up her husband reminded Beck he was treading on shaky ground. Not only was he stretching journalistic ethics by posing as a potential real estate client, but he was sleeping with another man's wife. He tried to run through his mind how his life got so complicated so quickly.

He looked at her natural beauty—the strong jawline that drew his eyes to those chiseled cheekbones—and her body's curves that made him constantly hunger for her. She was the whole package. But he felt a degree of unease. Was this real, or was he just chasing another pretty skirt? It certainly wouldn't be his first venture down that slippery path.

AFTER A LIGHT LUNCH at another beachfront café, they headed for Kindred's office near the back of the shopping center. Walking along the shaded sidewalk, Beck noticed a man in a white suit in the parking lot. He looked familiar. Beck's chest pounded. Could he be the same one with the binoculars from the other day? Coincidence? He remembered the short-brimmed, white straw hat and the tall, lean figure. He felt his heart pump faster, but he said nothing to Geneva.

The front of Kindred's law office had the same large plate-glass window as all the retail stores. It could have been a stationery store or a flower shop. Instead, large gold letters arched across the glass, announcing "Roger Kindred & Associates, Solicitors."

The office was tucked back in the corner of the shopping center, near a cigar bar and behind a women's clothing boutique. Beck pushed open the glass door. He saw a small empty waiting area and a vacant secretary's desk at the far end. The air-conditioning sent a chill down the back of his neck.

"Hello?" Beck said loud enough to be heard in the next room.

A young woman dressed in khakis and a short-sleeve blue button-down shirt came out of a side door. Beck saw a book-lined conference room through the open doorway behind her. She introduced herself as Kindred's paralegal. Her boss was running late with a real estate closing, she explained, and the secretary was out sick. Kindred should return in about fifteen minutes. She offered them coffee and cold drinks and disappeared into the book-lined room.

Beck stood fidgeting while Geneva sat on a couch and thumbed through old magazines fanned out on the waiting room coffee table. His hands became clammy. He felt a possible confrontation brewing. Game on, he thought. Pregame jitters, he told himself—the same feeling he got back in college just before a debate tournament. Then he and his teammate would step onto the stage and demolish their opposition.

Beck busied himself reading the various plaques on the wall: awards for good citizenship and lots of thank-you letters from charitable causes. He saw a picture of a Little League team that Kindred sponsored, a bar association award, grip-and-grin photos of a man—he assumed it was Kindred—receiving a plaque. He stepped to the next wall, where a dozen more photographs were hanging.

"Oh shit," Beck said in a whisper. "Look at this."

Geneva put down her magazine, rose from her seat, and walked toward him. On the wall was a picture of Jackson Oliver—Daniel Fahy's boss—and Kindred standing together on a ski slope. Beck recognized

Oliver, remembering the photos he had pulled up on the screen in the newspaper's library when he and Nancy were researching Fahy's secret Justice Department memorandum.

The paralegal reappeared with two glasses of ice water.

Beck turned to her. "Is Mr. Kindred a friend of Jackson Oliver?"

"Oh, he's his half brother," she said. "Mr. Oliver's father died when he was young, and his mother remarried a British gentleman."

"Really," Beck said. "I didn't know he had a brother."

"You know Mr. Oliver?"

Beck tried to take it all in. Kindred is tied directly to the Justice Department—to Dan Fahy's boss. What does that mean? Fahy never said anything about this. Was Fahy leading him on? For the first time, Beck had a bad feeling about his entire investigation. He needed time to think and to sort things out.

"I think I'm coming down with something," Beck said. "I'm beginning to feel nauseous. Do you mind if we reschedule our visit? I'm not feeling well."

Geneva looked at him, puzzled.

"I'll let Mr. Kindred know we will reschedule," the paralegal said. "There must be something going around. First our secretary and now you."

Beck took Geneva's hand and led her out the office door into the heat and sunlight.

26

"What am I missing?" Geneva asked as they walked down the sidewalk in George Town. What had Beck seen that changed everything?

"I'm not sure," he said. "I can't talk to Kindred yet. Jackson Oliver is a big wheel in the Justice Department. I'm not sure of his title, but I remember he used to work in the White House."

"I think you're right. I've met him before, at some White House function," Geneva said. "I think he worked for President Croom."

"Oliver is somehow tied to the deals with Bayard, and he's using his brother to facilitate them. That would explain why he delayed the Bayard investigation."

"He did?"

"Yes. That's how I got involved."

"I don't understand."

"Let's just say there are honest people who want to see this investigation go forward—or at least up until now I thought they were honest. If we approached Kindred with what we know, he would only alert his brother. Here—follow me." He took her by the arm as he pointed to a small outdoor beachfront restaurant covered by a giant canvas tarp. They ducked in and sat at the bar. The sun outside made the air boil, and yet a breeze off the water in the shade of the bar was moist and salty. Before two beers arrived, Beck was on his cell phone.

"Nancy? Any news?" He leaned against the bar staring straight ahead. "Uh-huh. Uh-huh."

Geneva sat next to him, looking out over the water. The view was pale blue, and the breeze on her face made her skin tingle. She closed her eyes, feeling alive and yet relaxed. She turned to Beck as he spoke on the phone.

"Bingo . . . I knew it. It fits. It's all coming together," Beck said. "And, Nancy, you'll never guess—Oliver is Kindred's half brother . . . Yes . . . I'm not kidding . . . that's right. His boss . . . Can you believe it? . . . I'm probably out of here in the next day or so . . . I'll e-mail you details . . . Right . . . Super . . . Okay. Anything else?"

"Leslie found what? Really." Beck was silent for what seemed like forever with his phone to his ear, listening to Nancy. "You sure? . . . Yeah, I've heard of them . . . Okay . . . Okay. Gotcha . . . Later."

Beck hung up. He picked up his beer and took a big gulp. He exhaled and wiped his mouth and mustache with his bare arm, then placed the beer deliberately on the bar. Geneva could tell something was wrong. He turned to her. His eyes narrowed. He gritted his teeth.

"I just got some very interesting news," he said.

"Oh?"

"It seems Serodynne is Lamurr's competition for the Pentagon contract. Were you ever going to tell me?"

Geneva could feel the blood drain from her face. Her head felt light; her heart raced. She knew this moment would arrive at some point, yet she hadn't prepared. She had let her feelings for Beck distract her.

"Jen?"

She looked up at him. Tears blurred her vision. "I'm sorry. It wasn't supposed to be this way." Her body shook as she attempted to talk. "Beck, I had no idea you were looking into my competitor's bid for the contract until dinner the other night. I should have told you then. I panicked. I didn't want to spoil our time together." Her shoulders sagged, and she looked away. She glanced around at the bar and the ocean, then she touched his arm.

He pulled back.

"I guess I should have told you."

"You guess?" Beck stood erect, towering over her. "Do you realize this could jeopardize my entire investigation? How will it look if it gets out that Serodynne is taking part in the *Post-Examiner*'s investigation of its chief competitor? I lose my credibility. I might as well pack up and leave now. Your company has a direct financial interest in seeing that Lamurr loses this contract and is found guilty of paying off Senator Bayard. Shit." Beck slammed his fist on the bar.

Geneva jumped. She had never seen him angry.

"Now I'll probably have to turn my story over to someone else on staff. Nancy will have my head. I'll be totally fucked out of my own story. I won't get credit for any of it. Shit." He leaned on the bar, grasping his beer in both hands and shaking his head. "I can't fucking believe this."

Geneva looked at him as he squinted into the bright sun reflecting on the pale blue of the Caribbean Sea, refusing to look her way. She hadn't realized how big a mistake she'd made by not telling him. She didn't understand the rules of journalism. He had trusted her, and now she had jeopardized their relationship.

And yet, she had just lied again. She had suspected before they even flew to Grand Cayman that Beck might be working on her story.

"Damn it," he said. "I should have checked on the Pentagon connection before I left DC. I was in too big of a rush to get down here." Beck shook his head. He looked at the bottle of beer on the bar in front of him, then pushed it aside.

He turned to her. "You were asking about my professional ethics yesterday when I pulled that little acting stunt with that old man. I defended my con, because it was insignificant to the big picture. This isn't. I crossed a huge ethical line with you several days ago and didn't even know it. I'm investigating your competitor, and you're helping me. That can't continue."

Geneva felt her chest ache, and she began to breathe heavily. She needed to will herself to take control. Grabbing her beer off the bar, she took a drink, and then a second, before she turned to him.

"Beck, it's not like I'm doing anything you couldn't do without me. I'm sorry. I don't understand your rules. I didn't come down here to ruin your story. I came here to be with you."

It was time she fessed up to more. She needed to judge his reaction. She needed to salvage this. "Beck, I should have told you something else too. The FBI came to my office shortly before we met and asked about Lamurr's relationship with Senator Bayard. An agent McCauley implied there was some payoff."

"Payoff?"

"Yes."

"Who is this guy?"

"An agent. You know the type—a big guy. Not a goon, but very tall. Maybe late thirties."

"What else did McCauley tell you?"

"Not really anything. He asked me if we had any financial relationship with Bayard and implied Lamurr might. Beck, I didn't realize we both held pieces to the same puzzle," she lied. "Honest, I didn't know. I came here to be with this hot man I just met."

He grinned.

Had she found a tender spot? She would push and find out. She couldn't lose Beck. She both wanted him and needed him. He was the key to her future. "I think you're one of the most fascinating men I've ever met. I don't think straight when I'm around you, and I've obviously made some bad decisions. One of them was not telling you about Serodynne as soon as I understood what your story was about."

Beck looked straight at her. His pale blue eyes sparkled in the reflection of the sea. Geneva felt herself weaken as she looked into them.

"This is both of our faults," he said. "We're personally involved. I'm personally involved. Things have just moved so quickly."

"Will you forgive me?"

Beck looked at her without blinking. She needed an answer, but there wasn't one.

Geneva bit her lip and attempted a smile. She slid off the barstool and into his arms and buried her face in his shoulder. He wrapped one limp arm around her. The other remained on the bar.

"I should have explained sooner why I was coming to Grand Cayman," he said. Beck pushed back and looked at her, wiping a tear from her cheek. "But why? Why didn't you tell me everything you knew sooner?"

This time Geneva didn't speak. She could feel her lower lip quiver as they stared into each other's eyes. She felt his faith in her slowly ebbing.

"Does anyone else know about Bayard and Lamurr?" he asked.

Geneva straightened and leaned against her barstool. "Serodynne's corporate counsel, Sue Nijelski. She told me to keep it quiet. She said a false rumor could harm Serodynne. Now it may not be so false. This could run into hundreds of millions of dollars in lost profits for my employer."

"You might be right."

"What do you mean?"

"My call with Nancy just now. Sunrise Meridian is a subsidiary of Lamurr through a company it owns called XAX Ltd. Our stringer in Venezuela checked the corporate records in Caracas where Lamurr has a mining operation. That's how Lamurr is funneling the money to Bayard's corporation."

"You're not making any sense."

"Lamurr is bidding on the Pentagon contract. It owns a mining company in Venezuela. That mining company owns a small solar energy company, which has turned into a real estate investment company called Sunrise Meridian here in Cayman. So all Lamurr has to do is tell officials of its subsidiary to work out sweetheart deals with Bayard. Lamurr is twice removed from the money transfer, but it really controls the whole process in return for favors from Bayard."

"Oh my God. There goes my Pentagon contract. He really is being paid off."

"Yeah, and I may not be able to do anything about it," Beck said. His disgust emanated from his sharp stare that locked on her while burning a hole in her heart. Then suddenly, he turned away and grabbed his warm beer off the bar.

Her turmoil lingered. Not even the warm gentle breeze or the soft melodic drumbeat of the languid ocean surf could wash it away.

27

Beck continued to eye her. She looked beautiful in another short sundress, this one dark blue with yellow flowers. The thin straps showed off her darkening tan and her cavernous cleavage. Her breasts alone were enough to undo him. He needed to start thinking about the task at hand instead of taking her to bed again.

"We can't undo what's already been done," he said. "But going forward, this has got to be strictly my investigation all the way."

"You're the boss."

He smiled. "Well, that's a first."

"You know what I mean, Mr. Rikki." She curled her lower lip in a mock pout. Slowly, a smile emerged between her widening dimples. Her act was sexy and endearing, he thought, and he immediately felt vulnerable to her charms. Not this time, he told himself. He needed to keep her allure in perspective. His first allegiance was to his story, no matter what he felt for her. And now he wasn't at all sure what that was.

"This story could become a family affair," he said. "The half brother facilitates the bribe for Senator Bayard. And what is Oliver's role? I think I'll be spending the afternoon looking through land records to see if any have Mr. Oliver's name on them. You can't be a part of that. How about you pull docs on land sales in Bayard's land development? There's no harm in that. Whether you pull them or I do, it won't change what they say. But you need to stay clear of my investigation from now on. You understand that?"

"Sure. I'll keep my distance. But what are you looking for now?"

"I'm tracking money and looking for an Oliver connection. I need a paper trail."

"Does it matter? I mean you still have enough for a story about Bayard taking payoffs. Don't you?" she asked.

"Yeah, but it could be a bigger story if it involves Oliver. I'll need to confront Kindred, but by myself this time."

"I understand."

He needed distance between Geneva and his investigation. This really didn't fix the problem, but right now he needed to keep her involvement hidden from Nancy and Baker, his managing editor, until he could figure out what to do. This could be one of the biggest stories of his career, and he wasn't going to let Geneva screw it up for him. One way or the other, he was going to find the truth about Lamurr's payoffs to Bayard.

Beck pulled his cell phone from his pocket and called Kindred's office. The paralegal said they could meet at one o'clock tomorrow. Beck apologized for becoming ill earlier and hung up.

As he stood to leave, he slowly slid his wooden barstool back into place, giving him time to look for the white straw hat. He saw nothing. He felt silly. He must be getting paranoid.

"Will your editor be okay with all of this?" Geneva asked.

"She doesn't need to know."

BACK AT THE GOVERNMENT records offices, Beck was determined to find ties to Jackson Oliver. Maybe Fahy's suspicion about his boss was correct.

Beck scoured computer documents for three hours. Then he requested the clerk bring old deed index books out of storage. He turned the musty pages carefully for fear he might tear the brittle sheets. He ran his index finger down the columns of entries, finding nothing. He scanned the faded decades-old handwritten entries, created long before records were typed, scanned, and filed in a computer. There was no Jackson Oliver anywhere—not a deed in any book, nor a corporate filing or tax record on any computer screen he checked. Nothing.

Geneva had better luck. She found more than two dozen lot sales in Bayard's development and dutifully made copies, stapled them together and stuffed them in her large canvas beach bag.

Beck loved her enthusiasm. He felt a tinge of guilt keeping her occupied with meaningless work and away from his investigation. But he knew he had to. And if she realized she was just doing busy work, she pretended not to care.

But he was still bothered by the lack of any paper trail tying Jackson Oliver to his brother's legal work on Bayard's sleazy land deals. There had to be something. But it sure didn't exist on this island. He had exhausted every avenue.

He'd been sitting at the computer terminal in the middle of the records room for so long running the details through his head that the screen went blank and he failed to notice.

What was he missing? It couldn't be just a coincidence that both brothers were tied to the senator. He'd been a reporter for too long to believe in coincidences.

Was there another possibility? What if Oliver wasn't tied to the senator at all? Beck didn't want to consider that possibility. He trusted Fahy, yet he had only Fahy's word to go on that Oliver was trying to kill the Bayard investigation. What if that was all a lie? But a lie to accomplish what?

Did Fahy have some ulterior motive Beck hadn't considered? Maybe he wasn't such a Boy Scout after all. Could there be something more sinister?

Beck didn't like where his mind was going. He decided to walk it back to the beginning.

He'd never met Fahy before all of this began. He'd never even heard of him. Was he being honest when he said he wanted an investigative reporter to go after the Bayard scandal, or could Fahy be targeting Beck for some reason? But why go after a reporter? Maybe Fahy was leading him on some wild goose chase in hopes he'd publish a bogus story that would quickly be discredited and ruin Beck's reputation. Many a reporter had been misled by a source, but not Beck. Oh sure, he understood his sources may not have the most honorable intentions in mind when leaking a story to him. That's why he always tried to verify his facts with a second source. Boy Scout or not, surely someone as politically savvy as Fahy would know that. After all, Beck had not only seen the redacted memorandum on the investigation, but Geneva verified it with her story of the visit from the FBI.

And Fahy's suspicions about Bayard were turning out to be true. The more Beck dug, the more dirty dealings he uncovered, just as Fahy suspected. So he was on the right track, and his political corruption radar was still strong. So Fahy really was the Boy Scout the papers said he was. Beck just didn't have the complete story yet on Jackson Oliver. That would come. And Geneva was right. He had a story, even if Oliver wasn't part of it. Beck needed to stop doubting himself and go with his gut. Oliver had to be involved. Beck was sure of that. He just couldn't figure out how.

Beck jumped when he felt two hands suddenly rubbing his shoulders.

"You okay? You seem tense and you're . . . staring at a blank screen," Geneva said softly. She leaned into him and ran her outstretched fingers down his chest and kissed him quickly on the cheek. As she stood, he could feel her breasts hidden under her lightweight dress press against the back of his head, her hands again kneading his tight shoulders.

She was trying to make up, he thought. But his focus was elsewhere. Right now he was more interested in the relationship between Jackson Oliver and David Bayard than his own with Geneva. He hated being misled, even if it was unintentional, and he did not easily forgive.

28

Beck again sat in the waiting area of Kindred's dark-paneled law office. This was going to be awkward. He had his normal pregame jitters. It thrilled him to pound an adversary with the most stinging questions. It was college debate team all over again. But for the moment, he kept his game face on and revealed nothing.

Kindred strode into the room in a pale blue long-sleeve shirt, dark tie, and rimless reading glasses. He greeted Beck with a warm handshake and pat on the shoulder, then invited his new client back into his office.

"So you're interested in some real estate," he said as he showed Beck to a seat and settled behind his desk, polished to a high sheen. An antique brass lamp with a dark green shade sat at one end, and an expensive pen set resided at the other.

Kindred leaned back in his big leather chair and placed his hands behind his head, his posture a bit too casual for a first meeting, thought Beck. The only thing missing was propping his feet up on the desk. Then Beck understood. Kindred was putting him in his place. Showing him who was top dog.

Beck noticed the sweat stains in the armpits of his shirt and immediately felt at ease.

"What can I do for you?" Kindred asked.

Beck surveyed his prey. This was always the most difficult moment, his journalistic Kabuki dance before he moved in for the kill. He looked at his unsuspecting prey. Kindred was short and overweight with a graying, receding hairline.

That was it, thought Beck. Kindred's legs were too short to prop up on his desk. Otherwise, he'd be getting the full treatment. Beck was all too familiar with the god complex. The shorter the god, the bigger the complex. This was going to be tough.

Time to drop the pretense and weigh in. He had to lay out his facts carefully and give Kindred the opportunity to respond to his findings. Beck could not afford to have him complain later that a reporter had misled him. That was Journalism 101.

"I'm a reporter with the *Post-Examiner* in Washington, DC, and I'm looking into some land deals you've been involved in."

"Really?" It wasn't a question, but a challenge. Kindred's upturned smile went horizontal. His eyes narrowed and zeroed in on Beck. The hands came down and took a defensive stance atop the glistening desk.

"I'm interested in Senator David Bayard's relationship with Sunrise Meridian and its parent company, Lamurr Technologies."

"As you no doubt have found in the public records, I have provided legal services to Mr. Bayard. You're entitled to anything you can find in the public records. Beyond that, I don't discuss my client's private business affairs, and I have no idea about any relationship with a Lamurr Technologies. I don't know the company."

Clever move, thought Beck. Complete ignorance about the source of all of the funds. Beck explained what he had uncovered. Kindred leaned back and then edged forward in his armchair again.

"You've never heard of Lamurr Technologies?" Beck continued.

"No, and again, I'm sorry, but I cannot go into detail about any client's business dealings."

"But it's all there in the government records."

"Government records are public. You're welcome to read anything you want into them. Just be sure you are accurate. We have libel laws in Grand Cayman that reach across the ocean. I would be very careful about anything I published if I were you."

Threats, thought Beck. Good, he was agitating the little man. "What about incorporating both Jersey Shore and Sunrise Meridian?"

"I'm a lawyer. It's what I do. Again, be careful with what you try to read into public documents." Kindred's voice was curt. The warm lilt of a gentlemanly English accent had disappeared.

"Was Sunrise Meridian originally set up as a solar power company or a real estate investment company?"

"You'll have to contact the company and ask them. I only do the legal work."

"But you are the company in Grand Cayman. According to legal documents, your office is the address for Sunrise Meridian."

"I'm only an attorney. I have nothing to do with the company beyond providing legal services. Again, be careful, Mr. Rikki."

This wasn't going anywhere, Beck thought. Kindred had found his defense and was adorning it with a forced smile and civil demeanor. The lawyer leaned his elbows on his desk and grasped his hands.

The sparring continued. Beck made three more attempts to get Kindred to open up, reshaping the same questions each time, trying to attack from a different angle. Kindred was no amateur. He dodged and weaved, citing attorney-client privilege each time and always referring Beck back to the public records.

Kindred was very sure of himself and grew more confident as the conversation volleyed back and forth and Beck failed to chip away at his armor. Beck sense Kindred could tell he was running out of revelations to serve up and was trying to toy with him. A hint of sarcasm perforated the lawyer's speech.

Finally, Beck decided to drop his big bomb. "I understand Jackson Oliver is your half brother."

Kindred paused and then spoke slowly. "There's no secret about that," he said as he adjusted his position in his chair.

Beck could see in Kindred's manner he had finally hit a nerve.

"What is your brother's relationship with Senator Bayard?"

"You'll have to ask him. I don't really know. Do they even know each other? You tell me."

Damn. Kindred had recovered almost as quickly as he had stumbled. Back to the old singsong rhythm of ignorance and attorney-client privilege, thought Beck.

"And like I told you," Kindred said, "I represent Mr. Bayard, and I do not discuss my client's private business affairs."

Beck could hardly hide a smile as he scribbled in shorthand on his notepad. He felt like he was back in college in the middle of a tournament. "Is your brother involved with Sunrise Meridian?"

"As I've told you before, what's in the public documents is public. Be careful, however, what you try to read into them."

A nondenial denial, thought Beck. "We're going to run a story with these facts. Would you care to comment on any of them? I want to be fair and give you every opportunity you need to explain what you know about these deals."

"Your offer is very generous, but I must decline to discuss my clients' business."

Beck thanked him for meeting with him.

"I feel like we have met under false pretenses," Kindred said. "My assistant said you wanted to talk about purchasing some real estate."

"And that's exactly what we did," Beck replied.

Kindred shook his head. He'd left himself open for that one—an unusual foot fault in their word tournament. A hint of a smile crossed Kindred's face. Score one for Rikki—a meaningless point in this game of gotcha.

They shook hands, a forced gesture of civility this time. Kindred locked his eyes on Beck, silently daring him to turn away. Beck squeezed Kindred's hand a little tighter and smiled broadly, signaling he had the lawyer by the gonads. The best part of it—Beck knew Kindred fully understood.

29

When Beck entered the penthouse, Geneva was in her normal state of undress, lounging beneath one of the large umbrellas on the terrace, reading a novel. Her body glistened from perspiration. She turned to him when he stepped out into the sunlight.

She stood and walked toward him. Even though she was naked most of the time, he still had not gotten used to her allure. Her breasts jiggled and her hips swayed as she eagerly padded in his direction over the stone terrace. Normally, that would set his desire on fire. But this time, he felt little. He still wondered if he could forgive her.

"How did it go?" she said, wrapping her arms around him and pressing her wet bosom against his chest. She gently kissed him.

He explained Kindred's defense. Not totally unexpected, but clever, he said.

"So you really didn't learn anything new?"

"I learned he's a good lawyer. The purpose of the meeting was to lay all my cards on the table and let him respond."

"I don't get it."

"I confront the subjects of my stories and give them a chance to respond to my findings. Even if they say nothing, that's a no-comment response I can use. The worst thing I can do is blindside somebody in print. That opens me up to attack for failing to get their side of the story."

"You have so many rules." She shook her head from side to side.

"That's the way the game is played. We try to be fair." He paused and looked at his surroundings, restless. Beck wondered how long it would take for Kindred to be on the phone with his brother. One of them would contact the Bayard campaign. Beck had just fired the opening salvo. He had poked his cell shortly after leaving Kindred's office to warn Nancy that Bayard's people would soon be alerted. She said she would notify the city desk to route any calls to her. They were armed for a fight. All Beck wanted to do now was get back to Washington and finish his story.

"I think we're done here. It's time to head home," he said. "I'll make the arrangements for a flight tomorrow. There's no more work here that I can see."

"Our last night in paradise. Let's make the most of it."

Beck looked at her and forced a smile.

THEY STARTED THEIR EVENING at the cigar bar near Kindred's office. It was after five, and Beck could see the law office was closed. They progressed to a nightspot on the roof of one of the other hotels on Seven Mile Beach and gazed out at the Caribbean as they sat at a small table nibbling on fresh sautéed grouper. The sun slowly descended behind scattered clouds. The evening was pink with brilliant streaks of orange piercing the pastel sky as it arched from the blue-green water.

There was nothing he could do about his story until he returned to DC tomorrow, so Beck decided to enjoy his last evening with this beautiful if confounding woman. Her beauty was without question. Those eyes and that lush brown hair that sculpted the perfect contours of her cheekbones made his heart skip. But just how candid was she? Was she deceptive or simply ignorant of the rules of his profession? He very much wanted to believe the latter, but his suspicious nature, honed over many years of reporting, still left him doubtful.

She was, after all, a lobbyist and a player in Washington's political merry-go-round. But he had to give her some benefit of the doubt. He didn't think she had had many dealings with the press before she had met him except to comment to some style reporter about a sexy dress she had worn to a charitable event. He wanted to shake her as hard as he could to find the truth, but what good would it do? There were no easy answers to finding this complicated woman's core.

She sipped her martini, and then grabbed Beck's hand. "Let's dance."

The band was reggae, something not easy to find on the island. The British and US cultural influence permeated the Seven Mile Beach clubs and bars. American rock and roll and new generations of British music dominated the club scene.

"You know a lot of Latin steps," Beck said after they returned to their table to catch their breath.

"I've visited the Caribbean a lot."

"Whereabouts?"

"I was here probably five years ago. We stayed on the east end of the island. It's much quieter there. I like this though. It's nice we can walk to some nightlife. And I'm with you, which makes it even nicer."

Beck smiled broadly.

"I've also been to the saints—Saint Martin, Saint Bart's, Saint John—and to Tortola and Abaco," she continued.

"Favorite?"

"Abaco. It's less commercial and more private than here. Less touristy."

"Nightlife?"

"It's more local island rake and scrape music and limbo dancing, which creates a more authentic island feel for me. But most of all, it's serene, quiet. That's what I love. It's as far from the Washington scene as you can get, but with all of the comforts of home. Of course, it was nice that we were on a private island across the harbor from the main island so I could have my. . . ah . . . privacy."

"You mean a place to skinny-dip and sunbathe in the nude."

"You've got me pegged. Enough rest now. Will you dance with me again, Mr. Kemper?"

He laughed. "Ms. Rikki, I would love to."

As they danced, Beck glanced at his surroundings—the view of the lights nearby and distant along the oceanfront. He twirled Geneva around and changed his position, now facing the bar on the other side of the dance floor. Only a few people sat there. A white straw hat sat atop the bar in front of an empty stool. Beck thought it odd and immediately thought of the man with the binoculars who had spied on them a few days before. Only an elderly couple was seated while a fat man in a flowered shirt stood with drink in hand at the rail watching the band. There was no white suit in sight. You really are getting paranoid, Beck thought.

He twirled Geneva again, but this time even faster and with more intent. She reacted with a puzzled look, and then went along, picking up her pace. Their dancing grew more intense, until the song finished. She stood still gasping for breath.

"That was quite a workout," she said. "Where did you learn to dance like that?"

"Let's go," Beck said softly. He paid the tab, and they headed indoors for the elevator. Beck looked back at the bar. The hat was gone.

WHEN THEY RETURNED to the penthouse, Beck nearly tore off Geneva's clothes. They grabbed at each other and were naked in seconds. He mounted her with little foreplay. He pounded her, mercilessly. He was rough, squeezing her breasts and thighs until she yelped from the pain. His aggressiveness, however, excited something inside her she had never experienced before. She grabbed his body and held tightly as he slammed into her. The spontaneity of the moment excited her, and she exploded with an orgasm while he continued his relentless pursuit. But then his unyielding siege of her flesh began to sting and surge through her body. She pushed back, pressing both hands against his chest, but her effort only exaggerated the fire of her throbbing pain. He either did not notice or did not care. He kept going until finally, finally, a husky growl thundered from his lungs, and he was done.

Beck collapsed on top of her, his head turned away. His full weight pressed against her, and she could not move. Finally, he rolled over on his back breathing heavily. She closed her eyes and said nothing. Then Beck shifted onto his side with his back to her, never kissing her good night, and fell asleep immediately.

She listened to the soft cadence of his slumber as she lay awake now staring at the ceiling. Her body ached from the rough sex. She understood now his work had come between them. He had never expressed his ire to her other than at the beach bar, but it was obvious he was still very angry. She'd hoped the episode had passed, but his aggressive lovemaking proved otherwise. She realized she did not really know this man. His rage, drive, and ego were bottled up behind a veneer of calm, wit, and gentle charm—the side of him she adored.

She had wounded his ego and endangered his story. If she'd only understood better, maybe she would have reacted differently. If only she could take it all back and start over.

She couldn't sleep, and her mind wandered. She looked at the shadows cast by the moon through their open window. Then she was sure she heard the clinking of their ice maker in the kitchen. Finally, she thought she heard someone passing by in the hallway outside of their suite.

She began to doze off as her thoughts returned to Beck. She wondered if their relationship was damaged beyond repair. All she knew was she now feared the man she needed and still desired.

30

As the morning sun cast its shadows on the beach below, the hotel maid propped open the door to begin her daily assignment. She grabbed a stack of towels, clean sheets, and bathroom cleaner from her cart, then turned to enter the hotel room. Walking head down toward the bathroom, a strange odor caught her attention. She looked up.

Her mouth fell open, and she gasped desperately, trying to catch her breath. Then a wail, like a dying animal, rose from her throat. She dropped her supplies on the carpet and staggered into the hallway and down to the supply closet where another maid was loading a cart with clean towels.

"The couple, the couple!"

The second maid ran to the suite.

She too screamed. There, only a few feet away, lay a man and woman, naked, drenched in dried blood.

INSPECTOR WAYNE TOMLINSON SCANNED the room for answers as the photographer shot stills of the blood-soaked bodies. The man lay faceup on the bed, a large stab wound right in the middle of his chest and his eyes and mouth wide open. Had he been able to scream?

Dried tears streaked his cheeks, and dried blood smeared both sides of his jaw, his ears, and his hand, where he must have attempted to grab his chest. He must have grabbed his head as well. Screaming in pain, no doubt, Tomlinson thought. He couldn't imagine the agony. Poor bastard.

The gash in the chest would have incapacitated him immediately. The wound would have penetrated the sac surrounding the heart, equalizing the pressure in the heart and the chest cavity. The guy never stood a chance. He had no more than ninety seconds to live with a wound like that, Tomlinson figured.

The assailant knew what he was doing. Obviously, he attacked the man in his sleep first. That way, the victim couldn't put up a fight. Blood had spurted all over the body and the bedsheets.

"Shoot a close-up of the face. Get the dried tears," he ordered.

"Why?" asked the photographer.

"I want to show a judge and jury the poor bastard knew he was dying and was helpless to do anything about it. It might come in handy when we catch the son of a bitch who did this."

Murder and violent crime were infrequent on the island, and the sight of the woman made him sick to his stomach. She must have been awakened by her mate's struggle and attempted to flee. Her body sprawled on the floor. What a beautiful creature, he thought.

Slash wounds cut across her forearms and both breasts; she obviously attempted to defend herself. She, too, had a stab wound to the heart, but also to the stomach. Blood ran down both legs. She must have been standing when fending off her attacker, he figured.

Blood splatter also covered the floor and the wall behind the bed where she must have been cornered, having no avenue of escape. And to top it off, the assailant slit her throat from one ear to the other, nearly decapitating her. Part of her trachea was visible. Spite for fighting her assailant? Tomlinson turned away.

The couple, he figured, were in their late thirties or early forties.

"Make sure you comb the bathroom. The killer might have left some DNA. He wouldn't have left here with all of that blood on him. He would have been noticed within minutes," Tomlinson told the crime scene tech.

Two officers escorted the maid who had discovered the bodies downstairs to the hotel's office, where they sat in a staff conference room attempting to question her and calm her down. Tomlinson left the crime scene to the photographer and stationed a guard outside the door. It was time to interrogate the hotel workers. He ordered the manager to gather all staff who had worked in the last twenty-four hours.

"I need the names of the victims too."

The manager nodded.

Tomlinson took over the manager's office. He ordered the island's makeshift forensics team to meet him there. The island's part-time coroner, a local undertaker, had been called in to examine the bodies. His assistant was the island's only crime scene technician, and the photographer freelanced for the department. Judging from the degree of rigor mortis, the coroner said, the murders took place sometime between midnight and 4:00 a.m.

The manager returned to the room with the clerk who registered the guests. "Mr. and Mrs. Beck Rikki," he told Tomlinson. "They've been here for three days. My clerk remembers them checking in."

The clerk nodded. Tomlinson sat the shaken woman down at the small conference table outside the manager's office. "I saw them on numerous occasions walking through the lobby, hand in hand," she said. "They were a handsome American couple and seemed very much in love."

"Was there anything unusual about them?" Tomlinson asked.

"No. Nothing."

"Did they act strange in any way?"

"No, they just came and went each day like all of the other tourists."

One of the officers came to the conference room doorway. "We've got the night crew out here."

Tomlinson instructed the desk clerk not to leave the building while he interviewed other staff. For two hours, he grilled the evening crew, and they each explained their actions during the last twenty-four hours. It was tedious, and they grew impatient as Tomlinson questioned them over and over about the same points of their nightly routine. Finally, he let them go home and back to bed. It was only then that he called the desk clerk back for more questioning.

"I'd like to see the hotel registration information," he told her.

"It's at the desk."

Tomlinson followed her to the front desk, and the clerk immediately printed out a page of information.

"Here you go," she said, handing him the page with the couple's information and a copy of their daily hotel charges.

He glanced over the information. Mr. and Mrs. Beck Rikki, it said. Had been at the hotel three nights so far. Were scheduled to leave today. Had a rental car with the valet. No unusual charges, no room service, not even a movie. Tomlinson thanked the clerk for her help and turned to head back to the manager's office.

"Oh my god," she screamed. "It's them."

Tomlinson swung around. "What?"

The clerk pointed to a couple exiting the lobby elevator. "It's them. It's Mr. and Mrs. Rikki."

Tomlinson bolted across the lobby in their direction.

31

"Stop!" Tomlinson yelled. Everyone in the lobby turned toward his booming voice, including Beck and Geneva. Tomlinson dodged three tourists and grabbed both Geneva and Beck by the arm. "Police. Come with me."

"What the hell," Beck said, pulling away.

"Police. Please come with me." Tomlinson held Beck's arm tightly and led them into the hotel manager's office.

Beck kept pulling his arm back. "What's going on?" he demanded.

"You're Mr. Rikki, right?" asked Tomlinson.

"Yes. Who the hell are you?"

"In room five forty-two?"

"Ahh . . . no. Who the hell are you?"

"Detective Tomlinson, Royal Cayman Islands Police Service." He showed his badge. "You're not in room five forty-two?"

"What's going on here? We're in the penthouse."

"I don't understand. Then how . . . who . . . was in five forty-two?" Tomlinson turned to the clerk.

She shook her head.

"Where's that manager?"

"What's all of the excitement about?" Geneva asked.

"The hotel has you booked in room five forty-two," Tomlinson said. "We thought you were the couple in five forty-two."

"Wait a minute," said Geneva. "I think I understand. We were going to check into five forty-two, but I asked if the penthouse was available when we arrived."

"That's right," Beck said.

"So I put it on my American Express card instead of on Beck's credit card. My last name is Kemper. I'm Geneva Kemper."

The clerk sat at the manager's desk and quickly typed into his computer. "That's right. We have Mr. and Mrs. Kemper in the penthouse and Mr. and Mrs. Rikki in five forty-two."

"Same people," Beck said. "When we arrived several days ago, you were shorthanded at the desk. Must have made the error then."

Tomlinson told them about the murders, leaving out the grim details. Just then, the hotel manager stepped back into his own office.

"Find out who those people were in room five forty-two," Tomlinson barked. "Clear the room. I need to talk with Mr. Rikki and Ms. Kemper."

The office was small and cramped, with too much furniture and a window overlooking the back parking lot. Tomlinson closed the door and sat behind the desk. Beck and Geneva sat on the flowered couch with their backs to the wall.

"What does this have to do with us?" Beck protested.

"Maybe nothing. Maybe a lot. I don't mean to be melodramatic," Tomlinson said, "but I didn't want to speak in front of the hotel staff. When we discovered the bodies this morning, I had the manager call in the entire night staff. The night clerk told us that around eight o'clock last night, a man came to the front desk asking for you, Mr. Rikki. The clerk called your room, or what he thought was your room, since the occupants of five forty-two were registered under Mr. and Mrs. Beck Rikki. It is policy here, as in all hotels, not to give out a hotel guest's room number. No one answered the call, which I assume the man asking about you already knew would be the case.

"This morning I had the night clerk reenact what took place when the man asked for you. Your room number is your house telephone number. Anyone who was the least bit observant could have picked up the room number when the clerk dialed. The phone is clearly visible to the general public." Tomlinson stopped and shifted his gaze between them.

"It is my belief," he explained, "that the intended victims last night were not the unsuspecting couple who now lie dead, but the two of you."

Beck's jaw dropped, and his eyes glazed. Geneva bent over, looking at the floor, her hand on her forehead.

"Oh my god," she said. "Beck, what have you gotten us into?"

Beck looked away, staring at nothing.

"Mr. Rikki, we need to discuss why someone would want to kill you and Ms. Kemper."

"I just can't believe this," Beck said.

"Why would someone want to kill you?"

Beck explained why he was in Grand Cayman and gave a cryptic account of his investigation.

"And you, Ms. Kemper. What are you doing here?"

"She came to help me," Beck said.

"Do you work for the newspaper too?" Tomlinson faced Geneva.

"No. I'm a lobbyist in Washington. Beck and I are friends, so I agreed to accompany him."

"Very well," the inspector said. "We will want to search your room, just in case. We need to make copies of your passports and driver's licenses. We will also need your telephone numbers in the States. Then you will be free to go."

He handed them his business card, and they exchanged information.

"We have a two-thirty flight out this afternoon," Beck said.

"I would be on it, if I were you," Tomlinson said. "We will be in touch if we need more information."

The three of them walked over to the lobby elevator and waited. Beck held his arm firmly around Geneva, her head on his shoulder. Tomlinson signaled one of his men to accompany them while he continued his investigation downstairs. After the elevator doors closed behind them, Tomlinson shook his head. He would do his best to keep them safe on Cayman, but he couldn't assure their safety once they left. He knew all too well the seamier side of powerful financial forces that made up the island's global business community. If this couple had gotten mixed up with them, leaving Cayman would not protect them, not for long anyway.

THE MAN IN THE WHITE LINEN SUIT sat in the small café looking out at the hotel lobby, drinking his third cup of coffee. Whenever possible, which was often, he liked to hang around after his man had carried out an assignment to assure himself all had gone according to plan. Like his bosses, he hated loose ends.

So when the hotel clerk screamed and he spied Mr. and Mrs. Rikki exiting the lobby elevator, he jerked to attention, carefully setting down his steaming cup of coffee while never taking his eyes off the pair. Last night he had called his man from the bar and was assured everything was in perfect order. He figured he would never see the couple again— at least not alive. Now the police were here, and so was the couple.

What had his man gotten wrong?

TWO HOURS LATER, with tumbling bags and no bellman, Beck and Geneva poured out of the elevator and into the lobby. They wheeled their bags and hefted their carry-ons toward the glass front door where the valet held their car. Beck tossed his bags in the trunk with the help of the valet and then noticed Geneva struggling with her roller bag. It was stuck in the closing hotel door.

"Here, let me help you with that," said a tall, thin man to Geneva. He looked vaguely familiar to Beck, but he couldn't place him.

"Thank you. Thank you very much," Geneva said. She turned to him and nodded appreciation.

The man helped the valet load the bags into their small trunk and backseat. "I hope you enjoyed your stay, Mrs. Rikki," the man said. "Be safe."

Beck thanked him. There was something about the man that didn't fit. Beck couldn't place it and shook it off. He had a plane to catch. He tipped the valet and hopped in the driver's seat and began to drive away. He checked his rearview mirror and saw the man talking to the driver of the cab in line behind them. Beck said nothing to Geneva as he turned the car onto the street. His eyes were glued to the rearview mirror.

Then he realized a complete stranger had just called Geneva "Mrs. Rikki."

32

Back again in the first-class section, Beck drank three Bloody Marys while Geneva tried unsuccessfully to sleep. He tried gently to talk to her and assure her they were safe. She turned away and curled into a fetal position with her back to him, facing the window. He thought he heard a soft sob, but when he tried to comfort her, she pushed his hand away. He felt she needed him right now, but he'd been so angry with her, she no longer wanted his comfort. He could not see her face, so he grasped strands of her luscious brown hair and felt guilty he had been so angry. How could he have ever been mad at this enticing woman?

When they finally arrived at Reagan National Airport late that evening, they stood at the luggage carousel in silence for what seemed like forever. After their bags finally arrived, they walked silently to the cabstand and took separate cabs to their separate homes. Geneva said nothing, not even good-bye, which made him feel even more unsettled.

Beck did not unpack when he got to his condo. Instead, he went straight for his liquor cabinet and humidor, grabbing a fifth and a cigar. After an hour on the balcony trying to erase the past eighteen hours, he staggered down the hall to bed.

He wasn't sure what he'd gotten himself into, but it was now obvious it was much bigger than he had first thought. Whatever Bayard and Kindred were up to, whatever role Oliver or Fahy might play in all of this, Beck was determined to find the truth.

"YOU LOOK LIKE SHIT," Nancy said.

"I feel like it. I didn't sleep last night." Beck squinted under the harsh fluorescent lights of the newsroom, waiting for his steaming twenty-ounce Starbucks to cool off. He took a sip—still too hot—and explained what had happened in the last twenty-four hours.

"I'm not in the mood to finish this story today," Beck said. "Those people were perfectly innocent, and they were killed because of my investigation. It's a political corruption story. Nothing more. And they were killed because of me. I can't deal with that right now."

Nancy pulled up a chair next to his desk. "You've been going non-stop for days. You're tired. Take a break. Look, there's no proof anyone was coming after you. It's a good story. You've got the goods on Bayard. Do you know anything about the couple?"

"I don't. I'm afraid to ask." Beck's head hung low, his eyes glued to the floor.

"Go home. Take the day off. Collect your thoughts. Get some sleep."

Beck drove home and crawled into bed fully clothed. He thought of Geneva lying naked beside him and finally crashed, sleeping for more than fourteen hours.

The sun was peering through the blinds when he awoke. He took a long, hot shower, trying to cleanse the memories of the police investigation from his mind and body. It didn't work. After he toweled off, he sat on his bed and called her.

"You okay?"

"No, I'm not," Geneva said. "I don't know what to make of all of this. What have I gotten myself into? I'm sorry. I can't talk right now."

The line went dead. He starred blankly at the small object in his hand—his only tether to her. No good-byes. She just hung up. He began to realize the toll the murder was taking on him too. He'd lost control of his story and he'd lost Geneva—the two loves of his life right now.

His phone rang.

"Geneva?"

"Meet me at the restaurant at nine," said the voice, and hung up.

It was Fahy. Beck stared at the silent cell phone, heart pounding. Immediately, he refocused. It was time to find some answers.

FAHY AGAIN WAITED AT A TABLE IN THE rear of the restaurant, away from the windows, his back against the wall. The smell of strong black coffee and the hint of cigarettes permeated Beck's nostrils as soft Latin music bounced off the restaurant's walls. Fahy did not stand to greet him, but kept his gaze downward and fingered his half-empty cup of coffee. Word must travel fast, thought Beck. He was eager to find out what Fahy knew.

The waitress took their orders, two eggs over easy and a bottle of hot sauce. Beck remembered the strong coffee from their first meeting. He was no longer an espresso drinker, not since his younger days when he thought it cool to drink out of a demitasse cup in Georgetown cafés. Nor was he a fan of strong African-brand coffees. He asked for an inch of hot water in his coffee.

"You've stirred up a hornet's nest," Fahy said. "The FBI is now in Cayman aiding local officials with the murder investigation. The two murdered were US citizens from Hartford, so we've got reason to get involved, and the Cayman government has acquiesced."

"Do you think they were after me?" Beck worried his question might make him appear vulnerable.

"You mean *us*, don't you? You and Mrs. Kemper?"

Shit, thought Beck. Nothing is private anymore. In the back of his mind, he had to figure the authorities here would know everything. Geneva was a target too. He felt embarrassed that Fahy would know about his love life. He heard his old metal chair squeak as he shifted uncomfortably.

Fahy didn't miss a beat. "Detective Tomlinson filled in the FBI. We're working to keep it as quiet as possible, but a murder can't be swept under the rug. Let's hope this doesn't make the local newspapers. If we're lucky, it will only make the news in Hartford, unless cable channels pick it up."

"Was it tied to my story?"

"Don't know yet."

"Why didn't you tell me about Oliver's half brother?"

Fahy paused and struggled with his words. "I wasn't sure of its relevance at the time."

"What else haven't you told me?"

"You know more than I do."

"I guess I should keep it to myself."

"That's probably not a bad idea. The less I know, the better." Fahy tipped his coffee cup to his lips, his eyes sweeping the room.

Beck's coffee arrived in a heavy, worn porcelain cup. He waved off the creamer. The waitress had forgotten. He took a sip and felt the steam in his nostrils clearing his head. "Where does the Oliver thread of this story go?"

"That I don't know. The FBI has found no shady deals involving him. I assume it's totally political. He's betting the odds. We've had eight years of a Democratic administration. The pendulum is likely to swing this year, and the Republicans may take control. He's a survivor, and I assume he's bet his money on Bayard."

"And having his half brother do the dirty work gives him cover."

"Precisely."

"God, don't you just love this town? Everybody's on the take. Everybody's frantically grabbing for their piece of the American pie." Beck shook his head.

"It is what it is."

"Am I in danger?" Beck looked into Fahy's deep blue eyes and, for the first time, noticed large bags slumping beneath them, marring his otherwise taut and angular face.

"Can't say. We haven't a clue who murdered that couple, but you're back in the States now. Whoever did it—and we're assuming they were after you—has got to expect they can no longer stop a story from being published. If that's the case, if it is Bayard's people or someone trying to protect him, they will shift into some sort of defensive mode."

Beck knew Fahy just might be trying to make him feel better, but he felt relieved anyway. "I'm not sure I even want to write the damn story. I feel awful about that couple. I feel responsible, and I don't even know who they are." Beck downed his coffee and grabbed the black plastic carafe the waitress had left on the table.

"It's best you not know. And you need to keep going. Did you find a connection to Lamurr?"

"Yep. Got it solid."

"Then you have an ethical obligation to go with the story. It's important we have honest, honorable public officials."

"God, you do sound like a friggin' Boy Scout—just like all of those stories written about you."

"I just don't want to see you sidelined by some false sense of guilt. Whoever killed that couple is guilty. Not you."

"Yes, but—"

"You are not responsible for their deaths. You did nothing wrong."

"But if I hadn't been there . . ." Breakfast was not sitting well. Beck blamed it on the hot sauce.

Fahy pulled a cheap burner cell phone from his pocket. He handed it to Beck. "If you need to reach me, use only this phone. It's one of those prepaid jobs with three hundred minutes programmed into it. It can't be traced back to you or me. I've got one that matches. Here is my number."

"This is a bit of cloak-and-dagger, isn't it?" Beck looked at him. "Is a burner really necessary?"

"Like I said, you've stirred up a hornet's nest in Justice and on the Hill. Remember a few years back when the Croom administration secretly subpoenaed all those news service telephone records? Now we have the National Security Agency routinely looking at individuals' e-mails and phone records. I don't want us caught in that dragnet, if and when this thing finally blows up. I may work for Justice, but I can get caught just as easily in any inquiry as you can."

Beck sat up straight. For the first time, he realized the risk Fahy was taking. Fahy could actually go to jail for talking to Beck, to say nothing of destroying his career at Justice if he were found out. Beck was not the only vulnerable one here. It made him feel more confident. Like it or not, they were in this together.

"Important people will be hurt by what you know," Fahy continued. "I don't think your life is in danger here in DC but be careful anyway. If I were you, I'd think twice about seeing Ms. Kemper in the near future, or at least until you've published your story."

"I don't think that will be a problem." He thought about her and realized he missed her.

"Be safe."

Beck tilted his head and looked at Fahy.

"What?" Fahy asked.

"Funny." Beck remembered now and felt a chill.

"What?"

"That's what this complete stranger said to us as we were leaving the hotel in Grand Cayman, right after we'd learned of the murders. It struck me as odd then, and you just stirred something in my brain."

Beck paused and pressed a hand to his temple. "He called Geneva by name—or at least the name he thought she went by—Mrs. Rikki. How would he have known that? And I thought I'd seen him on the island. He might have been following us."

"You're going after some of the biggest fish in all of government—hell, the world. Consider every possibility. You must be extremely cautious." Fahy looked up and again surveyed the room.

Beck turned to look as well. The waitress stood by the lunch counter, talking to the owner. Maybe half a dozen patrons were scattered throughout the restaurant. The Latin music pulsed from the cheap radio behind the bar. No one was within earshot of their conversation.

"I've never been tied to a murder before," Beck said. "I solve political puzzles. Destroy political careers. I don't investigate murders. My job is to describe a game of political chess where the stakes are little more than someone's reputation, not life or death."

"Now it's a game with big consequences," said Fahy. "And you've seen what the consequences can be."

"I don't feel sorry for the people I expose. I'm shedding light on their crimes, their conflicts. But these murders take things to a new level. Two people are dead, for Christ's sake."

"Just to be safe, cover your tracks. Cover your butt. Make sure your editors know where you are at all times. Make sure they have the information you've collected for your story and it's not all up here." Fahy pointed to his head. "Write it down somewhere and hand copies to someone else. And let everyone know that other people know what you know. That's your insurance policy."

Beck sighed. He took a sip of coffee and contemplated Fahy's advice. "You're right. Even if I don't publish it, I need an insurance policy. And then what?"

"If it's Bayard's people who came after you, they will say nothing and wait for your next move. They have to figure your paper already has the complete story. But if someone else is out to harm you, you must be on your guard. Change the locks on your door. Secure your windows. Be careful what you say on the phone. You and I might be under surveillance right now. If we meet again, be very careful to ensure you aren't followed."

"Jesus. What the hell am I involved in?"

"Right now you may be just a footnote in an FBI file. You're either on the edge of their investigation or right in the middle of it. We don't have answers yet." Fahy pushed his cup out of reach.

"A couple from Connecticut was murdered. You were not involved. The hotel made an error in identification. That's all. Oh, by the way, the couple was robbed of some expensive jewelry. Maybe that was an afterthought to cover the real motive or maybe that was the motive all along. If the FBI finds nothing else, the investigation will die just like the Connecticut couple."

Beck wasn't about to let this story die. He knew exactly what he needed to do. It was time to meet with Red and start writing.

33

The next morning, the headline on the front page of the business section of the *Post-Examiner* screamed the news. Just as Geneva had expected, Lamurr Technologies won the multibillion-dollar Pentagon contract to build unmanned aircraft, beating out the heavily favored Serodynne Corporation. An air force colonel in the Pentagon contracting office was quoted saying it was important for national security that more than one contractor be able to build its new drone aircraft program. The real news, she thought, was in the twelfth paragraph of the story where it noted Lamurr had strong political connections on Capitol Hill. Geneva shook her head as she finished the article. Typical reporter—he missed the real story.

Above the fold on the front page, she noticed a story about the Republican presidential candidates fighting for delegates now that the primaries were over and the national convention was nearing its end. Bayard was in second place in the delegate count behind Governor Ford Patten of Texas with convention voting set for today. She wondered what Harv was doing at the convention—and who he was doing it with.

THE MARKETS REACTED as Geneva expected. Serodynne stock lost 31 percent of its book value in a day. Lamurr stock shot up 22 percent. This was exactly what she had hoped would happen. Geneva laid her *Post-Examiner* on the desk and closed her office door. She called her favorite New York investment banker.

"Keith, you see the news?"

"Yep. We're looking pretty good right now. Your plan is brilliant. The stock is still moving in our direction."

"No one up there but you knows about us, right?"

"I'm not sure."

"What do you mean?"

"Let's take the money and run."

She was stunned. "Keith, what are you not telling me?"

There was a long pause, then Keith spoke. "We've got a problem. Bernstein recognized one of the names among our phony brokerage accounts. It was one of his former clients."

"Shit." Geneva leaned forward, putting her elbow on her desk and resting her forehead in the palm of her hand. Her eyes squeezed shut, imagining the worst. She took a deep breath. Everything could fall apart. If it did, she would never escape her miserable Washington life. "Why did you use an old account name?"

"I had to use deceased clients' information. It was the only way I could set up enough accounts in time to pull off our plan. I never dreamed the partners would remember a client from a decade ago. Who does that?"

"Is Bernstein suspicious?"

"I had to think fast. I told him it was just a coincidence the clients had the same name. Fortunately, I didn't use the account's real address. I don't think he suspects anything, but it makes me nervous. I'm not sure I want to continue. We've done great. We've made millions. Let's get out while we're ahead. I can't afford to get caught."

This was not enough. She needed more to assure she could afford a new life away from Washington and away from Harv. "Keith, we can't quit. Not now. We're about to increase our winnings exponentially. You need to think bigger."

"I don't know, Geneva. I'm nervous. Bernstein might recognize other names."

"Look. Cover your tracks. Even if you can't change the account names, can you change other information without anyone noticing?"

"I've already started."

"Good. Don't touch the money. Not yet. Let me check the lay of the land here in DC. If everything works the way I expect, you'll be able to start your full-time writing career sooner than you could have imagined. This will all be over soon."

He assured her he would do nothing until they spoke again. She hung up. Geneva had thought Keith was all in. Now he was getting cold feet just when she needed his expertise the most. She might have made a mistake pulling him in as her partner. But she really had no choice at this point. She had to figure out how to keep him onboard.

THAT EVENING, SENATOR DAVID BAYARD'S FORTUNES were no better than Serodynne's. Geneva watched on television as he lost the Republican convention vote by fifty-seven delegates. She knew enough from talking to Harv that the California delegation screwed him at the last minute. Harv had urged Patten to promise several ambassadorships and government jobs to the state's contingent in exchange for their support. Apparently Patten had taken his advice, Geneva thought.

Immediately after the final vote, she watched Bayard step to the podium in front of 2,286 screaming delegates, 2,125 alternates, and thousands of loyalists and members of the media. He asked that Ford Patten's nomination be declared unanimous by acclamation. The red, white, and blue Atlanta convention center roared with approval.

In Patten's hotel room that night, she knew Bayard would secure the nomination for vice president. Harv told her Patten's presidential elector counters had determined winning New Jersey in November was the safest path to victory, so Patten was forced to put Bayard on the ticket. He wanted Diana Lee, the senator from Florida. But with less than two months to go before the election, polls showed Florida was already leaning toward the Republican nominee. New Jersey was now the biggest battleground still up for grabs.

Geneva wondered what had happened to Beck's story. She had to believe he was still working on it, but she worried he might not publish it in time. That would mean Bayard's influence over the Pentagon contract would only grow, especially if he were vice president. She needed Beck's story to go public soon.

34

The next day, Harv was back in DC and smoking a Cuban on the penthouse patio in his lounge chair next to Geneva.

"Yes, I had an affair. Actually a couple," he said. "You're not to blame. I enjoyed the attention, dear. It doesn't change how I feel about you. You know . . . men."

Geneva was surprised how little his admission bothered her. She had known of his affairs for more than two years, long enough that she was done grieving over their relationship.

"Do you want a divorce?" She took a big gulp of her martini.

"No, dear. What I want is you—as long as you don't mind my little trysts on the side."

"If I did care, it appears it wouldn't matter."

He turned to her, brows raised, eyes opened wide.

"That's right. Harv, this comes as no surprise." She stared him down. She was probably the only human on the planet who could do that.

He looked away. "Oh . . . you have your trysts. I have mine. Fair enough?"

"Enough."

Harv fingered the stem of his glass, looking intensely at his wine as if examining it for clarity. "I have my needs."

"And I have mine."

"I still desire you, darling. In fact, I want to make love to you right now." Without looking at her, he placed his hand on her bare thigh and inched it upward. Geneva placed her hand on his and stopped him. He turned to look at her, and their eyes met. "Can we at least keep up appearances?"

"Harv, I don't wish to embarrass you," Geneva said. She knew in her heart things would never be the same between them. There was nothing left for her here.

They sat in silence for several minutes, watching the sun disappear over the Smithsonian. A car horn blared in the background. Naked, Geneva stood and walked into the condo. She mixed herself another martini. As she stepped back through the door to the patio, she studied the smoke swirling around the back of Harv's head. He held his cigar high in the air while sipping his favorite Australian red.

She shivered. It was as if their conversation had never taken place. She slowly spread her body on the lounge chair next to his. It bothered her that Harv did not notice. So this is how a marriage dies, she thought.

Her mind wandered to Beck. What was he doing? She wasn't ready to deal with him. She needed to know when—or if—his story was going to be published. It would determine her future since its publication would likely make her fabulously rich. But the murder had rattled her and made her feel unsafe about approaching him. And their last night together scared her as well.

She looked at Harv, her cheating husband, puffing away on his cigar. He'd been unfaithful for years. Then she thought of Beck, who once got too rough in bed. Where was her perspective? It wasn't the first time a man had gotten carried away in bed with her, but this was so out of character for Beck. That was the difference. He was loving, gentle, and funny—yet he was absolutely ruthless when it came to his job. Exactly, she thought. There was a line there, and she had crossed it and gotten a glimpse of both sides of this man.

Suddenly, she understood. It was so obvious. She was blinded by the loving attention Beck showed her. Of course that was it. Harv had ignored her for too long, and she was starved for affection.

She took another sip from her glass and felt better.

Geneva told Harv about Bayard and how Beck had tied the massive payments to the senator directly to Lamurr Technologies through its Venezuelan subsidiary.

"Do you think it could disrupt the campaign?" she asked.

"It could. But Mr. Rikki needs to be very careful. Tell him to double-check his facts. Bayard is a real bastard. He will stop at nothing. He will take Rikki down with him if he has to. It's personal with that guy. Bayard does not have a thick skin."

"Harv, he's a pro. Mr. Rikki's done this before. I think he will do all right." Mr. Rikki. That sounded awkward, she thought. But calling him "Beck" in front of Harv seemed too personal.

"Just the same, I'll ask around with some of my friends at the FBI and Justice and see what I can find out," Harv said. "It would be such a shame for Patten to lose the election because of Bayard. Patten is a good man."

"Who sold his soul to Bayard for a chance at the brass ring."

"Strange bedfellows, dear."

"Safe sex, dear." She took a gulp of her martini and smiled. She now understood exactly where she was going to go with all of this.

35

Amtrak's Acela Express arrived in New York's Penn Station exactly on time, one of the few Amtrak trains to ever do so. Geneva took the escalator to the street level and stood in the long taxi line for a ride to her favorite hotel.

The Algonquin was a boutique hotel on Forty-Fourth Street, famous for the Algonquin Round Table, a meeting place for writers during the 1920s and the Depression. Writer Dorothy Parker, whom Geneva admired, was one of the group's most famous wits and for a while a resident of the hotel. Rooms at the Algonquin were small, so when Geneva came to town, she always reserved Dorothy's larger suite.

About a half hour after she unpacked, Keith knocked on the door with his laptop in tow.

"Everything okay?" she asked.

"I think I've got all of the accounts disguised," he said. "So far, so good. This worked like a charm. I can move the portfolio assets very soon."

"Not yet. Let it ride."

"I still think that's a dangerous idea. We could lose it all even if we aren't discovered."

"We can make ten times what we've already made."

He sat at the small writing desk, and she leaned over his shoulder looking at the numbers on his laptop. They had done well. She could begin to see her future, but she wasn't there yet. She wanted to make enough money so she would never be beholden to a man like Harv. She never again wanted to suck up to anyone in power whose relationship was based solely on how big a political campaign check she could write.

"I don't know. Maybe we should cut and run," Keith said. "We have been successful enough. We don't need any more."

"Ten times this amount," she said. "Think about it. Now that will give you freedom to live the life you crave." Geneva knew he was right in one sense. This whole thing could still backfire. After all, they were dealing with risky stock options. They could be left with nothing—or worse, millions in debt. That would mean slaving in the Washington trenches for another twenty-five years—the rest of her life—squeezing out a buck to pay off a huge debt and make ends meet while living with a man she no longer admired or loved.

Fortunately, she was confident in the bets she had placed on Beck's cunning as a reporter. She needed only one winning number, she told herself, and she believed the odds were in her favor.

Keith showed her how he divided their cash into dozens of phony accounts to hide it from his firm's partners. They painstakingly went through each one to assure it was well disguised. The results were always the same—astonishing financial returns owned by plain vanilla investors, which was exactly what they intended.

"Enough," Geneva said. "Let's grab a bite to eat."

OVER MARYLAND CRAB CAKES in a nearby seafood restaurant, Keith again talked of pulling out.

"I've got a couple of million dollars to call my own. That's all I need."

"You need more. Unless you truly want to live in a shack on an island, a few mil at your age won't last forever. You'd better be a damned successful writer."

He didn't say anything, but his pleading expression reflected his reluctance to risk his windfall. Would he pull out of the deal? The money was good, but it wouldn't last her a lifetime. She couldn't take a chance Keith would get cold feet and defect. Not at this stage. This would not work without him. She felt desperate, but what could she do?

"Do you trust me?" she asked.

"It's not that, Geneva. It's that I never dreamed I'd be in this position so soon. I just wonder if it's worth the risk. I can't afford to lose this."

It was worse than she thought. She needed to do something to keep Keith in the fold. She reminded herself he was a nice guy and rather handsome. And she had repeatedly tracked his gaze as his eyes surreptitiously wandered down her chest during many of their conversations. She had what he wanted, and it was more than money. That may not have been part of the original deal, but this was business, she told herself.

When they finished their meal, she made an excuse about needing to go back to the hotel to look over more figures. She needed his full cooperation, and she decided she would do what she needed to secure it.

But as they walked down the hall to her hotel suite, she had second thoughts. She thought about Beck. She had to admit she liked Keith and this was necessary. She was too close to winning it all.

As soon as Keith closed the door to her suite behind him, Geneva took off her jacket, turned to him, and kissed him squarely on the lips. He stood, motionless, and then he held her tightly and kissed her.

She slid her fingers through his hair and caressed the back of his neck. His hands wandered to her chest. She let him fondle her, and she rubbed his crotch. He unbuttoned her blouse and quickly reached around, unhooking her bra. He bent over to kiss her breasts. Her nerves tingled, and she closed her eyes, enjoying the sensation. She then looked down on his full head of wavy hair as he feverishly devoured her. She moaned and began to call his name, but stopped herself. She realized she was about to call out Beck's name instead.

She lifted Keith's chin and kissed him passionately. But then she pushed back, taking his hands in hers.

"There will be time for this later," she said. She again kissed him, this time lightly on the lips. "We need to make some decisions first. We still have the rest of our plan to execute."

"And what is our plan?"

"Hmm. Well, it certainly has something to do with business," she said, gazing into his big brown eyes. "But I'd say we've entered a whole new realm of possibilities."

"I'd love to enter that realm," he said.

She felt his hardening body next to hers as she pulled him closer. "Right now you and I have a lot of work to do." Their mouths met in a long, aggressive kiss. Then she pushed him back and pulled her blouse closed. She sat down on the desk chair and turned to Keith, now sitting on the bed.

"We need to talk about our financial future," she said. "The stock options we bought to bet on the decline in Serodynne shares have made us rich. Now I want to do just the opposite with our money. I want us to bet on Lamurr's stock tanking."

"What?" Keith wrinkled his brow in confusion.

"We bet it's stock drops through the floor. If we take everything we have made so far and bet it against Lamurr, we will make more money than god. We will never have another financial worry again in our lives. You in?"

"But how do you know this?"

"I can't say. I just do. You've got to trust me."

"I don't know. Why risk it all when we have a sure thing already?"

"I've been right so far." She looked into his eyes. At least for once, she could tell he agreed.

She had not planned on seducing Keith, but she was desperate. She still needed the help of two men—one to make her financial play, and the other to pull the trigger. She felt comfortable Beck would publish his story, which would set events in motion. There was no doubt about his motivation. She was not so confident about Keith. She needed to reel him in carefully to keep him on the line. If that involved some foreplay, then so be it, she told herself. She smiled at the thought that she'd actually kept her clothes on to seduce a man.

36

Beck sat in a large glass-walled conference room off the newsroom with two newspaper lawyers and his editor Nancy Moore. This was the part of writing a big story he hated. They were going over the final draft—line by line—looking for any potential legal problems. He spent half of last night pacing his living room talking to Red and polishing this version. He was exhausted, and he didn't want to justify himself to a couple of legal nitpickers.

Beck looked at the big gun, Charles Curtiss, a rotund former law professor with a bald white fringe and walrus mustache. He was like all lawyers, Beck felt. He arrogantly hurled his legal knowledge in public to command attention with civilians who weren't members of the jurisprudence brotherhood. Beck conceded Curtiss knew his First Amendment stuff, but in his mind that still didn't warrant the fat man's smugness.

Curtiss had been the newspaper's attorney for thirty-five years. He sauntered among the elite in the command structure at the *Post-Examiner* and shared his box seats at Redskins games with Publisher Katherine Cunningham, Baker, and other members of the newspaper's executive team. There was a definite pecking order at the paper, and despite the fame and awards he had brought the *Post-Examiner*, Beck realized he would never upgrade to platinum status. He was just unwilling to play the suck-up game. He thought his work would speak for itself. But the *Post-Examiner*, he realized, was no different than the rest of Washington.

Beck glanced over at Roby Hedelt, who sat next to Curtiss. Usually, story read-throughs were left to Roby, an openly gay, forty-something attorney employed full time by the paper. She not only handled any day-to-day legal issues, but some libel work as well. Beck liked her, and often felt disappointed that such a taunt, striking woman was gay. God, if she weren't, he'd have asked her out years ago. But with his win-loss record in relationships, maybe it was just as well.

He would have preferred to deal with Roby, but the political impact of his story seemed so high Cunningham had asked Curtiss to sit in on the story meeting, and Roby deferred to him.

"You did good work," Curtiss said. "No malice that I can see. There's not a chance in hell they can sue us for libel and win. But I'm disturbed none of your targets would comment. All I see is 'no comment' throughout this piece. Not Lamurr, not Senator Bayard, not even Jackson Oliver. You couldn't get any of them on the record?"

"Would you comment to a reporter when you were about to be hung out to dry?" Beck answered.

"Now we'll have none of that kind of talk outside of this room. Not even to your colleagues in the office here. Understood?"

"I get it," Beck said, angry at himself for being too candid in front of the newspaper's judicial nanny.

"I can vouch for Beck," Nancy said. "He's played the game before. A little frankness behind closed doors among friends to assure we all know where we stand is not inappropriate in my book."

Curtiss looked like he was about to say something to Nancy and then thought better of it. "Then I'm satisfied," he said. "I think with these minimal changes you should be good to go." He handed Beck a paper copy of the story that Roby had clearly marked up. He noticed Curtiss made a couple of unnecessary edits to justify his legal retainer. Roby was kind in her edits. There were few red marks on the page.

Nancy grabbed the story out of Beck's hands, donned her reading glasses, and gave the edits a quick once-over. "Beck, whatcha think?"

"I can live with this." He felt relieved. The damage was minimal.

Beck wondered why he went through this charade every time he had a big story. Anyone suing the paper for libel had to prove the newspaper knew it was publishing erroneous information and recklessly went along with it anyway with the intent of harming the person who was the target of the story. So why did he need to sit here for all of this? He'd been threatened dozens of times with lawsuits, and no one had ever actually wasted money hiring expensive lawyers to take him and the *Post-Examiner* to court.

What a waste of his time, he thought.

THE CONFERENCE ROOM DOOR swung open, and Cunningham entered. A few years younger than Beck, with long, flowing blonde hair, she wore four-inch spike heels and a dress short enough to show off her well-toned elliptical-machined legs. She was damned attractive. Beck would give her that. But the recent divorcee tried too hard to look younger and sexy.

"We've got a situation," she said. "The Patten-Bayard campaign wants to meet with us next week to discuss the story. They can't do it until then, and they say their input is vital before we publish."

"It's an obvious delaying tactic," Nancy said. "We've got them by the gonads, and they know it."

"They want to kill it," Beck said. Was Cunningham really falling for this?

"Legally, it's sound." Curtiss laid his pen on the pages of his copy of the manuscript and leaned back in his chair.

"I can't take the chance," Cunningham said. "They say we are missing important elements of the story that will make us rethink the entire piece. We've been accused on too many occasions of liberal bias. If we publish a story like this against a conservative Republican weeks out from the election, I will have more scars on my backside than I'm willing to nurse." After a pause, she added, "We must get this right."

Get it right? More like kill it, thought Beck. I put my heart and soul into this for weeks and she's going to believe those slimy bastards? Shit. This wouldn't have happened if Bob Riggleman were still in charge.

Riggleman's niece had recently been appointed publisher. She was now responsible for the family business. Beck knew Cunningham's focus was on the bottom line. With the newspaper's sinking stock price, he could see how she might want to kill the story to save the paper from a potentially expensive lawsuit. What do you expect when you replace an old newspaperman with a Harvard MBA with no journalism experience?

"Next Wednesday at two. I'd like you all to meet in my office," Cunningham said. "Campaign officials will be there. Any questions?"

Even Curtiss was quiet this time. The pecking order was fully exposed. Cunningham was in charge.

She closed the door behind her.

"I can't believe it!" screamed Nancy. "We've got maybe a two-week window to publish before we are too close to the election."

Beck said nothing. He stood, dropped his copy of the story on the table next to Curtiss, and walked out, too angry to speak. He needed a drink and to calm down. All of his work—everything he and Nancy had spent what seemed like forever putting together for this story—was now in jeopardy. He shook his head. Now he was fighting a war on two fronts, yet he wasn't endangered by the opposition. He was being threatened by friendly fire.

37

"So what the hell happened?" demanded Serodynne CEO Brian Dymon. "We're already looking at a major implosion in the value of our stock. We're looking at large-scale layoffs in eighteen months. We will need to begin downsizing if nothing can be done. And by the way, Ms. Kemper, nice of you to join us."

Geneva had just failed miserably to slip unnoticed into the Serodynne boardroom a mere five minutes late. Her flight from New York to Minneapolis had been an hour late arriving, and she had raced to corporate headquarters, bribing her cabbie with a fifty to break the speed limit and risk a ticket for reckless driving.

She'd kicked Keith out of her hotel room around five the night before saying she had to prepare for Serodynne's board meeting. Then she'd overslept this morning and was the last to jump on the plane before the crew closed the door, just so the plane could roll back from the gate and sit on the tarmac for the next hour. Stuffed like sardines in coach and bouncing for nearly three hours through turbulence, she had wondered if her day could get any worse. Now she had her answer.

Legal counsel Sue Nijelski caught Geneva's eye. She gestured discreetly, silently asking if she needed to step in. Geneva slowly shook her head. She would handle this. She took a deep breath and began. "Yes. We have a problem, but I don't think this is over. I wouldn't start calling the funeral director just yet."

"Why's that, Geneva?" barked Dymon.

"I believe Lamurr's contract application is fraudulent. If we can prove it, we will win the contract back. We are the Pentagon's only alternative."

"Fraud? You've got to be kidding." Dymon stood and paced the floor, impeccably intimidating in his pinstripe Brooks Brothers suit. The sun streamed through the conference room windows, deceptively beautiful as it reflected off his shaved head and diamond tie stickpin.

"It recently came to my attention that the FBI is investigating Lamurr. They have traced potential bribes through Venezuela to a US senator involved in the contract." She knew she was walking a minefield. How much could she tell them? She needed to tell the board enough, but not too much that it might hint at her own involvement. "I don't have any names yet, but I'm working on it."

"Well, there can't be too many senators in that position."

"I have my suspicions about his identity, but I'd rather not say until I'm sure. The last thing we want to do is start rumors that may come back to bite us in the ass."

Geneva glanced at Nijelski, who remained silent and looked only at Dymon. Both of her hands were on the conference table, one wrapped around a pen, the other lay palm down with her index finger pointing directly at Geneva. Clearly, their earlier conversation about Lamurr and Senator Bayard remained between the two of them. Geneva felt relieved and more confident having an ally in the room.

"Well, we can't just sit here and do nothing." Dymon sat down and did just that. He stuck his hands in his suit coat pockets and leaned back, emphasizing a growing belly beneath his striped shirt and silk suspenders.

Geneva knew Dymon was one of those CEOs who sucked all of the air out of the room, which made her even more desperate to steer the conversation where she needed. It hadn't occurred to her until just now that he might do something stupid to affect the company stock and screw up her plan. She felt goose bumps on her arms. Fortunately, she was wearing a suit and no one would notice.

She paused briefly and began again. "It's my understanding the news media are onto this. If they publish or broadcast a story in the near future, we will have to do nothing." She wondered how much progress Beck had made on his story.

"And who is that?"

"Again, this is so sensitive, we need to wait. We are spectators. If everything works out the way I hope, we will win the contract by just waiting and watching."

Dymon squirmed in his seat. "I don't feel comfortable leaving this to chance."

"It's not chance. This is how Washington works. Things are not always as they seem. Sometimes there's order behind the political chaos, and that chaos is nothing more than a smoke screen."

"It's all smoke and mirrors as far as I'm concerned."

"I don't disagree. From Minneapolis, I can understand your point of view. Trust me. I am confident we can win the contract. I will stake my job on it." She felt confident in her bravado. She knew if they didn't get the contract, she would be out of a job anyway. Dymon would see to that. She knew he needed to blame someone.

"I'll take you up on that."

She saw an opening and felt she had nothing to lose. "And if I'm right, I want a one hundred percent bonus on my salary."

"Done," said Dymon. "Geneva, you get that contract for us, and you've earned it."

Perfect, she thought. He got sucked right into that one, and in front of the entire board so there was no backing out. Maybe her skills weren't as rusty as she was beginning to believe. So now she would either be out of a job soon or have an extra year's pay lining her bank account.

She looked over at Nijelski. Both of her hands were off the table. Geneva detected a slight smile on her face.

The conversation went on for another forty-five minutes, but Geneva would not budge on revealing names. The CFO went over Serodynne's numbers, and the officers discussed alternative plans with the board should they still fail to win the Pentagon contract. It was all the usual stuff boards did when faced with a potential crisis, Geneva thought.

She was bored and worried she wouldn't make her flight home in two hours. Then her mind wondered back to Beck. What was he doing? Was he deep in conversation with Red? It was time she found out what was going on with his story. And she had to admit to herself the one thing she had been denying lately: she missed him.

38

As Beck drove home, his cell rang. The readout said it was Geneva. He felt a surge of excitement as he turned onto Fourteenth Street and looked to see if any cops were watching. Cell phone use while driving was worth a hefty ticket in the District of Columbia.

"I'd like to talk," she said.

"Okay."

"Your place?"

"You comfortable there?"

"Of course."

She sounded like the old Geneva. His heart soared. He felt like it had been forever since he had seen her.

He hung up and waited for the light at F Street between the National Press Club building and the Willard Hotel. A tall man in a Panama hat glided through the crosswalk—unusual dress for this time of year, Beck thought. The man seemed to turn and look at him far longer than normal before continuing across the street. He had big, sad eyes and his hat, at least, reminded Beck of the man in the white hat in Grand Cayman. Before reaching the sidewalk, the stranger again looked his way. Funny, thought Beck, he's staring right at me as if he knows me. After his experience in Grand Cayman, he admitted to himself he was a bit on edge, but he was sure the man was staring at him.

A car horn blast interrupted his concentration. The light had turned green. Beck pressed the accelerator and headed for the Fourteenth Street Bridge.

BECK BUZZED GENEVA UP TO HIS CONDO and waited at the elevator in the hall. When the doors opened, she reached for him and they hugged. She said nothing but sobbed quietly, her head pressed against his chest. Beck held her tightly. He had been so focused on completing his story he nearly forgot how good it felt to hold her in his arms.

"Come," he said, holding her hand and leading her into his condo. They sat in his living room. Funny, thought Beck. They had never sat here and had a conversation. Usually, they would have flung their things on the furniture and ripped each other's clothes off by now. Today, they hadn't even kissed.

"How are you?" she asked. Beck noticed her eyes glistening as she wiped a tear from her cheek.

"I've been better."

"Me too. I'm sorry for not calling. I didn't realize how all of this would hit me. I fell apart. I blamed you, but I realize you're not to blame."

"It bothers me too. I've never been part of anything like this."

"Beck, I want us to work. I do. I've had some time to think. I've got my share of baggage, and I'm still sorting through it."

"Any progress?"

"A little. Try again? Us?"

Beck looked into her sad, longing eyes. His body ached for her. Yet he wasn't sure if he could totally trust her. Was she really that oblivious to what he did for a living that she hadn't considered the peril she put him in by helping him investigate her competitor? He found it hard to believe. And yet he looked at her and felt himself melt under her spell. He should give her the benefit of the doubt.

"Are you kidding? I'd love to try again." There. He said it. He lifted her chin and kissed her. He wanted her so much; he was ignoring the voice inside him.

She gripped his forearms and pulled him close. The kiss intensified. Beck's hands slipped down her back, and he tugged at her blouse. He then took her hand and led her to the bedroom. Finally, familiar territory for both of them.

AN HOUR LATER, THEY WERE on his balcony with cigars and marti-
nis. Geneva asked about his story.

"It's hung up with the lawyers and the publisher."

"What's wrong?"

"Bayard is stalling, and my publisher is skittish. We're supposed to
meet tomorrow. So I'm hoping maybe we will publish on Sunday."

"Why Sunday?"

"More people see it. The Sunday morning political talking heads
pick it up, which puts it in every newspaper in America on Monday
morning. It's all about marketing."

"I guess there's a lot I need to learn about the newspaper business."

He looked at her and wondered why now she was suddenly so curious about his work. But her questions exposed her ignorance of how his
profession worked, and that relieved some of his suspicions. "There's a
lot I need to learn about lobbying. How is your company doing? I saw in
the paper that the stock took a beating."

"I just got back from a Minneapolis meeting with the board to discuss
the situation. They are secretly making plans to downsize if necessary."

"If necessary?"

"Well, if your story runs, it might help reverse the Pentagon's decision. That's our only hope."

"Oh, I see." Beck's radar kicked in. Was Geneva here to see him or
to check on the status of his story? He looked for some sign of deception
in her body language, but all he could see was her flawless nakedness
waving a cigar in one hand and holding a half-filled martini glass in
the other. If she was deceiving him, he sure couldn't tell. And if she
were, would she ever admit that publishing his story would help her—or
at least her company? No, on second thought, she was innocent of his
unspoken accusation.

"If it ever gets out about you helping with the story, I'm toast for
sure," he said.

"If we don't get that Pentagon contract, I'm pretty sure I'm toast
too." She paused and set down her drink, turning to him. "Beck, I really

screwed up. I don't know what I can do to make it up to you. I want you. I don't want to do anything to jeopardize you or your story. I know how much this story means to you."

Yeah, and you too, he thought. You too.

39

The next day, Beck's desk phone brought more bad news. "The meeting's been delayed until Monday," Nancy said.

He eyed her across the vast cluttered newsroom.

She returned his disappointed glare. "Bayard's lawyers said they can't meet until then."

"Jeez." He was disgusted with his publisher. She was letting them manipulate her.

"But one good thing. Cunningham told them if they didn't show, the story would run as is. No more delays."

"Good. She's found her testicles."

"Give her a break. I was pissed too, but she's got to think of the entire company. All you and I have to worry about is the entire nation."

Beck laughed. "I like the way you think." Nancy always had a way of making him smile even when his world was going to shit. He loved that about her. But Beck also knew time was running out. Unsaid between the two of them was the impending election, just weeks away. Their publishing window was quickly closing.

Was there anything he hadn't considered? He thought about the Bayard campaign. There couldn't possibly be any truth in their delay, could there? He rolled every aspect of his story around in his mind looking for holes. There just weren't any he could see. He had his facts down solid. God, he hoped he hadn't missed something.

He felt anxious, so he decided to stretch his legs and get a sandwich at the deli down the street. As he crossed the intersection on Fifteenth

Street, a tall man in a black raincoat strode toward him. Their shoulders slightly bumped in the center of the crosswalk. Beck was in no mood to be friendly. "Can't people watch where they're—"

"Sorry, Mr. Kemper," said a voice from behind. "Crosswalks can be dangerous. We must be careful. Be safe."

Beck turned back. The stranger's graying hair flowed from under his black fedora and over his collar. A goatee and designer sunglasses covered his face. Beck could make out only a smile filled with a set of expensive, perfectly capped white teeth.

"Pardon me." The man tipped his hat, turned, and walked away.

A cold chill ran down his neck. Beck hurried to the curb, then looked back. The man was gone. What had he called him? Mr. Kemper? And he said, "Be safe." Somehow, this guy was linked to the man in Grand Cayman. Now he was sure he had been followed on the island and was definitely being followed here in DC. It had to be the guy he saw crossing Fourteenth Street the other day.

"RED, WHO WAS THAT GUY?" Beck asked as he paced his living room floor that evening. "This has to have something to do with my story. The man called me Mr. Kemper. I'm sure he bumped into me on purpose."

Beck paced more vigorously. Think, he told himself, but answers evaded him. He shoved his coffee table up against his couch to give himself more room. Thinking aloud sometimes took up a lot of space.

"Red, why? Who? What for?" He sped up, looking at Red, but got no answers. He stared at the ceiling, never stopping, walking faster.

Then he slammed his shin into Red. The pain seared through his bone. Beck bent over and rubbed the leg of his jeans.

"Damn it."

He felt light-headed and eased himself into his favorite leather chair. He did not move, grimacing, rubbing his shin vigorously until the throbbing subsided. When the pain was finally gone, he stood and nearly banged his head against the lampshade of his favorite floor lamp. It was out of place. No, that wasn't right. He'd knocked Red out of position.

He turned and looked at his chair. He grabbed her supple leather arms and realigned her so her two front feet fit back into their impressions on his oriental rug. Beck was no neat freak, but he had fidgeted for five minutes when he first bought Red trying to make her fit in the corner, the only space left in his living room. At first he feared he had measured incorrectly. But after a few adjustments, he had realized she was just a tight fit next to his lamp and magazine table.

He began to pace again, this time with a slight limp.

"Damn, that hurt."

No matter how hard he tried, talking aloud didn't help. He could not focus on the meaning of the stranger who had bumped into him—nearly accosted him—on the crosswalk. Why would anyone be following him at this point? Was it a warning? A threat? Beck had no answers, and he hated that.

He understood the what. Someone was keeping tabs on his progress. But the who and the how puzzled him. And why so blatant? Whoever it was wanted him to know he was being watched. Maybe they were trying to intimidate him. Or something worse. Maybe they were threatening him. He thought about it. That threat could involve Geneva as well.

He needed to take some precautions. This wasn't just a story he was working on with Red anymore. He'd entered dangerous territory with an unknown enemy who could attack without warning from anywhere at any time, and he would never see it coming. He felt numb with fear. He realized no matter what he did to defend himself, he would always be vulnerable.

40

Beck, his editors, and the company lawyers finally congregated in Cunningham's top floor office. It was Beck's first visit since Riggleman's retirement. He couldn't help but think about the last time he'd been there.

Riggleman had invited him up to talk about his Nordact arms story a few years ago. He had gotten some angry calls from a congressman whose district might be harmed by Beck's revelations, and Riggleman wanted to pick Beck's brain about some facts in his story.

It had been an innocuous meeting, but Beck was impressed with Riggleman's interest in even the most minor details. He also reassured him the newspaper fully backed his effort. God, it had been nice to have a boss like that.

Since then, the office had been repainted with warmer, feminine beiges and pale grays. A huge vase of tall fresh-cut flowers stood on a corner table, and the obligatory pictures of Cunningham and her three small children hung on the wall. In a corner, he spotted a photograph of her uncle and late grandmother, who had steered the paper to fame and fortune a generation earlier.

A generation ago, thought Beck. Yep. Times had certainly changed since he was a rookie reporter.

A photo of Cunningham laughing with President Croom hung prominently behind her large, modern desk. The word in the newsroom was a *Post-Examiner* staff photographer had cracked an off-color joke about a Republican senator just as he was aiming to shoot and captured their reaction for posterity. Of course Cunningham would not repeat the joke, but it had made the rounds of the building in record time. While he didn't have the same confidence in Cunningham as he did in Riggleman, Beck appreciated her salty sense of humor. Most reporters carried it in their genes.

The newspaper crew filed into the adjoining conference room one by one. The Patten-Bayard campaign lawyers greeted everyone like long-lost relatives, but the friendly demeanor did not last. The newspaper tribe lined up on one side of the large conference table, and four attorneys for the Patten-Bayard campaign sat on the other.

It reminded Beck of the divorce scene in any number of movies: the anxious couple sits across from each other, arguing over who gets custody of the family dog. He wondered what assets would be split up today or left on the table. This whole scene disgusted him.

Cunningham was flanked by the *Post-Examiner*'s two attorneys on one side and Nancy on the other. Beck sat next to Nancy. At the end of the table, Baker pulled a skinny brown cigarette from his breast pocket and tapped it on the table. He did not light up. Smoking was prohibited in the building. He snared it between his lips anyway and leaned back with his hands behind his head. He surveyed the room.

Gerry Vandevelde introduced himself as the lead attorney for the campaign and introduced the other attorneys. Probably here as window dressing. A show of force, Beck thought.

Before the meeting, Baker had instructed Beck and Nancy to stay silent. Speak only in response to a question from Curtiss, Baker told them, and don't be tempted to answer questions from the other side.

The campaign attorneys' first attempt was to kill the story based on patriotism. Really? Laughable, thought Beck.

The liberal media attack on a conservative argument followed. The newspaper attorneys tossed the objections aside with ease. Obviously, these campaign hacks had a list of objections to present in hopes one would get a hearing at the table. They needed to get serious.

Katherine Cunningham remained silent, watching and listening. When the campaign's attorneys tried to address her directly, Curtiss interrupted and cut them off. "All of your questions will be directed to me," he said.

The back and forth continued for nearly an hour. From Beck's perspective, it accomplished nothing discernable, except to allow the attorneys to claim their retainer. He thought that was even questionable, given this inept display. His initial suspicions seemed correct. There appeared to be no purpose for the meeting other than to delay publication. He was now beyond disgusted.

Finally, the sparring appeared to end.

"There is one more issue we wish to address," Vandevelde said. "Mr. Kelly, would you hand out the materials and explain what you found? We had hoped this meeting wouldn't go this far, but since you refuse to listen to reason, we believe this will convince you to hold your story until you get it right."

Beck studied Kevin Kelly, who had been introduced to them earlier. He was much younger than the other attorneys—probably in his late twenties. He flipped copies of three stapled pages to everyone at the table.

"As you can see," Kelly said, "you incorrectly identified the XAX Company as a subsidiary of Lamurr. It is actually a subsidiary of Capo Mining, a coal operator in Venezuela. The names are the same, but they are two different companies with two different parent companies. Therefore, there is no tie between Lamurr and Senator Bayard."

The room was silent as everyone on the newspaper side looked over the documents, written entirely in Spanish. Beck sat stunned. Did Woodard's stringer screw up? He was too good for that, Beck assured himself. He'd seen the paperwork.

It was difficult to tell if the documents were legitimate. They looked similar to the faxes Bobby Woodard had sent from the stringer in Caracas, but extra pages made it appear Capo Mining was the company's owner and not Lamurr Technologies. Could there be two XAX companies owned by two different parent companies? What were the odds?

Spanish or not, Beck noticed something. He stood, walked behind the others, then leaned near Curtiss and whispered.

Curtiss looked at page two of the documents and nodded, picking up on his tip immediately. He turned and faced the lawyers across the table again. "Do you really expect us to believe two subsidiaries of two totally unrelated companies, both of which have the exact same name, have the same five corporate officers? This is an obvious forgery," Curtiss said.

Even though he couldn't read three words of Spanish, Beck had remembered the officers' names because he had spelled them out for Nancy back when he was in Grand Cayman. Thank god he couldn't pronounce them. He might not have remembered how they were spelled. Maybe it was a good thing he never learned Spanish. Score one for the good guys, he thought.

"Mr. Kelly," Vandevelde said, "you found these documents yourself, is that not true?"

"Yes," the young lawyer said.

"And you went to Caracas, directly to Capo Mining and to XAX and to the local government offices, to obtain these documents?"

"That's correct."

"Are these forgeries?"

"If they are, then they were forged by the companies themselves in an attempt to deceive me."

"So it's our position, Mr. Curtiss, that these documents are not fraudulent, but certified copies of legitimate corporate filings from Venezuela that prove there is no tie whatsoever between Lamurr Technologies and Senator Bayard," Vandevelde said. "If you should print any story saying such, you will be knowingly and maliciously printing an egregious error of fact, and we will use whatever legal means at our disposal to expose the *Post-Examiner*'s irresponsible behavior. Are we clear on that?"

"Very clear," Curtiss growled in a low, deep voice.

Beck couldn't believe it. Bayard's sleazy lawyer might get away with it. How could Curtiss let this happen? He was supposed to be the newspaper's First Amendment tiger. Beck cringed. He wondered if those documents scattered across the conference room table, which no one could really decipher, were his story's epitaph.

The meeting broke up immediately, no handshakes this time. Cunningham spoke as soon as Curtiss closed the door behind the campaign attorneys.

"So, if there is even the slightest hint of truth to these documents, they have a good chance of winning a libel case against us," Cunningham said, looking directly at her lawyers. "No matter how dubious these documents might be we can't afford a lawsuit like this, especially if we have been warned ahead of time. However small the possibility is, they could nail us."

Oh great. Here it comes. The end is near, thought Beck.

Nancy burst forward. "But if we take the time to check these out, it could take us days, maybe a week or more," she said. "Either way, unless we can work extremely fast, it appears they will get what they want—no story before the election."

Here we go again, thought Beck. Cunningham is wimping out.

"Financially, if we lose, it would be a tough hit," Cunningham said. "But if we are wrong on a story of this size, we could take a much bigger hit to our reputation." She paused and looked at her fingers splayed on the table. A large ruby ring sparkled on her right hand. Beck looked around the table. They all sat in silence, their eyes on Cunningham, waiting for her to speak.

"Pat," Katherine Cunningham practically screamed for Patricia Wade, her secretary in the adjacent room. "Have the foreign desk find Bobby Woodard. I want him on a conference call in twenty minutes. Nancy, grab the copies of the documents the stringer found in Caracas. Charles, you and Roby have fifteen minutes to examine those documents and compare them to the ones Nancy has. Grab Garcia in the newsroom. He is fluent in Spanish. Beck, make a half-dozen hard copies of your draft. I want everyone at this table in twenty minutes."

Whoa, thought Beck. Where did that come from? Was he wrong about her? He hurried off to make copies.

TWENTY MINUTES LATER, Bobby Woodard was on a satellite phone from a small village high in the mountains of Peru. The reception was scratchy. Beck leaned forward and listened intensely to the speakerphone in the middle of the conference table.

"Bobby," Katherine said, "I need you to get to Caracas by tomorrow."

He explained it was a day's ride down the mountain.

"Then get there in two days . . . Pat, talk to the travel office and get him the first flight to Venezuela. Bobby, Nancy will e-mail you scans of the documents that your stringer found along with the documents the lawyers dropped in our laps today. Get all you can find on their origin."

Bobby said he'd try, but his remote location made travel problematic.

"Bobby, Beck here. How credible is your stringer? Could there be any truth to what Bayard's lawyers are tossing at us?"

There was silence over the phone. Finally Woodard talked. "I think he's a good stringer, but he's a stringer. He could have made a mistake."

Beck held his head in his hands. He hated uncertainty.

Garcia interpreted the documents for the lawyers. He found no clues to help their cause. Again, more uncertainty. Curtiss and Roby checked the wording of several paragraphs in the story to see if any verbiage could be changed to write around the issue. There was no way. Bobby needed to find more evidence two thousand miles away.

"Let me go down there," Beck said, turning to Nancy.

"There's no time," she said, slowly shaking her head. "We've got to rely on our people there. But stay in touch with Bobby's progress so we can move as quickly as possible."

Beck felt uneasy. He was losing control of his story.

He left with Nancy and waited for the elevator to the newsroom. "Wow. I've never seen Cunningham like that before."

"You just need to give her a chance," Nancy said as the doors opened. "I know these aren't the old days, but even in this new style of journalism, she can be pretty impressive at times."

"Maybe I'm wrong about her. But I'm still not happy."

"What do you mean?"

"The fate of my story. It's in the hands of a freelance newspaper stringer—a writer who couldn't get a full-time job here."

"Don't be so disdainful of the underclass. Remember, you were there once."

If she only knew how close he still was, thought Beck. They stepped into the elevator.

"We're racing to make a deadline," she said. "We have no choice in the matter."

Beck looked at Nancy as the doors closed behind them, leaving them alone. He knew she was right. Damn it. She usually was. All he could do was stay on top of this. He had no choice.

41

Beck talked to Woodard the next day while he was stranded, awaiting his flight after missing yesterday's plane to Venezuela by more than two hours. Beck could feel the clock ticking.

They set up a time to talk each evening. Woodard told Beck his stringer was working overtime trying to trace the second set of documents. He searched all of the government offices and found nothing. Woodard worked the phone too, calling the different companies to figure out what was going on. It was a slow slog. With three weeks left in the presidential campaign, Woodard still had no answers.

He told Beck all of the corporate officers whose names appeared on the subsidiary corporate documents all turned up missing. He also ran into a brick wall trying to interview XAX officials. It appeared everyone had been ordered not to talk with them, Woodard said.

After four days, Bobby caught a break. He found a disgruntled former XAX midlevel manager at home on a Thursday evening who agreed to talk, but not for attribution.

"I'll take anything," Beck said. Beck wondered if Woodward caught the desperation in his voice. They all knew the importance of the story not only to their careers, but to the newspaper's reputation.

Woodard told Beck his source handled many of the company's investments and some of its financial affairs, and was familiar with the payments to Sunrise Meridian. He confirmed Lamurr owned XAX. Sunrise Meridian was a shell company XAX used for various real estate investments, not just in Grand Cayman, but throughout the Caribbean. It invested in various currencies, while scouting for deals on different islands. He even showed him some paperwork, proving his point, but refused to let Woodard have it. He did, however, allow Bobby to take photographs of the documents with his cell phone. At last Beck had his paper trail.

Then Woodard dropped the A-bomb. He asked the XAX worker if he knew Jackson Oliver. "And guess what," Woodard said. Suddenly there was static on his phone, and the call went dead. Beck couldn't believe it. Woodard was about to tell him Oliver was somehow connected. But how?

Beck quickly punched the number in his cell phone. Nothing. Beck tried again. Shit. What had happened to Woodard's phone? He dialed again. And again. He stopped. Waiting. Woodard would surely call back. Beck grew impatient and dialed again. Finally, it was ringing.

"Beck?"

"Yeah."

"Something wrong with your phone?"

"Tell me about Oliver."

"My source told me they tried to do several deals with him in Costa Rica. It was Oliver who introduced Sunrise Meridian to Bayard."

Woodard was on the next flight to Costa Rica, and Beck was making final edits to his story.

LATE ON SATURDAY AFTERNOON, three weeks before the election, his story was ready. Beck's byline sat at the top, and Bobby Woodard's name was tagged at the end of the story as a contributor. Nancy did a final review. The copydesk did its job.

"You checked in one last time with Bayard and Lamurr?" Nancy asked.

"Just got off the phone. Told them what we had, and they still refuse to comment."

"Good enough for me. Baker wants us in his office."

Charles Curtiss sat with Baker in the managing editor's office with the final document.

"You've got a solid story, but I'm axing the Oliver connection. We need more proof," Curtiss said.

Shit, thought Beck. This was why he hated lawyers. But he knew it was the weakest part of the story. Woodard had not been able to find anything so far in Costa Rico with Oliver's name on it.

There was a long moment of silence as everyone looked at Beck for his reaction.

"I can live with that," he said. At this point, Beck told himself, it wasn't worth jeopardizing his entire story for one small piece. He could always follow up on Oliver later.

"Then it's good to go." Baker held another unlit brown cigarette between his fingers.

"It's still a solid story without the Oliver connection," Nancy said.

GENEVA RECOGNIZED THE CALLER on her cell.

"Beck, how are you?"

"It goes tomorrow."

"Congratulations. That's wonderful. You must be feeling good right now. And you're publishing on Sunday, your big news day."

"Yep. Gonna even make the marketing people happy. Am I good or what?"

"I'll stick with what."

Beck smiled. He loved her sense of humor. "I just got home and opened a beer. Care to help me celebrate?"

"Love to. See you in an hour."

Geneva hung up the phone and immediately called Serodynne legal counsel Sue Nijelski at home. "Sorry to disturb you on a Saturday night, but the *Post-Examiner* is running a story on the Lamurr contract tomorrow."

"That's great news. What's it all about?"

"I'm not exactly sure, but it's along the lines of what I first told you. I'm pretty sure it exposes Lamurr bribing a US senator. I don't have the details. I just heard it's finally running. We'll have to wait for tomorrow to learn more."

"I'll be checking online early tomorrow," Nijelski said.

"You may want to pass it on to the officers—and remind Dymon about my bonus." Geneva heard laughter on the other end of the line.

"You bet I will, girl. Let's hope this not only turns out well for you, but the company too."

Geneva was feeling good for a change. Her next call was to Amtrak. She got one of the last tickets on the early Monday morning Acela train to New York. Then she called Keith.

"The wheels are in motion. Keep an eye on tomorrow's news," she said. "Did you buy all of the new stock options?"

"Yes. Everything's ready. I did as you told me. Let's hope this goes the way you think it will."

She felt relieved. Her little seduction was working. But she also felt weary. There was still plenty to do, even if the stock market went her way. And she'd been wrong about Keith. He was a trooper—and a cute one at that.

And then there was Harv. What was she going to do about him? She cared for him, but she couldn't go on like this. And finally, there was Beck. Her feelings for him were stronger than ever, but she was deliberately avoiding dealing with him because Keith was too important to her right now. Her life was too complicated. This was still a balancing act, she reminded herself.

She turned her attention to her plan. She now had to wait for Wall Street's reaction on Monday. It could change her life forever.

But first, she had Beck to tend to.

42

Beck picked up his newspaper in the downstairs lobby of his building early the next morning. "Bayard Receives Millions from Firm that Won Air Force Contract," read the headline.

Yes, he told himself, this was better than sex—and he should know for he and Geneva were going at it until after midnight.

He rode the elevator up to his condo to find Geneva standing in the doorway in her normal state of undress, unconcerned should a neighbor step into the hallway.

"It's a good thing my neighbors aren't early risers on the weekend."

"Let's see if you can be the exception," she said. As he crossed the threshold, she grabbed his crotch and kissed him.

But Beck pushed back. "Hang with me for a few." He wasn't expecting a passionate early morning, and right now his story needed his attention more than his libido. He walked to the dining room table and laid the newspaper out in full. "I need to read this."

He felt a warm glow as he read the lead out loud to Geneva. "The Justice Department is investigating more than eight million dollars in financial payments to vice presidential nominee, Senator David Bayard, a Republican from New Jersey, from Lamurr Technologies, which recently won a multibillion-dollar air force contract overseen by Bayard's Senate Armed Services Committee. The money was funneled through a series of Lamurr subsidiaries."

He stopped and looked at Geneva. Even this early in the morning, with tousled hair and no makeup, she was still alluring.

"If your grin were any wider, I'd say someone split your face in half," she said.

He opened the newspaper to a spread inside. Two full pages of story and photos showed Bayard's oceanfront mansion, XAX headquarters in Venezuela, the developer's sign on Grand Cayman, and Lamurr's corporate headquarters in northern Virginia.

Kindred's office in the Cayman shopping center was shown and described as the home of the shell company Sunrise Meridian as well as Bayard's Jersey Shore corporation. Man, he thought. The production and design staff really played this up nicely.

Beck finally sat down and read every word. He liked the rhythm. He liked some of the edits Nancy had made to ease the story flow. She had a light touch with his copy.

He got up to get a cup of coffee from the kitchen. Geneva sat in his place at the table and read the story. When he returned, he took the rest of the paper, strolled into the living room, and flopped on Red. He reached for the reading lamp and immediately knew something was wrong. Red had moved. Or his lamp had.

Geneva looked over at Beck who was bent over looking at the floor under his chair.

"What?" she asked.

He didn't say a word, but stood and turned to look at Red. Both front legs were off the rug indentations. But he remembered putting her back in place after their recent collision. Had he moved Red for any reason since then? The maids? No. They were due this week. They hadn't been here.

Geneva, perhaps? But they were rarely in the living room, spending their time on the balcony or in bed. "Hey, have you done anything with Red lately?"

"Ah . . . no." Geneva gave him a curious look.

"That's funny." Beck looked behind his chair, then studied the tall bookshelves next to Red. He got down on his hands and knees and looked under his chair. He then stood up and pulled Red out of her corner. His reading light was plugged into an electrical outlet on the wall.

He pulled a Swiss Army knife from his pocket and used it to unscrew the outlet cover.

Geneva got out of her chair. "Beck?"

He turned and signaled silence.

Something was not right with the outlet. Wires were connected to a small object that had nothing to do with the electrical plug.

"Beck?" Geneva called again from across the room.

He heard the concern in her voice. Again he turned to her, putting his finger to his lips a second time. "Let's get dressed and go out for breakfast," he said, loud enough that he could be heard in every room.

Geneva nodded. They were dressed in less than two minutes and out the door. They rode the elevator in silence.

When they hit the ground floor, Beck said, "Let's walk."

"Can we talk?" Geneva asked.

"I think so." Beck held her hand as they walked swiftly along Old Town's narrow brick sidewalks, stopping to stand aside and let a young couple with a very large Doberman on a leash go by in the opposite direction. The neighborhood was a mixture of old homes and red brick condominiums and apartment buildings.

"What's going on?"

"We're being watched."

"What?"

"That was some sort of listening device hooked to my electrical outlet."

"Listening to our conversations?"

"I assume so."

"To us? To us being intimate?"

"Maybe."

"Oh my god."

Beck stopped at the corner, and they faced each other as several cars passed. "I don't really know. I think maybe we'll go to the movies this afternoon—anything but spending the day in my condo. What I do know is we won't be having any serious conversations there until I figure this out."

43

The next morning, Beck arrived early in the newsroom and went straight to Nancy.

"I think my condo is bugged."

"What?"

"I know. Sounds absurd, but I found something in an electrical outlet."

"Are you sure?"

"Sure, I'm sure."

"Hold on." Her voice was weary. She punched a couple of keys on the conference room phone. "Bob, got a sec? Beck and I need to talk." She hung up and turned to him. "Come on."

The discussion in Baker's office was also behind a closed door.

"But why?" Baker asked.

"All I can think of is someone wants to somehow stay a step ahead and use what they find to discredit my story," Beck said. "Can't imagine they get their jollies from watching sausage being made."

"This seems real cloak-and-dagger to me. A bit sensational. We're talking about a newspaper story. Politicians know better than to bug a reporter. That's political suicide. I just don't buy it."

"But what about the murder in Cayman?" Nancy chimed in. "This is not your regular political story."

Baker paused, looking at both of them. Beck wasn't sure if his boss was buying it. Then Baker finally spoke. "I've dealt with this type of thing before," he said. "Long time ago. I forget who we used. Let me talk with Bennett in security. We will have someone qualified over to your home this afternoon to do a thorough sweep of your place."

IT TOOK THE SECURITY CREW less than thirty minutes to locate four listening devices. Even in the bathroom. What did they think they would find there? Beck wondered.

It bothered him that whoever was spying on him had monitored everything in his bedroom, living room, and dining room, though nothing on the balcony or kitchen. Whoever it was didn't know his habits at least. But the bedroom. Should he tell Geneva?

The ponytailed technician held up a small device in his sinewy hand, the one Beck had taken out of the wall behind Red. He held it up to the light and admired its craftsmanship. "Oh, this is a beaut. Don't see these very often. They're expensive. You must have some important enemies Mr. Rikki."

Beck winced, thinking about what someone out there had overheard. "I'm afraid I might."

"Pretty sophisticated stuff. This could pick up every conversation within twenty feet and broadcast it a hundred yards or more. So whoever was monitoring this could be just about anywhere. Could be one of your condo neighbors or someone in a car down the street."

"How long has it been there?"

"No way to tell. It was hardwired to your electrical outlet, which doubled as an antenna. Could have been here a long time."

Thanks to Red, Beck had a good idea of just how long it had been in his condo—sometime after he bumped into her and put her back in place.

He quizzed the tech more. For someone who didn't consider himself tech savvy, Beck was drilling pretty deep about the details of the device and how it worked. He was in reporter's mode, only this time the story was about him.

He felt violated. This was his safe place and now someone had walked in when he wasn't here and looked at all of his stuff—his photos, his awards, his books, maybe even his personal financial files in the closet in the bedroom.

He wondered if anything had been stolen. But then, if these guys were real pros, they wouldn't rob him for fear of raising suspicions and being discovered. He'd check his condo anyway. He would change the locks again and invest in something more substantial. Maybe he needed his own security system.

And what had they heard? He didn't have the heart to tell Geneva that the sounds of their lovemaking—the heavy breathing, the moans, and her husky voice exclaiming his name—were probably recorded on someone's smartphone, entertainment for a bunch of perverts drinking booze somewhere.

And had they heard him talking to Red? Could they figure out his secret from his one-sided conversations? He needed to erase the thought. It made him feel ill to think about.

He called Nancy and explained what they had found.

"Then you're going to have to be a lot more careful. We"—she paused—"are going to have to be a lot more careful. Watch what you say in your home. Maybe you should start working more at the office."

Beck almost panicked at the thought. "I'll be fine. It's not like I talk to myself in my condo. Who does that?"

44

As Amtrak's Acela subtly leaned unnoticed into the track curves at nine-ty miles an hour on its journey to New York on this chilly Monday morn-ing, Geneva reviewed her plan. Everything had fallen into place. Keith had done his part, and Beck had done his. She needed to await today's stock market reaction and pray the Pentagon did the right thing. She was anxious. The end was now in full focus, but there were still so many things that could go wrong.

As soon as she arrived at her tiny hotel suite, she flipped on the cable news channel and began to prepare for her rendezvous with Keith. She stripped and pulled a tight black sweater over her head and slipped into her skinny black designer jeans. She looked at herself in the bathroom full-length mirror. Like a second skin, the sweater revealed plenty of cleavage and every contour of her body.

Perfect bait, she thought. She needed to reveal enough but not too much, so she could reel in her catch and keep him firmly on the line. She turned in front of the mirror, examining her profile. She had worked hard. Yoga, treadmill, free weights. They had helped sculpt her figure. She knew it wasn't all of her doing and silently thanked her par-ents for the family gene pool.

The news channel caught her ear. Something about the Pentagon. She stepped quickly into the living room and looked at the television.

"The Pentagon official stated that, due to this week's revelation that New Jersey Senator David Bayard may be taking money under the table from defense contractor Lamurr Technologies, the drone contract it recently rewarded to Lamurr was—quote—under review," the news-reader said.

Geneva pumped her fist. Victory, she thought. Wait till they hear this back at the office. What will old man Dymon think then? It's happening right now. The Pentagon is sending signals it will quickly reevaluate the politics of the situation. Serodynne should have the contract within the week, she thought. She was so excited, she wanted to share the news with Sue Nijelski, but then she heard the knock at her door. She checked herself in the mirror one more time. She pushed her breasts up, but without a bra, gravity put them in their proper place. This is as good as I get, she thought.

She grabbed the bottle of chilled champagne she had opened earlier and turned her back to the mirror to check her outfit one last time. Why was she so nervous? She was on the verge of winning. She was close—too close—she told herself. She couldn't afford a misstep now.

Geneva threw open the door and faced Keith, thrusting her body and the bottle of champagne forward as an offering.

"Wow." His mouth hung open.

"Don't drool. We have something to celebrate." She grabbed his striped necktie and pulled him through the doorway, then kicked the door closed with her foot. She set down the champagne, turned, and kissed him hard on the lips. Theirs was a long, passionate kiss, and he held her tightly.

Geneva finally pushed back, grabbed the Dom Perignon, and poured two glasses. "I was hoping for something nicer, but this was the best the concierge could find at the last minute." She took a sip and clinked their glasses, never pulling her eyes away from his. "Here's to our success," she said.

"Here's to us." His eyes wandered down her sweater. He made no attempt to hide his desire.

As much as she enjoyed his attention, Geneva reminded herself she was here for a purpose. The most difficult part of their plan was yet to come. They had to move the money and make it disappear, which would be risky.

"Watch this," she said, pointing to the television.

They both sat and watched the cable news channel as it announced a surge in Serodynne's stock value while Lamurr's dropped by hundreds of points.

"We're richer than god," said Keith.

"God and all the gods put together," Geneva said. "But not if we don't get busy and finish this. We need to start cashing out."

"When do you want to start?"

"Do it gradually beginning tomorrow. We don't want to draw attention to what we're doing."

"I can't believe I did this. I can't believe we did this. I can't believe we made so much money. This is more than I ever imagined. And I owe it all to you," Keith said. He looked into her eyes and kissed her. She let him, and they lay back on the bed and began to make out, his hand sliding under her sweater.

45

Beck hunched over his computer, sipping his fourth diet cola of the day and surfing the web for stories about the public's reaction to his Bayard story. He looked at the clock—nearly lunchtime, which always meant most reporters were missing in action from the newsroom.

Public reaction to Beck's story had been immediate. Letters to the editor ranted in large cities and small towns across the country—in red and blue states alike. By Wednesday, the national media outlets awakened to the coming storm and piled on.

Privately, Beck loved every moment of it. But Nancy had warned him not to gloat. He must be the poster child for humility in public. The last thing he wanted to do, she explained, was to destroy the credibility of his story by coming off as an arrogant ass. The media, she reminded him, weren't exactly beloved by most Americans, and especially by conservative Republicans.

Public opinion polls began to show a shift of discontent, but there was no outward display by the presidential campaign of candidate Ford Patten that he had even noticed. Dissatisfaction with his vice presidential choice, however, was now chipping away at Patten's lead. Bayard's future dominated the discussions on cable television political talkfests.

And Bayard refused to budge. Bastard, thought Beck. But then, if Beck were in his shoes, he'd probably do the same thing. He thought about Bayard squirming uneasily and knew he—Beck Rikki—was the cause of all of his discomfort. Beck basked in the feeling.

The familiar buzz of Fahy's burner cell broke the silence. Beck yanked open his middle desk drawer, remembering he had dumped the phone there for the day since it felt bulky in his pocket. The phone rang and vibrated, causing his collection of cheap pens to tremble and dance atop dog-eared reporter's notebooks, half-eaten protein bars, and a stack of crumpled yellow sticky notes.

"Meet me at two," said the familiar voice. He hung up before Beck could respond.

NEARLY TWO HOURS LATER, Beck found Fahy in his customary spot near the rear of the dingy restaurant dining room, his back to the wall. He wore a dark pinstripe suit—straight from the office, no doubt. He began to speak before Beck could sit down.

"You're going to be served with a subpoena later today, ordering you to disclose your Justice Department source. Oliver is behind it. He's mad as hell. You just *had* to put the Justice Department investigation in the lead of your story. Jeez. Why did you do that? I thought you knew better. Now he wants your head."

Beck felt panic. "He can do this?"

"Federal prosecutor. Federal judge. You bet. Now, our agreement is still in place, right?" Fahy's voice quivered ever so slightly.

It was the first time Beck had seen Mr. Boy Scout's confidence waver, which made him feel even more unsettled. "Our agreement's still good. I do not reveal my confidential sources."

"You're willing to go to jail to cover your source?"

"That's our agreement, although I admit I never seriously considered jail a possibility."

"Consider it." Fahy blew out an audible sigh and looked around the restaurant. Once again, they were the only Caucasians gracing its shabby interior. An elderly couple sat at a table in the middle of the room, and two teenagers, who probably should have been in school, pawed each other at the lunch counter, his hand well below her waist. Construction workers, in paint-splattered black jeans and work boots, sat at tables on the other side of the room, sipping mugs of steaming coffee—likely driven inside by the cold drizzle that had started during morning rush hour. None of the other restaurant patrons appeared the least bit interested in two white guys having a conversation.

"I've never revealed a confidential source," Beck said.

"And you've never been threatened with jail time if you refused." Fahy talked softly, almost in a whisper. Beck noted his Irish complexion seemed to have changed. Fahy's skin was blotchy, as if he had been in the sun too long or maybe had an allergy. Or maybe it was stress, Beck thought.

"Why the rush? The government never moves this quickly. What's got Oliver's shorts in a twist?" Beck instinctively lowered his voice too.

"Oliver wants to deflect attention from Bayard and make *you* the issue. No doubt he also wants to impress the man likely to be the next president of the United States. It's good politics and good PR, as far as Oliver's concerned."

The restaurant owner brought over two large white cups of black coffee and placed them on the table in front of them. No cream. No sugar. No chitchat. He walked back to his post, threw a dish towel over his shoulder, and leaned on the lunch counter to read the local Hispanic weekly tabloid. Something in Spanish screamed across the page. Beck wondered if it could be his story.

Fahy took a sip of his coffee.

"What about President Croom or the attorney general? Don't they have a say?" Beck warmed his hands on his cup.

"Oliver is going out on a limb. The attorney general's policy is pretty straightforward. The AG must approve any news media subpoenas, not Oliver. So I'm sure there will soon be some very unhappy people in the Croom administration. Oliver's quietly gone ahead anyway and is playing the odds. Without notifying anyone, he went before a federal grand jury late yesterday, rather than to a judge, to obtain subpoenas for you and your newspaper."

"Me? I have to go to court?"

"Had he sought permission from a judge, the judge probably would have made some inquiries, which probably would have resulted in the AG signaling to turn down Oliver's request. But he was shrewd. He went to the grand jury. And you know what they say about a grand jury—it will indict a ham sandwich. So imagine how difficult it was to get a couple of subpoenas issued for you."

"You saying even though I've done nothing wrong, I could go to jail?"

"Wouldn't be the first time."

Beck could feel his stomach churn.

Fahy looked over Beck's shoulder. Someone had entered the restaurant. Fahy held his gaze and said nothing for several seconds. Beck finally turned and looked behind him. It appeared to be just another construction crew member in splattered jeans and a light jacket. The man appeared to finally recognize the work crew at the far side of the room and head in their direction.

Fahy sighed loudly again and looked Beck in the eye. "Oliver is basically daring the attorney general to object, and the way I see it, Oliver has this whole thing figured out. If Croom and the AG say anything—try to kill the subpoenas—their motives will be questioned. Not only do they appear to be politically motivated this close to an election, but they also could be accused of being soft on crime. What politician wants that? On the other hand, even though Oliver has gone rogue, he looks like a man doing his job, searching for the truth. Who looks better in that scenario?"

"Oliver can get away with that?"

"Sure. What's he got to lose? His boss and the president are both lame ducks. In a couple of months, they'll be job hunting. This is all about Oliver sucking up to the next president of the United States."

"Isn't he just a government bureaucrat?"

"Oliver was a helluva prosecutor in his time. And remember, he served in Bill Croom's White House. He still has a reputation as a skilled trial attorney. Even as head of Justice's criminal division, he prosecutes one or two cases a year to keep his skills sharpened. So no one will question his move as anything unusual. Plus, it's a high-profile case. What self-serving prosecutor doesn't want a piece of that?"

Beck hadn't seen this coming. He'd hit Bayard and the Republican ticket really hard, and now they were using all of the government power they had amassed over the years to strike back. This sure wasn't in his high school civics book.

"What are Oliver's chances of being the next attorney general?"

"After they check his background, I'd say he'd have a tough time. They'll check with the FBI, who will hand over what they have."

"But they have nothing. I've found nothing on Oliver. Last time I checked, having a half brother wasn't illegal." Beck took a sip of coffee. It was bitter. Must be the bottom of the pot. Fitting, given the way things were going.

"Maybe Oliver sees this move as a way to protect himself," Fahy said. "This might be his only play for the office. Or maybe he's looking for the big paycheck at some law firm or lobby shop. This is Washington, after all, where people tend to delude themselves about their own importance."

"What about me? Will I have to go before a grand jury?"

"No. That's done. Your lawyer will demand a hearing to quash the subpoena. Oliver has already checked the docket to ensure they can schedule a hearing almost immediately. That will take place in a closed courtroom before the chief judge of the US District Court of DC. All parties will agree to that. Remember, we could have the makings of a constitutional crisis. The courts will move quickly to resolve it. I assume that's in your newspaper's best interest as well."

"This is new territory for me. I haven't a clue what to expect." Beck knew little about the grand jury system except that it was all done in secret.

"Think back to the Bush-Gore presidential election debacle," said Fahy. "The Supreme Court doesn't want to get involved in another fiasco like that. It lost a lot of credibility with the public in that decision simply because it involved political candidates. The pressure is on the federal district court to find the facts and do it quickly before the election. That puts pressure on Oliver to come after you and me immediately. This is now a race against the clock."

"Jesus." Beck shook his head. "I wish we could nail down Oliver's connection to Bayard. We'd be set then. Our staff writer in South America got a tip that Oliver was the one who actually introduced Bayard to the Lamurr people, but he couldn't find any of Oliver's real estate deals in Costa Rica to tie them together."

"Costa Rica? Oliver doesn't own property in Costa Rica. He's in Tortola."

"What?" Beck sat stunned.

"The Virgin Islands, not Costa Rica. Your source got it wrong. Oliver has been going to Tortola for twenty years. He goes down there every winter for three weeks. He usually goes down around Christmas and stays till after the Martin Luther King federal holiday. Whatever he owns, it's there. That's his Caribbean base."

Beck thought about it. "That makes sense. Both Grand Cayman and Tortola are British. Roger Kindred could easily help his brother with any real estate details on another British island. Shit. I've got to reach our correspondent and send him to Tortola."

"Well, you'd better be damned quick about it. Look, if you can give me anything—*anything*—on Oliver before the hearing, maybe I can head it off or slow it down."

"You'd do that?"

"I have a personal stake in this, same as you."

Beck realized what strange bedfellows he and Fahy had become. Now he might have to entrust Fahy with his future. The thought scared the hell out of him.

46

As he slid into the bucket seat of his Volvo, Beck punched speed dial on his phone. The rain had stopped, and the sun was attempting to break through the clouds, but the chill had not dissipated. He turned up the heat in his car.

"Shit!" Nancy said. "But we might be in luck. The last I heard Bobby was in Honduras. That should be a quick flight to the Virgin Islands. I'll get back to you."

The phone went dead. Beck didn't get to tell her about the subpoenas. He was scheduled to take the afternoon off. His editors had been urging him to cut back on his hours. Fat chance now.

He drove north toward Old Town Alexandria against the oncoming rush hour traffic. It was just beginning its daily southern crawl out of the District. He was back at his condo in under fifteen minutes thinking about all of those government workers sitting in traffic. Beck dropped his tweed sports coat and notebook in Red's lap and flipped on his satellite radio. Jimmy Buffett sang a song about an expat in Paris. Beck glared at Red and paced back and forth.

"Red. This is crazy. Can they actually send me to jail for doing my job? Do I have a choice? The first commandment of journalism says I go to prison to protect my source. I become a friggin' martyr for the profession. I make history and headlines. But I don't want to spend months of my life in prison for some principle. That's stupid. I don't have a cause. I'm not political. I just enjoy chasing down dirty politicians."

He stepped out onto the balcony and leaned on the railing, looking at the dreary sky. That fits, he thought. Nearly all of the leaves from the large pin oak—his privacy shield against the world—lay in a pile in the neighbor's backyard.

He heard small voices and glanced down in their direction, eyeing two children playing on a swing set in the neighbor's backyard. A young blonde girl jumped out of her swing and rushed to dive into the heap of leaves. Every fall, he lamented the disappearance of his private world on the balcony. It affected his decisions to enjoy a cigar since he did not desire the scrutiny of neighbors. And this was Old Town where politically correct was, well, politically correct. Cigars were frowned upon as his neighbors ate their yogurt, drank their craft beers and green tea, and practiced yoga. And what about Geneva? Jeez, she'd actually have to put on some clothes.

The thought of her naked brought a smile to his face. In many ways, they were alike. He was a private person who loved exposing public people's hypocrisy. Geneva too was a private person imprisoned in others' public hypocrisy. Somehow, he thought, maybe her nakedness was her way of rebelling, of cleansing herself of the slimy feel of the city.

Was she once a young idealist who ran smack into the wall of Washington's reality? Is that how she became a well-paid hack for a big corporation? She certainly made more than he did as a journalist. Without the royalties from his books, which provided him a comfortable financial cushion, he'd be in some shabby basement apartment near Dupont Circle like many of his colleagues.

Maybe the murders and this lawsuit were the foundation for his wall of reality. He always thought of his profession as a moral calling. Keeping the government honest and all of that preachy stuff. But how far was he willing to go for his ethical calling? To jail? That was a bit too much reality for him.

Nailing politicians was a game—a match of wits between good and evil. But this Bayard story was different. This was bigger than anything he had ever attempted. The ramifications were huge.

Beck was like Geneva, a misfit in this town. Yet both of them fed off its questionable ethical energy. While they weren't guilty of the types of crimes and hypocrisy he loved to expose, their fortunes and livelihoods depended on the continued existence of the town's sleaze factor. It wasn't just a living; it was their parasitic way of life.

Neither of them, he figured, had the guts to turn their backs on it. Sit on a beach the rest of his life? Please. Not as long as he could play the game. He was not a cliché. He might last a month in the sun. He wasn't so sure about Geneva. She could probably last a lot longer.

He grabbed his cell phone and called Nancy again.

"Bobby is on his way to the airport," she said. "He's—"

"There's more," Beck interrupted. "We're being served with subpoenas." He walked her through his conversation with Fahy.

"Shit," she said. "I'll notify reception, Baker, and Curtiss. We'll be ready."

"What do I do?"

"Hang in there, champ. These sleazeballs may have the entire weight of the government on their side to throw at us, but we've got the Constitution. The First Amendment is pretty powerful stuff."

He knew Nancy was usually good at calming him during a crisis, but her words rang hollow this time, doing little to soothe his anxiety. He'd never tread this territory before. He felt like a deer in headlights, not knowing which way to go and glaring at that oncoming big monster semi about to turn him into political roadkill.

47

The next day Beck examined Bobby's e-mails. They included scans of real estate documents with Oliver's and Kindred's names all over them. Bobby had spent time at the tax assessor's office in Tortola, he explained to Beck. He gleaned the government's assessment of the current value of each piece of real estate. He then hit the dusty deed books in the local courthouse.

"I always follow the money," Bobby told him over the phone from the island courthouse. That made Beck laugh. It was a familiar line from an old movie that reporters loved to quote after a few too many at the bar.

Beck printed out Bobby's e-mailed scans and laid them on a conference room table so he could see everything at once. He found one rental property purchased in 1995, financed through a mortgage company, and paid off two years ago. The other houses were bought in the last four years. All were financed by Sunrise Meridian.

But it was the final set of documents Bobby e-mailed that caught his eye: a property that was sold by and financed by Sunrise Meridian. It was owned by Jersey Shore Ltd., Bayard's company. The documents were notarized by the paralegal in Kindred's office. The property address was next door to Oliver's first home.

Beck called Nancy in and showed her the last document.

"Finally, we've connected them," he said.

"But what does this really prove?" she asked. Nancy bit her lower lip, contemplating the array of documents on the large table before her.

Beck took offense at her question. "It proves they both were tied to Sunrise Meridian and Lamurr."

"It doesn't prove Oliver had anything to do with Bayard's relationship with Lamurr or Sunrise Meridian. It shows only that they might have known each other as neighbors. We need more. Bobby's going to hate me. We need to send him back to his source in Venezuela with these documents."

"Shit." Beck shook his head in disgust.

"This won't hold up in any story. We really can't use it." Nancy picked up the documents in both hands and looked them over again. "It shows everything but a Bayard-Oliver direct connection. Hell, this wouldn't even hold up in court."

Beck remembered what Fahy had told him. Wouldn't it? he wondered.

"EXCUSE ME. MS. MOORE?" A tall, balding man, probably in his mid-fifties and wearing a zip-up rain slicker, stood at the conference room door. "Ms. Moore?"

"Yes," Nancy turned.

"You've been served." He handed her a subpoena, just as Fahy had predicted. He then turned to Beck and shoved a piece of paper in his hand without saying a word. He then quickly stepped out of the room and walked away.

"Nice," said Nancy. "Reception was supposed to call me and let me know when he arrived."

"This has never happened to me before," Beck said.

"No biggie. Curtiss will handle everything. Now give me that thing. I'll make copies for Baker and have the originals couriered to Curtiss."

Curtiss quickly filed a motion to have them dismissed. The subpoenas ordered Beck and the *Post-Examiner* to reveal to the court all of their sources for Beck's story. It was now pretty obvious to Beck there was no way Bobby could pull together information in time for a story on Oliver before the hearing.

And just as Fahy had predicted, the *Post-Examiner* was immediately granted an appeals hearing. Beck had to hand it to Fahy. He knew exactly what Oliver was up to. He was not only a Boy Scout and top Justice official, he was a political soothsayer as well.

Maybe, Beck thought, Curtiss could get the subpoenas dismissed. But no matter what, Beck was going to have to testify in court. And if the judge refused to dismiss them and Beck then refused to reveal his source, he thought he would likely go to jail. How in the hell, he wondered, had he gotten himself in this situation just by doing his job?

He needed to improve his odds.

Beck combed through papers and dozens of his notebooks in his bottom desk drawer looking for the burner phone. He finally found it in the middle drawer where he remembered putting it so he would know exactly where it was.

"Jesus," he mumbled to himself. "I'm losing it. Can't even find the fuckin' phone."

Cheryl Rose, sitting at the desk in front of his, looked up from her computer screen and glared at him.

"Sorry. Just talking to myself," he said, and felt his face flush. Too much to think about, he told himself. Too much going on.

He pocketed the small phone and headed for the elevator, which creaked and spewed strange sounds as it delivered him to the parking lot on the roof of the *Post-Examiner*. He looked around, scanning for reporters, who frequently visited this concrete oasis for a smoke and some downtime. The lot was empty except for dozens of sedans, vans, and SUVs with baby car seats and pet carriers strapped tight in the backseats. We all make lifestyle choices, thought Beck. He made the call.

"We need to talk," he told Fahy. "I may be able to help you."

BECK WAS ALREADY SEATED when Fahy arrived at the restaurant three hours later. He was at the rear table with his back to the wall in Fahy's usual seat.

Beck held a large manila envelope. The restaurant was nearly deserted. As usual, the owner stood behind the counter, looking busy. He was always cleaning something. Today, he appeared to pay no attention to them. He flipped on the radio, joining a salsa already in progress. They turned at the sound and glanced at the man, who gave them a faint nod and went back to his work.

"I really shouldn't be doing this," Beck whispered. "If my editors find out, they'll kill me. It could mean my job. Here's something we dug up on Oliver that ties him to Bayard. They're next-door neighbors, and both do business with Sunrise Meridian."

Beck slid the envelope across the table, and Fahy riffled through the pages, barely glancing at them. "The subpoena won't be quashed. I can guarantee you that," Fahy said. "I've already checked with court officials. The judge wants to see this through to whatever end."

"Can you do anything with this Oliver information?"

Fahy looked closer at the real estate documents from Tortola. "I don't know. I'll have to think about it. We'll see."

"Okay, but if it gets out that I gave you info on Oliver, it's probably my job. I need your word you won't tell a soul where you got this."

"Kind of ironic, don't you think?" Fahy said. He folded the envelope and placed it in his jacket pocket. "We both need to keep our sources a secret."

Beck knew this was stepping way out of bounds even for an investigative reporter who sometimes stretched his professional ethics just a little for the good of his story. Deceiving the old man in Grand Cayman who lived next door to Bayard was a white lie—nothing as serious as this. This was deceiving his bosses. But Beck wasn't about to reveal his source to any judge. That would be breaking the honor code of his profession: never burn a source. The way he saw it, he really had no choice.

He was the one facing jail time, not Nancy, not anyone else at the paper. Sure, they'd support him, but he could be locked in a small room like a caged bird for weeks or even months—or even worse. Could it get worse? How long would a judge lock him up? He was claustrophobic.

Just thinking about a small space and four walls closing in scared the hell out of him.

He realized he'd been staring down at the table in thought. It reflected decades of daily meals on cheap china, heavy chipped coffee mugs, and dull steel silverware. They were all etched into the surface of the faded Formica top. All that time, he thought. All those meals. The owner behind the counter trapped in this small, shabby restaurant every day—the same thing every single day. He understood that monotonous daily repetition could soon be his future. He felt trapped.

Fahy interrupted his wandering mind. "What a dilemma. Your job or you go to jail. Glad I'm not in your shoes."

Beck looked up as Fahy spoke. He felt like Fahy had somehow turned the tables on him. Up until now, Fahy was beholden to him to keep his secret. Now it seemed the other way around. Whether Beck liked it or not, they now had a mutual bond of codependence. Beck suddenly felt he had fumbled the ball. Maybe he shouldn't have given Fahy the information on the ties between Bayard and Oliver. But it was too late now. He couldn't undo what he had just done.

48

Not wanting to get scooped on its own involvement in the news, Baker ordered a page-one story covering the government's attempt to reveal Beck's source. Courts reporter Steve Giegerich quoted Publisher Katherine Cunningham's stilted official statement in his story: "When the government goes after the sources of stories whose veracity has never been challenged, it chips away at the foundation of democracy and every American's right to an open and honest government."

Beck thought it sounded a bit pious. But it was Baker's choice. He wrote it. Cunningham signed off, and Giegerich quoted it verbatim. In the tenth paragraph, Curtiss spouted something about setting a bad legal precedent. It sounded all high and mighty to Beck, the type of prose the press loves to hype in any challenge to the First Amendment.

When the Boy-Scout-in-chief of the public integrity division first leaked the story, Beck thought Fahy was the only one taking a risk. Now he understood otherwise. Beck knew all too well that, while the federal government couldn't attack the accuracy of his story, it could legally compel him to reveal his source. None of this, of course, made any sense. What good would it do to find out the story's source if the facts were still true? Welcome to Washington's political playhouse, he told himself.

There was no federal shield law for reporters—and not a lot of sympathy for pushy ones like Beck. Many had gone to jail for less. He thought of the *New York Times* reporter who spent a hot summer in the Alexandria city jail for refusing to reveal her source after a CIA agent was outed by a previous administration. He could end up like her. He wasn't in a strong position to argue with public opinion at the moment, especially since Bayard's running mate, Ford Patten, was leading in the public opinion polls.

When the subpoena story hit the important front stoops, sidewalks, and ambitions of Washington, cable television audiences across the nation heard and saw the swelling chests of American journalism. Beck tuned in to watch the early morning newscasts and coffee-addled talk-athons. Disheveled First Amendment scholars from local universities were awakened from their intellectual slumber to make their ninety-second disoriented comments.

By noon, it was clear to Beck the pundits, by a wide margin, were condemning the government's action. Only a few conservative commentators on Fox News wondered if Beck had revealed any classified information, which could have made his behavior criminal. That rattled Beck. But any rereading of the story would quickly dissuade that kind of thinking. At least Beck thought so. But then Beck knew facts and punditry were rarely on the same page.

Nationally, most of his journalism colleagues played the story as a battle between two titans—the overreaching government and the heroic press always ensuring the public's right to know. It was the type of fight the national media love: a test of wills over the First Amendment. Beck would have found it amusing had he not been in the middle of this mess. Raising the banner of a free press was not only an easy story for the cable windbags and newspaper op-ed pundits, but it also spiked ratings and improved profits. Beck was a one-man profit center for the national cable media right now—at least until the next white coed kidnapping, he thought.

The political bloggers went on a tirade, blasting Beck for harming their government and their future vice president. They operated out of ignorance and were truly representative of their audiences, Beck thought. They knew nothing of journalism's sacred rules and grand code of ethical fairness. Grabbing an audience and making headlines was their only concern—capitalism at its best. Beck understood their motives and dismissed them. But their criticism still stung. He was not accustomed to the limelight.

As for Beck's real role in all of this, old walrus face, attorney Charles Curtiss, advised him not to answer his phone. The newsroom operator screened his calls. He was not to comment to the press. Here he was, an advocate of openness and transparency, ordered to shut down and shut up by the *Post-Examiner*'s First Amendment eight-hundred-pound gorilla. His world made no sense. He was already a caged animal and feeling the walls close in on him.

God, if the world only knew the whole truth about Oliver's connection to Bayard. He had to figure out a way to get that story out.

49

Keith Crocker sat at his desk and stared at his computer screen, preparing to make his morning trades. He was thinking about yesterday, about kissing Geneva and touching her, and about so many other future possibilities, when bank partner Robert Gettlin stepped into his office doorway.

Keith looked up. "Can I help you?"

"Maybe," Gettlin said. "I noticed you set up a personal account for Geneva Kemper of Serodynne and her husband, Michael Harvey—Senator Michael Harvey—without consulting the partners. Do you think that was a wise idea?"

Keith was stunned. How did Gettlin find out about Geneva's trading account, and how much did he know about their scheme to enrich themselves? He stared in the man's direction, not focusing.

"Mr. Crocker." Gettlin's words broke the silence. "Are you going to answer my question?"

"Sorry," Keith said. "I've been concentrating on other work. What was your question again?"

"Didn't you think you should talk to the partners before you opened a personal account for a representative of a large corporate client? In this case, Geneva Kemper and Serodynne Corporation? And her husband is a US senator, for crying out loud."

Keith caught the sarcasm and exasperation in Gettlin's voice. He had to respond. "I was trying to remember the details of her account. She asked me to set it up. She's now my client. I didn't know I needed to seek the partners' permission to set up my clients' accounts—no matter who they were."

"But her company is a client as well."

"Serodynne is also mine, if you recall. You and Mr. Bernstein assigned it to me. No one wanted to deal with Ms. Kemper's quarterly dog and pony show anymore. If I remember correctly, you were seeking new lucrative accounts, and old stable ones like Serodynne were downgraded in importance. That's why you assigned it to me." Keith was on a roll, now feeling more confident with every word he spoke.

Gettlin shifted in the office doorway, hands dapperly positioned in the pockets of his expensive suit coat. "Why did you invest in options in her company?"

"It's a perfectly legitimate trade. She gave me a small amount of money to invest. After going through the financials of her company with a fine-tooth comb, which is my job, I decided Serodynne was not a good investment. So I bet against it."

"Is it advisable to have your client bet against her own company?"

Damn. He couldn't deny what was on the books, and Gettlin, obviously, had been snooping around.

"As you noted, she was my client. She told me to invest for her as I saw fit. I won pretty big. Isn't that what I'm supposed to do?"

"It just seems odd. I was checking the trade records, and you invested dozens of your clients in the same thing."

"When I see a hot opportunity, I try to make my clients money," Keith said. "Unlike the rest of this firm, which has a history of trading for itself and *against* its own clients. Hell, the firm wouldn't have had all of those financial problems five years ago had the partners been thinking about their clients instead of themselves."

He paused, bolder now, but also worried. How much of his trading had Gettlin examined?

"I was thinking of shifting some of my clients' accounts and maybe some firm funds into Serodynne or even Lamurr." Gettlin's tone had softened.

If they dumped a bunch of money into either company, thought Keith, it would surely draw the attention of the feds. It would be far too much activity beyond his small number of trades, which had never drawn scrutiny before. His and Geneva's plan could blow up before they had a chance to cash out.

"Forget it," Keith said. "The government moved its big Pentagon contract from Lamurr to Serodynne. There's no play left. You won't see any stock movement for a long time. I'm cashing in the gains for my clients."

Gettlin leaned against the doorframe looking at Keith and said nothing. Keith didn't know what to say and stared back in silence. Had he blown it?

"Nice work," shot back Gettlin. "Maybe we should do lunch some time and talk about some of your ideas. Perhaps you should rethink your future and get on the partner track. We could use some winners in this firm that benefit all of our clients."

"Thanks. I'm happy with where I am, but I'll take you up on that free lunch." Keith smiled at him.

Gettlin grimaced. Obviously, he had no intention of ever taking Keith out to lunch. Gettlin was sizing him up, or perhaps just looking for a good stock tip to placate top clients. Lazy bastard, thought Keith.

Gettlin turned on his heels and walked down the hall in that slippery way only a partner could manage. The blood pulsed in Keith's temples. He buried his head in his hands as sweat poured down his face. How had he pulled that one off?

The throbbing subsided. Was there something more to the conversation? If Gettlin was snooping around, maybe others were as well.

He needed to cash out as quickly as possible. There wasn't time to tell Geneva. He would just do it, but very carefully. He did not know who was watching.

50

Beck, his editors, and the lawyers stepped out of several yellow cabs at the plaza in front of the E. Barrett Prettyman Federal Courthouse on Constitution Avenue. Television satellite trucks blocked most of the curb. As Beck navigated around them, he recognized some of the blow-dried correspondents strategically positioned on the sidewalk doing live stand-ups.

There, they would breathlessly cablecast the judge's ruling to the elderly, the infirm, the retired, and the unemployed—all of those tired, poor, and huddled masses etched so famously inside the Statue of Liberty—who welcomed the daily chore of watching midmorning television at home in their sweats and pajamas while the rest of America left for work or class or shopping.

Funny, thought Beck. Only comedians and television journalists did stand-up. What did that say about the state of his profession?

As soon as the press horde recognized Beck and his colleagues, they swarmed, surrounding Beck and company with dozens of cameras and microphones and blocking his path to the courthouse.

Beck immediately felt his claustrophobia kick in. He closed his eyes momentarily, determined to proceed. Then he opened them and saw his attorney take the lead. Fortunately, Curtiss must have weighed nearly three hundred pounds and easily pressed through the mob scene, which stepped back to keep their expensive electronic equipment from getting crushed. Curtiss, it appeared, had been through this routine before.

He had earlier warned everyone not to speak publicly before the hearing. Beck kept apologizing to his colleagues, all shoving to get closer, as he stepped carefully behind Curtiss through the media mass to the courthouse's front door. Cameras and other recording devices were not allowed inside.

Curtiss stopped and turned to the cameras. "Pipe down," he yelled. "We'll have a statement after the hearing."

Now Beck sat in the chief judge's cavernous, windowless, ornate federal courtroom with Curtiss at his side. For the first time in his career, he had become part of his own story, and he didn't like it. And unlike all his other stories, he didn't know how this one would end. Would he become a sacrificial pawn in this judicial sideshow? He thought of all of the people who would dance in the street to see him taken down—and that included most of the subjects of his investigative pieces. God, that would be embarrassing.

Maybe he would make the history books. Unless, of course, the newspaper's attorney had some brilliant legal strategy that would spare him the privilege. Curtiss had yet to share anything of the sort. Frankly, Beck thought, he'd rather make a quick exit than history.

He thought about his colleagues who were not allowed into this closed hearing. The legal correspondents were probably pontificating numerous scenarios; it was all gamesmanship and showbiz to them. Just another day's work.

But for Beck, this was real truth or consequences. They'll go home and sleep in their own beds tonight, he thought. But he could end up on a concrete bench in a six-by-ten cell.

He shuddered at the idea. His body suddenly felt cold.

He did not belong in this place. He wrote the stories. He worked in relative obscurity. The only time his name appeared in the newspaper was his byline. The only time he appeared in public was for an interview on a cable news shows or on the dust jacket of one of his books. But now, he was part of the lead paragraph, and his picture was in nearly every newspaper in America.

For the first time, he felt like a victim. But hell, he knew he was responsible for his current state of affairs. Did his sources from his many stories feel victimized like this? He wondered if they felt this vulnerable, like they had lost control of the situation. Maybe his previous investigative pieces were too harsh, or maybe he was too self-righteous about his noble calling and not concerned enough for the welfare of the people he wrote about.

Was he now paying the price for his journalistic arrogance? Maybe it was time he reexamined his methods, his ideals. He had always thought he was the moral, righteous type—above the Washington fray. Now he wondered if that was just his facade.

He sat next to Curtiss at a long wooden table in this chandeliered echo chamber, waiting for a judge to march in and decide his fate. He had lost control of the story. That's what really pissed him off. His writing, his sources, his research talents—no good here. No additional interviews, no extra phone calls would make a difference. He couldn't write his way out of this one. He had shown his entire hand and now waited to see what cards the other guy had to play. At this point, he would have to rely on the skills of others.

When this was all over, no matter how badly it went for him, Beck was determined to examine his ways. Maybe it was time he changed—if that was even possible for him.

Nancy Moore and Robert Baker sat in the first row of the visitors' section. Nancy was the only person other than Beck who knew the identity of his source. Baker, the old warhorse, was seated next to her. He was a famous civil rights reporter and later the newspaper's London bureau chief in the day when newspapers made obscene amounts of money. He was one of the canniest journalists of his time, which is why Beck knew he deliberately never asked to know Beck's source. After Nancy, Beck admired him most for his cunning and ability to cut through a complicated story to immediately find its core.

Only Curtiss, the senior partner at James, Howell & Gordon, a graying, prestigious city law firm, sat with Beck at the table.

Waiting.

The double doors at the back of the room swooshed open simultaneously, followed by a commotion of expensive leather soles and male chatter echoing off the marble floor. Jackson Oliver, assistant attorney general for the criminal division, led a group of five down the center isle of the courtroom and to the neighboring prosecutor's table. He looked just like the photos in the old newspaper clippings. Oliver hadn't aged in ten years. This guy appeared more formidable than Beck had thought.

Beck spied Fahy among the attorneys. What the hell was he doing here? Guaranteeing that Beck kept his promise? If he thought he would talk, wouldn't he hide out far from the news media outside?

He looked none too happy to be there.

Chief Judge John Savage stepped deliberately from a side door.

"All rise," bellowed the bailiff.

"Attorneys, please approach the bench," instructed the judge.

Curtiss raised his eyebrows and looked briefly at Beck.

Beck caught the glance. Curtiss appeared perplexed at the judge's order. Oh great, thought Beck, his lawyer hasn't a clue. That's a good way to start this thing and exude confidence with your client. It was not the look he needed from his attorney right now.

Curtiss charged forward, joining the swarm of suits in front of the judge's bench, all with their backs to Beck.

From his vantage point at the defendant's table, Beck watched Oliver and Curtiss engage in a lively discussion, but he could make out only an occasional word. The conference dragged on forever.

"Then we're all agreed," the judge said, and the lawyers rocked their heads in affirmative obedience, took a step back, and returned to their tables.

"What's up?" Beck whispered.

"No big deal," Curtiss said. "Just some prehearing maneuvers."

"Gentlemen," said the judge, "as agreed, Mr. Oliver will step aside from this case, and the new lead prosecutor for the Justice Department will be Mr. Daniel Fahy."

WHAT JUST HAPPENED? Beck turned in his seat and looked for Nancy in the visitors' section. Her gaping mouth said it all. She tilted her head and shifted her eyes toward Fahy. Beck turned back. Fahy stood shuffling papers at the next table, not looking in their direction.

Beck glanced back toward Nancy and mouthed silently. "What the fuck?"

She shook her head slowly and looked away.

"Your honor," Fahy said. "In light of recent developments in this case, I would ask for a ten-day continuance. The prosecution needs to review the case, and we would like to examine the possibility of bringing in an additional witness."

"This case has national implications," the judge said. "I will grant the continuance, but not for ten days. I will give you two. We will meet again at ten a.m. sharp Friday."

Judge Savage banged the gavel.

Just like that, it was over—at least for a couple of days. Beck didn't move. He sat silently trying to take it all in. Now he was totally confused. What had Fahy done? Where was this headed? How could Fahy prosecute the source of his own leak? And if he did, and did so aggressively, was Beck still bound by his promise not to reveal Fahy as his source?

51

THE NEXT DAY, Beck met with the lawyers, Cunningham, Baker, and Nancy in the publisher's conference room. Cunningham sat at the end of the table with a copy of the morning's newspaper opened to a short, page-two account of the previous day's events. Baker, Beck, and Nancy were on one side of the table and the lawyers on the other.

"Fahy says he's bringing the property rental manager Beck interviewed in Grand Cayman up here to testify," Curtiss said.

"What can the manager say to make the prosecution's case?" asked Cunningham.

"I have no idea," Beck said. "I didn't tell him anything about any source."

"Then I'm not sure what Mr. Fahy is up to," Curtiss said. "I did find out Oliver was dismissed from the case because he also has ties to Sunrise Meridian and Lamurr. I don't know how the judge got that information, but I certainly hope it didn't come from anyone in this room."

Curtiss glanced at Beck, then Nancy, and finally Baker. Everyone was silent.

"We need to be ready for this, no matter what comes along." Cunningham rose and gathered her papers, signaling the end of the meeting.

"Beck?" Nancy said as they entered the elevator. She pressed the button for the newsroom, and the doors closed on them.

"It wasn't me."

Their eyes met. She held her gaze and then rolled her eyes.

"Look," he said, "the Justice Department has its own investigation going on. I don't know what happened."

"Yeah. Right."

Beck wondered if she bought it.

His talk with Red last night had begun to clarify things. Beck must have paced the floor and worn the oriental rug out for more than an hour. But he was happy with the results. It was obvious Fahy somehow manipulated the system—using Beck's leaked information—to set himself up as prosecutor. That had to be a good thing for Beck because they both had so much to lose. Beck now had to figure out how he could seize control of the situation from Fahy. He was determined he was not going to let others decide his fate.

52

Ford Patten needed a way out. No scandal was sabotaging his shot at the presidency. The Democrats were already threatening impeachment if Bayard became the next vice president, and the ticket was starting to lose traction in the opinion polls. Patten had an eight-point lead before the scandal broke, but now he was just four points ahead in one poll and two ahead in another. A third even had him in a dead heat. And he had just weeks left before Election Day.

But Bayard wouldn't budge. He went on Fox News and denounced the news media for liberal bias. "I've done nothing wrong. The voters have spoken," Bayard said. "The liberal media don't like it that a majority of Americans will elect Ford Patten as their next president."

Patten watched the interview on the television in his Cleveland hotel room as he readied to tour a roller bearing plant and then make an appearance at a campaign barbecue near the small town of Bucyrus. By the end, he was fuming. Bayard had kidnapped his campaign.

"That ass has got to go," he told his campaign manager. "I never liked the jerk. I wish I hadn't needed New Jersey. I should have just picked the woman from Florida for my running mate. We need a way out of this."

"Tell him privately that, if he does not resign, you will take the nuclear option and call for his resignation and a full-scale investigation," said his manager. "Tell him we will pull whatever strings necessary to ensure he keeps his senate committee chairmanship as long as he pulls out."

"We've got two days then to get it done. You call him. Tell him we won't go public with his resignation until after the hearing about the source of his scandal story. Maybe somehow, that hearing will save his ass. I can't see how, but we owe him that much. We must wait to be sure."

"We need to vet a replacement quickly."

"I'll take care of that personally," Patten said. "It's time I started making some calls."

"We can announce a replacement on Monday. That will give us a two-week campaign. We will poll voters about the effect of a new vice presidential candidate. Thank god most people don't care."

Patten shook his head and placed his hands on his hips. "They care enough that my lead in the polls has shrunk. We've got a lot of repair work to do and little time to do it."

53

Beck stuffed the burner phone in his coat pocket. He took Fahy's advice to heart and now carried it with him everywhere. As he prepared to leave his condo for work, he felt the rumbling vibration in his breast pocket and heard the familiar buzz.

"Listen carefully," said Fahy. "No matter what I ask you about your source tomorrow, deny it. Got that?"

"Deny it," Beck repeated.

"That's right." Fahy's voice was stern.

"Okay. Can you tell me why?" Beck felt uneasy.

"No, but be very, very careful. Pay attention. Ask me to repeat a question if you're not sure what to say, and stall if you need to. Remember, you are not in a hurry. Think before you speak. Speak slowly and deliberately. That will give you a little more time to think."

"What happened? Why are you prosecuting the leak?"

"I managed to slip the information about Oliver into the judge's secretary's in-basket the day before the hearing while she was in the ladies' room. As head of the public integrity section, however, I should have realized he would hand the case to me. But he didn't say anything until the session before the bench, which you saw. I was caught off guard when he appointed me to prosecute. My error. I should have set it up better. My only excuse is I had too little time."

"What's your plan for tomorrow?"

"Can't talk now. Stick with me, kid. Remember. Deliberate. Talk slow. Think it through. Stall if you need time to think. And number one:

deny everything—every accusation against you. Deny it ever happened. Even the smallest detail."

The phone went dead. Beck was confused. Exactly what was he supposed to deny? He was more determined than ever to get back in the fight on his own terms. He hated being a pawn in a game of chess between two lawyers. But at least Fahy's advice gave him a smattering of hope.

THE MEDIA AGAIN GATHERED outside the federal courthouse. As Beck stepped out of the cab, they pounced. It felt like a television perp walk, but he had not been arrested—at least not yet—and he hadn't done anything wrong, at least in his mind.

The reporters yelled over one another with outreached hands, extending microphones in Beck's direction and trying to get his attention and comments. Curtiss, the Walrus, fended them off. Fortunately, he used his mass again and easily pressed his way through the crowd, and Beck and his editors followed. Beck laughed, envisioning Moses parting the Red Sea, as the swarm of reporters and cameramen jostled Curtiss and Beck but allowed them all to pass.

The commotion stopped as soon as they stepped through the federal courthouse door. Baker closed it behind them, and there was silence. The lawyers, clerks, and paralegals standing in the lobby looked up to see what the tempest outside was about. Embarrassed, Beck felt the weight of everyone's gaze. They made their way through security and the awkward stillness toward the elevators that led to the courtroom.

As soon as the judge gaveled the closed hearing to order, Curtiss asked that the subpoena be quashed and the case be thrown out.

Judge Savage's expression said otherwise. "Mr. Curtiss, this hearing is about a government employee possibly giving classified information to Mr. Rikki. Your arguments bear no consequence on the merits of this case. We will proceed."

Fahy called Beck Rikki as his first witness. The silence of the room roared through Beck's head as he rose from the table and walked awkwardly toward the witness chair. He raised his right hand to be sworn in as the room whirled around him like a carousel. He took his seat, then watched Fahy fumble with some manila folders strewn across the prosecutor's table.

"Mr. Fahy?" Judge Savage appeared eager to begin.

Fahy still stood with his head down, leaning over his table and juggling papers.

"*Mr. Fahy?*"

Fahy turned. "Sorry, Your Honor."

"Are you ready to begin?"

"Yes, Your Honor."

Dressed in a charcoal-gray power suit, white shirt, and red tie, Fahy approached Beck. Beck was dressed almost identically. It was only the second time he had worn a tie since the party at Ellen Elizabeth's, when he met Geneva.

"Mr. Rikki," Fahy said, "I don't want to insult you. So I'll just ask. Will you reveal your source inside the Justice Department?"

"I never said I had a source in the Justice Department."

Beck saw the corners of Fahy's mouth turn upward slightly.

"You didn't?"

"No. I didn't. You did."

"Then how did you come to know about the Justice Department probe into Senator Bayard's finances?"

"A source told me."

"But not someone in the Justice Department?"

"I never said I had a source in the Justice Department. I never said I didn't." Beck grinned. He was getting the hang of this. He slumped slowly in the witness chair, beginning to relax.

"Are you denying you have a source in the Justice Department?"

"No, sir. Nor am I confirming it. If I were to tell you my source is in the Justice Department that would only help you track down my source. If I were to tell you my source is outside the Justice Department, that too would help you track down my source. I promised my source that if he—

or she or it, for that matter—told me the truth about Senator Bayard, I would never reveal his or her or its identity. I plan to stick to that promise." Beck felt he got a bit carried away with his answer, but it felt good to take the reins again, even if only for a moment.

"No further questions at this time, Your Honor. I reserve the right to recall the witness."

"Mr. Curtiss, do you wish to question your client?" asked Judge Savage.

"Yes, Your Honor." He stood and lumbered across the room to within a few feet of Beck.

"Now, Mr. Rikki, you've been accused of receiving classified information from a Justice Department employee. Just what classified information did you receive?"

"None that I'm aware of. And I never said I received any from a Justice Department employee."

Curtiss smiled. "Did you ever publish any classified information involving the Lamurr Pentagon bid on unmanned aircraft—so-called drones, if you will?"

"I not only never published any, I've never seen any."

"So if you've never received or published any information the federal government deems classified, why are you here?"

"I have no idea." Beck appreciated the way Curtiss was positioning his questions to make his case.

Curtiss looked at Judge Savage.

"You've made your point, Mr. Curtiss," the judge said. "Now move on."

"No further questions, Your Honor."

"Very well. Next witness, Mr. Fahy."

Beck looked at the judge. That was it? Judge Savage, sensing his confusion, nodded to him and said softly, "You may step down and return to your seat."

Just like that, Beck's part of the performance was over. His adrenaline rush dissipated. He slowly rose from the witness chair and stepped gingerly down from his stage. His ankle gave way, and he stumbled slightly before recovering. It was okay. He had no audience.

The walk to the defendant's table seemed to last forever as he reviewed his performance in his head. He was quite pleased with himself.

Then he heard Fahy call out to the court, "The prosecution calls Mr. Casper Agee."

Beck sat in his chair next to Curtiss at the defense table and tried to refocus. Everything seemed to be swirling around while he was locked in place.

A bailiff led the aging Grand Cayman real estate agent through a side door. Agee eased into the witness chair and was sworn in. He stroked his bald head and wild fringe and looked toward Fahy, awaiting his questions. Beck remembered their encounter in Grand Cayman and thought it odd Fahy would bring this forgetful old man to Washington as a witness.

Fahy told Agee to identify himself for the record. Agee did and then explained how he met Beck in Grand Cayman a month ago when he visited his office and asked about real estate.

"What did you tell Mr. Rikki?"

"He asked about Mr. Bayard's property. I told him it was leased by Sunrise Marshall—no—Sunrise Mabel. No, that's not right. Excuse me. It was Sunrise Meridian. He said he and his wife were interested in renting the place on the ocean. I told him there was a long-term lease on the property, but he wanted to look into leasing it anyway, so I sent him to Mr. Kincaid—excuse me—Mr. Kindred, the attorney who handles the lease. Sorry, at my age the names sometimes slip through the cracks."

"What is Sunrise Meridian?"

"It's a development company on Cayman island. Bought a lot of property and sold a lot of it to Mr. Bayard."

"And you told Mr. Rikki that?"

"If I remember correctly, he already knew," continued Agee. "Mr. Rikki had looked at land records before we ever met. That's right. He asked about the oceanfront house, a condo, a shopping center where

Mr. Kindred's office is located and—what else—oh, some acreage at the other end of the island."

"A development owned by Mr. Bayard?"

"I believe so. That's right."

"Mr. Kindred's office. It's located in the shopping center owned by Senator Bayard?"

"Yes. Mr. Kindred was also the attorney for Mr. Bayard and Sunrise Meridian."

"How so?"

"I think he incorporated both. Oh, not Mr. Bayard. Mr. Kindred incorporated Mr. Bayard's company, Jersey Shore Ltd."

Fahy stepped back to his table to review his notes. He picked up a piece of paper.

"Mr. Fahy?" Judge Savage asked.

"One moment, if you please, Your Honor."

"We haven't got all day."

"Yes, Your Honor."

Beck watched Fahy. He couldn't make out what he was up to or why he had called Agee as a witness. Beck couldn't fathom what evidence Agee had that Fahy wanted so desperately that he would fly the old man nearly two thousand miles to Washington.

Fahy turned back and crossed the expansive courtroom to within five feet of Agee, this time with a piece of paper in his hand.

"Did you talk with anyone else about Mr. Bayard's property?"

"There was this guy. He said he was from the FBI. He had a lot of questions."

"Thank you, Mr. Agee. No further questions." Fahy quickly sat down.

Beck was surprised the FBI had been in Grand Cayman. He had suspected it after the murder, but not before.

Curtiss leaped to his feet. "Mr. Agee. You said you talked with an FBI agent. Is that correct?"

"Yes, it is."

"And this FBI agent talked to you about Senator Bayard's property?"

"That's right, he did."

"Did he mention the government was investigating Senator Bayard?"

"Well, as a matter of fact, he did. I thought the investigation was all about Mr. Oliver. You know, that Justice Department fella. But I later realized it was an investigation of Mr. Bayard. You see, Mr. Oliver and Mr. Kindred, the lawyer for everybody, are brothers."

"You're talking about Mr. Jackson Oliver of the US Justice Department?"

"I believe I am."

"And his brother handled all of Mr. Bayard's Grand Cayman real estate deals?"

"I do believe so. Yes."

"Did you and Mr. Rikki ever discuss Mr. Oliver?"

"I think so, but I'm not really sure. You see, I got Mr. Oliver and Mr. Bayard mixed up."

"But you did mention the FBI investigation to Mr. Rikki when the two of you talked?"

"I believe I did."

"So Mr. Rikki learned about the government's investigation of Senator Bayard from you? Is that correct?"

"Well, I do believe so. We discussed it."

Beck couldn't believe his ears. They hadn't discussed the FBI. Where was this guy coming from?

Curtiss faced the judge. "Your Honor, it's clear from this testimony that word of the investigation leaked out as part of an FBI investigation. There is nothing sinister here. My client got the information, not from a government employee, but from doing his job as a reporter and talking with a citizen of Grand Cayman island. In light of these facts, I would ask the court to dismiss the subpoena for Mr. Rikki's source."

Wow, thought Beck. Curtiss ain't so bad after all.

Judge Savage sat in silence. He looked at Fahy and back at Curtiss, then stared at Agee. Finally, he lowered his reading glasses from his forehead and glanced down at the paperwork in front of him. Savage sighed and shook his head.

This was taking forever, Beck thought.

"The court must agree with Mr. Curtiss," the judge finally said. "There is ample evidence from Mr. Agee's testimony to refute the government's assertion that someone employed by the Justice Department leaked information—classified or otherwise—to Mr. Rikki."

The judge paused again. Finally, he looked directly at Beck. "Mr. Rikki, you have my profound apology that you've been put through this judicial and media circus." Savage waved his arm in the air as he spoke, as if pointing to the reporters standing outside the courthouse. "The Justice Department should have had enough trust in its own employees, or at least have done some due diligence, before assuming one of its own would break the law and give information to you about an investigation. There is no evidence to prove the disclosure of the government investigation ever came from a Justice Department employee—an employee sworn to keep the status of such investigations privileged. Mr. Rikki, you are free to go. This hearing is adjourned."

Beck breathed an audible sigh and slumped in his chair. His long national nightmare was over. This was a better-than-sex moment—the feeling he got when he finally published a major investigative piece. Then he leaped to his feet and grabbed Curtiss's hand and shook it hard. He looked over his shoulder at Fahy, who busied himself filling his briefcase with papers, not looking Beck's way.

Nancy reached over from the bar from the visitors' section and slapped Beck on the back. "Way to go, champ." They eyed each other a moment longer than normal. It was an acknowledgment. Only three people knew the truth, and all stood in this room. Fahy had pulled it off, and Beck was elated.

Baker triumphantly nodded to him, the unlit brown cigarette in his hand gesturing congratulations.

"Excuse us for a moment," Curtiss said to Baker and Nancy. "I need to confer with my client." He grabbed Beck by the arm. "This way."

He pushed Beck through a doorway at the side of the courtroom and into an empty witness holding room. Then he closed the door, dropped his briefcase on the table with a deliberate thud, and turned to Beck. "Now, if I was a law professor—which I'm not—and I saw what I just witnessed in any moot courtroom in any law school in America— which this was not—you know what I'd do?"

"I haven't a clue," Beck replied.

"I'd flunk the goddamn prosecutor."

"Really?"

"Now how does a prosecutor with as much courtroom success as Mr. Fahy screw up a case so badly?"

"He did? I thought he was doing fine." Beck suddenly felt dread. Curtiss must be on to them.

"Fahy served up Agee on a silver fuckin' platter. It's as if he wanted to lose this case. If I didn't know better, I'd say that's exactly what he wanted. Now why do you think a prosecutor would do such a thing?"

"Beats me. Did he have a weak case? I don't know the law." Holy shit. He's figured out what just happened, thought Beck.

"I'm sure you don't. And it's a good thing too. Because if someone aided someone who intentionally lost this case, that would be obstruction of justice. You know what that is?"

"Not really."

"That's some real deep shit that person would be standing in. That would make one helluva story for the *Post-Examiner*. Know what I mean?"

"You've lost me." Beck was beginning to feel panicky.

"Have I?" Curtiss shook his head and smiled and looked down at the polished mahogany table. He raised his glance and looked directly at Beck. "Son, you stick to writing your stories. Let me handle the law."

He knows. Oh shit, he knows. Beck was too stunned to speak. He just looked at his lawyer.

Curtiss picked up his briefcase and snapped the clasps closed. "Jesus," he said under his breath. He whirled his heavy body and strode out the door without another word.

Beck stood alone in the small room. He wondered what Curtiss would do. He'd just won a major case—one that would headline the national news feed for the next twenty-four hours. He wouldn't take his suspicions to the judge, would he? No, Beck told himself. It would do his lawyer no good to tell the world his client had colluded with the prosecutor to win his case. And besides, what evidence did he have to prove it? It was only his suspicion. And this was Washington after all, where reality never really is how it appears to the public.

Outside the courthouse, the media madhouse resumed. Curtiss instantly switched into conquering hero persona and positioned himself in the middle of the media mob on the plaza, surrounded by dozens of cameramen, reporters with outstretched microphones, and print reporters with their digital recorders and low-tech notebooks.

As Beck stepped out of the courthouse door unnoticed, he spotted his former colleague Kerry Rabidan near the middle of the scrum, grilling Curtiss. Beck quietly watched the scene from afar. What a zoo, he thought. What a crazy life. Beck's sense of relief overwhelmed him, and he felt drained.

"Yes," said Curtiss, "it's obvious from the evidence that no Justice Department employee leaked the story to the *Post-Examiner*." He went on to explain how word of the investigation was inadvertently leaked through a third party.

"Wasn't this Jackson Oliver's case?" Rabidan shouted.

"Yes, but the judge saw fit to replace him with Mr. Daniel Fahy."

"Why was that?" she asked.

"You'll have to ask the judge. Not my decision."

"But he originally was supposed to prosecute the case, correct?"

"He was," Curtiss said. "But like I said, I would urge you to ask the judge for any specifics on why he was replaced by Mr. Fahy."

Curtiss knows exactly what he's doing, thought Beck. He just lit a fuse under Jackson Oliver.

"One at a time, please," Curtiss yelled to the reporters as they shouted over one another. "I'll answer all of your questions." As the man reveled in the media attention, Beck found it hard to believe only moments ago his lawyer had accused him of obstruction of justice. Of course, Curtiss would never come right out and ask him what he had done. He couldn't, Beck remembered, because if Beck affirmed any obstruction, Curtiss would be bound by his professional ethics to go to the judge.

His lawyer didn't want the whole truth. It would complicate his narrative, Beck realized. After all, his case wasn't about the truth. It was all about winning.

Beck looked back at Curtiss working the crowd. Everybody wanted to take credit for a win—any win—especially in this town. Curtiss was now the star. Andy Warhol was right about fame. This was his fifteen minutes, and old walrus face was going to take full advantage of it.

Beck slipped unseen around the corner of the building with Nancy and Baker. They waved down the first cab and escaped the headline-obsessed mob.

His emotional roller coaster was finally over. It was time he returned to his world—one that made sense to him and where he was the captain of his own ship. Tomorrow, he told himself. After a good night's sleep to recharge his batteries. He wanted to be at his best again. There were still too many unanswered questions about his original story that he needed to explore.

54

That afternoon, a few hours after Beck left the courthouse, Bayard stood in a Senate committee room and announced he would sacrifice his political career and voluntarily remove himself from the party ticket rather than put Senator Ford Patten's presidential campaign and his own party through the distraction of dealing with the frivolous accusations against him. It was time, he said, to put America back on the right track, and Ford Patten was the only man to do it.

Beck and the entire newsroom staff were glued to their computers and the many flat-screen monitors hanging from the newsroom ceiling, watching the live feed of Bayard's announcement.

"Nice going," said Tom Reed, the paper's religion writer.

Another reporter yelled from across the room, "Way to go."

A couple of reporters began to clap, and several walked up to Beck to shake his hand.

Baker walked out of his glass-enclosed office to survey the commotion in the newsroom. He grabbed a straight-backed visitor's chair next to a reporter's desk and climbed on it, towering over the newsroom.

"There will be no gloating. None. Not a word. Is that clear?" he barked. He scanned the scattered reporters who froze in silence. "This is a tragedy for the nation, but it also proves why we need a free and impartial press. We should all take great pride in what this newspaper has accomplished, but I'll cut your balls off if I see anyone gloating. And that goes for you too, ladies." He scanned the newsroom again. With a satisfied nod, he stepped down and walked back to his office. The news-room returned to its boisterous calm.

Beck repressed a grin, silently absorbing the accolades and feeling the pride of his accomplishment. He had actually forced a US sena-tor—a vice presidential candidate—to resign. He'd never had a story this big before.

Nancy crossed the large room over to Beck's desk and in a near-whis-per said, "Good going. I think some of the crew want to take a trip down the block."

He smiled. He and a half-dozen other reporters headed for their favorite watering hole around the corner from the *Post-Examiner* for a not-so-quiet celebration. As he crossed the street, he spied the man with the graying hair and goatee, the one who had bumped into him days ago. He approached in an unbuttoned, dirty black coat and again came toward him in the crosswalk.

"You," Beck said, stopping in the middle of the street. "You."

"Hello, Mr. Kemper," said the man as he passed.

Beck pivoted his way. "Who the fuck are you?"

The man turned. "Nobody. Pardon me," he said in a Hispanic accent. He tipped his battered fedora, turned away, and kept walking.

"What do you want from me?" Beck screamed at the man's back.

Everybody turned to look at Beck as the strange man continued to cross the street, not looking back.

Nancy looked at Beck. "What the hell was that?"

"He's after me."

"Jesus, Beck. It's just another crazy homeless person."

"You don't get it," he blurted out.

"Look, you've had a rough week. Come on. Let's celebrate your victory."

"You don't get it," he said again. "I'm being watched."

She grabbed his arm, pulling him through the crosswalk. "You just need a drink," Nancy said. His colleagues instinctively gathered around him like a protective shield but said nothing. Beck looked again for the stranger who had disappeared into the crowd on the other side of the street.

"I'm serious. Someone has been following me," Beck said.

"Let's talk about it inside." She gripped his arm tightly, and Beck did not resist as she pushed him forward out of the street.

Nancy sat next to Beck at the bar and told the others they would meet them at the table in a few minutes. He could tell she was studying him.

"Do you really feel you're in danger here in DC?"

"You don't understand," he said. "I'm being followed. I've seen that guy before on the street." Beck then explained how he had confronted the man before.

"He called you Mr. Kemper. What's that supposed to mean?"

Beck paused and looked at her. He knew he could trust Nancy to keep things between them. So he told her about traveling to Cayman with Geneva.

"That would explain that old man's comment in court about your wife," Nancy said.

"Things got a little mixed up down there," Beck conceded.

"But why would anyone be following you now?"

"Why do you think?"

"Oh come on, Beck. That's Hollywood. This is Washington. Nobody spies on reporters here. The backlash would be too great. We've sorta got immunity, a protective shield in that department."

"I'd like to think you're right, but after my place was bugged and after running into this guy twice and seeing him on the street—something is going on."

After two hours of drinking, they stumbled back to the office. When they reached the newsroom, Nancy walked directly to Baker's office. A few minutes later, she stepped back into the newsroom and immediately walked over to Beck's desk.

"We'll have your condo swept again tomorrow," she said. "And the boss wants you to take a few days off."

"Really?" Beck shook his head in disgust. Oh great, he thought, they're humoring him, and they think he's nuts.

55

"I told you that you'd be sleeping in your own bed tonight," Geneva said. She had arrived at Beck's condo uninvited with a bag of groceries for a salad and a bottle of her favorite Malbec. She needed some time with him.

"I admit I was worried. My attorney pulled it off."

"I have something special for you."

"Oh?"

"I hope you haven't made plans for the weekend because I've rented a cabin in the mountains for us. My car is packed. I just need you to fill an overnight bag, and we're off."

"Your timing couldn't be better. My boss told me to take a few days off. I think I could use it. Sure we couldn't take longer than the weekend?"

If only he knew, she thought. "Sorry, I've got a busy week next week. I'd like to make the most out of the time we have."

AFTER A TWO-HOUR RIDE, Beck and Geneva sat in front of a large stone fireplace, with orange flames hugging split oak logs. The fire stole the chill from the mountain air. The cabin was little more than one large room that combined the kitchen, bedroom, and living area. The only other room was a spa, which consisted of a bathroom with a walk-in shower, a six-foot hot tub, and a walk-in closet. It was a couple's cabin to be sure, thought Geneva.

A bottle of red wine breathed deeply on the dinged copper kitchen countertop, cozying up to two tall stemmed glasses standing at the ready. Beck filled them, and they sank into the couch. Their eyes locked onto the flames.

Geneva nestled her head on his shoulder, and he wrapped his arm around her. She could tell from his body language that he was physically and emotionally spent. Geneva raised her head only to sip the wine and to kiss him and then returned to the warmth of his body.

Later, she prepared a salad of greens, spinach, olives, tomatoes, avocados, and green onions, mixed with an explosion of exotic spices. It was a recipe, she told him, she had learned while living in Europe. Afterward, Beck washed their plates and glasses while Geneva packed water bottles and a bottle of merlot into a green rucksack for tomorrow. Then they retired to the bed and made love slowly and rhythmically, and then quickly fell asleep.

The next afternoon the temperature was cool as they hiked the mountain trail. A cloudless sky provided clear views of the Shenandoah Valley below. They paused at every clearing to gaze at the vista. After a couple of hours of steady uphill climbing, they sat on a rock formation to rest and opened the wine.

Plastic cups in hand, they sat in silence and watched a single-engine white Cessna fly through a mountain pass below them and above the valley farm fields about a mile away. The plane headed west toward the mountain range on the other side of the valley. Slowly, it turned into a pinprick in the vast blue sky as it rode the air thermals, dodging puffy clouds and escaping beyond the next ridge.

"That's liberating," Geneva said, nodding toward the plane.

"What's *this*?" Beck asked, raising his plastic cup.

She nuzzled her face into his chest as she put her arm around him. "This is my security, my comfort."

He looked down at her. "Thank you. I guess."

Geneva pushed back silently, looking out over the valley, and grabbed his hand and squeezed it. Beck was a considerate man, a kind man, she thought. Yet he played some of the toughest political hardball in all of Washington. Politicians in both parties—conservatives and liberals alike—feared his byline. Could idealism really make him blind to her deception? She felt twinges of guilt. She pulled him to her and kissed him. She needed to absorb every aspect of this moment. She knew it must come to an end, but until then, she would savor every minute.

THAT EVENING, THEY DROVE DOWN THE mountain seeking comfort food at a small diner in the village they had passed through on the way to their cabin. Calling it a village was a polite misnomer for a town with no obvious zoning and glaring neon signs. Rather, a hodgepodge of rundown shops, convenience stores, fast-food joints, and gasoline stations on either side of a two-lane highway with a double yellow line begged for the attention of those passing through on their way to Pennsylvania's ski resorts.

The night was cool, and Geneva felt a slight chill and grabbed her sweater from the backseat of the car. The gray and wet of winter, which she knew brought potholes and loose gravel to the local streets each year, had yet to descend on the valley.

Bubbas and sturdy women, stuffed into tight sweaters spilling over the tops of their jeans, stopped to talk to friends on the sidewalk. A group of anorexic teenage girls, whose appearance in tight jeans, padded bras, low-cut attire, and raccoon-eyed mascara rendered an image leaning toward hookers rather than high schoolers, crowded a street corner. They smoked cigarettes, and Geneva heard them talking as they walked by about who wore what at Friday night's homecoming football game.

None of them fit into Geneva's high-octane existence in Washington where daily workouts, salon visits, and Botox injections kept women in fighting form to do battle in their image-conscious bubble of influence.

As they entered, she looked around the crowded restaurant at the other diners. Young people, middle-aged couples, two old men drinking coffee, and a couple of truck drivers in uniforms with their names embroidered over their right breast—all people who were unaffected by what she and Beck did for a living.

She could tell from Beck's expression as they waited to be served, he too was feeling it. "Different world, isn't it?" she said.

"Yeah. It's like once you're outside the DC Beltway sphere of influence, my work probably doesn't mean much to most people. You think about it, and you realize just what a small stage we play on. It's like we're nobody here. There's probably not one person here who knows about—or cares about—yesterday's court case or that a vice presidential candidate resigned."

It was obvious to Geneva that Beck was feeling unsure of himself, even after a major victory. "Hey, stud," she said to him, "you did well this week. You not only won your case, you took down a vice presidential candidate. You should be proud of what you do."

Beck gave a slight grin but said nothing. He looked into her eyes and she returned the gaze. It was killing her not to tell him the truth. She would wait until tomorrow. One more night, she told herself.

When they returned to the cabin, the night turned into the most passionate of their relationship. Geneva aggressively came back to him again and again, her appetite insatiable. For a while, she could tell Beck must have thought he had died and gone to heaven. And she wouldn't let up, sending him to heaven over and over again. They lasted for hours. Taking breaks and then starting all again. She did not stop until he finally said enough. Heaven could wait.

It was better than the hell she feared she was about to put him through. They lay exhausted, their bodies covered in sweat. Beck fell asleep holding her in his arms. She looked up at the glow of the fireplace embers bouncing around the wood beams in the ceiling. She couldn't sleep.

56

The next morning, Beck ventured down the mountain early and found the *Post-Examiner,* the *News-Times*, and the Winchester, Virginia, newspaper. He was hoping to find a *New York Times* but had no luck. Geneva had two cups of special blend coffee waiting when he returned. The fresh aroma of hazelnut mixed with the distinct smell of oak logs burning in the fireplace filled the room as they settled under the covers for some leisurely reading.

This was their first Sunday morning together in bed reading the newspaper, and Beck was enjoying it. He could see himself with Geneva doing this on a regular basis. Beck scanned the front pages. Patten was scheduled to announce a new running mate tomorrow. Bayard announced he would not give up his Senate seat. Kerry Rabidan's front-page story in the *News-Times* quoted Bayard saying he was not resigning from the Senate but had an obligation to fulfill his term. Funny, Beck thought. When did Kerry start covering politics?

He scanned further. There was nothing about Fahy's boss Jackson Oliver. What would ever come of that?

Geneva fried up some corned beef hash and eggs for Beck in a cast-iron skillet. She was quiet during their late morning breakfast, barely taking a bite of her English muffin. He knew they had to leave in a few hours. The last day of any vacation—even one this short—always made him sad. He couldn't get it out of his mind that it was ending and he was returning to his daily routine. Yet it was a routine he loved. Note to self: he needed longer vacations.

They sipped their mugs of coffee in silence.

"Beck, I have some bad news," Geneva said finally.

"Oh?"

"We can't see each other anymore."

"What?" He nearly dropped his cup on the table, spilling his coffee.

"Harv is going to accept Ford Patten's offer to replace David Bayard on the party ticket. I'll be surrounded by Secret Service twenty-four hours a day starting tomorrow. It will be impossible for us to be together."

"Shit. Your husband? Running for vice president? Do you have to do this?"

"Right now, I have no choice."

"Can Patten do that?"

"It's already been done. It will be announced tomorrow. I'm sorry. I'm so, so sorry."

Beck felt sick to his stomach. "It will only be a few weeks, right?"

"Depends. If he wins, I will be surrounded by Secret Service indefinitely."

"What happens to us?"

"I don't know. I don't know how long this will go on. I need your understanding right now. Please. I have no control over this."

Beck groaned. It was the only sound he could make. It was like being kicked in the stomach. He was struggling to catch his breath.

"So this weekend was?"

"To say good-bye. Yes."

"You've got to do something. What do we mean to each other?"

"I'm sorry, Beck. I can't walk away from Harv right now. It would be too awkward and too public. He needs me right now."

"What about me?" Beck tried to look her in the eye, but she glanced away.

"You know what I mean."

"No, I don't. I need you. I . . . want you."

"I can't right now. Maybe at some point later on we can get together."

"Maybe? At some point later on?"

"Look. This is just as difficult for me as it is for you. I was hoping for some understanding." She looked away.

"I'm sorry. I don't understand." Beck could not hide the anger in his voice, and he could tell Geneva was agitated too, but he didn't care. She'd just ended their relationship, and it hurt like hell.

A few hours later as they left the cabin, fog began to envelop the mountain. The weather darkened, and they rode back to Washington in silence. Beck kept his foot pressed firmly on the gas, trying to stay ahead of an oncoming storm.

AT TEN O'CLOCK THE NEXT MORNING, Ford Patten stepped up to the podium on a small stage in the packed ballroom of the National Press Club to introduce his old friend, Senator Michael Harvey, as his choice for the next vice president of the United States. Beck watched it live on one of the newsroom monitors. Geneva stood by Harvey's side during the announcement wearing a dark suit and gold necklace. Beck thought she looked fabulous. He thought about their weekend together and how perfect it was until the very end. He got that sick feeling in his stomach again.

After the announcement, Beck listened to the television commentators say Patten had made a brilliant choice in choosing Harvey for his vice president. At age sixty-six Harvey would never run for the presidency, and it was questionable if he would run for reelection for vice president in four years. Patten had avoided giving anyone in the party a clear advantage in the fight for a future party leadership role. It was a great strategy to keep peace in the party, they said.

Beck groaned as he listened. That meant if Patten won, which at the moment appeared likely, he'd have to wait at least four years for Geneva. The odds of them getting back together, he realized, were now very slim.

The next day, Beck scanned stories in the *Post-Examiner* and the *News-Times* profiling Harvey's career and talking about his twenty-year marriage to a woman nearly twenty-five years his junior. The *Post-Examiner* said Geneva would bring sex appeal to an otherwise colorless

Republican administration. She was described as a vivacious, daring, and handsome woman. The paper included photos of her in low-cut evening gowns at social events and descriptions of Harvey and Geneva as one of Washington's glamour couples.

The stories made Beck long for her even more. He told himself to stop and move on, but he couldn't.

Kerry Rabidan's story in the *News-Times* not only said Geneva gave sex to the city, but it outlined her career on Capitol Hill and as a lobbyist for Serodynne. Rabidan mentioned nothing about Geneva's latest Pentagon contract.

My god, thought Beck. Kerry Rabidan is covering everything these days. Maybe she's shifted to the political beat. He should call her and congratulate her.

But first he needed a distraction from his tattered love life. He would get back on his Jackson Oliver story. With the court case and his weekend with Geneva, he had left it alone for too long. He wondered if Rabidan was working on something, especially since she was among the media mob grilling Curtiss after his court case. She was too good to let that one go. He needed to get busy before she beat him to his own story.

BACK IN THEIR PENNSYLVANIA AVENUE penthouse, Geneva privately told Harv she would stay with him through the election and its aftermath, but then she was leaving. Out of sight of the rest of the world, she and Harv would begin to make arrangements for a divorce as soon as the election was over—win or lose. She told him she would not campaign and she would not move into the vice presidential residence at the Naval Observatory on Massachusetts Avenue if he won, but would stay in their condominium, guarded twenty-four hours a day by the Secret Service until their divorce was final and she could move out.

After she left Beck on Sunday, she immediately called Keith to warn him of what was coming. Keith nearly freaked out over the phone, worried about the public scrutiny. But she explained she would be out of this mess at the latest sometime shortly after the inauguration. He was to continue to cash in their options and move the money to make it disappear.

"Take your time. We can't see each other for a while, and it may be difficult for me to call you. And whatever you do, don't call me," she warned. "I can't chance us slipping up in front of the Secret Service."

Keith agreed, and her words seemed to calm him. But Geneva felt uncomfortable. She now had no choice but to put her complete trust and her financial future in Keith's hands. So far, he had done a good job, but only because she held a tight leash on him and their money. Now he would be on his own, and she worried if he would follow through without her constant prodding and stroking. She imagined the presidential campaign completely destroying her future. She just couldn't let that happen.

57

"What have you done for me lately?"

Nancy startled Beck from his thoughts. Seated at his desk with his feet propped up on three banker's boxes filled with files on the Bayard story, he'd been thinking about Geneva when he heard his editor's familiar refrain.

He turned to her and sipped his cold coffee. "I thought I'd give you the joy of my absence and take a little time off."

"Baker told me the exterminator checked out your condo again, and you're still bug free. Kinda nice the newspaper offers free extermination services."

"I was going to check and see if Cunningham offered free interior design to go with it. Like a package deal, you know. My place could use a facelift."

"And maybe a low-cost mortgage as well."

"Hadn't thought of that one. I'll ask personnel if they can set it up."

"If your condo's anything like your work space here, you'll need a bulldozer to redecorate."

"Yeah, but then I wouldn't have any use for that mortgage."

"You can't have it all."

"I keep trying."

"Try to make your way to the newsroom by Election Day. We need your services. You're responsible for this mess, you know."

Beck smiled. He wanted so much to gloat, but it wasn't good form, especially after Baker's speech to the newsroom. "I couldn't have done it without Senator Bayard's help."

"I'd say he was essential." Nancy paused with her hands on her hips. "Seriously. Be back here on election eve. They want you to make the rounds of the news channels and promote the paper."

Beck realized he was some kind of company prop, and he didn't like it. "You're not kidding."

"Not about that."

"Since when did I become the poster boy?"

"Since you ousted a vice presidential candidate. You're big shit right now."

"Then you should treat me like it."

"Like shit? I already do." Nancy surveyed his desk. "Jeez, how do you function in such chaos?"

Beck caught her glance and looked at his work space. "Okay. Okay. I'll find a twenty-gallon trash can and a shovel somewhere."

His desk was like a layered wedding cake. Files in manila folders balanced precariously atop several days' newspapers, atop month-old magazines, atop photocopies of who-knows-what. All of this teetered on a base of three hardback books Beck thought he remembered checking out from the newspaper morgue. Was it a year ago? Maybe she was right. It may be time for some spring cleaning in the middle of fall.

"And would you mind taking your feet off your boxes and out of the aisle? Some reporters actually work around here and use that aisle to walk to their editor's desk, unlike a certain reporter I know who forces his editor to make house calls."

Beck tried to hold back a grin. "Anything for you, boss."

Nancy shook her head and headed back to her desk at the far side of the newsroom. Beck looked at the mess again, wondering where he would begin, and then, thankfully, his phone rang, interrupting the thought.

"I pitched your publisher this morning to feel him out," his agent Judith Cover said. "We had a long discussion. You interested in doing a book about Bayard? I got assurances of a six-figure advance if you can write up a proposal this weekend. What say you?"

Beck perked up. "What say me? Me say you good agent. Me say yes."

"I thought you might. Told him I'd have it to him Monday by close of business."

"Of course me agent presumes a great deal."

"Your agent assumes you write more smoothly than you speak. Your agent assured your publisher of such."

Hot damn, thought Beck. Another big payday. And he could use his poster boy status on election night to promote his next book. Beck sat up in his chair and dropped his legs from the file boxes blocking the aisle. He saw Nancy on the other side of the newsroom nodding in approval, thinking he improved his posture on her account. He knew exactly what he needed to do—haul all this crap home and get it organized. He had a book proposal to write. And hell, he'd make his editor happy too.

"Monday morning. Just for you, Judith."

He hung up and checked the boxes. He also grabbed a pile off his desk and dumped it in the nearest half-filled box. In all, there were four boxes jammed with position papers, legal documents, land records, pages of campaign disclosures and financial records, and old clippings of stories that had never been scanned into the newspaper's computer system. The *Post-Examiner* could do without them for the weekend.

Besides, it probably would have taken him months to return them to their proper owner. Beck checked his desk drawer and tossed in a couple of reporters' notebooks. He would sort it all out at home, with Red's help, and be ready for battle.

AFTER LUGGING THE HEAVY BOXES to his car and telling Nancy he was checking out for the day, Beck went home. He stacked the boxes on the floor and on his coffee table, then plopped his body on the couch. He took a few breaths. He was in worse shape than he thought. He hadn't gone running for weeks—ever since this entire affair began.

He made a note. Tomorrow, jog a couple of miles. Get your wind back.

Beck reached in the first box and grabbed some file folders. In disarray, they spilled out onto the table and floor.

He tried to shove the coffee table aside with his knee, but it wouldn't budge. It was one of those heavy models with sturdy oak legs. He bought it because he liked sitting on his couch and propping his feet up, frequently forgetting to take off his shoes. The only thing he told the salesman who sold it to him was he needed something sturdy.

Beck knew he'd have to stand up to shove it aside. Instead, he got down on his knees and found documents strewn on his oriental rug under the coffee table. Shit, he thought, I've got a mess here. It would take him forever to organize this stuff.

He glanced at the pages, trying to put them in some semblance of order and realized the scattered pages were the busy work he had given Geneva while in the courthouse in Grand Cayman. He'd told her to make copies of any building lot sales in Bayard's island development, and apparently she'd found some.

Two words—Sunrise Meridian—jumped off the first page of one of the deeds of trust she had copied. That's odd, he thought. What was Sunrise Meridian doing financing the sale of one of Bayard's lots to someone else? He read a couple of sentences. Then a few more. His antenna went up.

According to the document in his hand, Sunrise Meridian had financed the sale of Bayard's building lots to other buyers. But why? One thing Grand Cayman had was plenty of banks and financial services companies.

"Red." He turned to his chair. "Why would Lamurr's subsidiary finance Senator Bayard's land sales in his development when any bank or mortgage company on the island would be more than willing? That makes no sense. There's nothing to hide here. Unless . . ."

He read on.

Decker Development. The name appeared not on one deed, but two. Geneva had neatly stapled them together.

The first document showed Decker Development, a Grand Cayman corporation, purchasing lot fifty-one in Bayard's development last November. The next document showed it selling the same lot the following March. It must have made a hell of a profit to unload so soon, Beck thought.

He thumbed through the pages farther. "Red, there's something wrong here. This Cayman company sold the lot for the same price it purchased it for four months earlier. With closing costs and real estate taxes, the company actually lost money on the entire transaction. What gives?"

He picked up another stapled set of deeds. Graver Partnership purchased a lot in June and sold it the following January. Again, for the same price. He kept reading. There were more than two dozen deals Geneva had copied and he had filed away. And funny, not a single lot was purchased by an individual. Instead, they were all partnerships and corporations—legal entities.

He began to understand what was right in front of him and grew excited.

"Guess what, Red. Our old friend Roger Kindred did all of the paperwork. I think we've got a pattern here. Kindred draws up the documents, and Sunrise Meridian finances the sales. I bet if I go back to Cayman, I'll find that Kindred created each of the buyers that bought a building lot. I'll bet they're shell companies."

He leaned forward over his coffee table. "Red, I think I've stumbled onto something. I was wrong. Bayard still has something to hide."

Beck felt the familiar surge of adrenaline. He had a spark of an idea, a clue to another story—possibly bigger than his first.

"Red, I told you Jen was special. I give her busy work, and she was so diligent, she found the key to this whole mess. Bayard is just a player, or maybe he's just a pawn on a much bigger stage." Beck paused, staring at the paperwork in front of him. It started to make sense. "I think I may have played right into their hands. But whose, exactly? If this is what I think it is, then we are heading down a whole different path."

The book proposal would have to wait. He needed to return to Grand Cayman immediately. He got on the phone. "Judith, I just need another week. I've come across something that is so big it could become the basis of my book instead of Bayard."

"What are you talking about?" she asked.

"I think Bayard may be the tip of the iceberg. I think the land deals are more than just payoffs for Bayard. I believe the senator or someone else used phony corporations to cover up a slew of fraudulent transactions."

"Slow down, Beck. You're making no sense. Now start at the beginning."

Beck didn't realize he was talking so fast. "They are laundering hundreds of thousands of dollars."

"Who is 'they'?"

"That's what I have to find out. I also need to find out where the money's going."

"I need more than that to go to your publisher. I'm still confused. You don't know where the money's coming from, and you don't know where it's going. How can I persuade your publisher to hold off on that tiny bit of information?"

"You've got to figure that one out."

"I need more, Beck. Your publisher's set us a tight schedule. He wants the book out in the spring. That's why he needs the book proposal by Monday."

Beck thought a minute. He had to have more time. He also had grown paranoid about talking over the phone in his condo. But Nancy had just assured his place was clean. "Judith, what if I can prove that millions in illegal drug cartel money was being laundered into US banks through fraudulent land deals to fund American political campaigns?"

"I'd say I'd have a bidding war among several publishers for that book. But can you prove it?"

"It's only speculation right now. I've got to go back to Grand Cayman to prove it."

"Okay. I'll see what I can do."

Beck hung up and immediately called Nancy and told her he was heading back to the Caribbean.

"What do you mean Bayard is out of the picture?" she asked. "What the hell are you talking about?"

"I think this is much bigger than Bayard. And if I'm right, I need to move now before the election."

"The election is only a few weeks away. Why do you do this to me? I was perfectly content with Bayard's meltdown. Now you want to blow up the rest of Washington."

Beck could hear both frustration and excitement in Nancy's voice. "Do you ever give up?" she asked. "The best thing about you is you always make me sweat a story right down to the wire. The worst thing about you . . . well . . . you get my point. You haven't got much time. Get moving—and keep me in the loop."

58

The Cash Cow's pilot was pissed. He didn't know his passenger's name, and he didn't know why he was out here in the middle of the ocean in a fishing boat, a good five miles off the coast of Grand Cayman. He knew his passenger as only the gardener—a wanton killer who he'd watched back at the jungle airport viciously swing a machete to clear not only brush, but also some poor sucker's mind.

The memory chilled him. He'd heard too many whispered tales from men around him, indiscreetly slurred after several shots of tequila. It wasn't like this gardener fellow lusted for the kill. It was worse. He was indifferent—a true psychopath dispassionately killing on command. It appeared the gardener cared only about one thing—his stupid plants. He would cut off a man's head without thinking, yet he'd nurse a plant back to life. What was with that? It made no sense to the pilot. It was a damned good thing they were on the same side.

Still, having a murderer on board made him uneasy. And that stare—that wild-looking eye. It just made the goon look more ominous. He was supposed to drop off the gardener at the Grand Cayman airport and return to Venezuela, just like he did a month or so ago. But at the last minute, the boss had told him to stay over a few days while the gardener attended to some unspecified business—something about tying up some loose ends.

He'd heard that one before. It was always "unspecified business." Whatever. His job was simple. Don't ask. Don't tell. It was his pilot's creed for survival. It had done well by him. He was making more money than ever keeping his mouth shut, and he figured he could retire to his cabin in the mountains in another year. No more ferrying drug money or drug lords—or whatever their dirty business was. He would retire at last. He'd seen a lot, perhaps too much, so it was probably a good idea to get out soon.

Word had spread quickly through the organization about the last time he'd dropped off this creep in Cayman. Apparently he'd killed the wrong person—some innocent couple in a hotel. How dumb was that? The pilot couldn't imagine killing two perfectly innocent people. Oh sure, some have it coming. He'd heard horror stories. And in this business, sometimes it's just business. But to fuck up so badly and to not give a damn. Collateral damage. That's what they called it.

The boss was more upset about it than this guy. Yet knowing the boss, he was probably more upset things didn't go as planned than about killing an innocent couple. Yeah, it was time to get out, to retire and get away from these fruitcakes.

But first he had to put up with this inconvenience. He was playing offshore chauffeur on a fishing boat to this malicious weirdo. He wasn't quite sure how he had gotten roped into this one. But as always, it came from the top. Just because he could captain a small jet didn't mean he could pilot a twenty-eight-foot boat. At least the boat had GPS so he could find his way back—if this guy ever stopped attempting to fish.

Attempting. That was a good description. The gardener hadn't caught a thing, and it was pretty damned obvious he'd never been deep-sea fishing before. But then what did a pilot know? He was more comfortable thirty thousand feet above sea level rather than three thousand leagues below.

The gardener sat in a fishing chair at the back of the boat, his seat belt undone and his big pole pulling his line through the water as the pilot churned the boat forward, glancing back every so often to watch, well, not much at all.

Just then, the gardener yelled. He'd hooked something—probably an old fisherman's boot or some flotsam from another boat. The pilot turned again to see a taut fishing line skimming across the small waves. A giant fish leaped out of the water about thirty yards from the boat. The gardener grunted and leaned forward, trying to reel in his line.

He turned to the pilot. "Come here. I can't hold it."

"What?" the pilot yelled back over the engine roar.

The gardener motioned for him to come closer.

The pilot slowed the boat, shifting too quickly into neutral, and the wake instantly rocked the craft, water splashing over the stern where the gardener sat on the cushy seat. The pilot grabbed a railing for balance. His inexperience was showing. As the motor rumbled on, he finally walked gingerly to the stern trying to keep his balance while the boat bobbed atop the waves.

"Here, I can't hold it," the gardener yelled in broken English with a heavy accent. "Bad back."

There was a pause. The pilot looked at the gardener, now covered in sweat or was it salt water? What the hell was he supposed to do with this fishing pole?

The gardener shoved it in his hand, and he felt an immediate tug. He grasped the pole tightly with his second hand, fearful it would slip into the water and be lost forever.

He turned to the sea. Then he tried to play the fish. He tugged on the line, and it tugged back again. The fish, whatever it was, was powerful. This was not going to be easy. The fish jumped again. It was large, but he couldn't make out what it was—as if he knew anything about fishing.

"Beer?" the gardener asked.

"Down below." The pilot glanced back to see the gardener disappear into the cabin. He then turned to the fish and began to tug again. Slowly, he began to reel it in. He'd never done this before. He'd only watched deep-sea fishing on TV. He pulled hard and then leaned forward and reeled in the slack in the line.

He started to get a feel for it. The fish ran about twenty yards to the side of the boat, and he stepped around to avoid getting wrapped up in his line. He was going to win this battle.

He caught a glimpse of the gardener stepping onto the deck and taking a swig of water from a plastic bottle. He thought he had asked for beer. He reeled in some more line.

"Hey, you're pretty good," said the gardener.

Perhaps the guy wasn't all bad, thought the pilot. Like him, the gardener had a job to do. It was just business after all—at least he'd like to think of it that way. He turned to the Gardener.

"Thank—" The words froze in his mouth. The gardener held a .45-magnum pistol about a foot from his face. The barrel was huge and black. "What the—"

He heard the blast, or at least part of it before everything turned black. He felt his face crack open in horrific pain as he realized he was the unspecified business. For an instant, his head was on fire. And then it wasn't.

59

Over a breakfast of eggs and corned beef hash the next morning in a Fort Myers Beach hotel, Beck sat in front of his copy of *USA Today*. He had five hours to kill before his flight to Grand Cayman. He'd left Washington so abruptly; he'd been unable to reserve an earlier connecting flight. Between sips of coffee and the day's news, he occasionally looked through the shade of the wide outdoor patio at the placid sun-drenched Gulf of Mexico and the glaring white sand beach that separated him from its quiet slap of repetitive humble swells.

"Excuse me," came a voice from behind page 2A.

Beck lowered his paper and looked at a very tall, muscular man with a salt-and-pepper goatee.

"May I bother you for a moment?" He was dressed in an expensive navy-blue pinstripe suit and a neatly folded red silk handkerchief peeked from the breast pocket. A bit odd for the beach, thought Beck. The stranger was broad-shouldered with perfect posture, and he wore a crisp white button-down dress shirt with no tie. His flecked gray hair flowed over his collar and was swept back from his forehead.

"I've seen you before," said Beck very slowly. "Who the hell are you?"

"Someone who wants to chat about Mrs. Rikki. Or was it Mr. Kemper?" The stranger smiled, showing off his perfect teeth. "May I?" The man gestured to the chair across the table.

Beck nodded. The man eased into the seat. Beck folded his newspaper on the table and gave him his full attention.

"Pardon me if I don't introduce myself. It's probably better that way. I'd like to talk to you about your intentions."

The stranger's Hispanic lilt and perfectly groomed goatee matched his regal bearing. This man didn't seem to fit the stereotype of a criminal, yet he had been following him for weeks, or so Beck thought.

"I can see you're puzzled."

"Yeah. You're the crosswalk guy. You've been following me all over DC. Who the hell are you?" Beck sipped his coffee, his eyes at full attention.

"Let's just say I have connections who have an interest in your fine work. Your investigation of Senator Bayard was right on point, as far as it went. But we believe you may again be embarking on an investigation."

Beck felt a chill. They knew. "What makes you believe that?" His stomach was churning, but he tried to keep his voice matter-of-fact calm.

"You see, I work for people who have been watching you closely— ever since you landed in Grand Cayman, and the moment you talked to that Texan who lives next to Senator Bayard's waterfront villa."

"Was he tied to Bayard?"

"No, just the opposite. We paid him to keep tabs on the senator. We try to stay one step ahead of Bayard's people most of the time."

"The guy in the white straw hat who followed me in Cayman?"

"One of theirs."

"Who are they? Who the hell are you?" Beck's head was spinning.

"Let's just say I used to be in your business. Sort of. I investigate and monitor things for some powerful people who have a great interest in you. You see, there is the permanent campaign infrastructure in the United States, and then there is the political underground known as political intelligence. That's where I fit in. We keep tabs on what's going on. We monitor situations, and yours became a situation we needed to monitor."

"So you're Democrats spying on Republicans? Or are you Republicans spying on Republicans?" In the shade of the covered porch, Beck looked for some tell in the stranger's expressive dark eyes, a clue as to who this guy really was.

Nothing.

"Does it matter? Both sides are in the same business. We do what we need to do to maintain power and democracy in America. Political power is about getting what you want. Otherwise, why would you need all of those lobbyists throwing money at elected officials?"

"So how did I come up short?" Beck continued to look for any signs that would give him a hint. The man's skin was smooth and tanned and lacked wrinkles to match the graying hair. Brown chest hair peeked up from his open collar. Who was this guy really?

"I'm not sure you did come up short. You got everything right—as far as it went. However, you needed to dig deeper to get to the bigger story. I believe you discovered the missing link yesterday."

Beck couldn't believe it. They knew everything he was doing. "How did you know that? How do you know what I was doing in my living room yesterday?"

"Who is Red?"

"You've bugged my condo again. What all have you heard?"

"Since 9/11, Washington has become one of the most secure cities in the world. Probably only London has more cameras and recording devices than our nation's capital. When people of power want to find out something about a private individual, there really is no one to stop them."

"You bugged my condo." Beck's gut turned from fear to anger.

"Yesterday, you figured out the true meaning of the land deals, didn't you?"

"You bugged my condo."

"Okay. Yes."

"When?"

"Does it matter?"

"It does to me."

"Yesterday, you finally figured out what was behind the land deals." The stranger paused, waiting for Beck to speak.

"It's a giant money laundering machine. It's a lot bigger than Senator Bayard. Large land deals churned over and over. Money changing hands. A lot of cash is being funneled into somewhere, and I think I know exactly where."

"Just like Watergate back in the 1970s. You follow the money."

"That kind of cash has gotta be drug money," Beck said. "Mexican? South American? That's the question. I don't think it will be hard to figure out or follow."

"You're sharper than we gave you credit for, which is why I'm here this morning instead of bumping into you on the street in Washington. You see, the land development project in Grand Cayman—if you want to describe some acreage and a few signs as a land development—wasn't anything of the sort, as you have figured out."

"Money laundering. I get it. South American?"

"Precisely. Building lots are bought and sold, over and over again, to shell entities, and each time they're given a different corporate name. The sales, which are perfectly legal, generate the necessary paperwork to bring cold hard cash into the international banking system in Grand Cayman without being questioned. It's South American drug money made socially acceptable."

The waitress approached and offered them coffee. Beck took a refill. "It made no sense that someone would buy a building lot and resell it six months later for no profit," he said. "Actually, by my calculation, they took a small loss."

"Precisely. They got a little sloppy there. Who is Red? We saw no one coming or going from your condo."

"Even I have my secrets. I'm not the only one who knows what I know, but there are some things you will never know." Beck stared at the silk handkerchief in the stranger's breast pocket. "Whose campaign coffers are the recipients of all of this drug cash? Your pin-striped friends?"

"You are quite perceptive." The man glanced down at his suit and sighed. He raised a thick eyebrow and continued. "Jackson Oliver's half brother, Roger Kindred, put the scheme together, and Oliver brought the senator in years ago to get a piece of the action. The brother continually incorporates shell companies and partnerships to buy the lots. No one checks the background of the owners because Kindred pays all of their corporate and real estate taxes promptly. The lots are churned constantly, and because expensive land sales are the excuse for the large bank deposits, nobody even questions them. Rather ingenious, don't you think?"

Beck's mind was racing. Why was this stranger telling him all of this? He smiled. "I have to give it to you. But sooner or later, even the Grand Cayman officials will get suspicious about all of those lot sales and not a single home being built."

"Precisely. There are already three permits to begin building houses. It will go slowly, and many years from now, when the development is built out entirely, it will eventually be sold off to real buyers. They will simply move the operation to another offshore location."

"How many operations already exist?"

"That's a good question."

"It's so efficient," said Beck, flattering the stranger, hoping to encourage him to continue. "Each bank deposit Kindred makes from a lot sale, while substantial, is routine enough not to attract anyone's attention. In a year's time, you've deposited tens of millions of dollars. And Bayard knew?"

"Of course. But not for a while. You see, Bayard had his own thing going with Lamurr Technologies, and he hired Kindred to do the legal work. He had no idea Kindred was Oliver's half brother. Kindred watched Bayard's dealings but did nothing for the first year. After he made inquiries, he figured out the true source of the senator's money. Kindred knew then that he—forgive the pun—had a 'kindred spirit' in Bayard."

Beck winced at the bad pun as he considered what motivated this stranger to talk so freely.

The stranger continued. "Kindred told his brother. Jackson Oliver immediately saw the political possibilities and pulled Bayard into the drug money operation. That's why Bayard, who came late to the presidential contest, could so quickly gear up and have a formidable campaign war chest. Bayard thought big, far beyond his own campaign. He envisioned a permanent infrastructure for a drug money machine to finance Republican political efforts of all types throughout the US."

"Jesus. The American political system, bought and paid for by South American drug lords."

"Is it any different than a political system bought by special interests? Drug money is just one more special interest. Granted, it is much larger than most."

"Yeah, but the Federal Election Commission monitors individual donors. Bayard could never get away with that."

"That's where you are wrong. Remember the Supreme Court decision that allowed corporations to make campaign contributions? 'Citizens United,' I believe it was called. That ruling allowed anyone to spend unlimited amounts on a candidate, as long as the money was not given directly to the candidate's campaign."

Beck shook his head. The stranger seemed to relish enlightening him. But for what purpose? The stranger continued. "When Bayard was contemplating whether to run for president, the Supreme Court had already handed him the keys to his secret money machine. He couldn't believe his good fortune. And it was a fortune. No one could trace hundreds of millions in Latin American drug money being laundered into the process to support him for president, which made the drug lords ecstatic. They figured they were safe to do whatever they wished. The cartels were about to add a US vice president to their payroll, and then you stepped in and spoiled their plans."

Beck suddenly felt vulnerable. There was far more to this than he had imagined. "Unbelievable," he said. "Someone who gives a few hundred dollars to a candidate must publicly disclose it, yet the South

American drug cartels can spend hundreds of millions to manipulate elections, and no one's the wiser."

"The future of secret campaign financing is already in full operation." The stranger sighed again and stared at his hands while he rubbed his fingers and thumb together.

Beck noticed that one finger on his right hand was weighted down by a massive gold ring embedded with a large diamond. It said Pennsylvania State University.

The stranger looked him in the eye. "You must get it right this time, or you will bring down the entire political system. Powerful interests on both sides of the aisle do not want to see this matter exposed."

"Democrats are doing it too?"

The stranger smiled. "As I said. I work for powerful people. They have monitored almost every move you've made in the past several months."

"I can't believe that."

"My purpose in coming here is to make you a believer. You see, you were in danger for some time, almost from the start of your reporting. Oh, not from my people, but from the drug cartels."

Beck tried to calm his nerves. He quietly placed his hand on his knee under the table to stop it from shaking. "Am I in danger now?"

"Ironically, no."

"Ironically?"

"The drug kingpins usually resolve their problems with a gun or a knife, and they leave a mess behind. You can thank Senator Bayard for you still being alive."

"That's hard to believe. I'd figure he'd want to personally kick my butt."

"It wasn't easy, but he had to explain to his South American business associates that what may be good for their business in South and Central America was not so good for him. If any harm came to you, it would bring out every investigative reporter in the nation. To say nothing of the Justice Department investigators. And who would they point their finger at?"

"I see." Beck leaned forward in his chair and picked up his half cup of coffee. He was so fascinated by the stranger's story, he failed to notice his coffee had gone cold. He signaled a waitress for a warm-up.

The stranger continued. "He told them that, if they want to keep the laundry in operation, they would have to play it his way. Money and power speak louder than revenge on a single reporter, and there are other politicians to be bought."

"So if I pursue it, your folks will come after me?"

"No. We think you should pursue it. Follow the trail."

"Why are you telling me all of this?"

"As I said, politics is a big business in the United States. It has many competing factions." He paused when the waitress arrived with Beck's coffee. She offered some to the stranger, but he demurred. "My people happen to be of a faction that looks down on Bayard's operation," he added when she was out of earshot.

"So you're only doing this to harm the other side?"

"Well, that is the business I am in."

Beck looked at the stranger. He seemed very matter-of-fact, even friendly, yet his words were cold. At least Beck now understood the stranger's motive. He wanted to use Beck's skills for his own purposes. Beck realized this guy was shrewd enough to know he would never walk away from such a big story. So they would use each other for their own purposes. He hadn't met a source yet that didn't want something in return for his cooperation.

"You are headed to Grand Cayman again? Yes?" the stranger asked.

"Yes."

"Then you may want to know there is an important meeting tomorrow morning at Bayard's mansion."

"What kind of meeting?"

"That is for you to find out. What can you tell me about Red?"

"Red knows everything. If something happens to me, Red knows what to do with the information."

"We will find Red eventually."

"I doubt that. Unlike me, Red works undercover. Just like you. That's why you haven't found him yet."

"And Red does not speak. I find that unusual."

"He is extremely cautious. Obviously, much more than me. He probably figured my place was bugged all along."

"Perhaps. Or maybe he is mute." The stranger smiled. "It does not matter. We will find him, just as we found you. It only takes time."

Beck felt cold. How long before they figured out there was no one named Red to protect him? "Why do you care if I am alive or dead?"

"Senator Harvey is concerned. He still loves Ms. Kemper. And she apparently has feelings for you. He is very protective of her."

Beck thought of Jen, wondering if he would ever see her again. But right now, he had something more important to deal with.

"Who is taking over the money machine from Bayard? I assume he can't do it anymore."

The man stood and turned to leave.

"Not so fast," Beck said. "Who murdered the couple at the hotel?"

"Oh that." He turned back to face Beck. "The man at the hotel in Grand Cayman who helped Ms. Kemper with her luggage as you were leaving—"

"Yeah? I remember that. He called her Mrs. Rikki."

"Precisely. He was an associate of the murderer."

"Why was he there?"

"Obviously, he was looking for you. The murderer had never seen you before. He relied on the room number, and the hotel clerk got it wrong. You're a very lucky man."

"Tell that to that poor couple."

"Alas, think of how the world would be different today if you were not alive. You have changed history."

Beck wasn't moved by the stranger's words. He still felt the guilt of the murders. "Did the murderer work for the drug cartels or was he working for Bayard?"

"He wasn't working for us. We were keeping an eye on his associate. Our man—the hotel valet—overheard him speaking to Ms. Kemper as you were leaving and saw your curious reaction. At the time, the killer's associate still hadn't figured out exactly what went wrong. All he knew was his people killed the wrong couple. As soon as you left, he hopped in the next cab. I suspect to follow you to the Grand Cayman airport and do you harm. But we intercepted him at a stoplight on the way when one of our people deliberately ran into the cab, smashing a fender."

"You wanted Bayard destroyed. But why?"

"My people have their reasons."

"Are you with Serodynne?"

"Perhaps. Perhaps not."

Beck's head whirled. Could Geneva be behind all of this? Could Serodynne want to win the Pentagon contract so badly that it would not only destroy Senator Bayard, but kill an innocent couple to get it?

"I can see you are slowly putting the pieces together," said the stranger.

Beck looked down at the table and fingered his mustache in thought. He'd never considered Geneva being behind any of this. But the more he thought about it, the more it made sense. Her connection was too convenient, and it had nearly destroyed his entire investigation. But he still couldn't bring himself to believe it. Could she have faked their entire relationship? That was too painful to even consider.

After a long pause, the stranger spoke again. "I can see you have a lot to put together still. I should leave you to your thoughts."

"Wait." Beck looked up at him. "Why the constant reminder? Why the subterfuge for so many weeks?"

"We wanted you to feel our presence. You can appreciate our abilities now, I presume."

"Yeah, but it didn't stop me."

"Precisely. My people did not want you to stop. They wanted you to destroy Senator Bayard. Our constant presence during the last month should have long ago convinced you we are serious about this matter. We will protect you. Do you want to spend the rest of your life looking over your shoulder?"

"Not really."

The man raised both palms in the air and looked to the ceiling. He then looked down at Beck, tilted his head, and raised an eyebrow—a salute to Beck's reasoning. "It has truly been a pleasure to meet you, Mr. Rikki. You are a great reporter."

"If I had been really smart, I would have gotten the whole story in the first place and . . ."

"And there is a possibility your story about Senator Bayard would never have gotten published. You did well."

"You knew exactly how far to let me play this string out so that your people got exactly what they wanted."

"If our paths cross again someday," the stranger said, "it would be my honor to buy you a stiff drink and a good cigar. But if you don't mind, I'll keep my pants on."

Beck's jaw dropped. He began to laugh. "What don't you know?"

"You have done your country a great service. You have saved it from an individual who was corrupting the system to take on enormous power."

"Only to be replaced by another corrupt individual, no doubt."

The man thrust his hand out to Beck. They shook hands.

The man pivoted and walked out of the restaurant. Beck moved to the window and watched the stranger step into the backseat of a black town car, its door held open by a driver in a dark suit. In seconds, they were gone, heading down Estero Boulevard. Beck strained to read the license. The car had government plates.

Finally, it was all beginning to make sense. Yet he still had several pieces of the puzzle to put together. He realized the stranger believed he was several steps ahead of Beck. No doubt the stranger thought he was pulling one over on him, but Beck knew better.

60

Fahy, thought Beck, as he returned to his table. Could the guy work for Fahy? Or maybe he was a fixer for one of the political parties. Beck had heard of such things before. He knew he could rule out ties to Bayard. The stranger was doing everything he could to destroy the man—or so he wanted Beck to believe.

But that didn't explain how the stranger knew all about his conversation yesterday in his condo with Red. Beck glanced down at his plate. His breakfast was cold.

Connect the dots, he told himself. The stranger bugs his condo a second time. But how? Baker just had it swept a second time, and they found nothing. Nothing.

Beck reached for his wallet to pay for breakfast. He found it in his Windbreaker pocket along with his rental car keys and Fahy's cell phone. He laid the phone and keys on the table as he rummaged through his billfold, seeking a twenty-dollar bill to pay the waitress.

He stared at the phone. The stranger knew about yesterday's conversation with Red. The stranger knew his whereabouts today. His brain lit up. He suddenly knew.

Jumping up, he dropped the twenty on the table and was out the door and in his rental car in seconds. The northbound traffic moved slowly. It took him fifteen minutes to get off the island and find a large shopping center with an electronics store. He inquired about cheap gray burner phones and showed the clerk the one he'd received from Fahy.

"We've got one exactly like that," the sales clerk said.

Beck jumped back in his car with his purchase and, in seconds, headed to his hotel, pressing his foot firmly on the gas pedal until he spotted blue lights flashing ahead. A cop stood on the side of the road, issuing a ticket to some poor guy with Michigan license plates. He slowed and went with the traffic flow, banging his hand on the wheel in frustration. He was eager to get back to his room to test his theory.

When Beck reached his hotel room, he laid Fahy's cell phone next to the new identical phone. Methodically, he took the back off each one, careful not to disconnect the battery. Fahy's phone had a heavy-duty, long-life battery. The phone he had just purchased did not.

Beck turned his attention to the phone he had just purchased and disconnected the battery. Two tiny screws held the guts of the device together. Using his tweezers as a screwdriver, he delicately twisted the screws and lifted the innards of the phone from their plastic shell. Looking closely, he examined a tiny circuit board and an object connected by a short dangling wire. He assumed it was a speaker of some kind. It amazed him how small everything was and how much manufacturers could cram into the body of a handheld phone.

After learning from his electronics school cadaver, Beck turned his attention to the real patient. He removed the battery and then delicately, ever so delicately, removed the screws, just as he had taught himself to do five minutes ago. He purposefully laid each of the parts in sequence on the bed, and then carefully pulled the guts free from the plastic body.

Oh Jesus, he thought, as he lifted the tiny device into the air. He recognized the tiny transmitter immediately, almost identical to the electronic listening device the technician had found in the wall socket of his condominium. His suspicions were correct. He took a deep, validating breath. His phone was bugged.

That's how the stranger knew about Red. Conversations at home, at work—wherever he carried the phone—were monitored. They obviously could track him with the phone's GPS as well. That's how the stranger knew where to find him today, whether on the crosswalks of downtown Washington or here in Fort Myers Beach, Florida.

And that answered his question about the stranger's business ties. The man worked with Fahy, who had given Beck the phone—not to talk privately, undetected, with him—but to monitor his investigation. Shit. How much did Fahy know?

He was certainly not the Boy Scout he portrayed himself to be, and not the benevolent source Beck originally believed. Fahy was spying on him. He was using him. But for what purpose?

Beck's adrenaline surged. His body shook involuntarily. The rush came, not from his excitement for the hunt, but from anger of having the tables turned on him. He was now the hunted.

He tried to think of all of the times he had carried the phone with him as Fahy had instructed. There were too many. He had to assume Fahy knew everything. They knew exactly where he was right now. Okay, he thought. How do I play this game?

Beck quickly reassembled both phones and left them in his room while he traveled down to the hotel lobby, carrying his own cell phone. He walked out onto the beach, hesitated, then pulled the back off his phone and unsnapped the battery. There was no eavesdropping device inside that he could make out. He told himself he now had good reason to be paranoid.

After waiting for his phone to reboot, he called Nancy. He explained his suspicions about the nonprofits allowing anonymous drug lords to dump tens of millions of dollars into the Patten campaign.

"Can you run some searches on independent expenditures on Patten and Bayard's behalf?"

She said she would get the research staff on it right away.

"For all I know, the Democrats may be doing it too," he said.

"Holy Jesus. The whole system may be corrupted."

"Can you also trace a government license plate for me?"

"Can try."

Beck gave her the plate number of the stranger's vehicle. "I'll be in touch," he said, and hung up.

He dialed his condo. When his ancient answering machine picked up, he punched in his personal code to listen to his messages and immediately erased all of them.

He liked the old machine because he could leave up to an hour of messages with no fear of being cut off. Sometimes when he was driving in his car and thinking about a story, he would call it and dictate some ideas before he forgot them. It was just so damned convenient for a technologically challenged writer.

Beck rode the elevator back to his room. Unbelievable, he thought, he'd been had. He was one of the best goddamned investigative reporters in the nation, and he had been manipulated like a string puppet. How many layers were there to this onion? Maybe it was a good thing he wasn't as good as he thought he was.

Back in his room, he picked up the bugged phone and called his condo again. Four rings later, his answering machine kicked in. He placed the phone on the windowsill, walked into his bathroom about twenty feet away, and began to talk.

"Red, it's Beck. The next time I call you, I want you to listen carefully."

He walked back to the phone and hung up, then immediately punched redial. When the answering machine picked up, he punched in his message code and listened. Beck heard his words to Red as clearly as if he had held the phone in his hand rather than them being transmitted from across the room.

He hung up, pulled Inspector Tomlinson's business card from his wallet, and called the number, remembering to insert the international code. The inspector was not in, he was told. Did he want to leave a message? He explained who he was and that he was inquiring about the recent double homicide in the hotel. She said she would pass on the message.

Beck turned off the phone and looked at it. Just how the eavesdropping device inside it worked—he didn't know. All that mattered was that it did work, because now he had a plan. He couldn't erase the wide grin on his face. He had just sent his first message to Fahy, and Beck knew Fahy was listening.

61

Inspector Tomlinson welcomed Beck into his office the next morning. He offered him coffee from a steaming pot on a corner table, surrounded by stacks of paper files. Beck took it gladly. It was strong, almost too much so.

His plane had been nearly an hour late yesterday, but he had still managed to race over to Government House and comb through more of Bayard's real estate files before the offices closed their doors for the day. In the few hours he pounded the keys on their computer, he traced every one of the buyers of vacant lots in Bayard's development—every corporate entity and partnership—and made copies. He spent his evening in a hotel room cross-referencing every corporate office, director, and partner, and didn't look out his window onto the Caribbean sunset once.

Of the thirty-one sales he found—Geneva had missed some—he discovered all of them shared the same names. The same people turned up as officers in one company and directors in another, and again as members of various partnerships. But the one name they all had in common was Roger Kindred, who created all of the corporations and partnerships, using his law practice as the mailing address for all. Clearly, this tight-knit group used the land transactions to launder dirty money. Beck didn't crawl into bed until well past midnight.

Tomlinson apologized for having to meet so early, but he had another engagement at eight thirty. In preparation for the meeting, Beck drove his rental car to police headquarters and left Fahy's phone and the newer burner phone in the glove compartment. His conversation with Tomlinson was private. He did not want Fahy or the stranger listening in.

No, Tomlinson said, the murder case was not closed. They had plenty of forensic evidence, but none of it matched their only suspect, Sancho Franz, the man Beck saw briefly in the hotel lobby that morning.

"The man in the white suit? With the white straw hat?" Beck asked.

"Word is, he works for the Mexicans," Tomlinson said. "Franz is a midlevel enforcer of some kind. Not really high up in the cartel, but at or near the top here, and that makes him dangerous—very dangerous. He likes to keep his hands clean, a step or two away from the dirty work. So he's hard to pin down. We have our suspicions, but unfortunately, we've been unable to directly connect him to anything."

"So someone working for him carried out the murders?"

"That's what we suspect. We traced a phone call he made the evening of the murders, to a telephone booth not far from your hotel. Believe it or not, we still have a few of those around. When we questioned him, he told us he dialed a wrong number, though he talked for nearly two minutes. He couldn't explain that. We haven't been able to figure out who was on the receiving end. I assume it was the murderer."

"The man who asked the hotel clerk if I was in my room that night?"

"That's correct."

"Were the staff able to give you a description of the man?"

"Only that he was Latino. The clerk said he eyed her strangely, and at first, she thought he was being fresh. Then she thought he was not especially bright." Tomlinson sat back and folded his arms. "So, you're back on the island because . . . ?"

Beck shifted in his seat. "It's personal. I feel responsible. They were looking for me."

"Not an easy thing to live with. I understand. But we're handling this investigation. Don't involve yourself. Your FBI has been around here asking questions as well. They think we are fools and can't do the job. You Americans think you're so special."

"Sometimes we're guilty of that, but not this time. I'm following up on the story that brought me to Grand Cayman originally."

"Your story made headlines here as well. You stick to that story. Let us conduct our murder investigation. No offense, but you're a reporter, not a police officer. You are not equipped to deal with this."

"I'm just here for my story."

"I don't think you understand. These people are killers. They tried to kill you once. What makes you think that a pen and notebook will protect you?"

"Don't worry. I'm careful."

"Are you? Your history says otherwise. You were followed almost since the moment you first set foot on this island."

"You're right. I'm not a cop. I work out in the open. I don't care if you or anyone else is watching me. I've got a job to do. I've been doing this for years. I know what I'm doing."

Tomlinson shook his head. Beck saw the look in his eye. He knew this time it was different. Tomlinson was probably right. Beck was into this far deeper than he had ever anticipated, but he was determined not to show any sign of uncertainty. He was more worried about his safety than he let on. He hoped he didn't give off a vibe that gave him away.

AS HE FINALLY TURNED WEST ON THE winding island road in the blinding early morning sun, Beck was again on the north side of the island, headed west to a familiar place—the spot where this all began, the place yesterday's stranger practically begged him to visit. He bounced along the nearly deserted, weather-beaten road, eyeing glimpses of the narrow beach that peeked at him between the dunes off to his right. Occasionally, he spotted a car on the shoulder—when a shoulder could be found—temporarily abandoned, no doubt, by eager swimmers and fishermen along with their coolers, beach towels, and umbrellas.

Three cars sat in the driveway of Bayard's mansion as he approached. Beck felt the surge. He slowed his car and found a spot to pull over just short of the senator's property.

He turned off the engine. He eyed a workman on his knees, digging with a hand trowel around a bush in the front yard of the mansion. A small plastic tarp lay on the grass, piled high with potting soil.

Now what? thought Beck. He pulled his baseball cap down low, stuffed the cell phones in his pockets, and stepped out of his car. Walking toward Bayard's house, he heard every step as his sneakers crunched on the crushed shells along the edge of the bleached, sun-drenched pavement. He felt them under his shoes, shifting ever so slightly as he took each step.

The last time he was here, Geneva had been impressed by his deception of the neighbor, Bridges, although now he realized the old man hadn't been deceived at all. Beck quickly needed another ruse. He didn't want to just walk around the Bayard mansion again. He needed to get inside.

His back to Beck, the gardener stood now, shoveling dirt back into a hole after removing a dying plant. Beck was no horticulturalist, but he recognized a dead plant when he saw one, even if he had no idea what it was. He spied a yellow hose snaking across the U-shaped driveway between the cars over to the gardener. It gave him an idea.

The gardener looked in his direction as he approached, so Beck picked up his pace, striding deliberately along the drive. Showtime, he thought. "I'm with the Water Authority. You having pressure problems?"

"No, sir," said the gardener, pointing at the hose at his feet.

"I got a call from dispatch. I'm here to check it out." Beck noticed a pair of work gloves the gardener wasn't using sitting on a wheelbarrow. He needed a prop of some kind. This would have to do. "Mind if I borrow these while I check?"

The gardener shook his head, squinting at Beck. But the sun was directly in his eyes, making it impossible for him to look Beck's way. Beck grabbed the gloves, approached the front door, and knocked.

It seemed like he waited forever. He knocked again.

Finally, a tall, bald man answered the door. "What do you want?"

"We're having some water pressure problems in the area. I need to check your pump and water heater." He slapped the gloves in his hand. "This is the Bayard place. Right?"

"Not now. I'm in the middle of a meeting," the man said.

Beck recognized the man's large, round Greek eyes. Though he knew the face from photographs he had seen while researching Bayard's background, Beck couldn't place him.

The Greek began to close the door, and Beck stiff-armed it. "Sir, if your water heater explodes, you won't be having a meeting—or a house, for that matter. If water is drained from your water heater, it could blow you sky-high."

The man growled something in Greek that Beck couldn't understand and then mumbled a profanity he could. He waved Beck through the door. "This way."

A short, stocky man and an attractive, older woman with blonde hair sat in the large living room, the same room he and Geneva had spied from the patio just over a month ago. Decorated in shades of white and pale blue, the overstuffed furniture was placed in a semicircle facing the Caribbean. The outdoor furniture, which had been stacked in the room when Beck was here last time, now stood on the patio outside.

They looked up from their discussion.

"Sorry, folks. Just checking on a water pressure issue."

They turned away and immediately ignored him. "In here," said the tall, bald man. He pointed to a utility room off the kitchen and rejoined the group in the living room. Beck immediately walked up to the kitchen sink and turned on the water. The sound interrupted their conversation again, and they looked his way.

Beck shrugged apologetically. "Seems okay to me. Bathroom?"

The tall man pointed to a doorway across the hallway from the living room. Beck crossed the room, trying to listen to their conversation. But they had stopped talking. Then he heard the woman, the slender blonde wearing designer reading glasses, complain about the public services on the island.

"I'll just be a moment. Sorry," Beck said. He turned on the water and flushed the toilet in the bathroom. He quickly scanned the room, looking for a spot where he could hide Fahy's burner phone. Nothing. It was all clean lines and no clutter.

He stepped out of the room and quietly crossed through the living area, heading toward the utility room just behind the open kitchen. A large water heater stood near the utility room door. Afraid he might be watched, Beck pretended to inspect it and twisted a few water knobs slightly. He then pulled his phone from his pocket and looked at it. Anxiety washed over him. Which one was it?

He pulled the second phone from another pocket. Shit. He couldn't tell them apart. Which one had the bug?

He hit redial on both. One called his condo. He hung up the other. He waited for the voice mail to answer, then hid the phone behind a bottle of cleaning liquid on a shelf above the water heater. He pretended to hold a conversation on the other.

"Yeah, it's me. Now listen up." Beck spoke loud enough so that everyone in the other room could hear him. "There's plenty of pressure here at the Bayard place. Might even be a bit too high. Can you have a tech come out here and adjust the meter?" He paused for effect. "Tell Red to keep better records next time."

"Something wrong?"

Beck jumped. The Greek was standing in the doorway behind him. Beck turned to him. "Sorry, I—you startled me. I didn't see you. The folks at the office apparently got their records mixed up. I think the issue is at one of your neighbors. I'll have to check next door. Some people can't keep their water meters straight. Everything seems fine here. Sorry to have bothered you."

A nervous surge shook his body. The Greek must see this, he thought. Beck knew he tended to talk too much when he was nervous. Had he overdone it?

The man blocked his way and stared at him. Beck paused. Standing in silence, he did not move. Was he on to him? Why wouldn't he let him leave?

The Greek continued to examine him. Then just as quickly, he stepped back, and Beck slid by him and strode quickly toward the front door. His heart pounded so hard he thought he could actually hear it.

He apologized to the Greek again and quickly pulled the door closed behind him. He turned to leave and stopped dead. The man in the white straw hat stood some thirty feet away with his back to Beck, talking to the gardener. It was Franz. Dressed in a white suit, Franz towered over the gardener, who was on one knee with his hands wrapped around a small flowery plant. From their animated conversation, it was obvious Franz and the gardener were acquainted.

"Hey, you." Beck heard a familiar voice from behind. He turned to see the Greek standing in the front door. "You left this." He held up the burner phone.

Shit, thought Beck. He stepped back to the door. "Hey, thanks, man. I would have been lost without this."

The Greek handed him the phone and grunted, then closed the door in his face.

Dread filled him. He'd been busted. His scheme was ruined. Beck had lost his only chance to tie the drug money directly to the campaign.

He shoved the phone in his pocket, disgusted with himself. Then he realized there was nothing there. His pocket was empty. The other phone, where was it? In the commotion in the utility room, when the Greek had startled him, he must have left both phones behind. Which one did he have now?

He closed his eyes, hoping there was a chance, then turned away from the front door. The Greek's voice had drawn the attention of the gardener and Franz, who now looked in his direction. Beck hesitated and turned his face away from them. Finally, he pulled his cap lower and walked quietly down the driveway, away from their conversation.

"Amigo," said the gardener.

Beck kept walking.

"Mister water supervisor," the gardener said in a soft voice.

Beck kept up his pace.

"My gloves," the gardener rasped.

Should he run? If he did, he would surely give himself away, but Franz would recognize him if he turned around. He looked up. The sun blinded him.

Beck thought about donning his sunglasses, but the yellow pair in his pocket would surely give him away. Damn, why didn't he fit in with convention and wear expensive stylish eyewear like everybody else? And then he realized. He didn't need sunglasses.

He turned toward the two men. They both looked in his direction, but the morning sun was still low in the sky and at Beck's back. The sun blinded them as it had Beck, forcing them to shield their eyes and look away.

Beck walked back toward the gardener and then picked up his stride. The workman still knelt on the lush Bermuda grass surrounded by a trowel, rake, plants, a pile of freshly dug dirt, and Franz's shadow.

He took several steps closer. Sancho Franz turned sideways, looking away from Beck, rubbing his eyes. The brim of his hat was not wide enough to shade his face.

Though Beck picked up his pace even more, he felt like he moved in slow motion, his feet encased in lead. He watched Franz for signs of recognition, but Franz continued to look away.

Beck stepped closer. Finally, he reached the gardener. He squatted to the ground, at the gardener's level, so that Franz would not see his face hidden under the brim of his baseball cap.

Beck handed the gardener his gloves. "Thanks. False alarm. The pressure problem must be at one of the neighbors."

The gardener stared at him. "*Gracias.*"

Beck gazed back at the gardener's pockmarked face. The man smelled of sweat, and his eyes seemed distracted, almost wild, and they looked right through him. Beck shuddered. Up close, the gardener looked menacing, not like a man who loved to mix his hands in the soil.

Beck glanced away. He stared at Franz's white shoes next to the gardener. They rocked back and forth on both heels, the cuffs of his white linen trousers rising over his pale, speckled socks with each impatient sway. It was the motion of a man in charge who had grown impatient. He needed to get away quickly before Franz discovered who he was.

In one motion, Beck stood, careful to keep his back to Franz, and stepped back into the protective cocoon of the glaring sun. The bright curtain safely enveloped him and blinded the two men's probing gazes.

He heard their conversation pick up again in perfect English. Franz was berating the gardener. "It's a good thing your hearing is so damned good, 'cause otherwise I'd have never hired you, you one-eyed bat."

Beck tried to control his pace and not walk too quickly. As he reached the safety of his car, the conversation faded, but his thoughts sharpened. Bad eyesight mixed with acute hearing . . . of course. What he was beginning to understand gave him goose bumps. That far-off stare. It was the look of death. The man breathing life into plants and shrubs at Senator Bayard's home had murdered the couple in the hotel and was still willing to kill Beck if he got the chance.

Beck slipped silently into his rental car and looked back toward the mansion. The gardener was on his knees, back at work, and the man in the straw hat stood in the doorway of the mansion. The Greek greeted him with a bear hug. Wow, he'd gotten out just in time. Franz surely would have recognized him in the house.

Beck was sweating profusely, despite the blast of cool air streaming from the rental car's AC unit. He pulled the cheap phone from his pocket and nearly ripped off the back cover to check the battery. Tension drained from his body. It did not contain the listening device. That one was still in the mansion. He couldn't help but smile as he wiped his brow. He immediately made a U-turn and headed back toward George Town.

He punched redial on his phone. "Detective Tomlinson," he said, "I think I know who your murderer is. The killer didn't see the hotel clerk dial the room number when she called it the night of the murder. He heard it. He has very keen hearing. And you mentioned something about one of the clerks saying he had a strange, almost wild look in his eyes. This guy has that too."

"Who are you talking about?" Tomlinson asked. "Where are you right now?"

"He's the gardener at the Bayard place. I suspect if you match his DNA, you'll have your man. And where am I? I'm out of here."

BECK WAS ON THE NEXT PLANE home. During a layover in Charlotte, while awaiting his connecting flight to DC, he called his landline at the condo. The answering machine picked up. He punched in his code to listen to his messages.

Fahy's telephone had picked up the conversation from the living room and transmitted it to Beck's answering machine, something he wasn't sure would work until he tested his theory in his hotel room in Florida. That's when he realized all he needed to do was to figure out a way to hide the bugged phone in Bayard's house and dial his own number.

"We've got the money in various accounts here." Beck heard Franz's distinct voice.

"Kertsos, have you all of your advertising time reserved?" Beck did not recognize this voice. It had to belong to the third man—the one who never got up from the couch. But as soon as he heard the name Kertsos, he finally remembered. He was the man at the front door. The Greek.

"Everything's ready." Beck recognized Kertsos's voice. "We just need the money moved immediately. I've got more than four hundred million in pro-Patten campaign ads ready to run, and we're still waiting.

You said we would have the funds two weeks ago. Betz, those ads won't run if we don't pay up front. And this Bayard fiasco has us clawing for every vote we can get. We've nearly lost a seven-point lead. If we don't get this money now, we will lose this election."

Betz? Who was Betz? Beck wondered. The unknown Betz spoke again. "You shouldn't have spent so much on your early get-out-the-vote drive. How much good does early voting do anyway?"

"You know that wasn't my decision. I'm the advertising guy," Kertsos said. "I don't do ground game. I wanted the money for advertising. That decision was made at the top. So now I'm short of cash. Don't blame me."

Beck remembered now. Kertsos was William Kertsos, the communications director for Bayard's defunct campaign. Beck had dug his name up from news clippings during his early research on Bayard. The press had labeled Kertsos "the General Store" for his ability to provide anything to a political campaign. His friends called him Wild Bill. If you needed something difficult done, you turned to him. But who were the others on the recording?

"Patience. The money will be moved this afternoon," Franz said. "I'll funnel the money through the ten nonprofits we discussed. Only those ten. They have shown they can move efficiently and quickly. You figure out how you want to distribute the funds. That's your problem."

"We will take care of that," came a woman's voice. It had to be the blonde, Beck thought. "All of our organizations are ready to move quickly as soon as the funds arrive."

"Then let's celebrate," Franz said. "There should be champagne in the fridge."

Beck heard his flight called and hung up. He would listen to the rest of it when he got home. See you on the front page, he thought.

62

Baker closed his office door behind Nancy and Beck and motioned them to sit down. Beck had arrived home late and was still sleepy from listening to the entire recording. It ran about thirty-five minutes before he heard the group leave the house.

Baker wanted to walk through the entire story before his midmorning story meeting with his editors. "What's that?" he asked, pointing to the object in front of Beck.

"My answering machine."

"And?"

"Listen." Beck turned it on, and they listened to all thirty-five minutes of the conversation, which meandered onto several topics involving the campaign. It also enabled Beck to identify all the participants. Laurie Frank was the attractive blonde sitting on the couch in Bayard's great room. She was Patten's assistant campaign treasurer. And Baker recognized the voice of Fred Betz, the campaign's polling guru, who was explaining to the group which media markets they would target with the drug money, based on his survey results.

"Tread lightly, people," Baker admonished. "Write deftly. Use a scalpel, not an ax. We really are dealing with the future of the free world. That's no exaggeration. We must be one hundred percent sure we get it right. Nancy, have you documented the nonprofits' spending?"

"They're all identified on the audio," Nancy said. "I've got three reporters nailing down their spending habits and media buys.

Altogether, I've got a team of six working on it. We should have it all pulled together no later than tomorrow."

So on a Friday, just over a week before the election and a day after the Walrus and Hedelt had gone over every word in the final draft with a sharp pencil, Beck awoke early and took the elevator downstairs to retrieve his morning paper. He didn't bother to look online. Not for something this big.

He pulled his paper out of its clear plastic bag and unfolded the front page and reveled in his work. The headline "Patten Campaign Funded by Drug Cartels" screamed across six columns at the top of the front page. Inside the paper, he found two more stories, four sidebars, several charts created by the art department, and one large graphic explaining the money flow. The stories covered every aspect of the money laundering scandal, from real estate deals in Grand Cayman to how much of the drug money the nonprofits were spending in support of Patten's presidential bid. He buried his face in the newspaper, reading every headline, still standing in his running shorts and T-shirt in the lobby of his condo building. Finally, he pushed the elevator button to go back upstairs.

He thought about how different this story was from his first. There was no waiting around to showcase it on a Sunday. The allegations were so important and the money trail evidence so solid, there was no talk of the *Post-Examiner* losing credibility by running the story this close to the election. If Nancy was concerned, she showed no signs this time.

The online staff had uploaded an edited version of the audio to the newspaper website along with still photos of Kertsos, Frank, and Betz. There were no file photos of Franz. Beck then flipped on his television. Even at six in the morning, the Friday morning news shows had already tossed their prepared scripts and were airing wall-to-wall coverage of Beck's funding scandal story. On his drive to work, talk radio talked about nothing else.

Barely more than a week before Election Day, and the cable news channels had their kidnapped white coed and shark attack all in one story. Beck felt giddy. He knew the cable channels could run with his story for days. Once again, Beck had provided them with a ratings bonanza.

"How do you keep doing this?" asked Tom Reed. Reed was the third writer this morning to drop by Beck's desk to congratulate him. Beck sat back, drinking it all in along with his morning coffee. He had left for the office early, as soon as he had finished reading his story. He secretly wanted to soak in the adulation of his colleagues.

He jumped online at his desk to check on the latest news. The Patten campaign had released a defiant statement denying all of the allegations. Beck made a few calls to check on the whereabouts of Kertsos, Frank, and Betz. They all had disappeared from the public stage. Then he switched to a new online website that ran instant polls. They were devastating to Patten's campaign. Prior to the story, Patten had a small, but comfortable lead. Hours after his story ran, Beck saw the public had begun to absorb the meaning of the *Post-Examiner*'s stories. Patten was now losing by a percentage point. Beck was amazed his story could have such a sudden impact.

"The nonprofits named in your story are not backing down," said Nancy. She had been following the aftermath of the story all morning and had reporters tracking the campaign's media spending. It had been the hit of the morning editors' meeting, she said. "Their ad buys, made before your story broke, are still running on broadcast television, cable, radio, and online channels in every battleground state. The news channels, which are getting rich off his campaign spending, aren't about to return millions in advertising dollars—dirty drug money or not." Nancy shook her head. "Journalistic integrity. You gotta love it. It just can't compete with an open wallet."

FOX NEWS INQUIRED ABOUT the origin of the audio. How had the liberal newspaper acquired a recording of such a meeting?

Baker hunkered down in his closed-door office with Nancy and Beck. Now they faced a journalistic dilemma. Using Fahy's phone to secretly record the campaign's private conversation, without the participants' knowledge, would never pass the smell test in a journalism ethics course. That was the behavior of the sleazy London tabloids, and they had ended up in court for their shoddy behavior. If Baker revealed how Beck had bent the rules of engagement, the story would be tainted. Political attack dogs would shift the media focus from the content of the story to the journalistic tactics used to obtain it. The newspaper had little choice but to respond to the questions.

Nancy and Beck sat in Baker's office trying to justify Beck's actions for more than an hour. Baker sat quietly, taking it all in. Finally, he grinned at Beck and tapped one of his brown cigarettes on the top of his cluttered office desk.

"You really could say this recording came through a confidential source," Baker said.

Beck grinned back. He knew exactly how to respond.

An hour later, the newspaper released a statement to Fox News and the rest of the media, quoting Beck as saying the recording came through a *Post-Examiner* confidential source. Clever, he thought, noting he used the word "through" instead of "from." No one picked up the nuance, however. Technically, it was the truth. Ethically? Well, that was another matter, Beck thought.

The media were satisfied, and that's all that mattered. They quickly shifted their attention deficit disorder to another facet of the story. The white coed was dead. It was time to look for another shark attack.

BECK AND NANCY had lunch in the cafeteria to get away from the madness in the newsroom.

"Look," she said, "I know you're all jazzed about this story and the reaction. You've done well, and you deserve the adulation. But you need to pace yourself."

"I'm fine. Really."

"I want you to stay that way. Take the weekend off. Lay low out of the spotlight and try to absorb what you've accomplished. You're beat. I can tell. We need you in fighting form for Election Day. Remember, you're the poster boy. We've got six reporters to cover this now. Take a break."

Beck had to admit he was exhausted. He left work right after lunch for his condo. When he arrived home, he grabbed a beer and sank onto his leather couch face to face with his flat-screen. He escaped into old mystery and action movies with an occasional break to catch up on the latest news about the Patten campaign. It was a bit otherworldly and just plain weird to hear newscasters refer to him over and over again in their stories. He even saw video of himself taken outside the federal courthouse.

He began to understand why Nancy wanted him to lay low. If he accepted all of the requests for interviews this weekend, he would be old news by Election Day. The paper needed his poster boy routine ready for election night. At the end of the day, he thought, it's all about marketing and making money, especially now in the endangered newspaper business.

AND NOW IT REALLY WAS THE end of the day. Beck was being miked in the studio for his third network television appearance of election night. He'd lost track of how many political pundits had already predicted a Patten loss on the morning talk shows. The drug story had saturated the public conscience so thoroughly that more than 90 percent of potential voters were aware of the funding scandal. Maybe Beck's stage was larger than he had given himself credit for back in that diner with Geneva. Patten was going to lose, and it was because of Beck. That was a heavy load to bear, and it had taken Beck a few days to grasp the weight of history on his shoulders. Nancy was wiser than he had given her credit for. She was right to suggest he take a little time off to prepare for this day.

His role tonight was to dash from one Washington television studio to the next to be interviewed by network and cable news anchors. The *Post-Examiner* hired a driver to carry him from place to place so he could tout the newspaper's accomplishments on a maximum number of media outlets. The last time he enjoyed any media attention was on his second book tour three years ago when his publisher mustered a half-dozen interviews in New York. His audience back then was miniscule compared to what he faced tonight.

Other *Post-Examiner* writers who had helped with the stories were also called upon to flaunt the newspaper. But, by now, Beck was the celebrity brand they all wanted, and the one the *Post-Examiner* was more than willing to promote as the face of the franchise.

The company marketing vice president instructed him to always refer to the web page audio to build traffic to the *Post-Examiner* website. During his first interview, Beck felt a little awkward trying to remember his lines and to promote the newspaper's website. The questions were all softball. It was election night, and the producers at one of the networks explained to him privately he was merely color commentary. The real star was the vote count.

By the fourth interview, Beck was a pro with the lines and website endorsements, easily dropping them into his answers and commentary. But by the fifth time he sat at a desk in a studio and clipped on his microphone ready to repeat himself again, he was feeling a bit abused by his bosses and had grown bored with this gig. This is not what he had originally signed up for. The adulation was fine, but he wanted to cele-brate *his* victory with *his* friends and colleagues. He felt alone as he sat in the cold, stark television studios with their hot lights glaring down on him in front of millions of viewers.

AROUND ELEVEN O'CLOCK ON ELECTION NIGHT, Beck trudged into the *Post-Examiner* newsroom. He was spent. He dumped his sports coat on top of his desk, flopped down in his chair, and looked around the frenetic room, taking it all in.

The political reporters not attending presidential campaign vic-tory parties or following important state and federal races around the country crowded into the newsroom, yelling at editors with updates and pummeling their computer keyboards, spitting out copy for the national desk as quickly as their fingers could move. Many of the crew huddled around televisions and computer monitors, watching the networks tally results and then rewriting story leads as quickly as numbers came in. Everyone on staff worked on election night. Phones jangled nonstop throughout the newsroom, bellowing like instruments in a ghastly off-key orchestra, building to a chaotic crescendo.

Beck loved the chaos. This was what the news business was all about. He walked over to the metro desk to check out the latest, but everyone was too busy to pay him any attention. He walked by the national desk, which had the lead story, and they ignored him as they inserted the latest state polling numbers into their copy. He felt like a fish out of water in his own newsroom. His colleagues were completing a story he had started. He realized he had no important role tonight. It was almost as if he wasn't there. Beck realized he felt very tired.

The television anchors babbling on the overhead monitors all predicted a bad night for Ford Patten. Projections based on exit polling showed he would easily lose the race once all votes were counted.

Beck's cell rang. He turned away from the commotion.

"It's Jen. I just had to call and say hi. And congratulate you on your story."

Beck no longer heard the turmoil in the newsroom. All he heard was the voice of the woman who, like no other, made him feel something very different. He gasped for air, and his voice failed him.

"Beck? Are you there?"

"Wow. It's been forever. How are you?" he blurted out. For so long, he had wanted to talk with her, and now he couldn't think of anything to say.

"I'm sorry. It's the campaign and Secret Service. I'm in a hotel waiting for the victory party. I borrowed one of my aide's phones to call you."

Aides, thought Beck. It had been only a few weeks, and she'd already acquired political aides. Their lives would never be the same. "Doesn't sound like there will be a victory."

"Doesn't matter to me."

"I've missed you." Beck's words again failed him.

"This hasn't been easy. Everything has changed. Are you doing okay?"

"I'm fine," he lied.

"Look, I haven't much time. It's crazy here. I'm getting bounced around like a pinball following the Secret Service wherever they tell me to go."

She must feel as isolated in the midst of her chaotic evening as he did in his, he thought. "Will I hear from you again?"

"Look, I have to go. My handlers say I need to go to the ballroom. Something's happening, and they want me there." She hung up without saying good-bye.

All the old feelings surged to the surface. It literally felt like forever since Harvey became the vice presidential nominee and Geneva was sealed in a Secret Service cocoon. The call made him realize just how much he'd missed her.

And yet, he had been so busy chasing the drug cartel story, he hadn't had time to think much about her. He knew he needed to slow down—have a real relationship with a woman that lasted more than a few months. But he loved his job too and wondered if the two could ever coexist. He believed Geneva was the first woman he'd ever met who appreciated his obsession. She understood his passion for his work—his calling—and that he was an adrenaline junkie. She actually seemed to admire his drive. And yet he still had this uncomfortable feeling she had an ulterior motive. There was no evidence, just a gut feeling since she was so close to his story, and now her husband had profited from his work. Yet Geneva seemed to take no pleasure in any of it. She seemed more like a free spirit in a buttoned-down culture trying desperately to escape conformity.

He stood near the edge of the large room facing a wall, his cell phone still clung to his ear. He hadn't moved since Geneva hung up. Then the cacophony of election night surged into his brain again, and he was back in the newsroom.

"Did you see this?" Nancy's voice came from behind him. He turned, and she pointed to the television monitor hanging from the ceiling. "Virginia's early absentee voting is going to tilt the state to Patten despite today's exit polls showing him losing badly. Illinois and Ohio look like they're going in the same direction."

Beck looked up at the screen and saw the Virginia tally showing Patten slightly ahead. He couldn't believe it. After all of this, Patten might pull this out?

The television anchorwoman quickly called a Patten campaign aide from the green room and put him on the air to talk about early voting. The tone suddenly shifted from contempt to respectful as the aide explained how the campaign's massive early get-out-the-vote drive was changing the outcome in many of the toss-up states.

"No one considered the impact of early voting, which took place long before your story ran," Nancy said. "Patten could have run up a big enough lead with voters weeks ago to win this thing. Wow, what a story that would be. He could still win at a time when a huge majority of the public now despises him."

"You're kidding. A crook wins the presidency?" Beck grimaced.

"Jeez. Never happened before. Has it?" Nancy said.

As the evening turned into morning, the projections migrated in Patten's favor. Gradually, Patten's electoral college count was climbing, getting closer and closer to the magic number of two hundred and seventy. By three in the morning, there was no decision.

Beck gave up. He was spent and had no stomach to hang out in the newsroom any longer and be unproductive. He drove home to crash, questioning his role in all of this. He'd lost the woman he loved, and he'd lost his adrenaline rush tonight. Now he was even questioning what had happened with his job. How did he get to this place? He was supposed to be on top of the world, yet nothing seemed to be going his way.

63

Daniel Fahy, still dressed in a plaid bathrobe and slippers, picked up his morning *Post-Examiner*, neatly tucked in its plastic bag on his front sidewalk. He opened it to the front page and read the headlines in the dim morning light. Two days after Ford Patten won the election by a slim margin, the nation faced a constitutional crisis. Patten was yet to take office, and the Democrats, who controlled neither the House nor the Senate, were already calling for his impeachment if he were to ever take the oath.

He flipped to the op-ed page. A *Post-Examiner* columnist called for the electoral college to dump Patten in favor of Michael Harvey. "The president of the United States is not elected by popular vote," wrote the columnist, "but by electors chosen by voters in each state. It's civics class 101. We can still fix this."

Fahy picked up the phone in his den and dialed the private number he had been given several weeks ago. "You read this morning's *Post-Examiner*?"

"Yes," said Michael Harvey.

"I assume you're going to do it."

"You assume correctly."

"Too bad about Ford."

"He's a good man."

"The presidency is a zero-sum opportunity. If he falters, that leaves only one choice," Fahy said. He hung up the phone and headed for the bathroom to take his morning shower. There would be no workout today. Instead Fahy flipped on the morning news. The idea was quickly taking hold of the public psyche. It was cited, paraphrased, e-mailed, and tweeted tens of millions of times, according to the newsreader. Governors and officials from both major political parties were already talking to local politicians and electors about a deal. The public outcry was real. The United States had to be saved from the drug-infested campaign of Ford Patten, said one television commentator Fahy heard as he was shaving.

Publicly, Fahy remained silent. Privately, he opened a back channel to President Bill Croom through Jackson Oliver to keep abreast of the Democrats' plans. The issue was so sensitive, Fahy knew Croom could not risk even the hint of collusion on a deal to shove Republican Patten aside and give the presidency to his friend Michael Harvey.

Congressional Democrats, however, had nothing to lose, Fahy realized. They couldn't win the presidency, but they could guarantee the man who beat them didn't win either. They could shift their electors' votes to Harvey. Fahy monitored the situation calling his various Washington contacts for updates and quietly passing along the details to Harvey's people. Harvey needed only a handful of Republican electors to make it work. Fahy quickly saw a deal emerge. Patten was out, and Harvey was in. The electoral college could do that, and no one could stop them.

Patten fought the movement, calling electors across the country. But it quickly became apparent to Fahy and others that there was enough public opposition to his dirty money path to office that he would never again reach the two hundred and seventy electoral vote plateau he had won on election night. Republican electors were loyal, but not legally bound to their candidate. All of them were being pressured in their states to vote against Patten to save the party. Fahy was amazed at how quickly it all came together.

Fahy talked to Democrats working behind the scenes. They knew they could not only swing a deal with disgruntled Republicans to elect Harvey, but they made it clear to Republicans they probably had the votes to kill Harvey's choice for vice president when he sent his nominee before Congress to be confirmed. So in return for the Republicans agreeing to oust Patten, the Democrats agreed to rubber-stamp Harvey's choice for the number two spot.

The deal was sealed. Harvey would become the first modern president ever elected with a large swath of both Republican and Democrat electors—and you couldn't see Fahy's fingerprints on any of it. Fahy preferred it that way.

Nearly a month later, the electoral college did its work, electing Harvey with more than three hundred votes. The Congress would vote on Harvey's choice for vice president when it convened for a new session in January. There was plenty of time before the inauguration.

GENEVA AND HARV'S LAWYERS worked quickly. The divorce was friendly, since they had no heirs and splitting their assets was relatively easy. They each knew what the other wanted, and ultimately, they agreed they would keep the penthouse together. Perhaps there would be evenings in the future where they could capture some time together over a bottle of wine and cigars, Geneva told him.

She turned in her resignation to Serodynne. She had already collected her bonus check—a full year's salary—after the Pentagon awarded the drone contract to her company. It made her smile. If they only knew, she thought.

She and Harv used their influence to expedite their divorce. A local judge agreed to handle the situation discreetly and quickly, and a day before the inauguration, they met at the condo with the judge and their attorneys to sign the papers. The Secret Service stood outside in the hallway.

After the papers were signed, they asked everyone to leave. For a few moments, they talked about their life together and how they both wanted something different now. Harv said he understood her need for privacy.

"Nothing like having it handed to you on a silver platter." He laughed.

"For both of us," she replied. "Who would have thought?"

They hugged. After one long, passionate kiss, they looked into each other's eyes and smiled. They were both getting exactly what they wanted. They didn't need each other anymore.

Geneva felt a sense of relief. Everything was finally falling into place. She promised to stay through the inauguration and then they would jointly announce their split. She would be gone before the news media even knew—leaving Harv to deal with the chaos and tabloid headlines. There was only one thing left to do. She would check in with Keith to make sure everything was going as planned with her money. Once she had her share, she would be home free.

64

Beck sat at his desk with his legs propped up, reading the paper. It was thinner now that the holidays were over. He turned to the style section and saw a picture of Geneva at some charitable fund-raiser with the president-elect. Every time she showed up in the newspaper, it felt like someone punched him in the stomach. He hadn't spoken to her since their brief conversation more than two months ago on election night. She would soon be the new first lady. Their relationship hadn't even lasted the requisite two months, and yet he thought she might be the one.

Beck had spent the last six weeks outlining his new book on the fall campaign, Bayard's money game, and the drug money flooding into American politics. He'd actually taken two solid weeks of vacation to write and decompress. His publisher wanted a first draft by April.

He had tried to call Geneva, but her cell phone had been disconnected—no doubt at the request of the Secret Service, he suspected. He didn't understand why she hadn't called him. He even called their mutual friend Ellen Elizabeth, who said she couldn't reach Geneva either. Beck found that hard to believe.

He knew it was over, and he had to move on. Yet he was struggling to let go. No woman had ever sunk her claws into him the way Geneva had.

A phone rang, then stopped. It rang again, and Beck realized it was his. He grabbed the receiver buried under a stack of papers on his desk.

"It's Rabidan," said the voice on the other end.

"Kerry, how are you?" Beck nuzzled the telephone under his neck as he sipped his morning coffee—the black crud he'd grabbed from the cafeteria downstairs. He looked around for a reporter's pad and stole one from Cheryl Rose's desk next door. "Hey. You've been covering everything lately. I've been meaning to call and congratulate you. You taking on the political beat?"

"No. Just general assignment."

"Well, your byline is everywhere. Congratulations. I don't think I've ever seen so many front page bylines."

"Thanks, Beck, but this is not a social call," she said.

What possibly could be business between them? Beck wondered. "Oh? What's up? You need help with something?"

Taking another sip of coffee, he thought about their past. When Rabidan first worked at the *Post-Examiner*, Beck had flirted with her. After a couple of times in the sack, he'd called it quits, although she admitted she would have done the same if he hadn't. They agreed they lacked chemistry. By some miracle, they managed to keep the fling quiet and maintained their friendship, helping each other on stories from time to time before she was downsized and immediately snatched up by the competition.

Beck adjusted the receiver closer to his ear so he could hear over the white noise of the newsroom. There was a long pause on the other end of the line. "What's up?" he asked again.

"We're running a story tomorrow that says you were sleeping with the future first lady, who was a lobbyist for Serodynne Corporation, at the same time you were investigating Serodynne's competitor, Lamurr Technologies, and its ties to Senator David Bayard. Care to comment?"

What did she just say? Beck's mind was scrambled, struggling to focus. Did Kerry just say that? He was stunned. How did she find out? Why was she writing this story? He realized his private life was about to become public fodder in a town full of gossips and enemies.

"Beck? Are you there?"

"Ah . . . shit. Kerry, why are you doing this to me?" He slammed down the phone, then buried his head in his hands. Immediately, he thought better of what he had just done.

He called Kerry back. "Off the record. Please don't run this story. You'll ruin my life."

"Beck, don't you think you had just a slight conflict of interest helping your girlfriend take down her competition?"

"It wasn't like that. It wasn't like that at all. She didn't know anything about it. At least at first. You can't run this story. It's complicated."

"Sorry. So seeing that I'm your friend, I'll ask again. Care to comment for the record?"

"Wait a minute. What about you and me? You're writing a story about a guy you slept with. Remember?"

"This is different, Beck, and you know it."

He looked at the telephone receiver and placed it quietly in its cradle. His life, as he knew it, was over. He could see it in his mind, the public humiliation that was about to come. He was about to become a laughing stock, a late-night punch line.

What was he going to do? Who told her?

Fahy. It had to have been Fahy. He must have called the *News-Times*. That son of a bitch. He was going to pay. Beck slammed his fist on his desk spilling his coffee on a stack of papers. No one was close enough to notice. Most reporters had yet to arrive.

Beck picked up his office phone and called Fahy's cell. He didn't care if it was traced to his newsroom landline. Fahy would probably be in his office, but this couldn't wait.

"Meet me at noon. We gotta talk."

"Tomorrow," Fahy replied. "Can't today."

"You son of a bitch, I need to talk to you now."

"I'm sorry. I can't. It's impossible. I have meetings with the new administration all day today starting in a half hour. What's got your tit in a ringer?"

"You know perfectly well." Beck slammed down the phone. That S.O.B. It had to be him. Fuming, Beck made a slow walk to Baker's office. He told him the entire story.

"Christ. You didn't see this possibility? Are you thinking with your dick? What the hell did you think you were doing?" Baker pulled out a cigarette from the pack in his breast pocket and lit up.

Beck had never seen him smoke before.

"I've got to go to Cunningham with this one," he said as he puffed.

Beck stumbled back to his desk. He didn't know how he would survive this. He eyed the back of Nancy's head at her perch across the newsroom but said nothing. An hour later, he saw Baker glance at him as he returned to his glass-enclosed office. He watched Baker pick up his phone, and he knew instinctively who he was calling. He stared as Nancy walked into the managing editor's office.

Fifteen minutes later, she emerged and strode sternly back to her desk. She did not look at Beck. Then one by one, each top editor's phone rang, and one by one, each marched into the boss's office. Every time an editor emerged, there would be a furtive glance in Beck's direction and then a swift turn of the head when their eyes met.

He felt disgraced. Everyone would soon be snickering at him behind his back, and he was helpless to do anything about it.

Little remained private in a newsroom for long. By midafternoon, it was apparent a good proportion of the staff knew the situation. Finally, his phone jarred him out of his funk, and he trudged into Baker's office.

"Kid. I hate to tell you, but I think you've done it this time. We need to do as much damage control as possible. Cunningham is not happy. She's already been on the phone to the publisher of the *News-Times*. The story is running front page above the fold tomorrow. Our friend Kerry has the byline."

Baker paused and rubbed his forehead. "Man, what were you thinking? Cunningham put her neck on the line for your stories. And look what you've done? It all looks suspect, like your motive was to screw Lamurr and help Serodynne win the contract for your girlfriend, the future first lady. Tomorrow, your reputation, and the reputation of this entire paper, will be under a cloud. Bayard supporters will be howling we were out to get their man, and I can't blame them for thinking that."

Beck hung his head, staring at the gray fibers in Baker's office rug. Cigarette ash slowly melted black spots in the synthetic fibers. He lifted his gaze. Two half-smoked cigarettes lay mashed atop Baker's desk in an ashtray Beck had never seen before.

"Senator Bayard may not be able to sue us for what you've done, but you may have just resurrected his political career. Tomorrow, he finds out he has a fighting chance at reelection in two years." Baker pushed the ashtray aside. "You know better. Reporters need to be unbiased, or at least appear to be."

Beck knew Baker was right. Why had he let it get so out of hand? The whole relationship just sort of happened before he got a grip on his own investigation. He felt his eyes glisten. He needed to keep it together in front of his boss.

"I'm sorry, kid, but you give us no choice. We've got to let you go. Go up to HR, and they'll help you with the paperwork. Cunningham has agreed to give you six months' severance, plus your unused sick leave and vacation. Pretty generous, if you ask me, but we want to recognize the good things you've done for the paper over your seventeen years here."

Baker rounded the desk and stuck out his hand. "Kid, I wish it didn't have to end this way. You're probably the best I've ever seen. Come in around seven tomorrow morning before the place gets busy and clean out your desk."

Beck couldn't believe what he was hearing. He'd just lost the best job in the world. He had nothing left.

After finishing up with human resources, Beck said his good-byes to several newsroom colleagues and editors. So many memories came to mind about so many good times working together. His relationship with each one would change. He knew that. They would still be part of the newspaper's family. And even though they were friends, he would now be the outsider, never sharing the same camaraderie again.

Nancy gave him a big hug. Tears streamed down her cheeks. "We did a lot of good together," she said. "Don't you forget it."

And then he broke down and sobbed softly, hugging her tightly with his cheek against the top of her head. He had disappointed his mentor, the woman he admired most—the woman who had backed him and trusted him and fought for him for so many years. He had failed her, and yet she was still trying to reassure him of his own worth.

BECK DIDN'T REMEMBER driving home. He stepped into his condo and lost it, sobbing uncontrollably, like never before in his life. He'd destroyed his career over a woman. How could he have been so stupid? It wasn't intentional, he told himself. It just happened.

Tomorrow, he would be a worldwide laughing stock.

"Oh, Jesus. What have I done, Red? The entire world will soon know. They'll never understand."

He placed his head in his hands. He remembered an aging bottle of sleeping pills left by an old girlfriend in the medicine cabinet. He could mix it with some alcohol. He had plenty of booze in the house. It would ease his pain forever. He wouldn't have to deal with tomorrow's wrath and eating humble pie for the rest of his life. He didn't see how he could ever get through the oncoming tidal wave of disgrace.

He walked to the cabinet above the kitchen sink where he kept his liquor. Behind the leaded glass in the carved oak door stood nine bottles of booze. Bourbon? Gin? Scotch? Vodka? They glared at him, inviting him to forget his problems for the moment. He grabbed the bourbon by the neck. He knew he didn't hold his bourbon well.

The pill bottle stood, short but stoic, in the medicine cabinet. He reached for it and read the label. "Do not take with alcohol." Why the hell not? No more Red. No more Nancy. No more . . . Geneva. No more . . .

He stepped into the kitchen and paused. "Why not?" he asked himself out loud. He looked at the bourbon bottle now standing alone on the countertop beckoning him, and then he glanced down at the bottle of pills, still grasped firmly in his hand. He quietly sighed, and his shoulders slumped. He unscrewed the bottle cap and slowly dumped the pills down the garbage disposal. He flipped the switch, and the whine of the motor crunching dry pills reminded him to turn on the water. Who was he kidding? He would take no chances. He would take his lumps. He'd figure out a way. He always had.

Beck smoked three Churchills before he drained the bottle. He tried to sleep in the dark on his balcony under two thick wool blankets, the empty bottle and an empty bourbon glass still on the floor by the daybed. With the last of the autumn leaves swept away by a thunderstorm long ago, he was fully exposed to the neighborhood—his only refuge, an empty bottle of booze.

In his haze as he surrendered to the alcohol, he thought of Geneva standing naked on the balcony in Cayman and forgot all about what tomorrow would bring.

65

Early the next morning, Starbucks black coffee in hand, Beck stepped into a near-empty newsroom. His head pounded mercilessly. Grumbling, he tossed most of his old story files in the janitor's fifty-gallon wheeled trash barrel, conveniently left next to his desk by the night crew. An appropriate burial site for his work, he thought.

It surprised him how few of his files he wanted to preserve. Seventeen years of labor, meticulously filed in cabinet and desk drawers, now lay pitched in a heap in one large trash bin—quite a showing for a lifetime of hard work.

Going forward, everything he ever did or said, including his obituary, would be accompanied by an asterisk. One mistake—one stupid mistake—and his career was over. His life was permanently labeled. Here he was, the sole heir to his legacy, presiding over the wake of his career in an empty newsroom with no one else in attendance. He'd been single all of his life, yet he had never felt so alone.

The newsroom outlaw was now an outcast. When you get fired, you learn quickly who your friends are, Beck thought. The phone hadn't rung once last night.

He remembered the dinner with Geneva in the diner near Winchester. He had wondered then if anyone outside the Beltway even cared about his work. Today, he knew. The evidence lay in a pile on the city desk—today's editions of major newspapers from all across the country waiting to be read. He could not bear to go near them.

He pulled on the top drawer filled with pens, notebooks, notes on various scraps of colored paper, and old files. Even after the stories disappeared, the files outlining his labor remained and brought life to his old investigations. On occasion, maybe every three or four years, he would open a file and reread it, reliving one of his greatest stories. They did not get lost in the unending grind of daily deadlines. His stories lived on in his memory and his notes—triumphs of his cunning and unbending tenacity.

Beck sighed, regret and nostalgia rushing through his body. He was like a dog with a buried bone. He couldn't let go. Not just yet.

He thought of his book publisher, and the regret intensified. Would he still be interested in a book after reading this morning's headline? Would Judy, his agent?

Most of his life had been off the record. Now it was a headline. This morning, as the world awoke to its morning coffee and newspaper on the front stoop, it would learn much more about him. He cowered at the thought and tried to think of something else.

Beck filled two banker's boxes with a handful of books, two coffee mugs, various notebooks, pens, and an old pocket calculator. His desk lay clear except for a battered company dictionary, used long before online dictionaries and spell-check were the norm. He had found it under a pile of loose papers on the corner of his desk.

There were also a couple of paperback mysteries Nancy had loaned him that he had never returned. He walked across the newsroom to her desk and left them on her chair.

By nine o'clock, long before most reporters arrived for the day, his desk was as empty as his career. He glanced at the newsroom one last time and hefted the contents of the last box. Seventeen years, he thought. He would never be here again.

The elevator doors opened, and he turned and pressed the button for the rooftop parking lot. The doors merged, forever sealing off this view of his old life. His newspaper career, like his old stories, had disappeared into the inevitable ether. Another deadline had passed.

WHEN HE RETURNED TO HIS condo, Beck didn't bother emptying the trunk of his Volvo. He grabbed his morning papers and went upstairs, locking his front door behind him. He laid the papers out on his dining room table for the full effect, then took several deep breaths before opening the first one.

The *News-Times* story was as bad as it could get. An Associated Press photo taken of him when he was heading into the federal courthouse was splashed near the top of the page. Next to his mug was Geneva's picture. God, this was bad.

Rabidan got a "no comment" from Harvey's presidential transition team, and there was nothing from Geneva. Obviously, she knew this story was coming, and still she hadn't called. Perhaps she was under such close scrutiny in the bubble that she couldn't contact him—at least that's what he wanted to believe.

He squeezed his eyes shut and tried to think of something else. Then he grabbed the *Post-Examiner*. Nothing about him, but a story at the bottom of page three caught his eye. Jackson Oliver had resigned as assistant attorney general for the criminal division.

"I can't believe it. That bastard. They got him." But unlike himself, it appeared Oliver would get to go quietly, his reputation intact. Welcome to Washington, Beck thought. Someday, he would expose Oliver. And then he caught himself. He would never get the chance.

He read on. The administration considered Daniel Fahy the leading candidate to replace Oliver at Justice. Shit. He couldn't even blow the whistle on Fahy for leaking his affair with Geneva. He had not only lost his career and his girlfriend, but his standing and the power that went with his job. The gravity of his loss was beginning to seep in, and he was struggling to figure out what he could do about it.

66

"You son of a bitch," Beck said when he approached Fahy at their usual table in the back of the restaurant. "You told the *News-Times*."

"Told them what?"

"About Jen and me."

"Are you nuts? We have a pact. The last thing I'd do is provoke you."

You're a liar too, he thought. "Then who did?"

"Who do you think?"

Beck sat down at the table. Without prompting, the buxom waitress brought him a cup of black coffee and asked if he'd like something to eat. He declined. And this time, Beck barely glanced at her ample bosom, her cleavage screaming for his attention.

"If it wasn't you, then I haven't a clue."

"Last week, I got a call from a very old friend seeking advice on how to place a story in the *News-Times* about you and Geneva."

"Who?"

"Her husband, Mike Harvey."

Beck almost dropped his coffee cup. He couldn't believe it. "Harvey? He wouldn't do that to his own wife."

"He said you pushed him to it. Geneva told him months ago about the two of you."

"But they had an arrangement. He okayed our relationship." Beck leaned on the table, closing the distance with Fahy.

"I know nothing about that. All I know is what he told me. Geneva apparently told Mike she didn't want to live in the political fishbowl with all the guards, the handlers, and the sycophants. She told him if he took the job, she would leave him. Obviously, the vice presidency meant more to him than she did. And now events have overtaken both of them. If she thought being the wife of the vice president was life in a fishbowl, imagine what she faces as first lady."

Beck shook his head, still not believing. "How do you know all of this?"

"I was one of his law school students thirty years ago. He taught a few classes at Georgetown at night. When I graduated, before I even passed the bar, he helped me get my first job at Justice. We've been friends ever since, and I was his personal Justice Department source for information. He also knew Oliver was blocking my advancement at Justice."

"You mean this was all a setup?" Beck leaned back. He eyed Fahy, looking for any hint of the truth.

"Are you kidding? No one knew how this would all play out."

"What was that whole business in the courtroom? That property manager in Cayman never told me about the government investigation."

"You know that, and I know that, but the rest of the world doesn't. The FBI came to me about the Oliver connection before you and I ever met. Oliver did his best to block the investigation, but he wasn't too subtle. And when the FBI told me his half brother was involved, I had every right to secretly investigate my boss. So I sent the FBI to Cayman before you ever got there. We interviewed the property manager. I remember the agent—"

"Was that McCauley? Jen told me about McCauley."

"Sorry. I can't say. Let's just say you have good instincts. The agent told me about that Agee fellow—the property manager. The FBI said he was reliable, but scattered and tended to mix up things."

"Yeah. I found that out too. I had to document everything he told me." Beck looked at the full cup of coffee in front of him and realized he badly needed a caffeine fix. He took a swig.

"So I told the agent to drag him back here for your hearing, threaten him if he had to. But that wasn't necessary. He was more than willing to take a free trip to the States, especially after I told him we would put him up in the W Hotel for a week. So I met with Mr. Agee the day before your hearing and reminded him several times about how the FBI agent had told him of our investigation of Senator Bayard. He said he only remembered the agent telling him about our investigation of Oliver, so I told him they were the same case, and he bought it. It was that simple."

"You mean the agent never told him about the Bayard investigation?"

"Of course not."

Beck shook his head in disbelief. "You manipulated the witness."

"It's all part of the job. We call it justice."

"That's what scares me. Behind the scenes, justice is twisted and manipulated. My case could have gone the other way."

"Not a chance."

They stared at each other in silence.

Beck shook his head. "You lawyers amaze me. And to think I wanted to be one when I was a kid."

"I've been meaning to ask, whatever happened to your source in Venezuela? The one that linked Oliver to Lamurr. We'd like to follow that lead."

"He completely disappeared."

"That means they got him." Fahy bit his bottom lip.

"You mean someone killed him?" The idea made Beck cringe.

"Probably. Or he's fled. Their tentacles are everywhere. Caracas is a very violent place. Another murder there could easily go unnoticed."

"What about the Cayman murders?"

"Oh, that's been mothballed. A bunch of fools down there running the place."

Beck said nothing about his conversation with Inspector Tomlinson. He assumed the gardener had been apprehended, which meant Fahy was either uninformed or lying. He suspected the latter. Beck seesawed from believing him to not trusting him.

The Boy Scout had said nothing about the taped conversation enabled by the burner phone. Obviously, he knew that Beck had figured it out. Yet would either of them confront the other, or would they continue to play this game?

The waitress eased a heavy plate of food onto the table in front of Fahy. She warned him it was hot. The smell of cheese and refried beans tempted Beck's nostrils, but he wasn't hungry. He would stick with his black coffee.

Fahy took an indifferent bite of his tamale smothered in chili. He wiped his chin with his napkin and continued with his mouth half full. "You might be out of a job, Beck, but you should count your blessings you're alive. You never knew how close you came. But you've done all the damage you can do now. Harvey made sure of that. I've no doubt there was some spite in his decision to expose you and Geneva, but he told me he wanted to protect her at all costs. He doesn't want either one of you in danger. The only way to assure that, in his mind, was for you to no longer be a reporter for the *Post-Examiner*, no longer chasing the drug money stories. So he embarrassed himself and his soon-to-be ex-wife to save you both."

"Ex-wife?" Beck's heart leaped.

"They are secretly getting a divorce. It will be announced after the inauguration. She wants nothing to do with Washington anymore."

Beck sat in silence. If that was true, why hadn't she called?

The waitress came by again and asked if they wanted more coffee.

"Black," Fahy said.

Beck watched as she also filled his cup, then looked at Fahy as she walked away. "Did Harvey have anything to do with this whole affair? I mean going back to the very beginning? Did the two of you hatch a plan to give Harvey the vice presidency—or the presidency—and use me to deliver it?"

Beck paused, brain spinning, and then pushed forward. "Of course you did. As soon as you tied Oliver to Bayard, the two of you conspired to bring me into the loop to carry out your plan. You needed outside help to make it all happen. The Justice Department couldn't do it, but I sure could. What an incredibly brilliant scheme."

Beck was searching, not sure what the truth was anymore.

Fahy smiled. "Not even I could pull that off."

Beck eyeballed Fahy. He was craftier than his aging government bureaucrat persona let on. The guy seemed to always be one step ahead of him. Beck kicked himself for taking so long to realize that. He thought of himself as the master of the inside play, yet this midlevel government bureaucrat had outmaneuvered him.

67

Geneva balanced the Harvey family Bible on her upturned palms on a bitterly cold Monday under a gray January sky as Harv stepped forward on the platform on the western front of the Capitol to take the oath of office. Later, after a luncheon with Congress and a long, colorful inaugural parade that lasted into the evening, Jen and Harv attended several inaugural balls and danced late into the night. As much as she enjoyed dancing, being on display for thousands at each ball was grueling. She and Harv would take a turn around the stage to one song at each event. She felt like a circus act. All Geneva could think about was never having to perform again.

Afterward, the Secret Service delivered her unnoticed to the condo. Harv slept alone in the White House.

THE NEXT MORNING, GENEVA stepped out of her condo and into the hall. The Secret Service agent stationed outside her door sat on a chair, reading her morning newspaper. When she appeared, he quickly folded it and handed it to her, feigning a sheepish look, as if he had committed some crime. While his role was different from her political aides, his behavior reminded her of the obsequious nature of Washington minions who coddled the politically significant every day, prostrating themselves just to be within arm's reach of power. Harv was right, she thought, power is the ultimate aphrodisiac.

And it hadn't changed even when her affair with Beck made the front pages and evening news shows of America. It was just one more scandal of many out of Washington. But this was the one time she had been thankful for the trappings of power. The Secret Service had kept the press at bay. Harv had arranged for the Secret Service to guard her until she left town. In moments, she would be persona non grata in Washington's social strata. To walk away was unheard of. No more aides and no protection. Many Washington insiders spent their entire working lives clawing to reach her social status, while Geneva couldn't wait to leave.

She stepped back into the penthouse and walked into her living room. It felt different without Harv there. She dropped her robe on a chair and stood naked in the middle of her living room. Then she picked up her phone and called Keith.

"Hey, hun, it's Jen. Are we all set?"

"Everything is in order," Keith said.

"Then I'll meet you at the airport."

"I'm so looking forward to this. I never thought this day would come."

"That makes two of us. You have saved me from this crazy world. See you soon."

She showered and dressed quickly. She felt giddy, as if a whole new world was opening up to her. Geneva wheeled a couple of suitcases over to the front door of the condo and opened it to the hallway. The limo driver was waiting and asked if he could assist. Without her having time to answer, he took her bags.

She checked her watch. She told the driver she needed to make a phone call and would be down in a few minutes. The Secret Service agent eyed her from his perch in the hallway outside of her penthouse, but he said nothing.

The driver expertly wheeled his black SUV across the Fourteenth Street Bridge. Through her tinted window, Geneva saw frost on the marsh and barren trees lining the George Washington Parkway. The morning sun had yet to melt it away. She fingered her leather jacket. She couldn't wait to ditch the coat for a more accommodating climate. She could hardly wait to get there. But first, she had one last difficult phone call to make to someone special.

68

Beck walked alone on the beach near the pier on Fort Myers Beach, squinting at a couple of bikini-clad women jogging his way on the hardened, wet sand near the edge of the gentle lapping waves. He fumbled in his pocket for sunglasses.

He had flown in yesterday to escape the hoopla of the inauguration, as well as his fellow reporters who were still hounding him for comment. Back at the condo, his answering machine was full of their messages seeking details of his affair with Geneva.

Beck wondered what happened to all of the newsroom colleagues who had celebrated with him after the drug money story. Not one had called. Journalism was almost as cynical as politics, or maybe, he thought, it was just a different form.

This was the first leg of his resignation tour, Beck decided. Florida first, and then wherever the tide took him. Someplace warm, he promised himself. It was still January.

Just before lunchtime, he sat at the near-empty bar at the pier, ordered a beer, and unfolded his *USA Today*. The headline screamed at him: "President Harvey Divorcing." Just as Fahy had said. He wondered if they still had a chance or if he and Geneva were just victims of incredibly bad timing. Yet Beck had to acknowledge he had brought it on himself, or at least his ego and his investigation had.

The story said the president and First Lady Geneva Kemper had officially divorced the day before the inauguration but decided not to disclose it until after the festivities were over. Beck pored over every word, though the only part that interested him was a sentence near the end about Ms. Kemper leaving Washington. Her future and final destination, the story said, were not disclosed. A spokesman for President Harvey said Geneva was seeking a "new beginning" and sought privacy away from Washington.

"I wonder," he said under his breath. He placed his elbow on the bar; his chin rested in his right hand. Beck smiled, remembering their time in Grand Cayman and their conversation about Geneva's favorite getaways. He was mulling over the idea when his phone rang. He fished it out of his shorts and read the display.

"Nancy, how are you?"

"I should be asking you that."

"I've been better."

"I can imagine. Look, I know this is too late to do you any good, but I thought you would want to know. My source finally came through on your license plate. The government car was checked out to an FBI agent named Patrick McCauley."

Beck closed his eyes. It all made sense. All the pieces finally fell into place. "That confirms my suspicion," he said.

"How so?"

"He fit Geneva's description. He tried to use makeup to hide his true age. Tried to make himself look much older."

"So now you know the FBI was involved." Nancy sounded hesitant.

"And he's tied directly to Fahy. When McCauley met with me down here in Florida, he already knew I'd discovered the fraudulent land deals were actually used to launder drug money. I was alone the day before in my home when I made that discovery. The only way he could have known was to have access to the listening device inside the phone Fahy gave me."

"So Fahy was using the FBI to plant his version of the story to assure you were on it and would bring down Patten. Yet you already had it figured out."

"Seems so. I guess they just needed some insurance. Nancy, think about what Fahy accomplished. It's breathtaking. He's the ultimate inside player. He not only had me take down Bayard, but then used McCauley to assure I got rid of Patten as well. And look who's left standing—Geneva's ex-husband, Michael Harvey."

Beck paused to consider all of this. What he left unsaid was that it was Harvey who took him down. Every last move was precise, and in twenty-twenty hindsight, totally predictable. Beck just had been too narrowly focused on his own story instead of the bigger narrative unfolding all around him. He had to give them credit. They were the best political chess players he had ever come across. Now, Beck knew exactly what their next move would be, yet he was in no position to do a thing about it.

"Beck? You there?" asked Nancy.

"Sorry. I'm still putting this together in my head. Despite everything, I've still got to protect that bastard Fahy as my source. How's that for irony? I have to protect him, yet now that he has no further need for me, he could let his drug lord buddies do with me as they please."

"Beck, you're scaring me."

Beck kept talking as if he hadn't heard her. "He would then be rid of the one person with knowledge of how he orchestrated the election to get his man in the Oval Office."

"Beck, you really are scaring me," she repeated. He could hear a tremor in her voice.

"Yeah, I'm starting to scare myself thinking about it. But early on, Fahy gave me one piece of good advice: protect myself. Have some insurance, he said. Back then, he was talking about protecting my skin from the drug bosses, which come to think of it, was in his best interest. My insurance policy was simple—just have you and the other editors at the paper know the details of my story to assure publication should something ever happen to me."

"Duh. So what do you propose now?"

"I need another insurance policy."

"Tell me what you need. What can I do?"

Her voice sounded stronger, like the old Nancy. Even when he was in exile, Nancy still had his back. It was hitting him now how much he would miss working with her.

"Would you be willing to hold a story—forever if need be—about our friend Daniel Fahy? Could you guarantee publication if something ever happened to me?"

"I think that could be easily arranged. What exactly are you talking about?"

"I'm going to write about my entire relationship with him from the very first day. If he harms me in any way, I'm certainly under no obligation to protect him then."

"I get it."

"You'll have the story later today."

"But, Beck, we've got to stay in touch. I need to know you're still okay. If I don't hear from you at least once a month, the story goes to press. Deal?"

"Fair enough. I'll e-mail you a draft shortly."

What a woman, he thought. He hung up, paid his tab, and headed back to his hotel. Red wasn't anywhere around, but Beck had no problem writing this story. He had lived it.

When he was done with the final paragraph and tapped a few keys on his laptop to send his story to Nancy, he felt elated and decided to celebrate with a few more beers back at the pier.

The bartender recognized him before he sat down and slid a Corona Light across the bar as Beck straddled a stool. Beck immediately took a swig. It was especially cold, like it had been on ice, and the crisp taste satisfied his thirst. He then pulled the new burner phone from his pocket and studied it. It matched Fahy's perfectly, except this one contained no hidden listening device. He glanced up to make sure the bartender was at the other end of the bar. He was tending to a beefy retired couple.

Beck quickly dialed a number he knew by heart. After five rings, voice mail kicked in.

"Danny boy. It's your good buddy, Beck. I wanted to talk with you about the Irish mafia. I guess you're not answering your cell phone anymore. But sooner or later, you'll check your messages. So here goes. Your guy McCauley makes a pretty good Latino. The accent, the makeup—was pretty realistic." Beck paused, giving Fahy a moment to let that sink in.

"You slipped up though, using the FBI to follow me. Very Nixonian, don't you think? Not your smartest move. I suspect a front-page story in the *Post-Examiner* would cause a furor on Capitol Hill and would put you and our new president in a very precarious position."

"Okay," Beck continued on Fahy's voice mail, "so you used me. I guess in reality, we used each other. I got my stories. You got your man in the White House. Just who played whom? I'll leave that up to you to decide. But to quote your favorite president, let me make one thing perfectly clear: Red has everything. And I do mean everything. If anything happens to me—anything—the complete story, with you smack-dab in the middle of it, goes public. Now I'm done. I'm walking away. But if I should suddenly disappear in a few years—hell, if I should stub my toe or get an unexpected nosebleed—everything goes public without any help from me. It's all on autopilot. So my health is now your number one concern. Are we clear?"

Beck hung up, paid his tab, and meandered out onto the pier, donning his yellow shades and blue Kalik beer baseball cap to shield his eyes from a blazing sun. He noticed the pelicans swooping low overhead as the tourists and fishermen leaned against the pocked concrete sides of the structure and baited their hooks. The faint stench of dead baitfish mixed with the gentle salt air breeze.

His phone rang. He grabbed the burner from his pocket and punched "Talk." But the ringing persisted. Shit, it was his own cell phone. He reached into the other pocket of his cargo shorts and checked the number. It was his agent.

"Judy, how are you?"

"Not good, Beck."

"Oh. What's up?"

"Your book. The publisher backed out of the deal. He said your firing and the controversy around your affair made it a hard sell."

"Shit." Beck turned, looking back to shore. "Wouldn't all the publicity about me make it easier to sell?"

"It would if you were willing to write about your affair."

Beck cringed. He knew that wasn't going to happen.

"The publisher said he's worried about your credibility."

"My credibility? Not one word in my story has ever been challenged."

"I know. I know. But we're talking about a publisher, and he thinks you're tainted goods and a bad financial risk."

"I've got two best sellers for crying out loud."

"I'm sorry, Beck. There's nothing I can do. Frankly, I wouldn't be surprised if he got a call from Washington that spooked him. Publishers are big conglomerates these days, and they are players in Washington just like every other big business. I'll try to sell it elsewhere, but it might be difficult in light of what's happened. Once one publisher turns down a book like this, the others tend to get skittish—especially if they think they can't trust the writer."

"Sheep. The publishing world is a bunch of fuckin' sheep." Beck watched a pelican swoop down to the water, scoop up a fish, and swallow it whole.

"Well, it gets worse. They want their advance back."

"All hundred thousand?"

"All hundred thousand."

"Well, there goes the Rolls-Royce."

"I'm glad you can see the humor in this, but there goes my commission as well."

"Sorry, Judy." Jeez. What else could go wrong? Beck bent over the side of the pier, looking out into the gulf.

"I'm sorry too, Beck." The phone went dead.

It was a beautiful day, but the bright blue sky, with only a wisp of clouds, didn't help his mood. How could things get worse? His career, his woman, his book, his financial security, and now his credibility—the only thing a reporter had going for him. All gone. All of it. And yet it was all based on a story that was rock solid. He didn't get one damned fact wrong. Not one. How can you write a great story that brings down a future president, and it destroy your own career as well? It made no sense to him.

He'd always felt so confident he was doing the right thing. Journalism—finding the truth—was his calling. But now he was not so sure. What difference did all of his work really make? It didn't change Washington. And now he was just another nobody who others found convenient to exploit.

Beck pulled the back off the cheap burner phone, yanked out the battery, and dropped it into the sea. It hardly made a splatter. He wanted nothing to do with it anymore. He glanced around. The tourists and the fishermen with their lines in the water were as preoccupied as the circling pelicans with their wings spread, gliding just feet above all of them, always eager to snatch their catch in their flabby gray bills.

He took one last look at the now useless phone and dropped it into the surf, watching it quickly disappear. Like his life, no one noticed. His concerns were not theirs. His world had come to a halt while the rest of the world kept spinning. He couldn't stop Fahy without revealing him as his source, and he couldn't ethically do that—not as long as Fahy continued to play by the rules. Even if he never wrote for another newspaper, in his heart Beck would always be a journalist and play by its rules—well, most of its rules anyway.

But now he had to move on. He needed to get over his pity party and get to that special place in his head again—where he felt jazzed—and his brain was on fire. That left him with only one option.

69

Keith Crocker looked at rows of suits talking loudly on their cell phones, seated on the morning shuttle leaving New York's LaGuardia Airport. Their destination was Reagan National Airport in Washington, and the ten o'clock flight was crowded for a Friday morning.

What were they worth? Not as much as he was. Keith smiled, thinking about Geneva and what they had done together. Even though he was much younger than her, they had this incredible connection. Well, she had twenty years with an older guy. Now she would have her chance with a much younger one.

He had never dated an older woman before. She made him realize just how much he had missed. Geneva opened up a whole new world. Okay, so they hadn't done it yet. So what? She said their timing wasn't right. Her life, she told him, needed to be less complicated. At first he thought she was blowing him off, but now he understood. Sex with the Secret Service in tow would have been a bit impractical. Now their timing was right. He was glad she was always thinking two or three steps ahead. He was richer than many of his firm's partners because of it. He smiled at the thought.

And he knew she was worth the wait. Just kissing her was an erotic experience. He never thought making out could be so exciting. She was better than any woman he had ever met, either in college or while living in Manhattan.

Suddenly, his thoughts were interrupted. The attendant announced they were ready for takeoff, and to fasten their seat belts, turn off all laptops, and set all cell phones in airplane mode.

He powered down his cell and checked his pocket for his ticket: a first-class seat from Washington, where they would meet up, to Grand Cayman via Charlotte. Geneva had sprung for it. He smiled. They had so much money, it didn't matter who paid. But she had told him she wanted to do him this one small favor, so she paid for it out of one of their new Grand Cayman bank accounts—the final destination for their fortunes.

Think of it as her way of saying thank you for everything he had done for her, she had told him. It was a sweet gesture, he thought. And thank you? He should be thanking her for their incredibly profitable relationship. My god, not only was he now rich, but he was about to have the most beautiful belle at the ball. What more could he ask for? Sex? He assured himself that was only a matter of hours away. He could feel his heart pound faster, just thinking of her.

In a little over an hour, they would be together again. Tonight, they would be having incredible sex on the beach, if he had his way. Tomorrow, they would begin figuring out how to invest their fortune and create a future for themselves.

Her plan, he recalled, had been so simple. Keith knew Geneva must have had some inside information, and it had been his chance for a huge score. Together, their initial take was nearly $10 million spread across all of their phony accounts. He had been ready to take his shares and go to the islands. But she had stopped him. "Trust me," she had told him. Now he was glad he had.

"Why take just a few million for yourself when you can multiply your nest egg many times over?" she'd asked.

She had instructed him to reinvest all of their funds, but this time, she'd added a twist. Instead of investing in Lamurr Technologies, this time she'd told him to buy options in her company, Serodynne. At first he had been uncertain.

But whatever Geneva knew, she had already proven to be a superior risk.

It was so simple, yet so clever, Keith thought. He should have thought of it, but he realized he would have needed Geneva's insider knowledge. And none of that mattered when he started to figure their gain. It was a gargantuan fortune—nearly $77 million. His share was somewhere around $12 million.

Then when Robert Gettlin showed up asking questions about Geneva's account, he'd thought the roof had caved in. But without really thinking, he'd managed to embarrass Gettlin, and thank god the man cared more about his golf game than his clients. He'd never followed up. Keith had actually intimidated him. He couldn't believe it.

But that experience and the time Bernstein had recognized a name on one of Keith's phony accounts had spooked him. He needed protection. So Keith had changed the information on two of his phony accounts—naming both Gettlin and Bernstein as owners—and never cashed them in.

His absence from work next week would spark an internal investigation, and eventually, the partners would figure out what he had done. But the investigation would stop there. They would not contact the feds for fear of implicating Gettlin and Bernstein. And would they really want any of this to see the light of day, especially with its close ties to a new president?

Finally, Keith was free to pursue his dream. No more Gettlin, no more Bernstein, no more Wall Street. He was going to write the great American novel—or at least some pretty lousy detective novels. He needed a lot of practice and experience to get really good. He didn't really care at this point. He had lots of free time ahead. His lifestyle was now his own, all his, and no one could disrupt it.

WHEN HE ARRIVED AT REAGAN NATIONAL Airport, Keith switched gates. Fortunately, his connecting gate for Charlotte was nearby. He had only a carry-on bag and his briefcase with his laptop. It was an island, he told himself. He didn't need much more than shorts, T-shirts, and sandals. And he could afford to buy anything he wanted—from clothes to shelter. Anything he wanted, he told himself, though he still found his newfound wealth hard to grasp.

At first, he thought of telling his landlord he was leaving for good and to sell off his furniture for the rent. But then he realized he needed to change his way of thinking about money and assets. He could afford to keep the apartment, even if he didn't live there. He could afford just about anything.

He glanced around the terminal, looking for Geneva. She hadn't arrived yet. He had a few minutes before the first-class boarding call. Those needing assistance were already on the Jetway to the plane. Then they called first class. He jumped in line, quickly boarded, and found his seat. The attendant offered him a drink, and he ordered a vodka tonic, then lost himself for a few minutes in a copy of *Wine Spectator* magazine.

Ten minutes later, the plane was still boarding, and he began to worry. He signaled the attendant.

"We have another twenty minutes before we close the door," she assured him. "We're actually a little ahead of schedule today."

The time ticked by slowly. He looked at his watch. Then looked again. Where was Geneva? Did she get the time right?

A young woman in a tight, low-cut tank top and designer jeans walked up to his seat. "Excuse me," she said.

Her cleavage was at his eye level. He managed to look up into a pair of crystalline green eyes surrounded by soft, smooth skin and thick blonde hair. He smiled at her beauty.

"Excuse me," she said again, now glaring at him. "I'm sitting in the window seat next to you."

"I believe there's a mistake. My friend is sitting here."

"No, I've got seat three-A." She showed him her ticket.

He signaled the attendant. "I think there is a mistake with this ticket," he said.

The attendant examined the young woman's ticket. "No, sir. This is correct. Is this not your companion?"

He was confused. Maybe Geneva couldn't get two seats together. He stood to let the young woman by, then Keith reached into his pocket for his phone. He'd forgotten to turn it back on after his flight from New York.

Had Geneva called?

He'd call her.

He pressed the power switch on his phone. Why had he done that? Why had he turned it off instead of just switching it to airplane mode? Old habits die hard, he thought. Now he'd have to wait for it to power up.

The screen was black. Then a small image appeared. Come on, he said under his breath. He hated that about cell phones. They always took forever to power up.

The attendant came over. "I'm sorry, sir, but we are getting ready to close the door. Have you heard from your party?"

His mind raced trying to figure out what had happened. "Come on, phone," he said under his breath. Was Geneva going to miss their flight? He looked down at his phone. He was still waiting for it to come to life.

"Sir?"

"Just a sec," he said, waving her off. The phone suddenly exploded with light. He swiped his finger across the screen, entered his pass code, and punched the telephone app icon.

"Sir, we are getting ready to close the door."

He checked his voice mail. Geneva had called about half an hour ago, while he was in flight.

"Sir, I'm sorry, but you must switch your phone to airplane mode."

Then it hit him. Without listening to her message, he knew what had happened. He jumped up, grabbed his briefcase and bag, and ran off the plane.

70

The driver pulled into the general aviation terminal at Reagan National Airport and was guided to a hangar where a private jet waited. She was the only passenger. The copilot and limo driver loaded Geneva's luggage in the cargo hold and helped her up the stairs before pulling up the door. Then she sat for half an hour as the pilot explained he needed to complete some paperwork and get his clearances from the tower. Finally, the engines whined and the plane shimmied as they taxied toward the runway.

"We are fourth in line for takeoff," the captain said over the intercom.

Geneva checked her watch and wondered about what she had done. Keith would be in the terminal by now. Just before she had left the condo, she had dialed his number to leave a message. She knew he was in the air at that time, and so she kept her message cryptic. She did not tell him she had transferred her funds out of the Cayman accounts just minutes before.

Truthfully, she had thought about taking everything but his original $55,000 investment. Let him work his way up the ladder as she had. But then she thought better of it. If he had something, he would not be inclined to seek her out. He could afford to leave New York and lay low. And besides, how much did she really need at this point? So she left him his entire share, enough money to enable him to disappear forever. And she knew he couldn't afford to make noise and come after her without admitting to authorities he was guilty of a major crime.

It ached a bit to admit she'd misled and manipulated Keith to ensure his cooperation. It was a side of herself she hated, the very essence of the life she was fleeing. This one last deceit, she reasoned, was worth the price to assure her own future.

It was over, she had told him in her message, and she'd apologized for doing it this way over the phone. He would have a great life, she'd promised, and then she had wished him luck with his writing and hung up. It was short, not sweet.

She had always expected something to go wrong with their financial deal, but Keith had followed her instructions to the letter, and it had gone off flawlessly. It had been so insanely easy. And her involvement was all perfectly legal.

Insider trading was still prevalent in Congress, and the Senate rules against it had been so watered down when no one was paying attention, that no elected official could effectively be prosecuted. So nothing she did as a wife of a US senator could be questioned.

She had instructed Keith to open her brokerage account using both her name and Harv's. Keith had never questioned why. So as far as the law was concerned, it was Harv's money—Harv's immune insider trading—even though he knew nothing about it and likely never would.

And if there ever were any rumblings, Harv could easily quell a Securities and Exchange Commission investigation. She knew the SEC, which was supposed to regulate Wall Street and discipline wrongdoers, was packed with Wall Street hacks and toadies. It had Wall Street's back all the way. Typical Washington ethics, she thought.

And as for Keith, he would keep quiet. Unlike her, Senate insider trading rules did not protect him. He could be prosecuted for receiving insider information and trading on it—to say nothing of the bogus accounts he had set up for himself.

Imagine. A starving writer who thought he could live high without earning it—before he ever wrote a damn thing. No one got to her station in life by skipping years of humiliation—the bending and bowing to others' unreasonable demands. The dues were expensive. Nearly everyone in Washington had to pay at one time or another. He was a writer. Even if he was from New York—especially if he was from New York—he should know better. Washington arrogance mixed with youthful exuberance, she thought. But she had given in and let him have his share. In the end, she reasoned, he really did earn it, and she would be forever grateful.

Geneva leaned back in her soft leather seat and closed her eyes. The jet banked into a turn, and she felt the sun's rays skate across her face. It reminded her of where she was going.

She opened her eyes and looked around the small cabin. The female flight attendant sat in the front of the plane. Geneva slumped in her large swivel seat, stretched her legs, and kicked off her shoes. She looked up, realizing she could barely stand without hitting her head under the low cabin ceiling.

"Would you mind turning around?" Geneva asked. "I'd like to change my clothes."

She pulled off her wool sweater and tight designer jeans and changed into a billowy white blouse and short, baggy navy-blue shorts. No underwear. She was finally comfortable.

"Thank you," she said to the attendant, who did not turn around, but waved her hand back at Geneva, signaling she heard her. "It's okay. Really," she told the attendant.

The attendant finally turned to acknowledge her. "Drink, ma'am?" she asked.

"Love one. Weed, please." Jeremiah Weed, Geneva meant, the blended whiskey she had given Beck back on Grand Cayman that had helped him sleep that night. An air force colonel in the Pentagon's contracts office had told her once how fighter pilots celebrated surviving yet another dangerous mission. Upon their return, they would toast one another with the Weed. She thought it was appropriate and had requested the jet service stock a bottle for her trip.

She swirled it around in her mouth and swallowed, feeling the burn. The late morning sun now stood directly overhead as she peered through the porthole at the wispy clouds between her and the earth five miles below. She set her drink down, leaned her head back, and closed her eyes again.

She thought about how she had intended on only befriending Beck and leaking him the story. Yet someone—she did not know who—had beaten her to it before they had even gotten to Grand Cayman. And now, as of this morning, she had severed her ties with the island, having moved her money to a bank in Great Abaco, in the Bahamas. There, it now awaited her and her private jet, which would land in another two hours.

The smile did not leave her face. Almost everything had worked out as planned. The only thing she hadn't counted on was falling for a newspaper reporter with a silly mustache who tended to talk to himself. He was now a casualty of her war—her biggest and her only regret. She thought about Beck for a long while. She missed him. It would have been nice, she thought, if he could have been part of her life.

And what would she do with her life now? She hadn't thought that through. She told herself she had plenty of time to figure it out.

Then the Weed kicked in, and she fell asleep.

Another mission accomplished.

71

Geneva stepped deliberately onto the rocking ferryboat in Great Abaco's Marsh Harbour marina and into her new life. The private jet arrived right on time, and getting through customs at the tiny airport took about a minute. The ferry would take her to a private cay about a twenty-minute ride across the large natural harbor. The boat captain, dressed in shorts and a wrinkled light blue fishing shirt, hefted her two large bags aboard the water taxi. She managed the carry-on and her briefcase.

She had rented a furnished villa with an option to buy, which faced the sunrise over the Caribbean. It was one she had admired when she and Harv stayed in a nearby cottage for two weeks seven years ago. It was five acres of privacy and three hundred feet of private beachfront on a private island. Finally, her piece of paradise. The $4 million asking price was now well within her means. She felt giddy, like a child, and almost laughed out loud for no other reason than sheer elation. She was free to do anything she wanted—absolutely anything, she reminded herself.

The Bahamian government and people frowned upon nudity on their public beaches, but a private island, by definition, set its own rules. And the weather and people were both warm and inviting. Unlike Cayman, it had seasons. In the winters, the temperatures sometimes dropped into the sixties. Summers were in the eighties. There were blue skies and sunshine.

She could go skinny-dipping any day she wanted, she told herself. And she could lie naked in the sun on the patio of her secluded estate, and no one would know she was there. No cars honking on the streets below. No presidential helicopters hovering overhead. Only the sounds of waves lapping on the shore. She would finally have her privacy, her peace of mind.

She looked out over the harbor. Abaco catered to hundreds of sailboats and private yachts that converged on the island each spring. Marsh Harbour became a beautiful enclave of money with ambition bobbing conspicuously at the end of an anchor line. The anxiety that created it all was temporarily left behind. That was something Geneva completely understood.

She remembered Great Guana Cay, one of the small islands that enclosed the harbor. It was known for Nipper's, a funky outdoor beach bar with music, a rickety dance floor, a small swimming pool, and ocean access far below via a sandals-only set of weathered and splinter-riven steps. She and Harv had spent several afternoons there enjoying the crowd, drinking exotic island concoctions, and dancing. She wasn't sure if she would revisit it in her new life. She feared too many memories. It would be strange without Harv.

Both to the north and south of Great Guana Cay were several private cays for residents only. Together, they enclosed the harbor, making it one of the safest havens for boaters in the Caribbean. Hundreds of boaters would take their dinghies to shore each day, party, and then return in the evening to their personal floating hotels to sleep it off. She looked forward to making new acquaintances—people who didn't pay attention to her previous life.

The breeze was brisk, and the temperature was warm on this January day. Geneva sat near the ferry's open stern, watching the luminous salt spray hurled by the powerful prop. Backlit by the afternoon sun, the spray glistened as the boat bounced and sliced through the chop.

A young blonde woman, maybe in her early thirties, and her two young, blond sons sat on a long bench across from her with their backs against the ferry's starboard wall. The boys swung their feet back and forth in rhythm as the boat rocked—their legs too short to touch the floor. Geneva wondered if she could have been that young woman if she had taken another path. She would now have had a family, maybe two young boys of her own. She sighed quietly, feeling the pain of loss and the effect her brother's death had had on her decision not to have children.

Instead, she had chosen a lifestyle of status built around disingenuous relationships and predicated on patriotic fervor. In reality, her life had been a vicious merry-go-round of self-interest masquerading as the public good. And what did she have to show for so many years in Washington? A divorce from a man she no longer wanted to be with. She had never envisioned herself at this point in her life being alone.

She wondered now if she had ever really loved him—or anyone else for that matter. Had she spent all of these years running away from her past? She felt a heavy emptiness. What had she done with her life?

Sitting next to the young family were some native laborers in T-shirts and gray trousers, their dark skin and clothes caked in white dust— probably from a day of laying block, building someone's beachfront mansion, she guessed. Geneva imagined them returning home to loving families on one of the cays. The laborers joked with the pilot, trading island gossip and news. This, no doubt, was their daily commute. There was no need for radio traffic reports every ten minutes to warn them of a horrific accident blocking the road ahead and suggest an alternative route. This wasn't the daily migraine of darting between lanes, cutting off another angry driver doing the exact same thing, and calculating a new direction to get home in time for dinner and a stiff drink. There was no road rage here.

The ferry slowed, and the wake and spray died down as they turned gently into a small cove. Private docks dipped their rickety legs in the water on both sides of the water taxi as it chugged slowly by. Finally, Geneva spied a larger concrete pier ahead where about a dozen people mingled, waiting to board or greet the young family, she guessed.

Looking at the mother and her boys, the giddy feeling Geneva had been experiencing left her body completely. A cold melancholy fell over her. She had focused on getting here, not on what came next. She hadn't even thought about dinner.

The boat bumped against the dock, knocking her slightly off-balance. The crew threw their lines to waiting arms on the dock. The locals knew the drill and aided the crew in tying the boat securely to the pilings. Only then did the captain help the young family step onto the platform.

The workmen looked at Geneva and nodded for her to go next. The captain tossed her bags up on the dock and helped her step from the rocking boat to the solid footing of the pier. She pulled her bags together around her.

Damn, she thought, she had forgotten. She needed a taxi to help with her luggage. Was there even one on the island?

"Madam, need some help?" came a familiar voice from behind.

She whirled around, recognizing that resonant tone. Her heart leaped. Beck was standing on the pier, not twenty feet away, shirtless and wearing khaki cargo shorts.

"How did you? What are you? Oh my god." Geneva dropped her carry-on bags and ran to him. They embraced. She grabbed him tightly around the neck and pulled his face to hers. He wrapped his arms around her and squeezed tightly, burying his face in her hair.

"I can't believe you found me." She nuzzled her face in his chest, feeling his warmth and inhaling the aroma of his body.

"You know me. I love the thrill of the chase," he said. "I just can't let a good story like this get away from me so easily."

She pulled his face to hers again and kissed him hard on the lips. She clung to him. She wanted to revel in this moment, this warm feeling. They kissed again. And again.

Finally, she rested her hand against his chest and pushed back, looking deeply into his eyes. She hadn't seen this one coming. Thank god everything did not go according to plan.

"How did you find me?"

"It was your ambition."

She froze.

He knew. How did he know? She had worked so hard to keep her plan a secret from him. Only Keith was supposed to know about the money, and she had taken precautions to assure he would never talk.

If Beck knew, who else knew? Where had she and Keith slipped up? Could this mean her plan to escape and live a quiet life in obscurity was in jeopardy?

Her head swirled. She couldn't think. She had no answer.

Beck tilted his head and studied her. "You okay?"

Geneva jumped—startled, realizing she was staring, her jaw agape. She must be a sight, she thought. She could feel her cheeks warming. Was she blushing? "Sorry . . . my ambition?" She stumbled over the words, struggling to regain control.

"Come on, Jen. You know. Your naked ambition."

"Oh. Oh. You mean . . ." She looked down and gently closed her eyes. She buried her face in his chest again and beamed broadly. Her heart stopped frantically pumping, and her pulse geared down to island time again. He didn't know. He didn't know about the money.

She remembered their conversation in Grand Cayman, telling him how much she loved this island. That explained how he had found her. Her secret was safe. He wasn't here about the money. He was here for her.

She pushed back and traced her index finger along at least two day's worth of stubble on his chin, then touched his mustache. That silly mustache. She hadn't realized how much she had missed it.

Beck motioned at their surroundings. "This is quite a place. It's a bit out of my price range though."

"Oh, it's not that expensive. Looks can be deceiving."

"I'd say. I still don't know how you do it. Escape Washington. Retire here. You're amazing."

"A girl's got to have a few secrets."

He smiled.

She gazed into his eyes. "You know, I'm free now."

Beck laughed. "No, you've never been free. You're one very expensive lady. You've cost me dearly, but you're worth every penny."

"I mean I'm single again."

"I know," he said softly. "That's why I'm here."

Geneva pulled him closer to her and rested her hand against his chest, their eyes still locked. She ran her finger across his chest, drawing a small circle where she felt his heart beating. "I need to be wooed properly, of course."

"That would mean flowers."

"That's a start."

"And I guess I need to dress the part. Do I need a tie to go with these shorts?"

She looked at him standing there bare chested. "Not exactly."

"Well, at least a shirt."

"Nope."

"Then sandals. Should I wear sandals?"

"That's not what I had in mind."

"Then, lady, I'm afraid I've got absolutely nothing to wear."

"You know just the right thing to say to a girl to make her feel special."

72

President Michael Harvey sat ill at ease behind the Resolute Desk, a nineteenth-century gift from Queen Victoria to President Rutherford B. Hayes. He shifted in his chair and glanced out of the large Palladian window at the dormant rose garden and White House grounds. The afternoon sun shone a spotlight on his new backyard on this cloudless January day. A marine in full-dress uniform stood erect on the portico outside in the bitter cold.

President John F. Kennedy was the first to bring the ornate desk into the Oval Office. Harvey rubbed his hands over the surface as he sat and surveyed his new official digs. He was in the Oval Office alone for the first time. The nonstop inauguration festivities had given him no time to examine his new surroundings. His own art and personal photographs already hung on the freshly painted walls. His shoes settled into the deep plush pile of the newly laid pale blue carpeting emblazoned with the dark presidential seal that he had personally chosen.

He felt giddy.

A note lay on the desk from former President Bill Croom, welcoming him to the hardest job on the planet. A nice tradition, he thought. What a powerful statement to the world. After more than two hundred years, this experiment in democracy still worked. This peaceful transfer of power, he thought, was a shining example for all.

Tomorrow, he knew, would be another day with both sides once again engaged in partisan combat. But for today, he could enjoy the moment.

"Mr. President." The intercom on his phone startled Harvey for a second.

"Mr. President, the vice president is here to see you."

"Send him in."

The Oval Office wall opened up.

"Mr. President," said Daniel Fahy.

"Mr. Vice President," said Harvey.

The men embraced and patted each other on the shoulder. Harvey returned to his chair behind the big desk, and Fahy eased his back into the visitor's chair on the other side.

"You look good sitting there," Fahy said.

"It was an extraordinary trip. I've got to hand it to you. I couldn't have done it without you."

"I could say the same to you. I wouldn't be here had you not put my name before Congress." Fahy ran his hand along the arm of his chair, feeling the rich fabric.

"No-brainer. With the original ticket up in flames, I needed someone whose integrity had never been questioned. You were the perfect choice for this town."

Fahy crossed his legs in a more relaxed position. "We both know who we have to thank."

"You're right about that. In fact, you were right about almost everything from the very beginning. How you planned this, how you were able to predict what would happen next, going all the way back to September—it simply astounds me."

"You need to remember, I've been watching crooked politicians for nearly a decade. People are predictable. I know how to exploit that to my advantage."

"And they call you the Boy Scout."

Fahy winced. "Not my choice of descriptors, but it's a label the media gave me years ago. I just decided to never give it back. They almost had me convinced."

"I still can't believe we pulled it off in time. Having McCauley jump-start it with Rikki the way you did really paid off."

"We had to assure the story got out before Election Day."

"How did McCauley do it?"

"He was an actor in college and worked undercover before we started working together. He's a natural. And I gotta say, your plan to nominate him as FBI director is a brilliant move."

"JFK and Richard Nixon set the example. They were constantly at odds with J. Edgar. That taught every president since then to keep the director close at all times. Thanks for the recommendation and for attesting to his loyalty."

"Teamwork."

Harvey shook his head and smiled, then laughed loudly. "What a business. What a way to run a country."

"The world," Fahy reminded him.

"You know what you—we—managed to do, don't you? You and I overthrew the government—"

"And nobody knew," said Fahy, completing the sentence.

Harvey stared at his vice president. There was an unspoken covenant between them—a secret to be kept. He reached into the side drawer of his ornate desk and withdrew a box of Cohibas. "Cuban?"

"Love one," Fahy said.

They both lit their cigars. Fahy savored the flavor and then spoke. "There still was a degree of luck involved in all of this. Your ex-wife turned out to be an unexpected asset. Being able to observe this whole affair unfolding at a very close range—much closer than we had expected—proved quite useful."

"It did. And she never knew," Harvey said. "Mr. Vice President—I like the sound of that—that proves to me just how agile you are. You'll be a great asset in the years ahead. But I do wonder about Rikki. Should I worry? Is this something we need to address?"

"Mr. President, he was better than I thought. After he helped us get rid of Bayard, he figured out on his own the connection between Patten and the drug cartels. He's a funny guy. I'd bet he thinks he's doing god's work. No, I don't worry about him. The only loose end is his accomplice.

Someone named Red. Not sure who he is. He's eluded us so far, but he knows what Rikki knows."

"That could be a problem."

"Not since you appointed me to head your new Presidential Commission on Campaign Finance Reform."

"Not the first time you've been appointed to investigate yourself, now is it?"

Fahy smiled broadly and took a puff on his cigar. The men looked at each other in silence. Fahy exhaled a long blue streak, the aroma of smoke mixing with the smell of fresh paint and the scent of chemical toxins from the newly laid carpet with the inlaid presidential seal.

Afterword

There is nothing to stop the flow of illegal funds into federal elections. Congress refuses to curtail the flow of secret money into the system. Presidential aspirants from both major political parties are more than willing to wink and turn a blind eye at financial transparency.

Thanks to the US Supreme Court's 2010 ruling in Citizens United v. Federal Election Commission, it is now impossible to trace the origin of these political campaign funds.

The possibility that drug cartel money has already infiltrated our elections is very real. No fingerprints. No trail. No problem.

Our elected leaders prefer it that way.

About the Author

Rick Pullen is an award-winning magazine editor and former investigative reporter for several newspapers who has worked in Washington, D.C. for most of his career. He lives in Fredericksburg, Virginia.

In 2015, he was a finalist for editor of the year. He was also named to the "Folio 100"—the one hundred most influential people in magazine publishing.

This is the first in his "Naked" thriller series. To learn more about Rick and his upcoming books, visit his website at www.RickPullen.com.